MAKE THE COSMOS
GREAT AGAIN

MAKE THE COSMOS GREAT AGAIN

Vincent P. Scully

Art by Robert Caldwell

Contents

L'Académie d'Escrime de Paris
1807 Fencing Manual
English Translation
Valid Target Areas of the Body

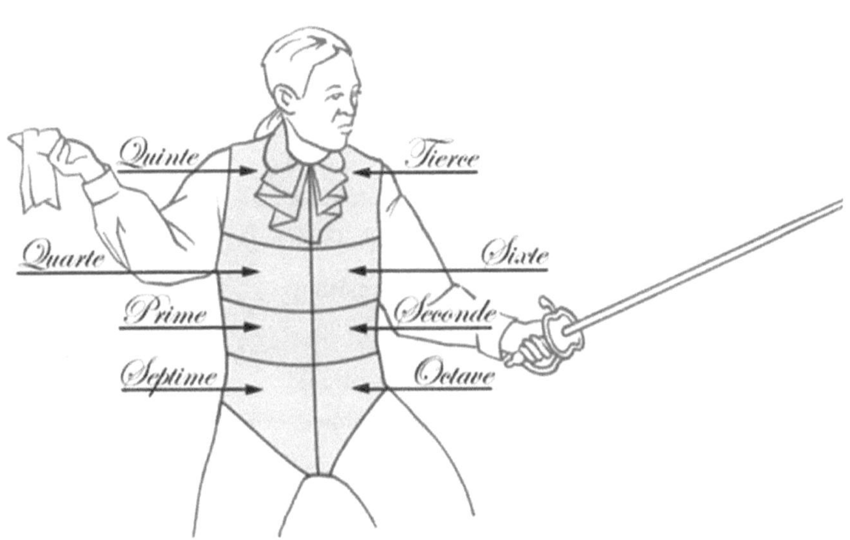

L'Académie d'Escrime de Paris
1807 Fencing Manual
English Translation

Parries

Prime (first position)
Lower right, palm down, tip down, cross body

Seconde (second position)
Lower left, palm down, tip down, straight out

Tierce (third position)
Upper left, palm down, tip up, straight out

Quarte (fourth position)
Upper right, palm down, tip up, cross body

Quinte (fifth position)
Upper right, palm down, tip down, cross body

Sixte (sixth position)
Upper left, palm up, tip up, straight out

Septime (seventh position)
Lower right, palm up, tip down, cross body

Octave (eighth position)
Lower left, palm up, tip up, straight out

L'Académie d'Escrime de Paris
1807 Fencing Manual
English Translation

Glossary of Fencing Terms

Attack. An extension of the point to threaten a valid target area.

Balestra. A forward jump that starts with the attacker pushing off the back leg as if lunging but ends with the rear leg recovered forward to replace the attacker in the on-guard position.

Compound attack. An attack with feints to different lines.

Corps à corps. The act of two fencers coming together in bodily contact, at which time the director will halt the action.

Coupe. The lifting of the blade over the opponent's blade to avoid a parry or change the line of attack.

Disengage. Dropping the point below the opponent's blade to avoid a parry or change the line of attack.

Double. An attack that makes a complete circle around the opponent's blade.

Feint. An offensive movement to provoke a reaction to open a line of attack.

Invitation. Intentionally opening a line for the opponent to attack.

Lines. The eight numbered valid target areas of the body.

Lunge. An attack using the back foot to push the attacker forward to land in a stretch, with the rear leg extending straight back and the front knee directly over the front foot.

On guard. The neutral stance of the fencer from which offensive or defensive actions can be taken.

Parry. A defensive movement of the blade to deflect an attack.

Passé. An attack that passes the target without hitting.

Riposte. A counterattack after a successful parry.

Salute. A gesture of respect to one's opponent at the beginning of a bout, performed by extending the point toward the opponent, pulling back to kiss the guard, then finishing with a downward cut in octave.

Take the blade. A controlling press on the opponent's blade.

A.	Mizen Topgallant		K.	Main Topmast Staysail
B.	Mizen Topsail		L.	Fore Royal
C.	Spanker		M.	Fore Topgallant
D.	Main Royal		N.	Fore Topsail
E.	Main Topgallant		O.	Fore Course
F.	Mizen T'gallant Staysail		P.	Fore Topmast Staysail
G.	Main Topsail		Q.	Inner Jib
H.	Main Course		R.	Outer Flying Jib
I.	Main T'gallant Staysail		S.	Spritsail
J.	Middle Staysail			

1.	Taffrail & Lanterns		11.	Waist
2.	Stern & Quarter-galleries		12.	Gripe & Cutwater
3.	Poop Deck/Great Cabins Under		13.	Figurehead & Beakhead Rails
4.	Rudder & Transom Post		14.	Bow Sprit
5.	Quarterdeck		15.	Jib Boom
6.	Mizen Chains & Stays		16.	Foc's'le & Anchor Cat-heads
7.	Main Chains & Stays		17.	Cro'jack Yard
8.	Boarding Battens/Entry Port		18.	Top Platforms
9.	Shrouds & Ratlines		19.	Cross-Trees
10.	Fore Chains & Stays		20.	Spanker Gaff

May 3, 2028

The Day We All Remember
Where We Were

Tʜᴇ ɪɴꜱᴛʀᴜᴄᴛᴏʀ ᴡʜᴀᴄᴋᴇᴅ Emmie across her forward calf with the side of his foil. Hideo Tanaka was an old school fencing master and had no qualms about a little physical punishment for missed parries. "You fence like turtle!" he exclaimed, his palm up and his face amazed.

Emmie nodded and came back *en guarde.* Advance, retreat, advance retreat, Hideo again extended in *quarte,* Emmie closed the line and Tanaka again disengaged to *sixte.* But this time Emmie circled smoothly into a *counter-sixte* parry and made a clean riposte to his flank in *quarte.* Her point caught on the instructor's leather chest protector as she lunged, her foil bending like a fishing pole. Hideo nodded, removed his helmet, saluted and bowed curtly to signal the end of the lesson.

Emily Bahtia, 32, pulled up her helmet, saluted back, walked off the *piste* to her open weapons bag, dropped her helmet and foil into it, threw her sweaty headband in as well, and lastly shook out her brown hair. After two hours of bouting and a thirty-minute lesson, Emmie Bahtia was ready for a beer. Her waiting friends were more than ready.

"*Il maestro's* a little grumpy today," said Connie. Connie Schwartzkoff was tall, blond and had a reach that made her one tough-to-beat epee' fencer. "That ole' samurai testosterone is up."

"Yeah, what else is new," commented Vanoune Rodriguez, the dark-haired saber fencer of the trio. "Let's go. How bout we try Lucas's? I know it's a tourist trap, but it's right here."

The three shouldered their bags and walked out of the Halberstadt Fencing Academy and into San Francisco's Presidio. San Francisco had inherited the base from the army forty years ago and it had opened it up to commercial and recreational use. Then, over the past decade, the Pacific Ocean had risen over thirty feet around the North Bay, giving the Presidio district a beachfront and making it even more popular. George Lucas had built a special effects studio, and now some dork supposedly named Joe Lucas had put a Star Wars themed bar right next to it and named it Lucas's. The name was in court but for now it was open, the beer was cold, and it was right across from Halberstadt, making it a popular watering hole for thirsty fencers.

They walked in past all sorts of Star Wars memorabilia and grabbed a high table with four barstools. Models of every empire and rebel space ship were hanging above them, along with way too many Princess Leias in the slave girl bikini she wore when she strangled Jobba the Hut. A robot C3PO rolled up, bowed, and tried to place menus on the table, but it whipped them down too fast and they slid across the table and fell to the floor. "May I bring you drinks? It said in a scratchy voice. The three women shook their heads at each other and grinned.

"C3PO! You missed!" said Emmie. "And it sounds like you need a throat lozenge. Where's that refined butler's voice?"

"Yeah, and how come you roll?" added Connie. "C3PO walked. You should walk for shit's sake. It's 2028, robots walk."

Unfortunately, C3PO lacked the aps for bantering with customers. "Today's special is a one-third pound burger, grilled to perfection, twenty-nine ninety-five."

"That's it?" asked Emmie. "You're a language droid and all you can talk about is the specials?" Emmie and her friends laughed, gave up on the robot and ordered burgers and a pitcher of IPA. Just as C3PO rolled off, a big group at the next table started yelling at the TVs. "Hey! Get the game back on!' and "You gotta be shittin' me! Only twenty seconds to go!"

Emmie looked up at the big screen over the bar and it was all snow and static. Suddenly it cleared up, but it wasn't the 49'ers game. Instead there was a thirty-something guy with chestnut hair tied up with a velvet ribbon, wearing a vintage uniform and pointy naval hat, standing in front of thousands of people, many wearing fantastic costumes.

Connie had been checking her phone and was unaware of what was going on, but now she too yelled out, plenty pissed off. "Hey, my entire phone just got taken over! All I get is fucking Comicon!"

"No shit," said Emmie." Look up—it's everywhere." Everyone in the bar stopped yelling as the uniformed guy started speaking.

"Greetings, my fellow Earthmen and Earthwomen. I am Rodney Wyckham, borrowing your communications system for a moment to send everyone on Earth a message from my planet, Freeport. Two hundred years ago, I accidently came to this planet with six ships of the British Royal Navy. Here the squadron won a war against its vicious rulers that were planning to attack Earth and created a free and peaceful planet we named Freeport. Since then, many beings from planets all over the cosmos have moved here and prospered." He stepped aside and gestured to the crowd behind him, which went wild like a circus menagerie at feeding time. While there were some normal-looking men and women clapping and shouting, there were also ants the size of sheep, moving bundles of vines, big balls of rolling mud, tall shiny humanoids like movie aliens, gorillas with empty eye sockets—all sorts of strange beings making all sorts of bizarre sounds.

What the fuck? Emmie thought. *Somebody hacked into network TV with one big-budgeted message! Must've spent a fortune—look at those costumes! And the size of the cast! But what's the message—dress up and be crazy? This is somebody's expensive joke?* The navy guy turned back to the camera.

"After two centuries of keeping to ourselves, we would like to help Earth, our mother world. We understand you have issues with rising sea levels and the resulting millions of refugees. My message to you today is that Freeport is open to immigration from Earth. For countries that are interested, we will set up transit portals so that your people can visit first to see what life here is like. We have constructed tourist attractions that showcase our abilities and pleasant accommodations. When you visit, you can see Freeport's burgeoning intergalactic economy and our vast stretches of available land, there are opportunities here for all. In addition, we offer Earth the use of our portals to trade with other planets, including advanced worlds that could halt Earth's climate change and reverse her coastal flooding. Working with them would save your planet.

"Just a few minutes earlier we contacted Earth's leaders, informing them of our existence and this upcoming broadcast to all the people of Earth. Over the next few weeks we hope to establish normal communications with your leaders—no need for more bursting in on your electrical communications. I leave you know, hopefully our two planets can establish beneficial relations, this initial contact can result in benefits for all. So, I won't interrupt your day any longer, Earth's screens will now be returned to their normal functions. I hope to see many of you in the near future." The guy bowed his head, tipped his pointed hat, and the TV went all snowy again.

The 49'er game came back on but nobody cared. Everybody started talking about what they'd just seen.

"Unbelievable!" said Emmie. "There's another world out there!"

You believe that?" replied Connie. "What a buncha bullshit! But who did it? And why?"

"Who do you think?" said an angry Vanoune, shaking her head in disgust. "Had to be America First. They hack us all the time."

America First was the political party that had formed after the 2020 election. It was now the dominant party in the seceded southern and midwestern states.

"Really?" asked Emmie. "I don't understand what this fantasy does for those whackos. It certainly wasn't anti-immigration. The aliens were great!"

"Wait!" yelled Vanoune. "Shut up, it's DiCarpaccio."

Everyone turned back to the TV which now showed Leonardo Di-Carpaccio, President of the Pacific States of America. He was the actor who had defeated Victor Triumph in the 2020 presidential election, resulting in the breakup of the United States of America into four independent countries.

"My fellow westerners and all good Americans across North America. I want to address you tonight about what you have just seen. A few minutes ago, every phone in the capital building here received a video from the same man you just saw. He informed us that he was on another planet and in a few minutes was going to contact all residents of Earth directly on our televisions, computers and phones. He said he wanted to set up interplanetary communication and open relations. He apologized for what he was about to do, interrupting all communications on Earth, but believed it was the best way to convince everyone that he was for real and to get relations moving along quickly. He also sent us pictures and scientific evidence that certainly convinced me that he is really on another planet. Later today my office will be releasing this message and a summary of its scientific evidence."

DiCarpaccio paused and shook his head, clearly overwhelmed, then continued. "Right now, I'm as bewildered as you are. But until I learn differently, I'm going to accept that this is an opportunity for our nation and for our entire planet. I will continue communications with them until they give me a reason not to.

"So that's all I know so far. I'll be meeting with my cabinet immediately, we'll hear more from our scientists, during all this we will be hearing more from this planet Freeport, and starting tomorrow I'll be updating you daily." He paused again and exhaled. "Quite a day, huh?"

Talking heads came on as the bar went dead quiet. The three women stared at each other, for the moment speechless. Finally, Emmie blurted out, "Un-fucking believable!"

Unserrenissima Venezia

T HE FRIGATE HMS *Righteous*, 38 guns, glided slowly to a stop in the center of the Grand Canal, her kedge anchor dragging across the famously shallow lagoon. Captain Rodney Wycham surveyed Piazza San Marco from his quarterdeck and had to admit that it looked exactly as he remembered it from his visit over 200 years ago. It was all there—the plaza's entrance flanked with two tall columns topped by the winged lion of St. Mark and St. George slaying the dragon, on the right the Doge's Palace, then further in the soaring Campanile, and finally St. Mark's Cathedral, the four Roman bronze horses taken from Constantinople prancing above its entrance. But this city before him was not Venice but an image, what the Fireflies called a *holograph*, caused by their electrical manipulations of the air.

He had seen the real Venice in '05 as a visiting midshipman aboard the frigate *Albermarle* under Nelson, when the man was just a captain. Despite the naval support Venice had given the Royal Navy against France, Nelson was there to tell the Doge of Venice that Britain would not be sending any troops to help fight the French. As a result, Venice, the Most Serene Republic, was overrun by Napoleon and became part of his Kingdom of Italy. While Nelson had explained to Lodovico Manin that he would be Venice's last Doge, Wyckham had spent several days ashore exploring the canals, alleyways, cafes and especially the taverns.

Piazza San Marco had always been the center of Venice, filled with strolling nobility, uniformed servants, colorful merchants, weathered sailors and all sorts of tradesmen, and they were all here again today, dressed like it was 1805, even though the year was 2028. However, this San Marco also had dozens of the stranger life forms that inhabited Freeport, including the seven-foot Slicks with their four arms, the blind gorillas with empty eye sockets they used for hearing, living blobs of mud rolling around, wolf-like Lycans lounging in the cafes, fish people, vine people, yard-long ants, and even the vile snakemen slithering about in their ridiculous corsair outfits. And hundreds of humans, mostly sailors from the fleet, including a marine band which struck up a lively tattoo once its director recognized Governor Wyckham.

Everywhere on Freeport, Human sailors mixed with aliens, and Wyckham had expected representatives of all the planet's diverse population at this epic event. What was new were the myriad groups of stiffly attired humans, including the current leaders of 2028 Earth, all arriving to celebrate the opening of contact between the two worlds. They certainly stood out, the men dressed in tight fitting black suits with long red cravats and stiff white shirts, the women in slightly more colorful jackets, short skirts that barely covered their knees, and pearls strung about their necks.

It was clear that the Human visitors were not comfortable rubbing elbows with all the various aliens. Wyckham watched as one older gentleman reacted in horror as the fishman next to him pulled out a handful of the live tiny humanoids they fed on and popped them squealing into his mouth. *Well, our visitors will get used to our colorful population soon enough,* Wyckham mused. *Everyone does.*

Most of the delegates from Earth were watching *Righteous's* arrival, though many of the males in the plaza were scrutinizing the scores of scantily attired Fireflies vying for their attention. The female delegates, despite their risqué skirts, were clearly discomfited by the Fireflies' dress and their overt sollicitations. Wyckham bit his lips. *Wish I could do something about that.*

Wyckham turned back to his ship. "Smartly done, Lieutenant Moore," he commented to the young lieutenant in charge of the ship as it anchored a cable off the San Marco quay. "My gig, if you would?" Moore nodded his head towards the maindeck, bosuns yelled, and hands scurried to form a side party and get the captain's gig over the side. Moments later seven crew and Lieutenant Moore lined up at the sally port and snapped to attention. Pipes squealed as Wyckham swung gracefully over the side and climbed briskly down the rope ladder to his waiting boat, his surgically and chemically maintained 200-year-old body responding like that of a twenty-five-year-old's, thanks to the medical administrations of the technically advanced Slicks. A fourteen-gun salute, the requirement for greeting an admiral, started firing a rolling volley from the shore battery. The jets of flame and ear-splitting explosions immediately captured the attention of everyone in the plaza, with humans and aliens both impressed by the thunderous salute. While Wyckham knew there was no battery there, just images of cannon created by the Fireflies' holo-graph projectors, he had to admit they looked and sounded very real. As the gun smoke cleared, he stepped out onto the quay right below the column topped by the statue of winged lion of Venice, the symbol of St. Mark.

Making a more dramatic arrival were a score of the Firefly leaders, glowing balls of bright light that floated down to the end of the quay. The energy beings could take the image of any person or thing, usually appearing on Freeport in the image of Human females. But having decided that it was rather unseemly for human images to fly, when traveling through the air they appeared in their natural form of pure energy. As soon as they lit on the ground, they changed into the human female forms they were known by on Freeport. And, thankfully, they were appropriately clothed for a state occasion, which certainly could not be said for the hundreds of their compatriots scattered about the square. While Wyckham was used to the shameless state of dishabille that Fireflies generally took in their quest for human copulation, he wished that just this once, the formal opening of relations between two planets, the Fireflies on Freeport could have been more discreetly attired, instead of the absurd tiny coverings that they wore over breasts and genitalia.

The leader of the Fireflies, in her normal form of a young Lady Tracy Brashton, Wyckham's childhood sweetheart, walked up smiling and gave him a curtsey as was proper for the Governor of Freeport. Wyckham made a leg, straightened up and surveyed the scene about him.

This was the first he had seen of this fantasy Venice, and despite the knowledge that nothing he saw was real, the vision of San Marco swept over his body like a warm, comforting wave. He hadn't been back to Earth since 1814, and to see a city that had given him such wondrous memories as a young midshipman was surprisingly gratifying. It was like revisiting an old friend, made the more wonderful since they hadn't met for over two hundred years.

"Good afternoon and welcome to 1805 Venice", Lady Brashton said with a friendly nod. "My race wants to thank you for allowing us to create this interesting destination for the many eager visitors from our galaxy to your planet. We hope your fellow humans enjoy it as well."

Hmmmph. He knew what the Fireflies were eager for, and it wasn't supplying enjoyment to Human tourists. The Fireflies constantly sought human seed, since each spermatozoa cell contained a unit of living force which the Fireflies could use to gain even more personal powers, adding to their ability to read minds and control senses. A successful tourist attraction on Freeport would bring in thousands of humans and more human males would visit the "taverns" that the Fire-flies operated both in New Venice and across the bay in Port Wyckham. *And she calls Freeport my planet?* This being before him was involved with so many important functions on this planet, from managing the transporters and gathering military intelligence to running dozens of businesses, that Wyckham often thought she was the real governor. But suspicious as he was, he had to admit that so far, the Fireflies' powers had helped bring peace and prosperity to the entire cosmos.

"My compliments, madam, for another job so well done. The capabilities of your race continue to amaze me."

She nodded graciously. "We always appreciate complements from the Captain Wyckham, the man who saved our race. Let's hope the effort we have made here will be helpful to the people of Earth as well." Her race and many others had been saved from the giant Draesh when Wyckham's squadron defeated the porcine giants and ended their brutal war against the entire League of Worlds.

Months ago, she had proposed the creation of a fantasy Venice in order to entice visitors from Earth, the idea being that many would later immigrate to Freeport. Today was the formal opening ceremony of the imaginary city, with delegations from Earth to see the city and to decide whether they wanted to establish commercial ties with Freeport. The Lady Brashton Firefly had set everything up by communicating electrically with Earth and today Wyckham would meet all its major leaders in person. Though he knew that on Earth everyone did all their communicating through electrical devices, he himself refused to use them. Wyckham believed diplomacy needed to be conducted in person, where a person's character and competence could be measured.

Wyckham was looking around the crowd of Humans before him, smiling and waving without a clue as to who was who. With all the visiting males clad in nearly identical black suits that were completely devoid of any decoration, there was no way to tell a leader from his manservant. Though one group that passed by was wearing yellow badges with a flag that Wyckham knew well, the yellow and gold flag of Spain. In 1804, a ball from *Righteous* had dropped a large version of this flag to the deck of *San Justo*, a big 74, causing the crew of the big ship-of-the-line to believe their captain had struck the colors and surrender to the much smaller *Righteous*. Wyckham still had that flag in his sea chest.

"Lookee thar. Them's the Dons," a nearby voice commented. Wyckham looked to his left and there was *Righteous's* Master Gunner, Peter Crawford. The grizzled old hand was at one of the plaza's outdoor cafes, deep into his cups along with several of his crewmates from *Righteous*. "Did ye know 'ey don't fook? 'Ey all be papists, and th' pope says no fookin!"

The man next to him put down his beer and looked at Crawford in disbelief. It was Barrows, a simple man, once a member of Crawford's gun crew. "Ye thinks I believes that? If 'ey don' fook, where d'ere babies come f'um?"

"It be th' storks what brings 'em," responded Crawford. "Ye been t' Barcelona 'n Malaga, ye saw th' storks ever'where, in the church towers, on all th' rooves, why d' ye think 'ey gots so many storks?"

Barrows nodded his head in acceptance. "Storks, 'ey? Aye, me grammum tole' me 'bout th' storks bringin' babes. So it be true aff'er all!"

Wyckham rolled his eyes and leaned over to speak in Crawford's ear. "Tell poor Barrows whatever nonsense you must, but do not use the word "Dons" on this day when we wish everyone to feel welcome here. We are no longer at war with the Spanish and they take offense at the term."

A sheepish Crawford knuckled his head in salute and responded, "Aye, Cap'm. Sorry, Cap'm."

The Brashton Firefly informatively joined in. "Actually, the term "Dons" has not been used to disparage the Spanish for over a hundred years and no longer upsets the Spanish. It's actually somewhat of a complement of their aristocratic heritage. In recent years it has even been used as a name for Spanish sports teams."

Interesting. Another thing that has changed over the centuries. Wyckham had once fought a duel with a Spanish colonel over his use of the word. He returned to surveying the visitors.

There was a large of party disembarking the *Indomptable,* the French 80 taken in the French invasion in '15, which had been sent to Earth to bring back delegates from the Western Hemisphere. Several men had run down the gangway into the plaza and were setting up a podium and electrical lamps on poles. An elderly, heavy-set man with bright yellow hair stepped to the sallyport, stuck his nose in the air, waved, then stepped down to the gangway. He pointed and nodded to someone in the crowd that he apparently recognized. Wondering who it could possibly be that this man already knew on Freeport, Wyckham turned around to look, but the area the man had waved at was empty except for a life-size statue. *Must have forgotten his spectacles. Quite embarrassing, saying hello to a statue.* Wyckham felt for the poor man but had only contempt for the American's staff. The whole bunch should be dismissed for allowing their man, obviously a national leader, to go out in public without his spectacles, especially at an event like this, the first meeting between the nations of Earth and another planet.

And apparently the poor fellow had even more serious health problems, because he couldn't even walk down the gangway. Instead, his staff had brought along a mechanized stairway, which was now turned on, giving the stationary man a short descent down to the docks without him moving a leg. Wyckham had no idea what disease could require a man to be moved down a twenty-foot gangway on a mechanized stairway, but it must be quite serious. An extremely beautiful and well-dressed young woman, obviously a specialized nurse, was following him down the gangway to catch him if he fell.

The man kept waving as he descended, then at the end of the ramp he bounded off and swaggered to the podium! Suddenly the man was healthy!

Wyckham couldn't believe what he'd just seen. This man wasn't ill at all, he was just trying to impress everyone by riding down a mechanized stair! Couldn't put one foot in front of the other and walk down the gangway like a commoner! This was a man who clearly fancied himself a great lord and always had to make a big entrance. He must be the pompous American president he'd been briefed on who was responsible for much of the calamity Earth was in.

Wyckham shook his head. Despite all the American nonsense about democracy, they'd elected themselves a king. One who seemed even more obsessed with his royalty than George the Third. And probably even more daft as well. Just about all of Europe's royal rulers had eventually turned out to be lunatics, and probably this king was no exception.

As the fellow dropped down the last little step onto the quay, a button at the bottom of his white shirt popped open, revealing what was clearly a corset. With his unbuttoned black jacket flapping open, the white band of the corset popping out was clearly visible, and without the restraining shirt button, it crept upwards as he advanced to the podium, becoming even more prominent.

Unaware of all this, the American stepped up and gripped the podium, which had an English coat of arms on it, while dozens of waiting Earthmen wildly cheered his arrival. The men who had prepared the podium now kneeled or stood to the side, all putting boxy devices to their eyes that had "Fox News" printed on their sides and aiming them at the big blond president.

"Hello to all Americans and to my followers all over Earth!" he proclaimed loudly, talking at the devices that were apparently transmitting electrical images back to Earth. "Actually, that's wrong, look here, turns out that I already have lots of followers in this place too, and I should've made a shout-out to them as well!" He stopped for a moment to wait for the cheering to die down. "But we made it here. Though I have to tell you the ancient wooden ships that brought us here don't compare to my new Boeing 877. Now that's the way to travel! But I'll put up with anything if it helps Earth, and believe me, I will get the best deals for us here, period. Guaranteed! Done deal!"

Wyckham couldn't believe this man was a world leader. He turned to the Firefly for confirmation. "So, I imagine this fleshy *poseur* with the circus hair and his paunch spilling out of his corset is the American president who started all the troubles in 2020?" Wyckham asked.

"Yes, that's Victor Triumph, President of a new confederacy of America's southern states. He also now claims to be the Emperor of the entire planet Earth."

"And he's not sick at all? Then what's that young nurse for?"

"No, he is not ill" the Firefly replied. "The woman is actually his sixth wife."

Christ, she's young enough to be his granddaughter! Wyckham now noticed the coat of arms painted on the podium with the word "Triumph" across the bottom. Sitting on top of the shield was a heavily bejeweled gold crown, with purple sapphires and leather for the cap, a crown for an emperor. But the three lions on the shield were definitely British.

"Where did he get this coat of arms?" asked Wyckham. "The House of Lords actually granted this man heraldry?"

"No. England originally granted this particular coat of arms to an American diplomat named Davies in 1939. Triumph liked it and just took it for himself, replacing the word "Integrity" with his own name."

Good Lord! The man just took another family's coat of arms and claimed it as his own? And further proves he has no integrity by replacing that word with his own name? *The cheek of the man! Some things are just not done, for God's sake!* Wyckham had no further interest in this charlatan. "Madam Tracy, would you be so good as to point out the delegation from Great Britain? They should be the easiest for me to welcome. After all, I am legally still a citizen of England. Might as well start there, what?"

The Lady Brashton Firefly started to respond, but before she could, a commotion on the far side of the square drew Wyckham's attention. A coach-and-four, the carriage heavily carved and guided pulled by four magnificent bays with red plumes bobbing on their heads, had emerged from behind the towering Campanile and was briskly heading towards the visiting diplomats. Many moved quickly out of the way as others, bodyguards for the Earth delegations, stepped to the fore with their arms wide, tying to divert the loping horses away from their respective charges. But the coach driver had apparently found his destination and brought the grand coach to a stop, thankfully before anyone was run over, right in front of a group of Americans.

"Who the hell is that, driving a coach and four at a full lope right through a crowded event?" Wyckham asked aloud, as much to himself as to the Firefly at his side. She too was surprised, but before she could respond, a garishly liveried coachman opened the carriage door and out stepped someone they both knew—none other than the real Lady Brashton.

Tracy Brashton had rejected Wyckham's interest in 1808 and married Baron Edward Kemp, a man much older than her but the patriarch of an old and powerful family. She and her husband had come to Freeport aboard a British invasion fleet in 1815, but when he left, she had stayed behind and started her own chain of brothels, gaining considerable renown on Freeport and the undying enmity of the Fireflies. What in Hell was she up to now?

She emerged from her carriage, assisted by two coachmen, and stood on its running board, waving to the crowd like a royal. She was attired in a long-pleated skirt which hung down from a wide bustle, and a tight-fitting bodice. As usual, she displayed an immense décolletage, thanks to Slick surgeons who had installed some kind of adjustable containers inside her breasts that she could fill with varying amounts of some viscous liquid. Today she had them extra full.

"'Bowsprit Tracy' got 'em big as barrels today," stated the nearby Crawford, using the hands' nickname for the woman who could vary the size of her prow. The sight of the beautified Baroness had him completely mesmerized, a not unusual occurrence around this woman. "Spillin' like a gale o'er th' bow," Crawford managed to sputter, almost swooning as he stared at her. And a stare from Crawford was pretty impressive, since his right eye bulged out like a big egg, the result of some birth defect or childhood pox. Many crewmen aboard Righteous insisted that his protruding eyeball was what made him such an accurate gunner.

Baroness Brashton always made a dramatic entrance at public events, and whatever one thought about the scale of the alterations the Slicks had made to her body, it certainly caused quite a stir in the plaza. Almost everyone hushed as they stared at her, including most of the aliens. Somehow, she had gotten many Slicks into her camp, despite their nonsexuality, and their surgeons had worked extensively for decades on all aspects of her face and body. From the chiseled cheekbones to the all-knowing eyes to the jawline of aristocracy, the results were better than Botticelli's Venus or even Canova's scandalous nude statue of Napoleon's sister Pauline Bonaparte. And with her protruding bust-line there was no mistaking her from anywhere in the plaza.

"Mr. Shillings! Welcome to my planet!" she called as she extended her hand towards the nearest group of black-suited humans. Standing there was a slim elderly man with short white hair, absolutely smitten, his mouth wide open in astonishment as he stared at her overflowing bosom. He managed to take a step forward and extend his free hand in greeting.

"Who's that old wobbler?' Wyckham asked the Firefly Lady Brashton at his side. She had worked for months on all the arrangements for this event and knew the identities of all the visiting politicians.

"Mark Shillings, President of the Midwest States of America," she responded. "A position he's held since the United States broke up in 2021. A devout Catholic, he's transformed his part of North America into a Christian theocracy. He closed the churches of other religions and passed laws based on the Christian bible, in particular laws against various sexual activities."

Freeport's Minister of Civilian Affairs, Thomas Obujimi, the freed African slave who was also Wyckham's personal valet, leaned forward into Wyckham's ear. "According to his letter of introduction, his primary reason for interacting with Freeport is to supply missionaries to help us convert our 'wayward alien races' to Christianity".

"*Hmmmph.*" As far as Wyckhan could see, holy rollers always bollocksed up matters whenever they got into government. He had seen the Church of England cause all sorts of problems in British politics, so he'd never promoted religion on Freeport, and no one seemed to miss it, even though many residents believed in some kind of divinity. While he'd fought America in 1814 and thought their democracy was a bad idea, he thought their nation's stand on separating church from state was a good one, and had quietly adopted that stance on Freeport.

Lady Brashton took Shillings's extended hand and moved hers up to his open mouth, indicating he should kiss it. When he hesitated, damn if the long skirt she was wearing didn't slowly part in front like the curtain drawing open in a Drury Lane playhouse, revealing the fact that she wasn't wearing any bloomers! And damned if the lips of her fundament weren't being held wide open by two red velvet strings tied to pearl brooches mounted there, apparently a statement of welcome!

Shillings now lost all control. He fell to his knees in front of her and started slobbering busses all over Lady Brashton's extended hand, babbling something about "a true queen" and "the female Jesus". Lady Brashton laughed approvingly as she surveyed the crowd, clearly basking in the attention. That was greeted by boisterous approval from hundreds of Wyckham's sailors, who were all frequent patrons of her taverns and knew the woman well. *Christ, probably familiar with every pore on her body!*

Shillings started to rise but managed to bump his head right into Lady Aston's left breast, knocking it free of her bodice, much to the delight of the crowd. Unfortunately, the immense breast easily got the better of the collision and it was Shillings who lost his balance, falling backwards towards the rear of the coach. The aged statesman's head banged right into the wheel hub and snapped back violently. Shillings slumped down to the ground, bleeding and out cold.

The crowd immediately hushed, realizing the man was seriously injured. Two Slick medics ran up—one knelt down over the prostrate human for a quick look, then pulled a small device and ran it over the hemorrhaging wound on the old man's skull. It was an electric cauterizer that Wickham had seen Slicks use before, a remarkable device, quick and effective at sealing wounds. But another Slick device was flashing and buzzing like an angry bee, and the two aliens spoke to each other in their strange clicking language, the alarm clear in their tone.

Now one of the men in Shillings's detail forced his way forward, waving a case and yelling at the Slick medic. "Step back from the President! I am the President's official physician. You are not authorized to administer to him! Get away from him now!"

But the Slicks would have none of it. Slicks were also the most technically advanced race in the universe, with the arrogance to match. They were physically intimidating as well, over seven feet tall with four arms, no facial features except for two small eyes and a slit mouth, and skin like wet porcelain that had gotten them their English name from the British sailors. Adding to that, the Slicks knew that the angry physician was unarmed, since the planet's transporters screened all travelers for weapons, and with no weapons a puny human was no match for one of the large four-armed beings. The translator device on the head of the taller of the two Slicks crackled to life.

"Your president man needs immediate surgery. Brain bleeding inside. We take him and save life. You stay here. Earthmen always hinder accomplishment. You all arseholes."

Well wasn't that great. In 1815 Sir Arthur Wellesley had invaded Freeport with an English armada that had required a Slick fleet to turn back. So visiting humans were no favorites to the Slicks, and this one had just arrogantly dismissed the doctor's understandable concerns with a demeaning English word it had learned from some sailor. Alien Tracy had emphasized to every being on Freeport the importance of etiquette on this day, and especially not to use colorful language with the delegates from the somewhat Puritan midwestern States, but as usual a Slick had acted as he pleased.

"Put him in my carriage!' instructed Lady Brashton. "It will bear him to your hospital the most speedily!"

Lady Brashton had the right of it. The Baroness's giant coach was here already, and with four bays was far better than the city's one-horse ambulances for barging through the crowd to the Slick medical facility north of the square.

The two tall aliens gently picked up the unconscious Shillings and started to place him on the carriage floor. The angry American doctor tried to stop everything by barging into the two Slicks, but his efforts didn't budge them. Several of his delegation then joined him and the Slicks turned around. To their credit the earthmen went right at them, but to no effect. The physician got thrown into the adjacent cafe for his efforts, sending food, drink, and a couple of patrons flying as well. One of them was Gunner Crawford, now in a fit after having his full pint sprayed all over. He got up and went after the prostrate Earthman.

"Ye foolish bugger, first ye try t' stop th' Slicks f'm savin' yer friend, then ye starts a fight wif 'em? Didn't ye notice th' thing is big 'iz a 'ouse, n gonna knock yer arse sideways?" he spat as he gave the downed American a solid kick in the stomach. He then picked up a chair and brained another human who was attacking the two medics. More of Schillings's party jumped in, and that got his drinking mates from *Righteous* into the fray, picking up their chairs and bashing a path through the fighting to their besieged shipmate. The fight was on.

The orange hair of the American president appeared above his sea of bodyguards, away from the fight, hoisted up by two of his guardians so he could see what was happening. A quick look and he started yelling out orders from his safe viewpoint.

"Save Shillings from those monsters! They're kidnapping him!" Following the order, dozens of his own black-suited guardians jumped into the fray, fists flying, several of them attacking Crawford.

Wyckham's mouth dropped open and he shook his head in disbelief. His carefully planned intergalactic event was turning into a cosmic brawl.

All sorts of aliens now jumped in, seeing the renowned Gunner Crawford under attack, each alien fighting in this own peculiar way. Slicks were grabbing humans and just throwing them sideways as they tried to get to the two Slick medics. Dozens of sheep-size ants swarmed over the fighting Earthmen, picking them up and carrying them from the plaza to throw them into the lagoon. Large octopi-like creatures, horrible looking beings with multiple eyes that Wyckham employed for all sorts of underwater work, were grabbing two humans at a time with their multiple legs and cracking their heads together. But hundreds more of the black-clad visitors from every delegation were yelling and queuing up to get into the fight. *Idiots. Penguins lining up for an unplanned jump into the sea.*

"Hey you Russians! And you Saudis, too!" shouted Triumph to some other guards who apparently followed his orders as well. "Get over there and shoot the hell out of those aliens! What they're doing is completely illegal!" He stopped for a moment, struck by a brilliant idea. "Yeah! Illegal! Illegal aliens! More illegal aliens! Shoot 'em for Christ's sake!"

Shoot them? With what? Over the past few months, Wyckham had prepared for any eventuality on this day, and one thing he'd made sure of was that no visitors on this day would carry firearms. All the delegates had been thoroughly searched before boarding Wyckham's ships back on Earth, not to mention having their thoughts scanned by the mind-reading Fireflies as they arrived. Triumph could tell them to shoot all he wanted, but none of his lackeys had a gun.

The fact that Triumph was unaware that his security detail was unarmed had Wyckham shaking his head in bewilderment. Jesus, more evidence that the man's staff was terrible! To omit telling Triumph this? A minor detail not to worry about? Or maybe it was just that kings didn't listen to anybody.

Forget it man! You've got a plan for a riot, now get it underway!

"Minister Rawlins, the provosts? I'd admire you separate the two sides and escort our visitors to their quarters."

"Aye, captain", his lifelong friend and captain of the big 136-gun *Trinidad* replied. Although Wyckham was now both admiral and governor, Pierce Rawlins still addressed him as captain from their years together on the frigate *Righteous*, which Wyckham still commanded.

Rawlins turned to his assembled officers in their formal uniforms behind him. "Captain Hamilton, the provosts if you would? Get them right into the middle of this mess and separate the two sides. Right quick now!"

The youthful-looking captain next to him nodded, barked out orders to several bosuns behind him, whistles blared, and a dozen of the mudmen rolled into the melee', followed by scores of sailors. The big balls of mud struck first, rolling right into the mass of humans and absorbing them into their bodies until only their heads protruded. They continued to roll along, bashing the humans' heads on the paving with each rotation, until they could pick up no more, then they rolled over to the canal, convulsed their insides, and shat the muddy humans into the water, sometimes an impressive distance, all the time yelling in their fart-like language. One particularly large fellow managed to expel Shillings's surgeon further than any of the others, resulting in farted congratulations from his peers.

"Jesus, they're having a bowel moving contest," Wyckham muttered under his breath, shocked again just when he thought this day couldn't get any worse. Wasn't this simply a wonderful way to welcome visitors? Turning them into shite? He'd be hearing about this from his both his guests and his own counselors, that was a certainty.

Meanwhile, the human provosts, mostly bosons picked for their size and authoritative voices, were bellowing, "Vast all fightin'! Back 'way fum th' coach 'r I'll flog yer arses raw!" as they started thumping the rioters right and left with their canes. The efforts of the mudmen and bosuns quickly got the attention of the rioting crowd, and the combatants quickly separated, though each side continued yelling at each other in a variety of human and alien tongues. The end of hostilities allowed the coach and four to head for the field hospital with Lady Brashton riding up top with the driver, the smirk on her face discernable even from Wyckham's vantage point across the plaza. *What was she up to?*

Christ. Another day on Freeport.

Diplomatic Issues

An hour later, Wyckham was in the council chamber of the Doge's Palace, surrounded by magnificent gilt-framed frescoes depicting the Serene Republic of Venice's historic battles with Saracen Turks, Constantinople's Orthodox Christians, and her own Catholic neighbors. While he knew none of them were real paintings, just electrical images, he had to admire the attention to detail the Fireflies had achieved in this recreation of seventeenth century Venice. They'd done it not just in architecture but also in the paintings, sculptures, frescoes and mosaics. His brain told him it was all real—the marble steps he had climbed, the paintings and sculptures by renaissance masters he could touch, even the moldy smell that permeated the new city. But they were all images sent to his brain by the Fireflies. The marble steps were actually metal scaffolding that antmen had built, the artworks were all just those electrical images called "holo-graphs", and even the smell was a false signal sent to his nasal nerves.

The whole idea had come from the Fireflies. After the invasions in 1815 by French and British fleets, Wyckham had stopped opening portals to Earth. But the Fireflies had ways of observing any planet, and they'd steadily reported to him on the major developments occurring on Earth. He'd been able to follow events on Earth for 200 years, watching the nascent American republic lead the world into a period of peace and prosperity.

But all that had changed in the early 21st Century. There were too many means of unrestricted electrical communication, and various radical political factions around the world had embarked on an agenda to spread fear, anger and hatred of others for their own benefit. Britain broke with the rest of Europe, the United States broke into four separate nations, and constant border wars broke out. International cooperation on most issues ended, including the effort to slow global warming, and the rising of the oceans on Earth had inundated many coastal cities. In the late 20th century, the more advanced and wealthier nations had started to address the problem caused by too much fuel burning, but in the early 21st century a new wave of politicians withdrew their nations from the international climate agreements, and millions had perished or lost their homes. And the saddest loss was the renaissance city of Venice, one of the most beautiful cities on Earth, completely destroyed by rising sea levels and violent storms.

Firefly Tracy had always pushed Wyckham to re-establish contact with Earth, expressing her humanitarian concerns about the growing problems there. But Wyckham knew her race also wanted increased access to human males with their inexhaustible supply of life-containing spermatozoa, since the Fireflies could harness the life energy in male seed obtained through sexual intercourse. With the millions of tiny cells that they could receive from every instance of copulation, the Fireflies had access to more life energy than some entire civilizations possessed, which they used to increase their own powers considerably. Their increased abilities had been key to success in the ongoing wars with the Draesh, the thirty-foot monstrous pigs that terrorized the entire cosmos by devouring whole populations for their life energy.

For two centuries, Wyckham had denied the Fireflies' entreaties for contact with Earth, but now the world's crises had pushed him to action. While world war had not yet broken out, the Firefly Tracy had convinced him that it was only a few years off, and with weapons that could quickly destroy the entire planet, Earth was in mortal danger. But Freeport could step in, reducing Earth's immediate problems by accepting its refugees and reducing its heat retention through League of Worlds' technology. Freeport could show the nations of Earth how peace, prosperity, and the advancement of civilization could be achieved by cooperation with other worlds.

First of all, Earth needed homes for millions of displaced people, from bankrupt businessmen in flooded London to impoverished farmers underwater in India. Freeport was an immense and mostly uninhabited planet with lots of arable land, except for the developed area around Port Wyckham and some remote highland areas where a few thousand Draesh still hid out. Several million aliens had settled on Freeport over the years, mostly refugees whom Wyckham had welcomed, but in his opinion the place needed more humans to emphasize its human foundation.

Not to mention that Freeport was an incredibly valuable world and various members of the League of Worlds had ambitions for it. Several worlds, especially those in the Slick and Lycan systems, were constantly pushing their races to immigrate there and gain influence over the planet's intergalactic politics. If nothing changed it was only a matter of time before one of those planets would use its immigrants for a *coup d' etat* on Freeport. But a hundred million more humans on Freeport would stop that in the one way that the League would accept—a majority of the popular and militarily unthreatening humans.

For months, Wyckham had developed the plan with all the alien leaders on Freeport to accept immigration from Earth. The effort began in May when the Fireflies had simultaneously interrupted every electrical communication network on Earth, sending his greeting and pictures of the planet along with images of Wyckham's sailors and all the other alien races on Freeport. The communication effort continued for months, with messages every day telling the history of Freeport, from its days as the home world for the evil Dreash to its last two centuries as a center for trade, science, the arts, and tolerance. The final enticement to at least visit Freeport was the electrical reconstruction of the city of Venice, offered as a tourist destination just as the original Venice had become. This day, October 1, 2028, would be the first day for visits to Freeport and its New Venice, with transportation portals opening in over two dozen cities.

At first, after their initial astonishment, the nations of Earth took different positions on the proposal from another world, with some excited by the possibilities and others reacting with fear and belligerence. But after the two coastal US nations, along with Great Britain, France and Germany announced that they would send delegations, most of the major countries on Earth joined the pack, afraid they would lose out on commercial and military opportunities. The new year came, the humans had arrived—and the grand opening had all gone to shite.

Seated at the long, carved benches around the room were members of each Earthly delegation, representatives from each race in the League of Worlds, and prominent citizens of Freeport, both human and alien.

The visiting humans were somewhat uncomfortable seated next to the various aliens, which was understandable given that many had large teeth, frightening countenances, strange languages, and overpowering body odor. They were focusing on the pitchers of water on the tables before them, fighting down the urge to flee. *Well, they'd have to get used to the way things are up here if they want our help.* Wyckham's sailors had quickly become comfortable with aliens, and with time these new visitors would as well. But just in case there were problems today, Wyckham had red-coated marines with bayonetted muskets stationed about the room. Wyckham stood and called the meeting to order.

"Ladies and gentlemen, welcome all to Freeport. This is the world where all beings in need find a safe place to live, myriad career opportunities, exciting scientific research, and stimulating arts. This city of Venice shows what can be achieved…"

"Bull-shit! Buncha bull-shit!" It was one of the delegates from the southern American nation, a pudgy middle-age man with tousled hair and in need of a shave, standing and furiously yelling, spittle flying from his lips. "We come here and the first thing you do is kidnap a world leader? Where is President Shillings? We demand you give him back! Immediately! No fucking around! Get him back to us now!"

Christ, can't even get the meeting started. Wyckham turned to a nearby Slick, Freeport's head surgeon, wearing nothing but a belt bearing electrical medical devices. "Mister 2256, can you bring us all up to date on President Schillings?" The Slick rose to address the crowd.

"I am number 2256," he stated, thinking to impress the humans with his high ranking in Slick society. No one reacted. "Your leader having surgery," the tall alien spoke through the translator horn implanted to his head. "Had oxygen shutoff to brain—what humans call 'stroke'. Most of brain went dead but we reconstitute, will be all finished tomorrow. All memories will be returned."

That only enraged the angry delegate further. "What? One of these chromed lizards is poking around in Shillings's brain?" He turned to Wyckham. "What kind of idiot are you to even let these dangerous beings on this planet, much less let them run off with an important world leader and dig into his brain? Filthy things are probably brainwashing him! Get Shillings back to the Midwest delegation now! Our own doctors will take care of him, not these monsters!"

Wyckham leaned over into head Firefly's ear. "Now who is this belligerent fellow?"

"Sherman Bamming, Vice President of the Confederate States of America, the American south," she replied. Wyckham nodded in recognition. Over the past few months, alien Tracy had told Wyckham everything that her race had learned from listening to electrical communications on Earth, especially over the last twenty years. With regard to Bamming, Wyckham knew he was the man who had masterminded the ascent of Victor Triumph, the last president of the United States and a divisive man who started Earth's breakdown thirteen years ago. Thanks to him, Victor Triumph was elected to the USA's last presidency, and later declared himself Emperor of Earth, constantly inciting his followers worldwide to revolt against their governments. He and Bamming, both graduates of America's finest universities and wealthy New York businessmen, moved to Texas when America broke up, changed their image to rural cowboys wearing large hats and bearing silvered pistols, and won the elections to run the southern nation."

Thinking of Victor Triumph brought up a question Wyckham had wondered about.

"Victor Triumph? That's the man's real name?"

"No," the Firefly replied. "He lost the presidential election in 2020 when it was discovered that his real name was Ronaldo Rumpero, an immigrant from El Salvador. In the 1950's he had dyed his hair, bleached his skin, changed his name and entered politics, using funds that his father made from smuggling illegal immigrants.

"His political career began with his weekly TV show, an electrically transmitted play in the 90's, called "Go Fuck Yourself", which was sent into people's homes and became extremely successful. Scenes of him severely beating foreigners and newspaper reporters were wildly popular with certain sectors of the American populace, and they elected him president, with Mark Shillings as his vice president. During the final months of his term as the nation's leader, American forces conquered northern Mexico and occupied some border areas in Canada. To win over undecided voters before the 2020 elections he started brief wars with north Korea and Iran."

Hmmmph! Wickham snorted in disgust. Of course the man had invaded his neighbors and started wars with distant nations. That's what royalty did, since their blood was better than everyone else's and that gave them the right to conquer weaker nations.

"Then in 2020 his actual El Salvadoran nationality was discovered by a Washington newspaper", the Firefly continued. "Having started his political career on an anti-immigrant stance, this discovery went over poorly with his base of supporters. He denied the accusation but was unable to produce a birth certificate, and DiCarpaccio won the election. He promptly declared the election fraudulent, started his America First party, and led an armed insurrection that broke the United States up into four smaller nations—Triumph's southern-based Confederated States of America, Shillings's Midwest States of America, the New England States of America and the Pacific States of America. Relations are not cordial between the coastal nations and the other two, and they often fight border wars. Triumph still sends out a constant stream of electrical communications pushing his agenda of fear, anger, and worldwide discord."

And now he was here, along with his court and this Bamming fellow, thinking to spread their nonsense on Freeport. *Hummph!*

Before Wyckham could respond to Bamming's tirade, the chief Slick surgeon replied. "The President Shillings has recovered enough to communicate. I take your doctor to him now. He sees he does fine. Would have died with your doctors, your doctors incompetent." With that he turned and headed for the door, assuming the member of an inferior race he was addressing would follow him as ordered. But no way was Bamming allowing Schilling's physician to walk out the door alone with that frightening monster.

"Our doctor should go off alone with that thing? Forget it! He needs security for a trip through this dangerous place, but thanks to you my bodyguards are useless, they, don't have a single gun! Give him some of those big balls of shit that you use for security, and make sure they have orders to protect him!"

So even though this Bamming had made it clear what he thought of Freeport's aliens, he'd witnessed how effective mudmen were in a scrap and wanted them on his side.

Wyckham addressed a large mudman at the door. "Chief constable Bubbler, can you have two of your fellows escort the surgeon here to the hospital along with Mister 2256? Have them make sure they return promptly and safely?"

Bubbler replied through his translator using sailor's English that he'd learned from selling aphrodisiac sticks from the rabbit worlds to Wyckham's sailors.

"Aye cap'm, though what 'iss bugger's worried 'bout 'z beyond me ken. Let's go," he instructed the surgeon. He then spoke in his farty language to two nearby mudmen, who replied with similar repulsive sounds and rolled towards the door.

After a brief hesitation, Bamming apparently decided the physician was safe in this "shitball's" care and nodded to the surgeon, who followed the three aliens from the chamber, leaving a trail of slime across the floor thanks to his recent swim in the murky Grand Canale. Maybe the meeting could now get underway?

"Ladies and gentlemen, may we resume? The purpose of this gathering is to establish relations between our two worlds. First of all, we wish to insure to you that we have only peaceable intentions, our main goal is only to aid a troubled Earth, our home planet. There are members of the League of Worlds who can assist Earth in managing its current atmospheric problems. And also, many of my sailors would like to visit their descendants in England, people they've never..."

"Atmospheric problems?" Christ, it was Bamming again. "You mean 'global warming' I suppose? You've had secret meetings with the coastal nations, haven't you? Earth doesn't have any climate problems, just God's normal weather cycles, which mankind has experienced many times over the centuries. We don't need your help with our weather! We're here to trade with you. Our nation has oil and all sorts of other goods that we'd like to trade for your..." he stopped for moment as some delegates on the other side of the chamber began to grumble... "technology."

Now the complaining from the other group became audible and one of its members shot to his feet. He was a handsome man, tall and trim, around sixty, with wavy hair and a well-trimmed goatee. His group immediately hushed up in deference to this man.

"First, I want to thank Governor Wyckham, the beings known as Fireflies, and all the other diverse and fascinating races that have invited us here today," he stated in a calm, intellectual tone. "My name is Leonardo DiCarpaccio, elected in 2020 as President of the United States..."

The southern and midwestern delegates exploded in self-righteous fury.

"Bullshit! It was rigged!"

"What about the emails?"

"Lock him up!"

Wyckham leaned over to the lead Firefly. "This fellow here is the 'movie star' you told me about? Became famous for acting in the electrical plays?"

"Yes," she replied. "He beat Triumph in America's 2020 election, causing the Midwest and South to split from the federal government, after Triumph persuaded his followers that DiCarpaccio was a criminal because he used the wrong communications device when he first entered government."

Wyckham could understand people being unhappy with leaders who hurt their country with wars or repression, but he was puzzled about the importance of electronic communication etiquette. "What was the problem with the communications device he used?"

"We fail to comprehend that as well, but millions of Americans became enraged over it for some reason," she replied, putting a confused viz on her holographic face to match her reply. "Possibly he selected the wrong color for his communicator? These devices have become a personal identity statement for many Americans."

So a nation broke up because of the color of an official's communicator? Wyckham began to doubt the wisdom of having invited modern humans to Freeport.

DiCarpaccio continued, apparently used to assaults from the Southern and Midwestern neighbors. "We differ with our fellow Americans" (that released a chorus of anger from across the room—'Don't call us your fellows! You're no American!'), but the actor continued, "on the issue of climate change. The West and our New England friends are having their coasts inundated and our agriculture is being destroyed by drought. We seek any advice and assistance you can provide, as opposed to the gentlemen across the room. And you should understand that the "technology" they want is advanced weaponry, mainly for use against us."

The Midwest legation erupted in denials but the Southern contingent basically confirmed his statement. "You're goddam right, and when we get them, you're done!" and "San Francisco gonna get burned into glass!" Now an elderly white-haired gentleman stood up in the middle of the New England delegation.

"I'm President Arnold Sandberg of New England, the proud nation of socialized medicine and equal opportunity." That upped the fury level in the room but Sandberg continued unfazed as had DiCarpaccio. "New England also is here to seek aid on climate change, clearly Earth's greatest problem. All our scientists agree that…"

The southern and midwestern delegations now started throwing their glasses and pitchers of water at Sandberg, who had to duck, and the two coastal delegations responded with their own missiles. Several diplomats started wrestling, and all the other groups seated between them, both human and alien, stood up and headed for the exits, trying to avoid the barrage of glass filling the air and shattering all over the room.

Christ, another brawl. "Who are those people trying to get out?" Wyckham asked the Firefly. "Is the British contingent here?"

"Yes, the young man there with the jacket over his head is Britain's prime minister, Alistair Cochrane. I have spoken with him a bit and he seems a decent and rational man."

Alistair Cochrane. In the history of the Royal Navy, his ancestor, Thomas Cochrane, was the most famous officer after Nelson. Thomas Cochrane had been on Freeport in 1815, performing incredible acts of valor during a battle with the Draesh, at one point personally leading an attack inside the portal cave. After he left Freeport, Wyckham learned from the Fireflies that he had gone to Chile and Uruguay with one frigate, built a small fleet from local sources, and pretty much single-handedly won those two nations their independence from brutal Spain. Wyckham had so looked forward to meeting the hero's descendant. But first there was the matter of the chaos in the room.

"Captain Morrison, it's time for that volley, if you would?"

The captain of marines nodded acknowledgement to Wyckham and bellowed out, "Detail, ready!" Over a dozen of the red-coated marines around the room put their big Brown Bess muskets to their shoulders, their captain yelled, "Salute!" and the muzzles were raised, "Cock firelocks" and hammers clicked, then "Shoot!" and they fired a volley at the ceiling. The bullets flew through the holographic ceiling without causing any damage, their frescoes still perfect.

The blast was amplified by the attending Fireflies, made to sound as if it really was echoing off real walls. The noise was so loud that everyone froze and jammed their palms over their ears.

"That will be enough!" Wyckham roared through the billowing smoke. "Since you can't seem to gather without battling one another, "marines will escort you to separate waiting rooms! You will get a schedule for meetings one country at a time! Now get out of my sight!"

Wyckham walked over and took Cochrane's arm before he could leave. "With your exception, Sir Alistair. Might we have a word?"

Around them the fighting delegates took one look at the marines, and especially their accompanying mudmen, and immediately became meek as sheep. The smoky room was completely silent as they were herded to their apartments in the palace. Cochrane pulled his jacket down and Wyckham got his first look at the man.

Damn if he wasn't the spitting image of the man Wyckham had known 200 years ago. The same bulbous nose, tightly pursed lips, brown eyes, and of course the red hair of a true Irishman.

"There's a small reception chamber right over here where we can have some privacy. I need someone that I trust to tell me the recent history and lay of the land in Earthly diplomacy. The room is stocked with refreshments I think we both need right now. Bring anyone you wish. Representatives of the other races here on Freeport will be joining us."

Cochrane, still a little shaken, nodded his agreement as Wyckham turned to his valet and Minister of Civilian affairs, Thomas Obujimi.

The former African had been a slave in 1814, managing a plantation near Baltimore. A foraging crew from Righteous offered to set him free if he signed up with the Royal Navy, an offer he immediately accepted. While he was a terrible seaman, he made for a perfect valet, with his experience at plantation mansions dressing aristocrats and running balls. Over the past 200 years here on Freeport his management skills had brought him to the highest levels of government, though he continued his duties as Wyckham's man, claiming that "The Governor would show up at state meetings dressed in Navy slop-trousers and smelling like day-old fish if I didn't keep careful watch upon his toilette and dress."

"Mister Obujimi, could you find the members of the Governance committee and ask them to join us and the British delegation in the Doge's office forthwith?" Obujimi nodded crisply and set off about the hall to assemble the various humans and aliens who represented all the major races on Freeport.

Ten minutes later everyone was in the magnificently appointed Doge's office, Cochrane and his associates marveling at the mahogany paneling, statues of Greek gods, and frescoed ceilings. Seated on plush velvet sofas along with Cochrane and three of his assistants were Freeport's most important leaders—Pierce Rawlins in his position of Minister of War, Thomas Obujimi, the Firefly leader in her image of Tracy Brashton, Slick number 2256, Bubbler the mudman, the leader of the ants who went by the name of Worker Queen, the chief of the native Goshen named Dreashpalone, and Wulfe, one of the wolf-like Lycans, an old friend who had played a key part in defeating the Draesh in '14. Also present were representatives of the gorillas, fish people, the boulder beings, the twining ivy, and the octopi. Wyckham stood and opened the meeting.

"Sadly, it seems that there are politics galore among our Earth visitors, which shouldn't have surprised me, though the level of rancor is above anything I can recall from when I was last there. So I've invited the Prime Minister of my old country, England, to give us some background on the people and nations that we will be dealing with if we want to resettle millions of humans and help Earth with some of its problems. May I introduce none other than the descendent of Thomas Cochrane himself, Alistair Cochrane?"

That produced a volley of cheers, clicks, farts, and other indications of welcome in the many strange languages common on Freeport. Every being on the planet knew the name of Thomas Cochrane, the man who almost single-handedly expelled a French-Dreash attack in '15. Most famously, he'd stood up from the rubble of a battlefield to chat with a Dreash while behind his back loading a half-buried thirty-two pounder. He then fired off the big gun, downing a hovering Dreash warship.

Cochrane stood up and nodded to his cheering fans, then made a circuit around the room to introduce himself to each individual. To his credit, he seemed to be comfortable with every strange being he met, unlike most humans who reacted with fear and rejection when first meeting Freeport's aliens.

"So Prime Minister, if you would be so kind, please take a few minutes to bring bus up-to-date on the major developments on Earth since 1815? Obviously, you cannot cover all the major issues of 200 years, just a brief summary?"

"Well, I can do that," the Prime Minister replied in a heavy Irish brogue. "But where's that refreshment you so kindly offered this thirsty Irishman? God knows I can use a drink after that shit-show out there!"

So Alistair had another common trait of his ancestor's besides looks. Obujimi magically appeared with a full tumbler of caramel-colored liquor.

"Would American whiskey be satisfactory?" the minister valet asked. "Thomas Cochrane had a taste for it as I recall."

"Faith and begorrah if your man doesn't know me already!" Cochrane gleefully said as he took a long gulp. Then he settled back to answer Wyckham's request.

"You want it short? The whole place is really fucked up," he stated bluntly. "That about sums it up. The story of my world is a sad one, because for 190 of the last 208 years, the world steadily improved. Slavery was mostly abolished by 1865, the rule of royalty was gone by 1918, Europe gave up war in 1945, and medical advances raised lifespans throughout the 20th century.

But by the end of that century, everything changed. Social media, personal electrical communication, had become so powerful that a single person could send messages to millions of people in seconds. Everyone was obsessed with their phones... ah, their communication devices, and certain political factions used them to spread baseless accusations. A few disgruntled and angry bombasts were able to gain millions of followers with constant blarney, primarily the belief that all government officials were criminals giving your money away to undeserving neighbors, either those across the street or in the nation next door. Some nations also used the power of this new kind of communication to destroy governments. Russia and China, run by calculating tyrants, put their state's power into spreading false news and interfering with elections, successfully contributing to the dissolution of democratic governments around the world. Not only did the United States break apart, but wars broke out almost everywhere.

"I'm embarrassed to say that Britain was one of the first countries to become irrational, voting to leave the European Union in 2016, which resulted in a prolonged economic recession and naval skirmishes with Holland and Sweden. Prussia broke from Germany and conquered Alsace and Lorraine, Russia quickly took back the Baltic states, Triumph's Southern Confederacy invaded Northern Mexico, and the Midwest states, prodded by the Southern Confederacy, attacked Canada and annexed much of Saskatchewan and Alberta. Prussia even tried a landing on East Anglia, but the Royal Navy persuaded them that was a bad idea—those that survived, anyway."

Cochrane paused a moment to address his dry throat problem with another sip. "Mister Triumph, now the self-designated Emperor of the World, presides over the Triumphant League, an association of militant states with old grudges to settle. Besides his Confederacy and the Midwest States, members include Russia, Prussia, Italy, Austria, Hungary, Poland, Northern Korea, Serbia, Turkey, Saudi Arabia, Venezuela, Argentina, and a host of tyrannical African states. Standing against him is the North Atlantic Treaty Organization, comprising the two coastal American nations, Britain, Germany, France, Spain, and several eastern European countries. Japan, Australia, and Scandanavia usually ally with this group as well. There is also an organization called the United

Nations that includes almost all countries, though most member countries break its rules whenever they feel like it."

He took a pause and sighed. "Now Earth is now fully Balkanized. The smaller nations conduct border wars whenever they feel like they can get away with it, invading both members of the opposing alliance and members of their own group as well. But if war breaks out between any two major powers, the rest of the big powers and their vassal states jump in. World war hasn't yet broken out, but we've had some close calls over the last ten years. If it happens, it could be an unbelievably destructive war that would make most of Earth uninhabitable.

"Adding to all that, the constant burning of fuels has heated up the entire planet, melting polar ice and raising ocean levels. Besides Venice, hundreds of large coastal cities have been made uninhabitable, forcing populations to move inland and fight over the reduced arable land. In addition, the increased planetary heat caused widespread drought in South America and Africa, and the nations there often fight water wars.

"So that's it, in a nutshell. I'm here, representing England. We were the first to vote to hurt ourselves when we withdrew from the European Union, resulting in the end of foreign investment and the devastation of our economy. After a few years of turmoil, we had learned our lesson and voted out the idiots who'd created the mess, and now we're electing rational people to government. I was barely elected, thanks to the fame of my famous ancestor, in a close race against Bernard Hill, a well-known entertainer whose only skill was performing pratfalls. But while our political problems are ebbing, we immediately need a place to settle about eight million refugees from Manchester, Portsmouth, Liverpool, Weymouth, Dover, and a dozen other coastal cities. And we'd love to work with your lightball friends and the other… ahhh… unusual peoples that we see around here to address our climate problems. Your top lightball here," he nodded to the head Firefly, "has told me that several members of the League of Worlds are familiar with atmospheric creation and management, that they routinely do it whenever they colonize a new planet. Certainly, the United Nations and NATO are interested in this, even if much of humanity thinks we don't have a climate problem, Triumph and the rest of his wankers insist it's just normal weather changes and the oceans are going to recede all by themselves any minute now. But many nations would welcome your assistance."

Christ. Earth Balkanized, for God's sake. Alien Tracy had been able to observe Earth's climate problems from her observation point from light years away but hadn't seen the chaos occurring between its nations. Would it be possible for the Fireflies to work with his old home planet without Freeport getting attacked by one of its fanatical nations? If this Triumphant League didn't believe there was a problem, no way would those countries allow a bunch of frightening aliens to tinker with their climate. Hell, these rogue nations are probably here to just to observe and plan a takeover of Freeport, with its invaluable transporter technology and vast deposits of gold and natural resources.

And he could just imagine what kind of armaments these constantly warring nations possessed. They probably had flying ships, beam weapons, rockets that aimed themselves, and bombs that could destroy an entire city—weapons that many alien worlds had developed in civilizations even younger than Earth's. In contrast, Freeport was prohibited from importing or developing new weapons, though Wyckham had done a few things in secret. But with wooden sailing ships and single shot guns, any nation on Earth could take this planet in a heartbeat if they were able to get their weapons past transporter screening. No race had been able to do that in 200 years, but humanity had been at war on Earth for centuries and might have developed electrical devices that could outwit the transporter's safeguards.

Yet he still wanted to help Earth. His own race was in trouble, for Christ's sake, and he could help them by arranging for assistance from other planets. Both the Slicks and Lycans routinely manufactured atmospheres for barren planets they colonized. They could produce a breathable, healthy atmosphere on a planet within two or three years, depending on a variety of factors, such as the size of the world and its distance to a sun. Cleaning up Earth's existing atmosphere should be relatively quick and easy. And he could start the process with England, led by a man he believed he could trust.

"Prime Minister Cochrane, you have been most informative. Let's meet again soon. I certainly believe we can help your country and your planet. Minister Obujimi will meet with your assistants and begin planning the first wave of English immigrants. For now, I must meet with all the other delegations, but mayhap we can meet for dinner later? I'd like to spend more time with you to learn more about the present circumstances on Earth and to discuss climate solutions."

Cochrane nodded agreement and stood up to leave, stopped as he realized his drink was not empty, downed it quickly and headed out the door.

Wyckham decided to bring in the visiting delegations in order of civility. "Thomas, the Pacific States delegation, if you would."

Obujimi exited and returned within a few minutes with Leonardo DiCarpaccio and four members of his staff. After the obligatory introductions, all sat back down and President DiCarpaccio addressed the group.

"First of all, my deepest thanks for inviting the representatives of all humanity to come here to this magnificent reproduction of one of our lost treasures, the city of Venice. If we achieve nothing else but travel between our two worlds, so that humans can once again marvel at this jewel of our history, our relationship will be a wonderful success."

Well, this fellow doesn't seem so bad. Maybe another nation he could work with alongside England?

"But yes, I would like to accomplish more, both for the citizens of the Pacific States and the rest of humanity. Firstly, my country has several million residents that lost their homes when southern California went underwater. Our attempts to resettle our urban flood victims into agricultural inland areas have not been very successful. Understandably, those who had previously lived in Los Angeles and other urban areas couldn't live in areas without lattes, sushi, and decent internet speed. Do you have these things here? I was told this was an advanced civilization, but all I see is clothing styles from ancient history and soldiers carrying weapons from the American Revolution. And do you have anything like a Starbucks?"

Latte? His people need Italian milk? Sooshy? What's that, a child's game? Fast internal nets? Whatever could that be? And Star bucks? Male deer that have stars on them? What would urban residents in the crowded cities of 2028 Earth do with deer? Maybe it wasn't going to be so easy to work with this nation after all.

"In addition to our own issues," DiCarpaccio continued, "we are a compassionate nation and gravely concerned over the plight of those in Africa. Before I was elected, I ran a foundation to feed and help sub-Saharan Africans, but climate change has wiped out the farmers there and the problem is now overwhelming. I understand that this world has fertile soil and a good climate for growing food. Earth has at least 300 million starving Africans that with very little help could produce vast amounts of food here."

Jesus! 300 million! Wyckham had been to Africa many times and knew the man wasn't lying about its natives' ability to work land under difficult conditions. With the abundant water and mild climate on Freeport, not to mention the increased sunlight from two suns, the planet could easily feed the increased population that immigration would bring. Hell, it probably could feed many local systems!

"We will certainly take your proposals under consideration. Mister Rawlins, let's you and I put together a list of the kind of skilled people we need here on Freeport and a schedule for settling them. And Thomas, I assume you would like to get involved in the African matter?" Thomas Obujimi had been an African prince before he was abducted by Arab slavers and bore strong feelings for his fellow African peoples.

"I would most certainly take up the topic with all my strength," he replied. "And I thank you most heartily for this opportunity to help my brethren."

The Pacific Coast President turned to Obujimi. "Let me warn you that modern Africa is a continent with many small nations you'll have to deal with," DiCarpaccio replied. "Most have corrupt governments that will demand all sorts of gifts, funds for their personal enrichment or advanced weapons to invade their neighbors. Only then will they allow you to traipse off with half their populations, even though it will be to those peoples' immense benefit. It won't be easy, believe me, I've worked with them for years."

"You need not worry about them. Before we were abducted, my family had dealt with African leaders for generations They will do as they're told when it's an Obujimi telling them."

Wyckham had no doubt that Obujimi would be successful in his efforts. Any reluctant tyrant would soon find an angry and well-armed revolution knocking at his palace door. Wycham turned back to Di-Carpaccio. He wanted to hear more about the political situation of the four American states.

"So what advice can you give me for dealing with the other American states? The southern group seems to be a handful. What about the others?"

"You'll find the New England folks more or less reasonable, we generally work with them on most issues. The Midwest, not so much. It is now almost all rural. The region lost most of its cities when the population ignored the radical increase in violent storms and didn't build levees along the rivers and the Great Lakes. Chicago, Milwaukee, St Louis, and dozens of smaller cities are underwater. The rural populations didn't seem to care, President Shillings convinced them that it was God's way of punishing sinful city folk, and they pretty much rejoiced over the thousands of urban deaths and refugees in their own states. And since they are devoted Christians and the bible says nothing about other worlds, they and their president will follow Victor Triumph and reject your assistance.

"Then there's the south. Seems they never forgave the north for winning the brutal civil war of the 1860's and in 2020 jumped at the chance to start it all over again. They welcomed Triumph and his family as their rulers when the USA broke apart and promptly attacked Virginia and Mexico. While Triumph's military efforts have now stalled, he continues to put out his fearmongering message of dystopia and anger to the world, and it continues to gain followers. 'Got a problem? You didn't do anything, it's your neighbor screwing you.' Works for millions. And it really resonates in the southern states where bitterness over the American Civil War still lingers.

"You should understand that while many nations are here to get help with refugees and climate change, Triumph's and his mentor Bamming are here for one reason only—advanced weaponry. I don't know what they think you've got, maybe they just guess that any planet that mastered space travel must have advanced weapons as well, but they're here to get whatever hi-tech weapons you and any other worlds may have."

Wyckham believed the man completely. *Hmmph!* And maybe there's been some kind of unauthorized communication between Earth and Freeport to aid this dangerous nation? While the League of Worlds put on a great face of inter-word unity, the fact was that many alien races had ambitions on Freeport. With all sorts of natural resources, especially the materials to make fuel for their ships, not to mention the Draesh transporter that had revolutionized space travel, it was an inter-galactic plum ripe for the picking. While there had been no attempts at a coup-d'-etad, over the past two centuries both Obujimi and the Fireflies had uncovered spy rings among Slicks, Lycans, the Snakemen, and several other races. For centuries the League was content to let this valuable world be ruled by the unthreatening humans, but if any race thought it wasn't getting its fair share of Freeport's riches, that could change overnight. And an alliance with millions of immigrating humans would be perfect cover for a takeover by one of the alien galaxies.

Wyckham's thoughts were interrupted by some yelling and the sounds of scuffling right outside the office door. Now what?

"I believe discontent has escalated with the Midwest delegation," DiCarpaccio dryly commented. "There was a mess brewing out there when I came in, sounds like it's gotten worse. Their physician returned from visiting the Midwest President and reported, sending the whole delegation bat-shit about something. You should probably deal with them now. Let me make my exit and we'll follow up with you on the issues. Good luck dealing with my Midwest friends, hope you get them cooled down. As with any theocracy, relations with them can be difficult, with God is on their side they tend not to compromise with sinners like you and me."

DiCarpaccio made his farewells around the room and Wyckham's personal marine sentry unbolted and opened the door. But before the western president could make his exit, a mass of people and aliens, Triumph among them, burst into the room, with red coated marines struggling with both the Midwestern and Southern delegates. The sentry prepared to bash the nearest one with his musket stock, but Wyckham grabbed his arm in the nick of time, then bellowed out in his best captain's voice to the rest of the scrum.

"Belay that! 'Vast fighting or I'll throw you all to the mudmen! Every one of you! Enough!" His voice was so loud in the small room, amplified by hidden Fireflies, that all fighting immediately stopped.

The scene looked like a roomful of Venetian statues taken from the plaza. Marines with muskets ready to swing, black-suited humans with fists cocked, all frozen with their eyes bugged out at the violence of Wyckham's order and the threat of a trip inside the dreaded mudmen.

"Marines will separate all combatants!" Wyckham ordered, and the marines, shoving with their muskets, quickly herded all humans to one wall and the aliens, mostly Slicks, against the other. "Now what in hell's going on here?"

An irate Triumph shoved a marine's musket aside, shaking his head. "Get that ridiculous antique out of my face, you ancient loser" he muttered to the marine as he stepped forward. *What a surprise, he's involved in this cockup*, thought Wyckham. Triumph pointed at one of the Slicks.

"These eggheads say they're going to keep Shillings! Maybe forever! I demand they return him to the Midwest delegates, his people! Now!" With that, Triumph grabbed a seat and sat down, nose high like a king on his throne.

Wyckham turned to Slick number 2256. "What's he talking about?"

"Human president now healthy, in love with human Tracy Brashton," it replied. "Says he stays here with her till end of time. This man's guards try abducting him, we stop." It then looked right at Triumph. "'All beings on Freeport have freedom of choice'—League of World's statute number 3059."

So Schillings had apparently fallen ass-over-tit for Baroness Tracy Brashton. Over his time on Earth, Wyckham had seen many a supposedly devout Christian fall for women of ill repute the first chance they got, and this old geyser hadn't stood a chance against Tracy Brashton's onslaught. Wyckham's very manipulative childhood sweetheart had snared another beau, and this time it affected interplanetary relations. He was getting increasingly angered that she had been in contact with Schillings before his arrival—clearly he'd recognized her as soon as he arrived in the plaza. What was she scheming up? *Control, Wyckham, control! You've got every race in the cosmos here to meet with Earth. Stay calm, carry on.*

"They drugged him!" yelled a furious Triumph. "They screwed with his brain! Now he doesn't know what's good for him!"

"Schillings suffer severe stroke," the chief Slick countered. "Brain was dead from lack of atmosphere. Our surgeons restore cerebral function exactly as before stroke. Same memories, same beliefs, same person."

Wyckham didn't trust Slick politicians, but he did thrust their surgeons. Slicks considered themselves the best at everything, and while that made for some very one-sided politicians, it certainly was true for their medical personnel. They may not have ever taken the Hippocratic Oath, but their medical research and practices were the best in the entire cosmos, and Wyckham had never seen a Slick physician put politics over patient care.

However, Wyckham certainly doubted that this American bigmouth would believe that. From what Cochrane had explained, one of the core beliefs of the new politics of the breakaway American states was that no foreigners could be trusted. If they couldn't even get along on Earth with slightly different humans, the chance they could work with strange-looking races from other planets was probably nil.

"President Triumph, I suggest you simmer down," Wyckham told him sternly, fed up with the man's constant belligerence. "It's your chance to tell me of your issues, President DiCarpaccio and I are done. Tell me your concerns".

DiCarpaccio nodded goodbye and headed out, muttering as he passed the orange head of the seated Southerner, "Hope you get your weapons, Vic". Triumph responded with a raised middle finger, a gesture that Wyckham had never seen before but assumed was not friendly. The Midwest delegates applauded his gesture with laughter and congratulations. "Way to show that faggot, Victor! You're the man!"

Triumph now stood, surveyed the crowd like he owned everyone, and very loudly started to complain. "Now listen here, Mr. Captain or Governor or whoever you think you are. Ever since we arrived here, we've been treated unfairly. You chat with the Brits and the west coasters, probably offering them all sorts of trade and technology, but we get no respect. Shit, we had to break the door down just to have a talk. Don't you know who I am? You better just listen to what I say or you're gonna have real problems, believe me."

Triumph was a different man without TV cameras around. Of a type Wyckham was very familiar with—royalty. Wyckham had worked for decades to make sure that the concept of aristocracy, the belief that the rich and powerful had superior blood lines, did not get established on Freeport. While he had never thought much of American democracy, he couldn't argue with their abhorrence of kings.

Kings were always obsessed with their image, trying to make history that proved their families were superior to everyone else's. And that usually led to war. Inbred and deranged, there was always childish competition between kings, such as whose city had the biggest walls and most beautiful gates. When that pissing contest settled nothing, the walls had to be tested, and war between kings was almost constant. The people often initially liked a new king because of the land and booty that an aggressive one could take from his unprepared neighbors. But kings never understood that conquered peoples would never love them and were always surprised when those they subjugated eventually banded together and fought back. Their big walls never kept out the determined, and all the horror and hardship of war came back upon each aggressive king and his people. Now one of these lunatics had come to Wyckham's door with a list of demands. Disgust welled up in his gut and he exploded in anger.

"NO, YOU LISTEN, TRIUMPH!" Boomed Wyckham, as he drew his sword and bashed the flat down on the desk in front of him. That certainly got the loud American's attention. Wyckham tried to calm himself but he couldn't resist raising his weapon to point at the demanding human in front of him, who jumped up and backed away, looking pretty frightened. "This is a peaceful world where all beings have personal freedom and are treated equally no matter where they came from. It's clear you don't share those basic beliefs. So we really have nothing to talk about. While I expect many nations from Earth will be sending visitors and immigrants to Freeport, this world is not open to your belligerent nation nor its so-called Emperor. There will be no trade between us, no contact. We will open no portals to your states, and from now on no officials from the Midwest or Southern American states will be brought here."

Triumph, having retreated behind a line of his personal guards, now seemed to regain some of his former bombast. "You little… you think you can keep me out? While you trade with the enemies of my great nation? Sell them all sorts of weapons from your alien friends? Completely unfair! You have no idea the fire and fury you risk!"

Wyckham, cooled down a little from his outburst, looked straight into Triumph's eyes. "I understand you like travel bans, Mister Emperor? So this one is for you. Get yourself and your people out of my sight and back to the docks. Call your personal litter or however you get carried around, God forbid you should travel by foot like we mortals. But get out of my sight. Have a nice trip home."

Wyckham nodded to Bubbler, the head mudman. Two of them rolled up and that was all Triumph and his people needed to see. Several of his party, heads bandaged from their earlier trips inside mudmen, yelled out farewells and made beelines for the door.

"Holy shit!… We're leaving… Ahhh!… Nice meeting you…!," and they were gone. Good riddance.

But Wyckham didn't hear Bamming's whispering to Triumph and his aids while marines escorted them back to the docks.

"Everyone take a look at this place. A world at the center of interplanetary trade, and full of gold. And all they have to protect it are wooden ships and 200-year-old cannons."

And then, in what must have been divine coincidence, a big snake slithered up with a folded wax-sealed paper that would start the Confederacy off on interplanetary conquest.

"Message from Baroness Brashton," it stated as he handed the paper to Triumph.

◆ ◆ ◆

Over the next four hours, Wyckham and Freeport's officialdom met with delegates from most of Europe, with the exception of a few small or newer countries that met with a lower tier of administrators. The larger, older nations were for the most part pleasant to deal with, very thankful for any help that Freeport could give them on immigration and climate. Besides the two coastal American nations, all the member states in the NATO alliance seemed to have gotten through their nationalist phases, had rebuilt functional governments, and appeared capable of fruitful relations with another planet.

But the rest of the world would not be invited to Freeport. Over the course of the discussion, it was revealed that besides the southern and midwestern American states, Eastern Europe too was in turmoil, Scandinavia was involved in a four-year war pitting an aggressive Sweden against all its neighbors, and most of the new world was a mess, with Canada a desolate wilderness due to climate change and the Central and South American nations controlled by drug cartels. None of them had even sent delegations. Nor had China or Russia, despotic nations that had been spared nationalist takeovers since they had restricted the electrical information that had brought down the western governments. Both were happy with the current weakness of other nations and didn't want another world assisting them.

That evening, over a long supper with Cochrane, Wyckham learned more specifics about the last ten years on Earth, mostly numbers for the grim "butcher's bills" that the planet had endured. Twenty-eight million killed in wars, eighty million from disease and natural disasters, a hundred and twenty million from starvation, over two hundred million refugees. But clearly, Europe was on the mend and trying to lead the rest of world out of the nationalistic morass. If his advisors representing the various races on Freeport agreed, this planet would be a partner in that effort.

The following day started with a meeting to propose this partnership to his ministers, the same prominent beings that had met with Wyckham and the humans yesterday. While the human visitors had a day off touring the sights of Venice, Freeport's leaders sat down in the Doge's chamber once again to discuss whether they should help the humans. As he usually did in meetings, Wyckham started by polling each faction on their starting positions.

"My esteemed colleagues, it's now time to hear your feelings on the issue of reopening contacts with Earth. Naturally, I am in favor. They are my people and they are in trouble. Rest assured, not all humans would be welcomed. I suggest we do not accept officials from countries with unstable or aggressive governments. At the top of that list would be the southern American Confederacy. I would ask the Fireflies to scan the brains of all visitors. But I ask for your honest and unbiased feelings on the matter."

As the leader of the most important race on Freeport, Firefly Tracy began the aliens' statements. "Welcoming races in distress is one of the founding principles of this world we have created. Over the past two centuries, it has accepted millions of beings fleeing galaxies torn by war, planetary catastrophes, and corrupt governance. Without exception these immigrants have been a boon to our world, bringing their different skill sets to the work force and setting up trade with their home worlds. Humanity is now clearly in trouble, and it is our duty and our opportunity to accept them as well.

"My race would be happy to operate the Venice fantasy, attracting millions of human tourists to visit Freeport, some of whom will undoubtedly decide to return and live here. My race could also staff the transporter, and we accept our Governor's request to scan all humans as they arrive for any thoughts of conquest or other malfeasance. Any visitors planning actions against us will not get past the docks. The human invasions of Freeport that occurred two centuries ago will not be repeated."

Humph! Left unsaid was that Venice would be the universe's largest brothel, with thousands of Fireflies in enticing forms harvesting immense numbers of human spermatozoa for their own purposes. Every one of those little wrought iron balconies on canal-side palazzos would have Fireflies reading the minds of the visiting males in the hotels across the canals, then posing in whatever female form was irresistible to each individual.

However, they had been using his sailors in the same way for decades, and though all that devoured energy from tiny sperm cells had been used to dramatically increase their powers, Wyckham had to admit that they had always used it as a force for good, mainly fighting the interplanetary threat of the Dreash. All Dreash ships were now isolated in distant galaxies, and the Dreash living on Freeport had returned to a primitive existence in the planet's vast interior, just as they did eons ago before they created the first transporter and started stealing technology from other galaxies.

"My race says let humans come also," added number 2256, the top Slick on Freeport. "Freeport humans defeat Dreash, save cosmos. Freeport needs more Humans," it spat out of its crackling translator.

It was true that there were relatively few humans on Freeport. Only a few dozen women had arrived in 1815 before trips to Earth were banned, and while the human population had expanded, its few thousand individuals were nothing compared to the millions of alien refugees. But Wyckham knew that the Slicks' thoughts weren't due to a soft spot for humans. With one of the most powerful militaries in the entire cosmos, the Slicks just wanted to make sure that Wyckham's weak human force held the planet instead of another more powerful alien race. Was it the Slicks who had been making contact with Earth to make this happen?

"I agree also," stated Wulfe the Lycan through the translator strapped to his furry head. "Get more humans on Freeport. Done a good job so far, should have themselves some real females and make more cubs."

Wyckham did trust Wulfe. He had turned the tide of battles twice against the Dreash, and had been a responsible businessman in Port Wyckham for the entire time since the human takeover. The Lycans only enemy was the Dreash, though they had fought occasional border wars with some of the Slick planets.

"Fook yes, I sez." It was Bubbler, the top mudman on the planet, speaking sailor's English. Over the last two centuries, mudmen had traded intergalactic aphrodisiacs to Wyckham's crewmen in exchange for purified water from the sailors' many distilleries, and had learned their dockyard English. "Jes' keep out any wankers like them whats invades us 'n th' past."

Having the mudmen on board was important. They were virtually indestructible and made great allies in any fight. Wyckham had always made sure to keep them happy and was reassured to find them going along with his proposal.

Next up was Worker Queen, representing the ants, Freeport's best workers.

"More humans fine". Short, but actually fairly verbose for an ant. They believed in activity—to them conversation was a waste of time.

Fish, the Gorillas, the twirling ivy vines, stonemen—they all made brief acceptances of Wyckham's proposal. it seemed every group was onboard with the idea of accepting human visitors and immigrants. Freeport was going to do its best to save Humanity.

But it would make sure it did not put itself in danger. While New Venice would welcome human visitors, it would be prepared for attack just as Port Wyckham was, with plenty of big guns. Just in case some Earthmen acted as they had in the past.

Interplanetary Invitation

THE BIG RUSSIAN beat Emmie's blade and lunged hard in *octave*, extending her point at Emmie's right flank. Emmie made a small retreat, circled her blade back up, parried the attack *contre-sixte* and thrust a lightning *riposte* in *quarte*. Her opponent tried to pull her foil back in time to parry but only managed to drag her electrified point in a late *remise* across Emmie's flank. Colored scoring lights lit up on both competitors' helmets. "Alt!" the director called out. "Attaque du gauche, parrad, riposte non, remise oui, touch a droit. Un, zero." *Riposte no? You gotta be shittin' me!* thought Emmie at the ridiculously bad call. She'd parried the attack, made an immediate riposte and hit. Couldn't get any simpler than that. The goddam French director said her riposte had first missed and her opponent's late remise then had right-of-way. How could he screw up anything so simple? Another instance of French bias in favor of Europeans over any American. Modern fencing had originated in France and was dominated by Europeans—most Europeans believed Americans just couldn't compete.

Emily Bahtia, tech worker and amateur fencer, had put a lot of her social life here in San Francisco on hold the last few months, training for this tournament, one of the five Grand Prix events that determined qualifiers for the Olympics and World Cup. If she could beat this opponent, Elena Kalovich, she'd make the quarterfinals and be a shoo-in for the US team. But this French director was one of those biased Europeans who was tough on Americans, and he was going to give this bout away if she gave him the chance. *Just have to make sure he can't find a way to get away with bullshit calls,* thought Emmie. If only one scoring light came on, there could be no doubt about which fencer scored. Couldn't let the Russian hit at all, no matter how out-of-time or how long after a halt.

She and her opponent returned to their *en guarde* lines. "*Enguarde? Pare? Alle'!*" the director called, and the bout resumed. Emmie immediately feinted a wild running' attack in quarte but pulled up in the *en guarde* position before getting within her opponent's parrying distance. The Russian went for the feint and rushed a parry across her chest, her blade hitting nothing and going wide. Emmie lunged, scored on her opponent's wide-open chest, then immediately pulled back before her opponent could land her point anywhere on her *lame'*, the vest-like garment of woven aluminum that registered hits on the torso, the valid target area in foil fencing. Only the green light on her helmet came on.

But the asshole director just stood there without saying a word, as if he was trying to come up with a way of denying the point to Emmie. But after a few seconds he finally stated *"Attack du gauche, touche."*

Goddam right, touch to the left! There's only one light on! Duh!

Emmie was now pretty pissed off, and when she became angry, she was a human tornado on the fencing strip. As soon as the director started each phrase with *"Alle'"*, the French word for "begin", Emmie exploded from the *en guarde* line, chasing her opponent down the strip until she either scored or forced her off the end of the *piste*, which also counted as a touch. Within a couple of minutes, the score was five to one for Emmie, the director announced "Bout", and the match ended. Emmie took off her helmet, shook hands with the big Russian, and joined her Halberstadt Fencing Club teammates, Vanoune Rodriguez and Connie Schwarzkoph, at the side of the *piste* where they'd been cheering her on. They'd known each other from the UC Berkeley fencing team where they'd competed together for three years. After graduation they'd landed jobs in San Francisco, joined the Halberstadt Fencers' Club, and spent countless hours together touring the country, competing on the Olympic qualifying circuit.

"Kicked her ass," said Connie. "Shouldn't have pissed you off."

"Wasn't her fault," replied Emmie as she threw her helmet down. She pulled off her sweaty headband and threw it into her weapons bag, then untied her hair and shook it out. "Fucking frog director just won't give a touch to anybody he doesn't know, especially an American". Using the word "frog", a disparaging name for the French from the British naval fiction that she read, showed how angry the politically correct Emily was.

"Yeah, well now that he knows you, maybe you'll get some calls," added Vanoune, the Indian woman who was the third member of the fencing triumvirate. "That's it for today. Let's boogie, we need a beer."

The first day of competition was over. All three had won enough of their bouts to qualify for tomorrow's round of sixteen, Emmie in foil, Connie in epee' and Vanoune in saber. They headed out the main entrance of the Moscone Convention Center to the Google stand and piled into one of the bubble-shaped self-driving cars.

Waymo, Google's computerized driver, greeted them in his pleasant voice through the car's speakers. "Hello, Emmie, Connie and Van. How did the tournament go?"

Usually the three women would give Waymo shit or talk dirty to him, but they were too exhausted for any suggestive banter with the computerized chauffeur. It took all their efforts to wrestle their stuffed weapons bags into the small vehicle, which could barely accommodate them and their gear even though it had no driver's seat or steering wheel. Finally, Emmie replied, "Yeah, we're fine, Waymo. Just take us to the Brixton," as she managed to get seated with her weapons bag on her lap.

A few minutes automated drive got them to the Brixton, an old but still popular bistro on Union. They threw their long weapons bags down on the linoleum floor and plopped down into the hard chairs, exhausted and famished after a long day of competition. Each of them had fought nine long bouts with only an occasional sip of Gatorade and bite of banana. A male waiter came over, gave them menus, and asked if he could bring them a drink.

"'A' drink?—Do we look like we'd settle for 'a' drink?" asked Emmie, sweat still dripping off her nose. "A pitcher of Anchor Steam for starters."

When the waiter brought the pitcher, they all dove for it, play-fighting over who got the first glass, then ordered gourmet burgers and San Francisco garlic fries. "And an order of your deviled eggs with crab, can't pass on those," added Connie.

"To American fencing," proposed Vanoune. They clinked glasses, took long gulps and passed around the pitcher for refills. While waiting for their food they reviewed the day's bouts, both their own and other competitors'. "So glad I didn't have to fight that big Hungarian, said Connie. "Shit, what is she, six-three? Shapova says she hits like a train."

When the food arrived, all three tucked in and silence reigned. While eating they watched the end of the second period in the Warriors game on the bar's many TV screens. All San Francisco was excited over this game, the first one in which retiring all-star Steph Curry would be playing alongside his daughter Riley, the first female in the NBA. The whole bar had gone wild every time Riley made a basket, outscoring her father ten to eight as the first half ended.

After several long commercials, the usual halftime news brief came on. Emmie was puzzled as pictures of Venice came onscreen. Rising oceans had covered the iconic Italian island three years ago—what was up? A headline flashed over the shot. "Venice in outer space!"

"Hey you guys, shut up for a second. More from the new planet. Let's hear this."

Everyone in the Brixton clammed up, staff and customers alike, and focused on an excited John Dickerson from CBS News. "More messaging tonight from Freeport, the planet that has just blown away all us Earthlings ever since their first contact last week. Now they're opening a tourist attraction for us to come visit! Venice! Actually, it's New Venice, a holographic recreation of the medieval city, in all its glory."

Emmie, a history buff since she learned to read, was thrilled. Venice resurrected? She'd cried when Venice, a place she had always planned to visit, was lost in 2024 to the rising seas before she had the chance to go. She took in every detail—Piazza San Marco, the Domo, the Doge's Palace, even the gondolas—it all looked perfect.

A video of a stroll across Plaza San Marco played as Dickerson kept narrating. "It's got everything our own Venice had—the canals, the plazas, the palaces, the statues, even old sailing ships. But it's got something our Venice never had—aliens!"

Every jaw in the bar dropped as the screen showed a variety of absolutely astonishing creatures in a 15th century Piazza San Marco. There were crabs the size of Great Danes with separate heads on spindly necks, humanoid shapes composed of thousands of buzzing bees, rolling balls of mud speaking cockney English, tall silver featureless creatures fresh out of "The Revenge of Vader's Grandson" the latest Star Wars movie—the amazing parade went on and on. And most of them were workers, wearing 15th century dress as they staffed the many shops, waited on human tourists in the cafes, baked bread in the bakeries, and worked construction in the plaza. The screen returned to a clearly astonished Dickerson, who shook his head and continued.

"Since they want to attract humans to immigrate from Earth, everything is pretty cheap, especially gold which is common on Freeport, and they will accept all major currencies. Tourists will be taken there free on old British sailing ships that will enter portals here on Earth and get instantly whisked off to this planet thousands of light years away. For lodging they've linked up with Airbnb and all their restaurants are on Yelp. And in the interest of attracting younger visitors, New Venice has all sorts of entertainment options, including this giant dance club staffed by aliens!" The screen switched to a bar inside an immense classical hall with tall marble columns along the walls. Two seated men in old sailors' uniforms were being served drinks by one of the Star Wars types with shiny silver skin and four arms. Having shoved two drinks across to the Brits, he leaned on the bar with its lower arms and froze motionless, like a robot waiting for its next order.

The two men looked into the camera and lofted their opaque green drinks. "Eere's to ye! When ye comes up 'ere, make sure ye git ye'selves one 'o these, a Sailor's Slam! Distilled f'um wildflowers 'n Freeport's magic seawater." With that, the two men put the glasses to their lips, downed them in one gulp, and smacked their lips. "One o' these 'll fix ye oop right quick!"

The camera turned back to the bartender's face. The creature had no facial features except for two vertical slits holding bright yellow eyeballs and a small slit for a mouth. On its head was a horn shaped speaker which barked to life in a monotone computerized voice as the being looked into the camera. "Sailor Slam best investment for inebriation. More brain-destroying compounds per glass."

The camera zoomed back to show a potted plant on the bar. Suddenly it opened its flower, revealing two rows of nasty little teeth, then cocked back on its stem and lunged at the camera, going for the cameraman's fingers. The video shook wildly but stabilized quickly as the cameraman jumped back, recovered his balance and resumed filming, the audio proclaiming "Fucking plant bit me!" The bartender entered the scene, grabbed the offending plant with one of his upper arms and nonchalantly chucked it behind him over his head. It fell right into a rolling trash bin pushed by a uniformed octopus corkscrewing its eight arms along the floor. Motionless, still leaning on the bar with its top two arms, the bartender summarized. "Plants on this world may offend. But as our Governor states, 'Just another day on Freeport'."

John Dickerson came back on. "And by the way, the planet has even set up cellular service so our phones will not only work on Freeport but will be able to send calls and texts back and forth to Earth. I can see what's coming here—a huge competition for who's the first to send back a selfie with an alien!" Dickerson continued discussing travel details as more photos scrolled by showing a beautiful unspoiled world with vast oceans, dense forests, spectacular mountains, and another city built in Gothic style with high walls and towers.

The planet Freeport had introduced itself to Earth by breaking into all its commercial broadcasting just a week ago, with an old British naval officer explaining the planet's existence and history. The tale of a British naval squadron that had conquered the planet's evil rulers two hundred years ago and set up a hospitable planet was the biggest story in the history of Earth, and it had just gotten bigger. This was just too cool!

The broadcast went to commercial and the three women looked at each other. Years of bonding as both fencers and friends had given them the ability to gauge each other's thoughts. And this time they were all thinking the same thing. Emmie yelled, "We are goin'!" as all they high-fived each other across the table.

Another Great Deal

Triumph couldn't believe he'd gone along with Bamming on this. Taking a ride in a small boat in the ocean off Miami to meet with some woman from another planet? Couldn't even take a decent-size cabin cruiser, New England's naval patrol might get him? He hadn't thought much of the note he'd received on Freeport about meeting with this old British woman, but Bamming was sure this was a super opportunity, and here he was getting a face full of spray as the flying speedboat bumped across the waves.

But Saul Bamming had proved time and time again to be a loyal genius, and Triumph didn't doubt that this trip would pay off. It was Bamming who was responsible for his present position as World Emperor. In the early morning on November 4th, 2020, when he was ready to give up and concede after all the networks including Fox had called the election for DiCarpaccio, it had been a phone call from Bamming that turned everything around.

"Victor, this is bullshit and you know it! No way you lost! Look at the crowds of Americans you get at your rallies! This thing was rigged and you know it!"

But he was too exhausted. "Sure, it was rigged, but I'm done. It's been hard enough running the country for four years with all the shit-heads out there, and now they'll all say I lost. I can't face four more years of disloyalty. I need a rest from working every afternoon, five days a week, yakking with fucking news reporters on the lawn. I'm going to work on my golf game and win Augusta, show the world."

"Victor, you can save the world. Don't let the lying scumbags win."

"How? What can I do? I'd call out the Army to break into every polling station and do a fair ballot count, but the stupid generals have already told me it's against the constitution and they're not onboard."

"It's easy. Just go out there right now, in front of all the major networks, tell everyone the election was a disgrace, you're forming a new nation based on fairness and ask everyone to join! Every southern state and most midwestern ones will follow you—they're crazy about you! All their state legislatures are loyal, and any governor in a pro-Triumph state that doesn't let his state join up will get voted out of office pronto."

Then Bamming sealed it. "And don't just settle for America. Go for the whole world. Declare yourself World Emperor and many countries will follow you—you're the chosen one!"

That did it. He went out to the podium at his Mira del Pozo campaign headquarters and gave the speech that changed the world.

"My fantastic supporters! What we have witnessed tonight is the greatest theft in the history of the world! The rigged system says that I just lost the election when we all know that's a complete lie. Look around you—you and your fellow Americans have packed every one of my hotels across the country, yet the crooks in Washington tell you you've lost. What bullshit! I know the truth, you know the truth—we won! Our data shows us at 62% and 327 electoral delegates—a landslide!" Triumph paused as the crowd went wild.

"You know, I tried to work with the Washington swamp but no more. Tonight, Victor Triumph declares the formation of the Triumphant States of America based on truth and honest American values, with me as its leader. I call on all Americans that want fair treatment to push your state to join up! No more Washington Socialists taking your guns (the NRA group up front cheered wildly), allowing Sharia law (the born again Christians started chanting 'Death to Moslems!'), banning decent-size drinks (the small business owners yelled their approval), giving your money to loser immigrants (the bankers nodded approval), supporting affirmative action (that got a standing ovation from the White Nationalists), letting other countries rob us (all the millionaires shouted their approval), or killing babies that haven't even been born yet! (which got the whole crowd going ape-shit). Fuck those assholes! Finally, we're gonna have a country for decent Americans!"

With each promise, the crowd had exploded in applause and cheers, finally peaking in a deafening crescendo. A huge guy in a cowboy hat waving a confederate flag managed to yell above the hundred-decibel crowd.

"Texas is with you fer sure, Vic! Make Dallas your capitol! We'd be honored!"

Someone passed a cowboy hat and holstered six-guns up to the stage and he put them on, showing the world his new position and image. Within months, everything had turned out just as Bamming had predicted. In a worldwide media campaign, the disheveled media mastermind got the secession speech to go viral and millions all over the world were converted into loyal followers. Following the example of the southern US, dozens of new nations declared independence, as Prussia split off from Germany, Calabria left Spain, Italy divided up into Naples, Florence, and the Papal States, and all of these new countries declared allegiance to Emperor Triumph. In addition, with America weak and divided, Russia annexed the Baltic states and China took back Taiwan, both of them maintaining cordial relations with him as they invaded. And now, again thanks to Bamming, here was Victor Triumph about to rule not just another country but to take the first step to rule a completely new world.

Bamming, a former navy officer, cut power and the craft slowed to bob gently in the light swell. "These are the coordinates in the note," he said as he stared at the GPS screen. "We're here."

So how long would they have to wait? Triumph didn't like being alone on a vast sea with almost no security. "When are we getting the fuck out of here? I'm getting seasick in this little piece of shit."

He didn't have long to wait. Before Bamming could respond, a long line appeared in the air right above them and started to descend like a curtain, leaving behind a growing window into another world.

"She's here!" yelled an excited Bamming. But instead of the woman they were expecting, a gigantic monster fell out of the window and dropped to the surface just yards away in a thunderous splash. The creature bobbed back to the surface just as Triumph wiped the sea water from his face, giving him a close up view of the towering beast looming above him.

It was the size of a Queens brownstone, its face very pig-like, with a large flat snout and foot-long tusks protruding from its lower jaw. It had a body like a huge gorilla, with lots of hair and bulging muscles. The webbing between its clawed fingers explained why it was so easily treading water, with similar webbing on its pumping legs.

But the most frightening thing about the beast was the small pointed demonic ears. Along with its ferocious countenance, it certainly looked like a giant demon from the deepest pits of hell. The fact that a smile slowly grew across its face did nothing to comfort Triumph.

"Skipper! Hit the gas! Get the hell outta here!"

Bamming slammed the boat in reverse and it leapt backward, throwing Triumph to the floor while Bamming managed to hang on to the wheel. Just as Triumph got up and Bamming went to turn the boat away, a small wooden boat roped to the huge creature also splashed down to the surface. Its only occupant was a woman, the same woman whom Midwest President Schillings had disappeared with back in New Venice.

"I'm here," she yelled, "Don't run, he's friendly."

The immense pig smiled further and nodded, though Trimph thought it might just be looking forward to dinner. But Triumph calmed down when, astonishingly enough, it spoke in English.

"Please relax," the immense demon said with impeccable diction. "I am Brak, leader of the Dreash, the rightful residents of Drez before the British took it from us. I know that to humans we appear frightening, but I come bearing good will. Give us a chance to explain our plans—we want to help you invade the planet now known as Freeport."

That immediately caught Triumph's attention. And the woman, the super-hot 10 plus from the incident in New Venice, also piqued his interest, no way a woman with looks like hers could be ignored. The big guy pulled the woman's boat up close and she started speaking.

"I am Baroness Tracy Brashton, you may have seen me with Mark Schillings in New Venice. I contacted him before he came to Freeport, his infatuation gives us an opportunity to cooperate for mutual gain. Once I get him, I will keep Schillings amused so he does not surface. You claim the Midwest President was abducted and invade Freeport.

"My companion here, Brak, has built this new transporter here, and it will ferry your armed forces to Freeport. He is the leader of the Dreash, the race that created the transporters millennia ago, only to have them and their entire planet taken by Wyckham and his aliens. With your modern weaponry and the help of the Dreash, you will easily defeat Wyckham's feeble military. After your victory, you leave us to rule the planet. In exchange you will receive the exclusive rights for trade with Freeport, plus the military and technological assistance which will give you victory over your enemies on Earth.

"To get started, you must arrange for Schillings's disappearance into my control. Tomorrow he gets released from the hospital. After he gets picked up, have his security people get him back to me. Over the next few weeks, we can work out plans for the invasion."

She tossed them a small device. "Here is a communicator. Push the red button to turn it on, then follow prompts. But now I must go, staying any longer will risk discovery for all of us. Talk to you soon."

With that, the big monster swam back through the portal, towing the Baroness in her boat behind him. As soon as he was through, the window rolled up, leaving the three astonished humans speechless.

Finally, Bamming spoke. "Oh, baby baby baby! Manna from heaven!"

The Big Weekend Arrives

Two months after the new planet opened for visitors, the big day had arrived for Emmie and her friends. It was a Friday, early afternoon. Emmie, still at work, surreptitiously checked her phone and replied to Connie's text, letting her know she would be at the dock on time. Her boss Ralph had called a stupid meeting for Friday afternoon, just to grandstand over getting the Uber account, and it was running long. If he caused her to miss this trip just so he could suck up to the visiting Marketing VP, OMG she would kill him.

It finally ended at 4:30, giving Emmie enough time to take a Lyft over to the Ferry Building. She was surprised when a new Icar3 pulled up in front of her office and a door popped open. *Wow, didn't know that Lyft had these already!* This trip was starting off great! The Icar3 had a work station, a full-size bed, and a fridge. Nothing that she would use today, but these Icar3s would be great for longer trips.

After twenty minutes in traffic the car pulled up to pier 41 just in time for Emmie to board a huge wooden ship, with *Nuestra Senora de la Santisima Trinidad* painted in gold leaf across the back. Just as she ran up the loading ramp some sailors on board started to pull it up. Consuela and Vanoune were already somewhere on the main deck of this big wooden vessel, an old warship that would take them to this New Venice—on another planet! Besides the hundreds of passengers on deck were big cannons and about a hundred men, yelling and pulling on ropes as it prepared to set sail. This was just too cool!

"Em!" It was Vanoune, waving from their seats near the front. She was dressed in a dark business suit as was Connie next to her; they both worked at Wells Fargo and like Emmie had come straight from work. "Over here!" Emmie, in the yoga pants and sweater that were standard work attire at her social media company, excitedly ran over and stuffed her carry-on under her seat.

"Fucking barely made it!" Emmie groaned. "Jerkoff Ralph called some bullshit meeting. Made us all watch while he brown-nosed some visiting mucky-muck. But I made it! We made it!" The three young women high-fived each other three times and then chanted "The Three Femateers! Me too for you two!"

They'd been intrigued months ago when the world heard another planet had been discovered and was open for tourism, but no way were they going to be the first to go, instead waiting to see what the first visitors posted about their trips. Soon it was clear that travel to Freeport was not only safe, but the most awesome experience ever reviewed on Yelp, and they began finalizing a trip. When the new planet announced its first New Venice Halloween Party during an eighteen-hour night, that did it. Despite her mother's warnings, (For God's sake, Ems, won't the Martians get you?), Emmie and her friends had begun the process to visit a foreign planet. It had taken three weeks to get travel approval from Sacramento but booking the actual transit to Freeport was easy. No visas were necessary, they just booked seats online for one of Freeport's sailing spaceships, and now they were off for what they expected would be the most amazing party ever.

About two hundred tourists were getting settled on deck when a good-looking young man with his long red hair tied in a pony tail, wearing a bright blue coat with red tails, a black cocked hat and tall black boots, moved to the front and addressed the crowd. "Ladies and gentlemen, welcome aboard, welcome aboard, grab a seat if you would, any seat will do, please keep your luggage with you. We'll be underway shortly." The young officer waited a few moments for the last passengers to get seated, then began a quick instruction in space travel.

"Lieutenant Moore, at your service." With that, he stuck out a leg and bowed.

"Connie, check him out!" Vanoune said under her breath. "You know you can't resist those boots!" Connie responded by fanning her face and pretending to faint. Emmie, a foil fencer, couldn't help but notice the gentlemen's small sword hanging from his belt.

"Look at that sword he's got," Emmie whispered to her friends. It wasn't a military weapon, it was a gentleman's small sword, used for personal protection. "Think he's any good with it?"

Without thinking Emmie had blundered into the crosshairs. Connie and Van jumped at the opportunity to needle their friend.

"We're not even moving yet and Ems needs to check out some guy's point control?"

"Really, Em, go get him! Right in front of a boatload of Iowans!"

But suddenly they realized that everyone else on the boat was quietly staring at them, and they immediately clammed up. The George Washington guy loudly cleared his throat, gave a final stare at the troublemakers and turned back to the rest of his passengers. "Oops! So much for that guy," muttered Van.

"Welcome aboard for the quick trip to New Venice," Lieutenant Moore continued. "About a minute after the *Trinidad* gets underway, expect to see a big square hole appear in the air right in front of us. We will enter this portal and drop a few feet into the waters right off our version of medieval Venice. The old girl here will bounce around a bit, but nothing she hasn't handled hundreds of times. So fasten your chair restraints, settle back, and you'll be on another planet in less than twenty minutes."

A tugboat nudged the big ship from the pier, crewmen scurried up a spider's web of ropes, and sails snapped open at the tops of the three masts. Passengers gasped for a moment as the *Trinidad's* deck tipped a bit, but the big ship immediately steadied and moved out into the San Francisco Bay. The passengers nervously laughed it off and returned to taking selfies.

Then, just as predicted, a gigantic square hole appeared in the air in front of them. Though the three women had seen videos of Freeport's transporter in action, they were still completely amazed. Through the portal ahead they could see another world, with two bright suns beaming in a partly cloudy sky, their warmth easily felt by the ship's passengers even though they were still on Earth. There were puffy clouds above, a bright blue bay below, white sand beaches with waving trees in the distance, some rocky points, and large flocks of bright red birds flying around. Unbelievably amazing. If Emmie looked to her right, she could still see Oakland, but through the big hole ahead was the planet Freeport, light years away.

The ship gained speed as the water flowing through the portal grabbed her, then her bow suddenly dropped as she entered it. It was like the moment at the top of a roller coaster, and many passengers whooped and yelled, bravely holding their arms up in the air as the big *Trinidad* plunged through the portal. The ship shuddered as its bow hit the waters of the other planet and made a huge splash down each side. Some passengers got lightly sprayed, laughing at the experience, just like a water ride at Disneyland. As the ship settled in the water and the mist cleared, Emmie and her friends had their first view of New Venice.

The holographic city was right off the bow, looking exactly like the pictures her parents had shown her of their 2010 honeymoon in Italy. Two columns dominated the entrance to the huge plaza ahead, one topped with the winged lion of Saint Mark, the other with Saint George slaying the Dragon. The pink marble Doge's Palace stretched along the right side of Piazza San Marco, with its dozens of delicately carved windows and pointed arches. Further in stood the multi-domed Saint Mark's Cathedral, the four giant bronze horses that Venice took from Constantinople in 1204 standing guard above the entrance. Above them were numerous statues of Christian saints, medieval doges and Renaissance admirals. Framing the rest of the plaza were columned loggias filled with bars and restaurants.

Sailors above spread more sails, the deck tilted further, and the big ship picked up speed as it headed towards the Venice docks. Other old wooden ships were arriving, leaving, or tied up there already, though none were as large as the *Trinidad*. Fifteen minutes later the sails were furled, and the ship slowed to a crawl, the short voyage ending as it bumped up against a wooden dock. Several gangways were lowered, and the hundreds of passengers grabbed their bags and quickly headed down onto the dock, joining a mass of other people exiting two other docked ships and heading into the plaza.

The women had previously reviewed Freeport's informational videos explaining that there would be none of the ubiquitous paperwork or rigorous inspections needed for visiting other countries on Earth. The only examinations were being done by several dozen men and women, each with a slight white glow about them identifying them as Fire-flies, the energy beings who could take the form of humans. Colorfully dressed in the clothing of Renaissance Venice, the men in black cloaks, stockings, and tricorn hats, the women in striking gowns covered with lace and jewels, they weren't real people but only holographic images.

And in place of complex vetting to make sure no "bad guys" were arriving, these aliens were simply reading everyone's minds! They did see one tourist get grabbed when a costumed greeter pointed him out to some red-coated marines. Thy quickly grabbed him and put him back on a ship.

Google Maps worked just fine on this planet and the triumvirate had no trouble finding their Airbnb apartment, a ten-minute walk from San Marco along the Canale l'Barcaroli, along the way marveling at the gilded 15th century palazzos lining the canal. The Renaissance apartment was magnificent, with high ceilings, large ornate windows and antique furniture. Consuela plopped down in front of a mirror and started applying some eye makeup.

"What are you doing, girl?" asked Emmie in exaggerated derision. "Don't have to worry about your appearance here, remember? They're gonna take care of all that."

"Shit, forgot!" laughed Consuela. "Automatic Earth habit. Gotta forget all that, huh?" Consuela closed her carry-on and the three headed back to San Marco. Entering the plaza at the opposite end of the docks, they walked up to a large colonnaded building marked with the emoji of an eye and "Imaging Station" carved into its stone lintel. A banner stretched above the entrance stated, "Get Your Halloween Costumes Here!"

"This is the place," said Vanoune as she hooked her friends' arms in hers. "In we go, ladies!"

At the entrance, a handsome man dressed all in black, except for a ridiculous collar of white lace as big as a pizza, walked up and bowed to the three women.

"Madams Bahtia, Rodriguez and Scwartzkophf? Your new bodies await you right here, just go on in and you will be directed to an imaging device," he said as he opened the door to a sixteenth century government building.

"Oh my God, our 'new bodies'! It's really happening!" laughed Vanoune. Emmie and Consuela shouted their approval as the three entered an ornate room and were approached by another of the alien holographs, this one a stunning woman dressed like a queen.

"Do you three want to edit yourselves in separate rooms or would your group like to stick together?' she asked politely.

"We better do this together!" answered Vanoune. "Emmie here will end up looking like a Market Street 'ho' without the two of us around to make sure she's decent!" Emmie laughed and jabbed Vanoune with a finger like a fencing attack. "Another nasty comment like that and your new image will have a second bellybutton!" All three went *en guarde* and pointed their index fingers at each other, laughing as they bobbed and feinted.

The holographic Venetian, a vacant smile on her face, was waiting patiently for a chance to finish the standard directions. Finally, the three celebrants noticed and quieted down, allowing her to continue.

"Go in right here, stand in front of a mirror and the body you selected back on Earth will be displayed. To make changes, just think of them and they will be displayed, the scanner over the mirror will pick them up. When you're satisfied, just press the 'select' box on the touch screen and that image will appear on your body. You will then see images in the mirror of the outfits you've previously selected, just touch the image of the clothing you wish to wear and that will also be transferred to you. Though you will appear in that outfit, again it will just be an image, the clothing you are wearing now will actually still be on you. Remember that nothing is permanent, there are changing stations throughout the city, and you can easily change your body or clothing anytime you like."

Simmering with excitement, the three friends entered an empty room with mirrors along the walls. As each stepped in front of one, the bodies they had preselected weeks ago back on Earth appeared in the mirrors, completely unclothed. Around the edges were photo suggestions for alterations to her face and body that she could select.

Emmie smiled at the version of herself she saw in her mirror. It wasn't a surprise, she'd worked on this version of herself over the previous weeks, but it was the first time she'd seen the image life-size, and she couldn't help but smile. While she'd never been obsessed with her appearance, it was fun to be someone entirely new. Her face was still identifiably her, though she'd gotten rid of some premature crow's feet and taken a little off her nose. But her body was considerably changed, a sort of warrior princess, with an additional six inches in height, wide shoulders, defined biceps, rippling abs, and thrusting breasts. Muscles and boobs, just what she'd always dreamed of as a kid watching Wonder Woman movies. She selected the image and whoa—there it was, right on her!

She ran her hands over her body, knowing it all wasn't real but marveling at how real everything looked and felt. Her hands said they were touching breasts, and her breasts were feeling the touching, but the truth was that she was still fully dressed and just running her hands over the clothes she'd been wearing. What her brain said was happening were only electronic messages sent to her brain receptors through nearby holograph amplifiers.

Several outfits that she had selected before now popped up on the screen. She selected the one with a fringed brown leather vest, a tight jeans miniskirt that was unbuckled at the top, and stiletto party boots.

Eagerly she stepped back to present her new self to her friends. But next to her, Vanoune was apparently gone, replaced by… oh my God, Vanoune was now Mystique, the X-men character played by Jennifer Lawrence, wearing nothing but blue paint! The actress had always fascinated Vanoune, ever since the X-Men films she'd watched as a child. Vanoune had followed her careers in movies, philanthropy and politics ever since, and now she'd taken the chance to actually be Jennifer Lawrence.

"Make way for the star, bitches!" she cried out. "Or Mystique will kick your asses!" She struck a provocative pose, slouching to one side with hands on hips, her face and body covered in blue scales and nothing else. "Check it out! Jennifer Lawrence!"

Just as Em gave her a high five, Consuela stepped back from her mirror, and there was Marilyn Monroe wearing the white dress from the famous photo over a street grating. But more amazing was the poetic license Consuela had taken with Monroe's bustline. Though it had been considered more than ample in its day, Consuela's breasts were the size of cantaloupes! Emmie and Vanoune were speechless, for once unable to come up with a quick jibe at their friend.

"Whoa, check these babies out," said Consuela as she shook her shoulders to make the giant breasts sway back and forth. "Always wanted boobs, but no way I could have them at the bank. Oh my God, could you imagine me walking into the Monday morning Risk Management meeting with these? The stuffy accounting assholes shitting themselves?"

"Fuckin' A," agreed Vanoune. "William Fargo and Henry Wells are turning over in their graves! Probably from desire—I bet they were both old pervs."

After a quick laugh, the three women spent the next few moments probing the prominent features on each other's bodies, finding Emmie's muscles rock hard, Vanoune's skin rough and scaly, and Consuela's breasts soft and natural. Even though they knew it was all just holographs, their senses of sight and touch told them everything was real.

Then it was more high fives, hooked arms, and a walk across the piazza to the Café Florian. The first bar of the weekend.

Doge Rodney Wyckham

Wʏᴄᴋʜᴀᴍ ᴀᴡᴏᴋᴇ ɪɴ his apartment in the Doge's palace and stretched contentedly, staring up at the ceiling fresco. Maybe a Bellini? For a fake room it certainly was beautiful. There were ceilings twenty feet high with ornate moldings, paintings by Titian and Tintoretto on the walls, and chairs with intricately carved mahogany arms upholstered in colorful velvets. Obujimi was standing there, the perfect servant, waiting with a tray of coffee, croissants, a soft-boiled egg and fruit. Wyckham arose, still stretching, and walked over to open the doors to his little balcony.

It was another beautiful day on Freeport, with both suns up in a clear sky and rain squalls over the distant hills. He walked onto the balcony and gazed along the Canal Canonica to see a typical morning scene in New Venice. Below him, a continuous line of gondolas filled with tourists were getting poled along by various aliens in striped shirts and black hats, the gorillas and octopi looking particularly comical in gondolier dress. Along the *fondamente*, the sidewalk along the canal, were more tourists following maps on their electrical devices or examining the shops and restaurants. To complete the authentic Venetian scene, small flocks of holographic pigeons had been created, circling and landing just as they had in Venice for centuries. Wyckham had to admit that the Fireflies had created a perfect fantasy, with surprisingly few problems. Probably this morning's Governance Committee meeting would once again have nothing serious to discuss.

But maybe not absolutely perfect. Wyckham saw one of Freeport's wild raptors that the local natives called "Tarren", which translated to "Winged Teeth. This was a big one, with a six-foot wingspan, big teeth and apparently a matching appetite", because it was diving down at blurring speed towards a pigeon that was flying by. But the pigeon it was aiming at was only another hologram, and by the time the Tarren realized there was no pigeon to hit it had splattered itself all over the very real ground. Several tourists were hit with bloody gore and the sharp shafts of broken feathers.

There were several more raptors flying around the palace courtyard, frustrated with their wasted efforts diving at non-existent pigeons but fortunately not crashing into the ground. *Maybe these pigeons weren't such a good idea?* One particularly large Tarren was momentarily too tired to fly anymore and decided to grab a rest before flying back to attack altitude. Gliding along a line of 15th century statues, it flared its wings and came to rest on the head of the last figure in the row, which unfortunately was not a statue but a distracted tourist with a bald head who was focused on his communication device. The human felt the bird flapping but thought it was just another pigeon.

He called to his companion, "Honey, get this, quick!" While his companion attempted to make an electrical picture with her communicator, the raptor realized its claws were grabbing flesh. Curious, it bashed the man's scalp open with its beak, clamped on the torn skin and ripped off a saucer-sized chunk of meat, swallowing it with sudden jerks of its head. The man started screaming and tried to shake the big bird off, but it held on with its sharp talons and kept chewing on its tasty morsel. Many other tourists started running away from the poor man, adding their terrified shrieks to the growing turmoil.

But the raptor's lunch was suddenly terminated as a red-coated marine rushed up, planted his musket muzzle right on the bird's chest and pulled the trigger. The Brown Bess fired off with a big crack and a cloud of white smoke, and the big bird was blown to shreds, the result being more screaming tourists hit with more bloody gore and sharp feathers. Two Slick medics rushed in and started ministering to the poor fellow with the partly missing scalp, more marines arrived to check the other tourists, and waiters from the cafes began cleaning up those who had been splattered with dampened dinner cloths. *Christ. Well, at least the emergency services are prompt and citizens are helping out as well.*

But Wyckham shook his head, realizing the damage this incident would cause. Discourse all over Earth would immediately focus on the incident. Wyckham could just imagined the first page of the London Times electronic newspaper: "Wild Animal Attack on Freeport—Is It Safe?" With the tourists' damned communicators, everyone on Earth would know the story within minutes, and immigration to Freeport would suffer.

Yet this planet was safer than a church! Even with a population that was over three million and extremely mixed, with beings from dozens of planets, Freeport had almost zero homicides. Never had any problems until the tourists came! And whenever some tourist stared a fight or or fell into a canal, the newspapers back on Earth would paint Freeport as a war zone, and tourism would drop. This incident would be the worst yet. He would bring up the Tarrens at today's council meeting.

His gaze wandered down the Canale Canonica and surveyed the small iron balconies on the palazzos, originally built for aristocratic youth to flirt with each other, now filled with dozens of Fireflies trying to attract the attention of male tourists strolling below. They were all in the forms of Venetian noblewomen, their hair long in dangling curls topped with elaborate headpieces and wearing lacy ball gowns with tight bodices.

"Buongiorno, capitano! A little morning cruise?"

"Si, your sails set for a big blow?"

"Tighten your cable, sailor?"

Disgusted, Wyckham turned away before the inevitable display of raw flesh and the even cruder discourse began. Every Firefly wanted some of Wyckham's seed, believing that he was the best of the humans and his sperm cells must be extra powerful. But for Christ's sake, he was 252 years old!

Yes, for the first few years on Freeport he had certainly had liaisons with several Fireflies, often in the forms of famous queens and duchesses. What the hell, he was a sailor! But those days were long gone. While the Slicks had prolonged his life with repairs to his physical body, his desires were no longer that of a 28-year-old. And continuous debauchery was just not something that mannered men did—that was something the lower sorts aspired to.

As was usual over breakfast, Obujimi switched into his Minister of Civilian Affairs mode, reporting the previous day's numbers.

"Another good day yesterday, even though we were up against the baseball playoffs in San Francisco, which caused an eighteen per cent drop-off from the Pacific States. Total tourists 8,334, 1,550 took the promotional tour, immigrant arrivals 4,571. Also, 135 Drunk and Disorderly arrests, 96 needing medical services, and 33 assaults. No fatalities."

For its last few centuries of its existence on Earth, Venice had become known as the city of festivity and romance. Under Firefly pressure, the Governance Council had agreed to continue this image, promoting New Venice as a party destination, the place for Earthers to forget their problems and have fun. But the extreme drinking and wild carousing of New Venice's younger visitors had taken Wyckham by surprise. Fights had become common for the first time on Freeport.

Then there was the brazen debauchery in public areas. The Fireflies had insisted that New Venice have a policy that no act of affection would be illegal, mainly to help their harvests of human seed. The result was a shocking public display of drunken intercourse and other acts even worse. Was all this discouraging older visitors? Mature humans made excellent immigrants and Wyckham didn't want to lose them. Maybe it was time to bring this up to the committee? *A second problem to discuss.*

Obujimi continued with his daily morning report while Wyckham picked at his boiled egg and sipped his coffee. All three passenger ships were scheduled for six round trips each between New Venice and the ports of New York, San Francisco and London, making for a busy day along the new Venice docks. The *Cornelie* was still overdue from its mapping expedition in Freeport's south, but Freeport's seas had been up for days and she'd probably had to go into irons and wait out the storms. Its Captain, James Harrison, Freeport's leading explorer, was also an experienced sea captain, having manned a successful privateer in the Second American War, and the Governor wasn't concerned about his ability to weather a storm.

With the end of breakfast, Obujimi snapped back into his valet role, bowing and scraping as he helped Wyckham with his toilet and dress, though not missing any chance to criticize Wyckham's attire, especially whatever he felt was inappropriate. He'd gotten upset over Wyckham's dress at the annual Navy ball a few nights ago, and now he seemed to bring up the subject constantly.

"And Governor, I must also say your insistence on your captain's uniform yesterday was completely inappropriate for the ceremony greeting Earth's climate scientists. I'm gone for one night and you go out looking like a fool? My God, a lowly captain! All the talk in the taverns last night was how ridiculous you looked, just not befitting the ruler of an entire planet. Even the slovenly young American tourists were talking about it. The blue silk suit with the Governor's sash would have been correct for such an occasion. I suggest you listen to me for once. Sir."

Humphh. It had been a meeting of 21ˢᵗ century scientists and scholars dressed in the miners' pants they called "jeans" and equally crude flannel shirts. In governor's regalia he would have stood out as a stuffed-shirt royal. But Obujimi was a 19ᵗʰ century aristocrat at heart and believed powerful people should dress to impress at all times. No doubt it had been Obujimi's numerous agents stirring up discontent over Wyckham's dress in the city's taprooms last night.

"My regrets, of course I should listen to you. Next time I'll wear my governor's pajamas. Maybe with the Governor's seal on its arse?"

Obujimi indignantly reverted to his quiet servant role and did not respond. Wyckham suspected he was already forming more negative stories about the governor's shocking dishabille for his agents to disseminate around the city tonight. But for two centuries those same agents had brought valuable information to Wyckham about the Dreash fleets and other important goings-on in the cosmos, so he would let them pursue Obujimi's mission to change his dress habits as long as they continued to uncover intergalactic plots.

Wyckham and Obujimi descended the stairs to the Doge's office, which he had taken over as his own and was the venue for Governance Committee meetings. He nodded to the marine sentry flanking the door, as rigid as one of the winged lion statues all over the city. Wyckham had instructed the marine sentries to no longer bang their muskets on the floor and bellow out "Sah!" when he arrived—that was just too loud for this dignified building. And the Fireflies had even projected dents from the muskets onto the marble tiles to add reality, in Wyckham's opinion ruining a magnificent thirteenth century mosaic floor.

Greeting the varied beings in the room, Wyckham took a seat at the head of the ornate Byzantine table surrounded by carved chairs that put most thrones to shame. Obujimi closed the door, went to a dais in the corner, opened a large tome on the top, started writing it in with a quill pen, and called the meeting to order.

"The one thousandth, three hundredth and forty-third meeting of the Freeport Governance Council is hereby opened. Noted as present: Governor Wyckham, the Firefly Lady Brashton, Minister Rawlins, Slick number 2256, Lycan ambassador Wulfe, Mudman leader Bubbler, prominent ant Worker Queen, and Thomas Obujimi, Prince of the Zulu and Minister of Civilian Affairs. Noted as absent; Minister of the Interior James Harrison."

Wyckham addressed the council. "Once again, we meet as New Venice continues to prosper, thanks to the endeavors of all here, especially due to Firefly Brashton and the efforts of her fellow Fireflies, who have built this wonderful fantasy which brings smiles to depressed Earthers and needed immigrants to Freeport. But for once I do have some issues to bring up. First, I've noticed some messy incidents caused by local fauna trying to eat the holo-graphic pigeons that…"

But Wyckham had to stop as the door burst open and none other than James Harrison, the big missing American, burst into the room, his fringed leather jacket and britches filthy, with an exasperated sentry vainly trying to hold him back.

"Freeport is under attack! By a combined force of Draesh and Americans!"

Party Moves

WELL, THIS IS more like it!" Emmie's mood changed immediately as the three women walked through the colonnaded entrance of Baroness Brashton's. They entered a magnificent long foyer, its walls lined with statues, to a stairway that descended to the main hall. Reaching the head of the wide marble stairway gave the three a breathtaking view of the vast party facility. The giant interior was all neoclassic, its inner wall covered with marble pilasters reaching all the way to the fifty-foot ceiling. The three levels of suites around the circumference were all marble as well, built over arched loggias topped by thick cornices that crowned each one. The central hall alone was the size of Madison Square Garden, with many other large halls branching as well. A pounding dance beat seemed to be booming from every direction, sort of techno-rock with wild crescendos of instruments they didn't recognize. There must have been several thousand dancers on the recessed floor, most wearing wild costumes on their new holographic bodies. A dozen circular bars on twenty-foot-high stepped platforms loomed above the undulating mass of partygoers, surrounded by tables and their own small dance areas. The private suites along the walls were filled with more sedate partiers drinking and watching the gyrating circus below. Dozens of small stages holding the club's entertainers hung from the ceiling at varying heights, some with humans performing extremely suggestive dances. The nearest one, about thirty feet above them, had a very attractive couple in black body suits with dozens of holes cut out, doing handstands as they ground against each other upside down while grabbing onto a brass pole.

"Oh my God!" blurted Vanoune as the three stopped under the entwined couple. "Are they fucking?" A moment later it was clear to them that the holes in their suits were there for a reason. "Holy shit, they ARE fucking!" exclaimed Connie."

The Café Florian had just been OK. Emmie, Vanoune and Consuela had eaten a light meal of Venetian specialties, pasta and seafood, which were good but not as over-the-top as a typical San Francisco meal. And the wine certainly hadn't been much for a restaurant in a supposedly Italian city. Apparently, aliens didn't make good wine. And the bar at the Florian had been a bust, pretty dull, full of older tourists from Nebraska marveling at the restaurant's architecture. Though it had been fun to watch the amazement on their faces as the three outrageously-bodied movie star clones passed by on their way out.

But now came the main event. Soon after the first tourists had visited Freeport, Baroness Brashton's had quickly achieved notoriety on social media as THE club to hit in New Venice. Founded by a 19th century aristocrat turned madam, the club was the place to see and be seen, known for its lavish size, opulent architecture, and wildly uninhibited dancing. It was also famous for its popularity with aliens, nicknamed "The Star Wars Bar" by human tourists, and there were aliens dancing around the bars and on the small stages dangling from the ceiling. As they headed towards a nearby bar, the ladies went right under a little floating stage with two of the big mud creatures pulsing to the music, their bodies stretching and contracting like they were being squeezed. Suddenly they moved together and melded into each other, turning into a single large mudball that started violently shaking. After a few moments, the ball split back in two beings that just sat there, bobbing gently like they were recuperating.

"Did I just see what I think I saw?' exclaimed a slightly amazed Vanoune. "Alien mud sex?"

"I'm betting yes!" answered Emmie. "Watch, I bet now they have a cigarette."

Still chuckling and shaking their heads a bit, the three friends climbed up the steps to the first bar, threading their way through a mass of dancers bumping and grinding on the terrace around the circular bar. While most were garishly rebodied humans, there were a surprising number of aliens, especially the tall Slicks, enjoying the dance floor as well, some dancing with fellow aliens but many dancing with humans as well.

As they crested the stairs, they realized that this was the bar run by the Slicks. The women had researched Brashton's before coming on this trip and knew that each bar in the club was run by one of the alien races common on Freeport. The bartenders here were typical of the Slick species, around seven feet tall, with four arms, pearlescent smooth skin, unclothed, and having no facial features except for large diamond-shaped eyes and a small slit for a mouth. The bartender they approached looked exactly like the others, only differentiated by a chrome badge with the number "3,623,785" on it.

"Welcome to Brashton's," it said in a scratchy voice through the translator device strapped to its head. He stared straight at Emmie. "What is your poison?"

This was just too cool, getting drinks from a giant alien who looked like he was fresh from Area 51. His black eyes seemed to be boring into Emmie's brain. "I don't know, what do you recommend, handsome?"

"I drink a mental stimulant from my planet made from green mold. Humans do not like. House drink is Sailor's Slam, shot of blue liquor made from local tubers. Made by Human sailors on Freeport."

"I'll pass on the mold thing. Everybody down with the sailor drink?" Emmie asked. They nodded and Consuela laughed. "Do us up, Mister Slick!" The alien's four arms immediately started whirling around like a robot in a bottling plant, grabbing glasses and bottles from an overhead rack, filling the glasses with blue liquid from a hose dispenser, topping them off with lemon wedges speared on little plastic swords, then finally banging the glasses down on the bar. The whole process took just a few seconds, leaving the three San Franciscans duly impressed.

"Three drinks in less than a heartbeat!"

"A new NCAA record!"

"My kind of guy! You cook?"

The three clinked glasses and downed them in a gulp, then immediately cleared their throats to soften the burning of the fiery liquor. But all three had noticed the little plastic sabers in their cocktails, and whenever that happened to the three fencers, it always resulted in one hell of a scrap.

Emmie was the first to lunge for her weapon, though her two friends followed quickly. She whipped the little sword out of her drink and took a cut in *sixte* at Vanoune. Van made the parry with her little sword, giving her the right to reply to Em's attack. But she delayed for a split second, which Emmie used to make a body feint at Consuela, whom Emmie knew would be about to stab her in the back. While Connie froze for a second, Emmie had slyly left her point in line behind her back, which Van's hand blundered into as she lunged for Emmie's exposed back.

"A touch, a touch, I do declare," Vanoune declared. "But this bout's mine!" The three fencers continued poking at each other while they debated the veracity of Emmie's prediction.

But the comic sparring had caught the attention of the Slick bartender. "You fight same way as Moore. You only other humans that do?"

Moore? "Who's Moore?" Emmie asked. "Wait, wasn't he the officer on the ride over?"

"Yes. Great fighter, hero of Hollow Mountain. At that battle two hundred years ago, Moore saved Wyckham's life, fighting off dozens of Krag with his sword."

Emmie had read about Hollow Mountain. The final battle for Freeport had been fought inside a hollowed-out mountain, where the British under Wyckham had taken the Dreash command center and held it against repeated counterattacks from them and the Krag, their crab-like minions, until the League of Worlds fleet arrived and won the day.

"Your bootboy is a hero!" exclaimed Vanoune to Emmie. "You better go after that guy before Connie snags him!"

"Shit, a mere lieutenant?" Emmie shot back. "Forget that, I'm goin' for his captain. He's the governor of the whole planet and wears those hot boots, too!". All three had a laugh. Social media had gone wild over the dashing Governor Wyckham after his world-wide telecast on Earth. People magazine had declared him "the Universe's Most Eligible Bachelor".

Another Slick moved up to the bar next to Emmie. The words "Welcome to bar of…" came out of his translator but he then finished the sentence with some strange clicking sounds from its little slit of a mouth. "That is our word for ourselves in our own language. You Humans call us Slicks. I am greeter to our bar. You may ask questions of me and record image."

Cool! Emmie had researched all the aliens they would meet on Freeport and especially these Slicks, who were certainly the most imposing. That they had a PR flack greeting humans was surprising, since they were the most powerful race in the known cosmos and known for their arrogance. She and her friends jumped at the opportunity to have their first chat with a real alien, asking the usual questions—what they ate (very little), what they did (research and exploration), their life span (almost infinite), and what they thought of humans (mostly dimwits but a few were great fighters).

They ordered a second round and insisted on buying their alien companion a drink. He ordered one in his clicking language and the bartender furiously whipped him up a glass of horrible-looking green sludge.

"Jesus, what's that you're drinking?" asked Consuela. "Smells like low tide at a landfill." Rising ocean levels had invaded many landfills back on Earth, making them notoriously smelly during low tides.

"Drink name translated is 'Brain Food'. Makes drinker smart, not stupid like human drinks".

"How about making you a bit… ah… randier?' asked Emmie. "Don't you want to like…, uh, have fun when you go out to a club like this?"

"Randier?" The Slick had to wait for a second as his translator searched for the word's meaning. "Ah—sexually promiscuous. Slicks asexual, no gender like humans, all same. Reproduce in laboratories. Notice no genitalia." The naked alien stood up and spread his legs slightly to show that there was indeed nothing there, just more glossy skin.

"Now that's a picture, ladies!" Emmie said as she handed the bartender her phone. "Get in here, ladies!"

Consuela and Vanoune stepped to the Slick's sides while Emmie dropped to her knees, pointed a hand at the alien's crotch, and made a shrugging face with her other palm up in a "nothing here" pose. Consuela joined her in a similar pose while Vanoune hugged the Slick with one arm and put her other palm up in a shrug as well.

After posting some shots to their Facebook pages (Earth had installed WI-FI modems across Freeport and on buoys at transporter gates), they finished their drinks and set off into the vast hall for another bar. The next one they hit was run by the mudmen, with several behind the bar and more rolling around its perimeter. They maneuvered through them and dozens of tourists, got to the bar and were greeted by a six-foot ball of mud.

"Lookee 'ere", the thing barked through its translator's horn. "Three purty lasses, an' wit' a mighty thirst too, I reckon."

While it was odd to hear an alien talking like a cockney on the London docks, Emmie and her friends knew that the mudmen had learned English from 18th century sailors. It still took the women a few moments to actually start talking to a giant ball of mud—no eyes, no mouth, no arms or legs, just an undulating ball of brown slime. Finally, they managed to order three more Sailor's Slams. The mudman bumped a panel with its bulk and some kind of drink dispenser whirred to life, dropping three shot glasses on the counter and filling them from a robot arm. The mudman did manage to form some of its mud into an appendage and push the drinks across the bar. Right on cue, a mudman greeter rolled up to the new arrivals.

"Welcome to th' mudbar. Ye in'trested 'n a mud bath? Floral, sulfur, salts, gots it all right 'ere." Some of the creature's mud formed itself into an arm and pointed back at its body.

"Mud baths? How… cute," Emmie answered. "But no thanks, we're just here for a drink, don't want to do something that'd make us shower afterwards."

Consuela was interested. "Wait a minute! I love mudbaths! But don't your clothes get all filthy?"

"Don' need to bathe afterwards, mum. No mud sticks t' ye, all 'r parts sticks wit' us. Jes' jump inter any mudman ketches yer fancy." The friendly creature formed an arm and gestured to its right. "Pick anyone ye sees, though ye kin jumps inter me if ye likes?"

What the hell was it talking about—jumping into a mudman? This thing was hitting on her? But when Emmie followed the greeter's arm, she saw what it was talking about. Along the bar were several other mudmen with the people's heads sticking out of them, mostly female heads. As she watched, a giggling African American woman stood in front of her friends as another mudman rolled around her, wrapping her in mud until only her head protruded from the brown mass, then started undulating its body. The motion was irregular, at times washing around like waves in a muddy lake, or vibrating rapidly, convulsing in staccato shock waves from one side to the other.

The mudman next to Emmie kept trying to close the deal. "If ye thinks jes' sittin' 'n a tub o' mud is relaxin', jes' think how good it feels wit th' mud movin' around ye. All ye 'oomans loves it."

Well, the black woman was certainly having a good time, laughing with her friends, who were all wearing tee-shirts celebrating "Shiela's Bacholorette Party". Emmie and her friends watched as Shiela described her experience in real time.

"Oh man, this is very soothing! The floral smell is delightful, it just blends with the pervasive warmth…" then her eyes went wide for a moment, getting a volley of laughs and comments from her friends. "Is that 'pervasive' warmth or 'penetrating' warmth, girl?" and "Maybe you should forget the wedding and move up here, I don't think you need Brent anymore!"

But Shiela wasn't paying attention to them, her mind was elsewhere. "Oh my God, now that's reee-ally good! Oh… my… God! Is this legal?" With each phrase her eyes went wider.

Consuela, who had a lower tolerance for alcohol than her friends, was enthralled by what she was seeing. Emmie cracked, "Connie's thinkin' about it!" Just what you need, girl! You know you like your sex dirty!"

Emmie and Vanoune were hysterical, falling over each other from laughter, while Consuela just kept her eyes on the pulsing mudman. Finally, she rolled her eyes, shook her head, and muttered, "Get me out of here! I can't resist mud baths!"

Still laughing, Emmie and Vanoune began pushing and shoving her, pretending it was taking all they had to move a resistant Connie. Van yelled "Go—Connie he's not for you! He flunked out of med school!" and Emmie stating, "If you think your dad went berserk over that Bangladeshi guy, just wait 'til you bring Pigpen here home for dinner!"

Consuela finally accepted the humor of it all, leaving them all laughing and ribbing each other as they walked up to the next bar. This one was much bigger than the first two and more happening. Even the stepped base surrounding the bar was covered in hundreds of dancers, mostly humans, though aliens of many species seemed drawn to the spot as well.

"This one's the Fireflies' bar," stated Vanoune. "Where all those hot energy beings try to hook up with human guys." Sure enough, there were hundreds of young men on the bar's stepped base, its dance floor, and at the bar. But they were outnumbered by women, many of them in the most outlandish holographic bodies a mind could imagine. Some were incredibly tall, seven feet or more, others had rippling muscles on their arms and legs, gigantic breasts were common, and all had magnificent faces with penetrating eyes that took your breath away. And most were crowned with long hair in complex hairdos.

Vanoune was lesbian, so this was the place she had been waiting for. But this bar looked interesting to Emmie too, with all the good-looking guys around, and a tipsy Connie was definitely down. It took some shoving, but within a couple of minutes they'd managed to push their way to the bar and order three more Sailor's Slams, this time from a towering female bartender in a bronze bikini and wearing a horsehair-plumed helmet whose name tag proclaimed her as "Athena".

It would have been interesting to talk to the Firefly bartender, but it was time to party with some fellow humans. Drinks in hand, they leaned back against the bar and took the scene in.

The three women went to a lot of bars in San Francisco, checking out each new one, looking for the latest hot place. After a quick scan of the scene, Emmie decided that this bar was Vegas meets the DNA Lounge, an old but still hip club in SF. Just plain cool. Looking out over her new breasts into the mass of partying humans and aliens, she shook her head in amazement at it all. The hall was just magnificent, all marble columns and tapestries. The music in the huge room sounded like vinyl, with a slight echo and reverb like they were in a cave. And how could you beat a dance floor covered with wild aliens and unbelievably stunning people? With a good buzz going, Em decided things didn't get any more chill than this.

An incredibly good-looking guy walked up to the bar, nodded at her, and ordered himself a Moscow Mule. He was even taller than the new Emmie, with dark short hair, chiseled features and a tight body. Then an inebriated couple behind Emmie momentarily lost their balance and fell into her, pushing her into the new guy, enlarged breasts first.

"Now that's a friendly greeting!" The handsome guy said. "My name's Brent, REALLY nice to meet you!"

"Jeez, 'scuse me," Emmie said with a laugh. "Folks behind me lost it for a sec. But I'm Emmie." She stuck her hand out and they politely shook.

"Yeah, it's always a zoo at the Firefies' bar. I'm always afraid I'll get shoved into one of those gorillas. They're so big and don't look too friendly."

"Actually, I think they're pretty mellow," she responded. Emmie had read about every alien species on Freeport and told Brent that the blind gorillas were almost Budda-like in their kindness and tolerance of others. Brent was interested and asked her what else she knew about the other aliens in the bar, which Emmie explained from what she'd researched. Then they went through the usual banter about themselves, briefly describing their careers and where they were from.

Brent lived in Burbank, California, where he worked at a start-up developing improved medical diagnosis apps for iPhones. Further questions revealed that he was actually the founder, and though the company was only a year old, it already had two dozen employees and was doing quite well. Emmie liked it that she had to probe to find all this out, he wasn't one of those big-ego entrepreneurs that gave you his card as soon as he met you. In turn, he seemed impressed that Emmie worked with some of the same software as he did.

This guy was getting her energy up. "C'mon, let's dance!" she said, and pulled him away from the bar to a space on the bar's steps. Next to them two fish people were grinding together like they were flapping on a dock. Emmie was an athletic dancer and Brent wasn't half bad himself—they both got into it, and soon they were spinning around with a little playful bumping. After a half hour or so they fell against each other for a moment, exhausted, then wove their way through the packed crowd back to the bar.

Emmie melted against Brent at the bar. What a night! Everything she'd hoped for. Who knows where things were going with Brent? But what was Freeport's slogan on their TV ads? "Freeport, galaxies away—what happens doesn't even get back to the Milky Way!" She gave Brent a dreamy look—but he wasn't looking back, he was looking over her shoulder. Em turned and suddenly her night was ruined. There stood what had to be a Firefly, since she was over eight feet tall, incredibly beautiful, with six-pack abs and beer keg boobs! And Brent couldn't take his eyes off her!

She was dressed in a Vegas showgirl costume, all dangling jewels and little else, with big raven hair wrapped into a feathered rhinestone headdress. The goddess passed by Emmie like she wasn't there and brushed her giant breasts right across Brent's face.

"Good evening. Tonight I am Betty Grossman, your 7th grade school teacher. Would you like to dance and then copulate?" And then the goddam slut pulled away the pearls hanging over her crotch to show her labia, which opened wide like they had a mind of their own! As Brent stared they began undulating, just like a jellyfish on a National Geographic special!

Brent was speechless. His eyes were wide open and locked on the Firefly, mostly focused on her chest. Finally, he managed to get out a few words.

"Betty…Grossman… I don't believe it! My fantasy Betty Grossman! I daydreamed about you every day of my teenage life, just like this, my teacher with the body of Galaxa, my favorite superheroine! You're incredible! Unbelievable!"

"Let us dance." The fantasy school teacher hooked an arm in Brent's and guided him to the dance floor, where she put her long arms around him and started ferociously grinding her body into him.

So that was that. Emmie was really pissed. She'd landed a great guy, only for this fucking snake of a hologram to slither off with him! Son-of-a-bitch-piece-of-shit!

Connie and Van had been standing nearby and saw it all. They walked over to Emmie, shaking their heads in sympathy.

"Shit, girl, I thought things were going pretty good for you there," said Van. "He was a catch. Too bad superwoman schoolteacher showed up."

"Yeah, same thing happened to me," complained Connie. "It's hard to compete with these goddam alien holograms. They just take on incredible images, they can dream up anything."

Though the women were half gone, the comment hit all three like a thunderbolt. Shit, they could play that game too!

"Didn't I see one of those changing stations in the lobby?" suggested Emmie.

The Worst Possible News

THE PROBLEMS OF fake pigeons and drunkenness in New Venice suddenly meant nothing as the stunned group listened to James Harrison, the American privateer who had remained on Freeport 200 years ago rather than go back to London for his hanging.

"Two days ago, I was ashore about 100 miles south of here with eight of my men and the native leader Dreashpalone, surveyin' the height of the local mountain range. As I returned to the shore to get back aboard the *Cornelie*, what do I see in the air but a portal, bigger than ours, pouring gigantic metal ships onto the water and small flyin' craft into the air above them, all of 'em bristlin' with weapons. All around the sea and air are already full o' these things, musta been over a score of 'em. And all aflame in the middle was the *Cornelie*, burnt down to the waterline and sinking. Musta been a hundred corpses in the water, though we did see four boats taking prisoners. We stayed hidden for a day, watchin' the activity through our telescopes. What do we see but some Dreash, about thirty of 'em, come swimmin' up to a gigantic ship with a flat maindeck, clearly designed for the flyin' ships, and they climb aboard. Uniformed humans come out an' have a chat with the big pigs, real friendly-like, this is all planned. All the ships were flying this flag I sketched."

Harrison held up a paper showing a red flag bearing a blue "X" with thirteen white stars on a red background. The Firefly Lady Brashton immediately spoke up.

"That's known as the 'stars and bars'. It's the flag of the Triumphant States of America, the southern states of the previous United States."

Hummph. Triumph has invaded. No surprise, he had made it plain that he was going to pursue the riches and advanced technology on Freeport, and since he couldn't get it peacefully, he was doing it by invasion. Goddamit! Despite the Fireflies' best efforts, somehow the banned southern states had secretly communicated with the Dreash, constructed a transporter, and brought a fleet to Freeport! And the *Cor-*

nelie, Wyckham's fastest ship, was gone, along with her crew of both humans and aliens. Some of those men had been with him since 1811. Wyckham shook his head and forced his attention back to Harrison as the American continued.

"We watched fer a day, stayin' hidden in the brush along the shore. Some o' their ships did have some damage from comin' through the transporter, especially the big mother ship for the flyin' craft, she was listin' n' had some boats 'round her stern. I 'spect she dragged her stern comin' over the lip o' the transporter, prob'ly got her hull scraped an' maybe rudder damage too. After a day watchin' 'em and pickin' up four of *Cornelie's* survivors who made it to shore, we went back inland to a tribe o' friendly Garoshen. Dreashpalone got us guides and mounts, some o' their big armored cattle, an' with those tireless beasts under us we made it back here in three days."

God bless the Garoshen and their domesticated giant animals. It turned out that the armored beasts had existed on Earth millions of years ago. Earth tourists called the giant three-horned beasts *Triceratops*, members of a species called *Dinosaurum*. In the late 1800's their bones had been found all across Earth and were now displayed in museums. To see living ones was the highlight of many humans' visit to Freeport. Wyckham liked the beasts because they made for superb mounts in a fight.

"This here's Frank Dawes," Harrison continued, motioning for a sailor behind him to move forward. "Gunner's Mate on *Cornelie*. Describe to everyone the attack on your ship." Somewhat intimidated by his audience, Dawes stepped forward, nodded and saluted with a knuckle to his head.

"Sirs, Cornelie were anchored 'bout a 'af mile off shore, waitin' fer cap'm 'Arrison 'ere, when Topman James calls out f'm the crosstrees 'at dere be Dreash 'n th' water one mile south. Lootenant Willowsby calls th' ship t' arms, ever' ones lookin' south, when doan' a big portal opens right 'boves us. Right away, 'fore any ship drops through, rockets come out'a th' big hole, burnin' white 'n makin' a big wooshin' sound, all 'eaded right ats us. They all hits at once an' explode, the ship turns inta hell, fire ever'where, never seen th' like 'n all me years 'n th' navy, no sir, like no fight I ever sees. Me 'n a few udder 'ands git blown o're th' side, we climbs onter some wreckage 'n float to'ards shore. Topman James 'ee doan make it."

Wyckham looked down and pursed his lips. Topman James was the keen-eyed lookout who had first spotted the first Dreash 200 years ago when *Righteous* fell through a portal in the English Channel. *Stiffen up, Wyckham. You've got this man's report to listen to.*

"We're watchin'," Dawes continued, "we sees four flyin' things come slowly through, makin big 'ammerin' noises, 'bang bang bang', as 'ey fly. Den comes 'eze great big metal ships, no masts, droppin' mebbe thirty feet to th' water, a score of 'em. Den comes a big roar an' two small flyin' ships comes through real fast, like Wulfe's li'l flyin' boat, big orange flames comin' outer th' sterns. Fine'ly comes 'iss ship big as a town, gots lotsa th' flyin' craft on 'er flat deck, n' starts t' drop through, but she 'its 'er stern on th' bottom o' th' portal and heels t' port. She rights 'erself in th' water, but by th' time we gets t' shore she's listin' t' port ag'in, she's takin' water. Th' two fast flyin craft come in t' land on th' listin' deck, one does but th' udder one falls off th' side an' sinks real quick."

Dawes tried to continue but he started to cough, his throat parched from a long dusty ride. Immediately Obujimi handed the man a glass of whiskey. Dawes drained it eagerly and got his voice back.

"Thankee sir, thankee, t'were a long ride today. So," he continued, clearing his throat, "We makes it to shore 'n joins wit 'Arrison an' 'iz men. Fer hours we watch small boats f'um th big ship workin' on th' stern. An' then up t' th' surface comes 'bout a dozen Dreash, talkin' t' th' men aboard likes they're ol' friends, then they dive under an' starts workin' on th' stern, too. We leave with 'Arrison that night, las' we sees they still workin' on th' stern an' th' ship ain't movin'. "At's what we saw." Dawes knuckled his forehead again and took a step back. Wyckham nodded and spoke up.

"Captain Harrison, Mate Dawes, we owe you both a great debt of gratitude for getting here so promptly despite such a difficult trip. Rest assured your timely intelligence will be put to use." Wyckham turned back to the council.

"We are now at war with this Confederacy. As you all know, calling in the Slick navy or any other League forces will turn Freeport into a battleground. While they would quickly rout this human invasion, I doubt they would leave. Every world in the league wants an excuse to take this planet, our four-armed friends probably more so than any other. But other members of the League would not tolerate any take-over and would invade, bringing us devastating warfare.

"So we must kick these rabid Americans out on our own. We have to show the League that this planet can defend itself and keep it open to all. I've expected this day since we re-established contact with Earth and been planning for it, but they've surprised me with this second portal. Yet I'm sure this worthy group gathered here can again emerge victorious. Let us discuss tactics.

"As we know, their primary weapons are their rocket powered air-ships, which they had probably planned to launch by now. With their mother ship out of service and immobile it seems we have an excellent opportunity to sink it and remove this threat. I suggest that the Fireflies once again make a bubble, take our squadron under the surface right into that bay and sink that mother ship along with any other target of opportunity. As matters get too hot, which I'm sure they will, the Fireflies reform the bubble and get us the hell out of there." He looked at the head Firefly. "Your thoughts, madam?"

In the final battle in the original war with the Dreash, Fireflies had turned their inner energy into a huge electric bubble that enveloped the British ships and transported them underwater to a lake right inside Hollow Mountain, the Dreash control center. The six ships suddenly popped to the surface, facing a rock wall of ledges covered with dozens of Dreash and their Krag minions operating electrical sensors, communicators and distant weapons. The first British broadside wrought havoc, bringing down part of the cave's roof and destroying the enemy's ability to direct its forces, taking out most of the foes in the control center. Though Dreash reinforcements quickly arrived and almost destroyed the entire squadron, League ships soon broke into the weakened mountain and won the day. While HMS *Zeus*, an 84, was sunk and its admiral Sean O'Neal killed, the action won the war and allowed the creation of Freeport, an interplanetary commercial hub based on the use of the Dreash transporter. Now Wyckham wanted to repeat the tactic that won that battle.

But Firefly Lady Brashton quickly dashed his hopes. "Sadly, with the presence of Dreash in this enemy fleet, I don't think that will work a second time. At Hollow Mountain, the Dreash were taken by surprise and didn't immediately recognize that my race was present in the bubble. They won't make that mistake a second time. And being that close to them on this mass-based world, they can take control of us immediately, physically moving our bubble with your ships inside it to wherever they want. Probably right into the nearest sun."

Well that was a risk he couldn't take. Wyckham surveyed the room and saw similar feelings in the eyes of his advisors. And now another voice started yelling behind him. "You have an emergency, my friend!" Who's this now? Christ, it seemed it was impossible to hold any kind of meeting without someone bursting in.

Wyckham turned to the door to see Cochrane, the British Prime Minister, trying to get past the sentries and into the council meeting. "Lucky for you, Governor, your mother country offers assistance in your hour of need. I'm here with... oh, for God's sake man, you know me," he said to one of the sentries still trying to hold back the fast-moving Cochrane. "I'm the Earl!" he bluntly stated, looking the sentry straight in the eye. The sentry released him, and he turned back to the room. "Wyckham, no more of this nonsense! I'm here with DiCarpaccio! Let us in! We raced up here to warn you. You're under attack!"

A nod to the sentry and Cochrane was released, striding into the room while adjusting his ruffled jacket, followed by DiCarpaccio, Amaerica's west coast president. Behind them were a dozen men and women in various military uniforms, all inside a tight cordon of Wyckham's marines.

"Governor and ministers of Freeport." He began. "Excuse us for bursting in. Four days ago, satellites... picture-taking devices flying high over Earth... from the United Kingdom and the Pacific States observed what can only be preparations for an invasion of your planet. In the middle of what was supposed to be war games conducted by the Confederate states, a portal opened up in the Gulf of Mexico and was entered by an amphibious armada led by the Texas National Guard, along with elements from other Confederate states. Their fleet included four destroyers, two missile frigates, two amphibious assault ships, a dozen transports, a nuclear-powered submarine, and an aircraft carrier. We estimate a total of twelve thousand personnel and fifty aircraft."

"Yes, it's an invasion," agreed the American president. "Our militaries immediately conferred. We assumed this force was going to Freeport, and it was decided to immediately send a delegation of military experts here via your daily portals off London and San Francisco to warn you and offer military intelligence and advice. Freeport has been a lifesaver to our two nations, with its help on refugees and climate change, and our two nations have an interest in keeping this world under your control. The specialists we have brought with us are familiar with the enemy's weapons capabilities and can instruct you in countering them."

Then he took an even graver tone. "Though the simple fact is that you have no chance of beating them, given their weapons and yours. You face a choice. You can call on your alien allies for assistance, though I understand that there are several very powerful planets that would love to get here and claim territory. Or, England and the Pacific States can ship all the necessary forces here to assure you victory."

DiCarpaccio paused and gathered himself. He leaned over and looked Wyckham in the eye. "I know you're worried that we are interested in conquest as well, and I know that many on this planet will question my assurances that an Anglo-American army would not stay. I assure you that the chance to pin down Triumph's military here and destroy it is our only military mission here. Destroying Triumph's fleet would end the biggest threat to our own nations. All we want from you is trade."

DiCarpaccio stood up and addressed the room. "So, simply ask yourselves—who do I want to land armies on this world, humans or aliens? To save your world we need permission from you immediately. You have an imminent invasion to deal with and we need two more days to assemble forces and get them to the portals. I suggest that you select officers to meet with our military experts and get a quick education about the forces you face."

"Meetings?" snorted Cochrane. "Jesus, no time for that! That carrier will be operating in a day at most, and when it does their planes will sink every ship here. And you call for meetings?" Cochrane continued as he took the floor. "Lucky for you I'm here. I've got a few ideas."

The Thomas Cochrane that Wyckham had known two hundred years ago was a master at improvising battle tactics. Did his ancestor also possess that ability? Wyckham motioned for the man to take the floor. "Please go on."

"Governor Wyckham, don't let our Yankee friends convince you that you can't beat these foes. You've fought more powerful foes before—beat a whole planet of gigantic hi-tech monsters that were about to wipe out Earth! So attack! Put some of your ceramic 32 pounders, their crews, and Greek fire cartridges in the mouths of those friendly gigantic whales that you have around here. Tie the guns to their big teeth so the crews can haul the guns out and fire them, the whales can absorb the recoil on their huge tongues. Then swim out to the carrier's location; you'll be ignored, a school of fish. On the enemies' sensors these clay guns of yours will look like debris or teeth in the big creatures' mouths—they only look for metal. When you get a mile off, surface, start firing until they counterattack, then dive and swim away. Your Greek fireballs will be deadly for ships. Two or three hits on the carrier would surely destroy it. Triumph's fleet won't know what hit them.

"Now I suspect my friend Leonardo here thinks I'm crazy. But I've read my ancestor Thomas's diary explaining everything that happened here in 1815, and he described the incident when your Firefly leader talked to whales and after only a few minutes of clicking back and forth they all swam off, located and scouted out the enemy, and reported back to her. But let me ask the Firefly leader herself." He turned to the Firefly Lady Brashton. "How long do you think it would take to train several whales to accept artillery in their mouths and execute an attack?"

She responded immediately. "The most difficult part is to assemble them here, I don't know how many are nearby. But I can send underwater messages to them, relayed by the many dolphins on this world, and with their fast swimming speed I should be able to assemble a dozen here in an hour or two. Explaining our plans to them would only take minutes. I would imagine the main delay would be caused by the time needed to place guns in their mouths and secure them for firing."

Wyckham quickly considered the details. This could work. The whales on the planet had been brutally hunted for centuries by the Dreash and bore a visceral hatred of the giant pigs. They loved the humans for taking control of the planet and pushing the surviving Dreash inland, far from their aquatic habitats. They'd do anything the humans asked, especially joining an attack on the detested Dreash and their new allies. They could swim at thirty knots for hours and wouldn't register on any of the Confederacy's sensors as a weapon. And New Venice already had numerous cranes along the docks that could load artillery into their spacious maws. The *Trinidad* was in port and it wouldn't take more than a couple of hours to transfer a dozen of her guns into the whales' mouths.

Wyckham addressed the council. "Anyone see a problem here? I think it's one cracking idea!" Nods appeared across the room. Wyckham turned to the British Prime Minister. "Maybe once again a Cochrane has saved our world?"

"Well, hold your praise until I name my price. I insist on going along in a whale. Wouldn't miss this fight for anything."

"Done! I'll be there as well." To fight alongside another Cochrane was a memory Wyckham would cherish. He wouldn't be surprised if the Irishman sunk a ship or two single-handedly.

Wyckham quickly assigned tasks and dismissed the council members and the American delegations, but Harrison asked to remain.

"One more moment of your time? And possibly our Firefly friend could remain as well? You both gotta see this." He yelled out a window. "Lieutenant Barton! Bring him up."

A minute later, what walks into the room but Harrison's lieutenant leading what was obviously a baby Dreash! No human had ever seen one, it had always been a mystery how and where the Dreash raised their young. Though only about four feet tall, it had every feature of their breed—the porcine head and tusks, a gorilla-like body, webbed hands and feet, and the demonic pointed ears. But unlike adult Dreash, it seemed to have an amiable disposition—it followed Barton around like a happy dog, smiling and drooling, eagerly looking about, clearly enjoying a new adventure.

The Lady Brashton Firfly leaped back in terror, her hands reaching up to her head as if it were about to explode. Dreash could take control of a Firefly's mind when in close proximity, and even though this one was small, her first reaction was complete panic. But almost immediately she relaxed, her hands dropping back to her sides.

"It has not attacked me. Whatever makes Dreash aggressive and dangerous to my race has not yet been instilled into this one." She moved up closer to the creature and damned if it didn't jump up and try give her a big hug. But with nothing to grasp but an image, it's clawed hands just waved about fruitlessly, searching the air in front of him for his new friend. She calmed him down by patting his head as she continued.

"We have always suspected that the electrical balls that give Dreash so much power can only be installed in adults. Apparently, the procedure is also what makes them malevolent, since this one is still just an amicable child."

Wyckham knew what she was talking about. In his first encounter with the Dreash in '15, he had examined a corpse shredded by his artillery. All throughout its body were yellow metal balls, sparking and buzzing, even though the creature was quite dead. It had always been believed that these balls were responsible for their mental powers, such as their ability to absorb knowledge from any living being they devoured and communicating with each other. But could this creature help Wyckham in fighting its own race? He looked intently at the juvenile beast, for the first time noticing many bruises and cuts on its face and body, though they all seemed to be healing.

"Well done, Captain Jamison. I'm sure we can put this captive to good use. Poor fellow looks a little worse for wear. Was the hasty return trip difficult on him?"

"No, not at all. But when we picked him up, all these wounds were fresh and bleeding. We had to stich him up, which he actually bore well, clearly knew we were helping him. He's thoroughly enjoyed the ride back and is healing remarkably fast."

Apparently child raising was pretty tough on young Dreash. Knowing the Dreash, that didn't surprise Wyckham one bit. With care and affection, this little Deash could become a very grateful ally.

"Madam Brashton, might we install a translator on the little fellow? If we could communicate, we can quickly determine how he might help in the coming fight."

"Yes of course," she replied. I will take him to the Sick medical center off the plaza. Could you assist in his transport, Captain Jamison?"

"Certainly mam. Though he's quite obedient. Feed him live rats and you'll have a friend for life."

"Really? Then your assistance will not be necessary," said the Firefly.

Then, in a somewhat frightening display of the Firefly's power that Wyckham wished he hadn't seen, a rat strolled out from behind a tapestry and sat down in front of her, obviously under her mental control, offering itself up for the young Dreash's lunch. Clearly the Fireflies had gained more power over the years than Wyckham had realized. She headed out the door with the rat at her side and the excited Dreash bounding after them.

An hour later the council and their visitors were at the New Venice docks, watching the big guns getting loaded into whales. The Firefly Lady Brashton had stuck her head under water, summoned some dolphins with a series of clicks, and within an hour whales began to arrive, swimming about the San Marco quay and communicating with Lady Brashton in their own clicking tongue. One at a time the massive creatures, at least twice the size of whales on Earth, pulled up to the dock, Captain Rawlins sent gun crews from *Righteous* into their open mouths, and a dock crane lowered the big 32 pounders onto the immense animals' tongues. Each whale took on a lieutenant in command, with the exception of the first one which Cochrane boarded as first officer. Then it slowly swam away from the dock to make room for the next whale, the gun crews inside its open mouth tying up the guns up to the animals' large lower fangs.

These cannons were not the simple cast iron guns that had landed with the British squadron 200 years ago. Constructed by the planet's industrious ant men, they were made of a dense brown clay from the planet's interior. When it dried out It was incredibly strong and hard, able to withstand the power of Freeport's black ooze propellant which produced a massive explosion when ignited. In a clay gun it was capable of shooting ten miles and accurately for two.

And what they now shot was devastating. While they could fire solid balls of iron roundshot or grapeshot, they usually fired cartridges of two chemicals which turned into a white-hot fireball when mixed. Captain Harrison had found the stuff while exploring the planet's interior, when he was saved from a Dreash by natives spitting the stuff from hollow tubers. This Greek fire, as the Brits had named it, would burn through anything—four feet of stone or even several inches of steel.

The Firefly was teaching hand signals to each beast as it was being armed and crewed. As Wycham watched, she finished with her current student, the six crewmen in the beast's mouth signaled to her that the gun was secured, and the crane pulled away to pick up the next gun on the dock. Lady Brashton started signaling—she extended her arm and pointed into the canal while holding her hand open like the open jaw of a serpent, then held her hand up. The whale understood immediately—swim into the canal with open mouth, then wait. The Firefly turned to Wyckham as he walked up.

"I am teaching the whales a few basic signs so you may communicate with them. I cannot go with you to provide that service, Dreash would detect my presence and the all-important element of surprise would be lost. Let me show you the signals. Tap the teeth in its mouth in the direction you wish it to move. Tap the tongue to dive, the roof to surface and open their mouths. The whales have already been instructed on the mission—they will swim towards the enemy mother ship and will start squealing when they get within one mile. Signal them to surface and open their mouths and you may fire your guns."

A gun from the open mouth of the last whale to leave the quay fired off a test round. Captain Rawlins leaned over to Wyckham as he kept his eyes on the gun crew in the whale's mouth.

"Our gun crews will be conducting live fire drills until the squadron leaves, getting their beasts used to the sound and recoil. Can't say I wouldn't need a little practice if I had to relax as a 32 pounder went off in my mouth, what? Hmmm…appears that the big fellow took it alright." Indeed, this whale had Lieutenant Moore aboard as commander, who waved a thumbs up at them to confirm that all was well.

Indeed, while the big whale had jerked slightly when the gun in its mouth went off, it hadn't disturbed the six-man gun crew inside, who were now rapidly sponging out the gun barrel, worming out debris, and ramming the next load home as if in battle. The cooperative whale leveled its tongue to facilitate running the gun out, and the gun fired again in less than a minute from the first discharge. Lady Brashton was clicking loudly to the creature and it was answering back.

"How did the big fellow take that?' Wyckham asked her.

"The whale said that was fun," she responded. "I had described every detail of what to expect, so it wasn't really surprised. With its size, it's like having a hot pepper in your mouth."

She paused for a moment, receiving a second message. "However, this whale has objected to being called a "fellow". You should know that the whales here are all females. I asked for females because the males in this species are not as intelligent as the females, a trait I have noticed in most physical species. Her name translates to "High Breacher".

Hmmmph! Wyckham was going to argue the point but suddenly a pod of dolphins popped up right in front of them and started rapidly clicking at the Firefly. She clicked back, clearly trying to settle them down, and finally the pod let one dolphin carry on a long conversation with her.

"What's that all about? Do they need some fish or something?" Wycham asked.

"Nothing so simple. The dolphins have a string of messengers in the water all the way to the bay where the invaders are, and they report that the enemy mother ship is almost level, and there is lots of activity on its deck."

President DiCarpaccio had been watching from the back of the group but now stepped forward to Wyckham. "That's bad news. They'll be resuming flight operations soon. And once they do, you'll have jet planes bombing the crap out of you. You need to attack soon before they can launch their aircraft, plain and simple."

Wyckham believed the American was in the right. He walked to the end of the pier and called out to all the sailors standing in giant open mouths.

"Men of Freeport! I have just received word that the foes who want to conquer our planet are preparing to attack with airships. We must attack their mother ship before they do, and you..." he counted the whales swimming about with artillery protruding from their mouths, "eight guncrews are all that we have ready to stop them. I'm going along with you inside this fellow… ah, female here," he said as he pointed to the whale below him getting its gun installed, "When we are about a mile off from the target, I signal to my whale to open its mouth and attack the enemy, she will signal your whales to do the same. Fire at will until the mother ship is clearly sinking, then turn your fire on any other large ship the bastards have brought here. When the enemy recovers from our surprise appearance and starts firing back, I'll have my whale contact the others to dive and swim off. If I and this big girl here fall, keep fighting until you see the fight has gotten one-sided, then tap the tongue of your whale's mouth to dive and flee. Don't stay too long! They have weapons that will decimate you in seconds once they start firing. You've all been in plenty of fights and know when it's time to retreat. Don't get yourselves killed for nothing, there'll be more fighting after this, and we need you. So I'm getting into this big girl here and off we go! Freeport and victory!" The gun crews standing in the eight open whales' mouths cheered as Wyckham stepped down into his whale's mouth and the last ropes were removed. Lady Brashton finished clicking to the whales and addressed Wyckham as he was climbing aboard.

"The whales are all ready. I translated your speech to them, and they are now eager for battle. Though your whale wants to know that she is not a girl, she is actually over 100 years old."

Good Lord but these female whales take offence easily!

"Let's prepare them further," commented DiCarpaccio. "The firepower they are about to encounter is beyond anyone's dreams. But if Miss Firefly can communicate with them through the chain of dolphins, let's train them further while you're traveling. I'll bring up my military experts to describe each of the enemy ships and their weapons capabilities. She can inform these dolphins here and get this information passed along the chain to your whales as they swim. These animals need to know what to dodge and when to flee."

"Capital idea! Get your best experts up here, Mr. President. But now I must leave, time is of the essence." As he prepared to descend into the mouth of the whale at the dock, Wulfe moved forward out of the crowd. "How about having me above in my scout craft? I could drop a few presents on the invaders," he suggested through his translator.

During the second battle for Port Wyckham, the wolfmman had used his captured Dreash scout ship to drop thirteen-inch mortar shells on the Dreash defending the transporter cave. Loaded with the explosive black ooze, the bombs had allowed Wyckham's force to attack it. With its provenance as the vehicle that had turned the fight around, the League of Worlds had allowed it to remain on Freeport, though devoid of weapons. As the only space ship in New Venice, it was a popular tourist attraction that could now be used in this battle.

DiCarpaccio disapproved. "I wouldn't do that, Governor. The enemy fleet has long range radar, they'd see him coming as soon as he took off, it would alert their defenses. Stick with the whales, they're your only attack force that they might ignore."

Wulfe nodded his head in understanding as Wyckham looked him in the eye.

"Do not worry, Wulfe. We'll surely need you and that ship later: this fight is just beginning. Keep it fueled and armed, ready to fly." He then stepped down into the mouth of the huge whale to be greeted by Gunner Crawford and his old gun crew, the best in the fleet.

"Another fight alongside my savior Crawford. I must say there's no one else I'd rather have at my side in a desperate scrap. How many times do you think you'll save my life today, old friend?" he said as he patted the man on his back. Crawford had saved his life thrice during the original war with the Dreash—once using the bow carronade to blow away a giant Dreash attacking Wyckham, another time when he cut the scrotum off one as it was about to swallow the captain, and a third time when he fired a 32 pounder up another one's arse just as it was about to drop a gigantic turd on Wyckham.

"Don' think eye'll 'av t' save ye today, cap'm. Wif' 'ese clay guns an' th' Greek fire, th' buggers don' stan' a chance, sor, no chance a' tall. We'll be fryin' fish for lunch o'er their burnin' ships, we will." With that he went back to getting his gun loaded and run up to the big mammal's teeth.

Surprisingly, also present was James Harrison, still looking bedraggled from his three days ride on the back of a Triceratops.

"Yep, I'm goin' along too, wouldn't miss this for the world. Haven't used this rifle in combat yet, couldn't think of anyone I'd rather shoot than these arseholes who invade our peaceful world." The ants had made him a special flintlock rifle of the same clay as the naval guns. It used the powerful black explosive to shoot balls of Greek fire over a mile. Harrison had even mounted a telescope on top so it could shoot accurately at long range.

Crawford lit some oil lamps, the whale closed its mouth and headed out into the bay with the seven others behind, Freeport's answer to an invasion by thousands of Americans with high-tech weapons. Wyckham settled down in the creature's mouth for the two-hour trip.

Bridge of *CSA George H. W. Bush*

Victor Triumph felt like crap, and he looked like it too. First of all, he wasn't getting his usual four hours sleep. It was hard enough for him to fall sleep on the fancy Swedish mattresses in his hotels, and trying to sleep on a cot inside a tipped aircraft carrier with the continuous hammering of repair work was nearly impossible.

He'd tried to pass the night tweeting, but all he'd managed to come up with was a tirade against the Guatemalan judge assigned to his latest public molestation case, in which the female plaintiff had unfortunately turned out to be a Silicon Valley CEO with top lawyers.

"This is another foreign judge treating me unfairly, they all do it. Maybe just once I could get a judge who was born here? And this case is totally bogus. Everybody on the airplane knew it was consensual. The truth is that I was minding my own business and she propositioned me! Happens to me all the time!"

And the food really sucked. There hadn't been time to stock the ship's galley with Big Macs, Domino's pizza, and good New York croughnuts. And while he did look good in front of the Fox News cameras with his admiral's uniform, unlike his normal suit jacket this one had to be buttoned so he'd had to tighten his corset, and the damned thing was killing him.

Beside him on the bridge of the huge aircraft carrier, staring out at the assembled fleet, was Stan Bamming. Four days aboard a listing ship had him looking worse than usual, and that was saying something for a man known for his bloodshot eyes, cheeks with permanent stubble and hair like a bird's nest. But even with the discomfort of seasickness, he wouldn't let himself or his boss move to another ship. "Victor, we've got to be here, on the command ship, looking in charge. Can't have the news showing us away from the action. This is the very first interplanetary war. This is big. You want to go down in history as humanity's intergalactic Commander-in-Chief. You have to be in control. You're the man!" So Triumph had remained on the *George H. W. Bush,* acting like he was managing the repairs, though the mundane matter of repairing a ship didn't interest him in the slightest.

But why it was taking them so long to get this boat fixed? How hard can it be to fix a propeller? It had happened once on his yacht and they had it fixed in an hour! Though the deck was finally leveling out and it appeared that they would be launching jets soon. Then he'd show the pitiful jerks on this planet who thought they could fuck with Victor Triumph. He'd never lost any fight in his life and this one wouldn't even be a contest. His modern hi-tech task force versus a bunch of old Brits with a few ancient cannons? Not even close.

A group of top officers had congregated around a sonar screen in front of him, pointing at some images with concern. Something more important than fixing the propeller was happening. Triumph barged into them to find out what was going on before they screwed things up. "What's going on here? Anything you'd like to tell your commander-in-chief?"

"Eight blips on the long-range sonar, sir," the fleet captain replied. "About one hundred feet long, speed five knots, random zig zag pattern, depth approximately 150 feet, issuing clicking sounds, occasionally surfacing. Not sure what to make of them."

"They're just whales, for Christ's sake," commented Bamming, the navy veteran, always on the bridge looking over everyone's shoulder. He turned and addressed the Admiral, Buford Jackson, and the nearby officers. "Didn't you big brains read about these things? They've got them all over this planet."

Also monitoring activities on the bridge was Brak, the leader of their Dreash allies. While the thirty-foot Dreash couldn't fit inside the bridge, it was loitering just outside, an advisor to the force trying to take back his old planet. It spoke to them through an open window.

"Kill them. These whales are all enemies, part of Wyckham's alliance. They are large and ferocious. Do not underestimate them. Kill them all—now. Don't let them get close."

The cameramen from Fox News moved in to record the discussion. Triumph believed in direct communication with his base and allowed them to film all operations despite the objections of the navy commanders. Bamming pulled Triumph aside and spoke under his breath.

"Don't listen to the big pig. You kill a bunch of whales, it'll cost you three to five points easy. Everybody loves whales, especially the moderates in Virginia and Florida you're trying to flip. You just can't kill whales, for Christ's sake. Be worse than when you cut funds for the special Olympics."

The Special Olympics. Shit, that had been a fucking disaster. Cost him two points, even in the south. Nodding agreement, Triumph turned back to the sonar screen as the operator spoke up. "Lots of small blips coming in now, in front of them. Looks like a school of small fish that the big blips are pursuing."

"See?' said Bamming. "They're just feeding, no threat to us." Triumph nodded agreement and turned to the cameras.

"I've decided that these blips are simply whales, God's creatures, following a school of fish that they're feeding on. Though they have sided with the bad guys here, they pose no danger to a modern naval force and will not be bothered, you navy guys understand?" he said, looking briefly around the bridge. "Acting decently is why the Confederacy is great. And isn't this something? No other president has brought real-time combat decisions right into your living rooms!"

The huge Dreash outside the window shook his head, sneered at them, then turned and dove over the side into the water some 100 feet below.

"Pissed off their leader," commented Triumph.

Bamming grinned. "It's what I do."

A lieutenant came onto the bridge, walked up to Jackson, saluted and reported. "Deck list under two degrees and stable, propellers 100 per cent, clear to resume flight operations, sir."

"Thank you, lieutenant. Get her into the wind, five knots, launch crews on deck and F-23's to the elevators. Commence 'Operation Americans First, Aliens Last'."

Triumph beamed. The name of this operation was the best one he'd ever come up with. Actually, the name was Bamming's idea, but he'd made it real. Starting in 2015, he'd constantly worked to generate hatred of alien immigrants, and switching that hatred to aliens on other planets had been an easy transition for his base.

Sirens clanged and the energy level on the bridge now went into overdrive, with some officers leaving, others arriving and reporting, all talking into their headset mikes. The pilot turned the ship into the wind, engineers called out power requirements from the nuclear reactor, weather officers were reporting wind conditions, and sonar operators plotted a course through the shallow bay. This was exciting! Really big!

With the sonar operators gathered in front of the short-range radar watching for hidden shoals, Triumph had a clear view of the long-range radar across from it. It looked different than it had just moments ago. The large blips had spread out into an arc and the small blips had disappeared. And the large blips were moving faster, much faster. Right towards the *George HW Bush*.

"Hey! You guys! What's going on here? Somebody better look at this!"

But no one paid any attention to him. Fucking idiots were all on their headsets and couldn't hear him. Triumph grabbed the nearest sonar man by his hair and shoved his face into the long-range sonar shroud. "I'm the President, Goddammit! Listen to me! Look at this!"

The sonar operator had lost his glasses in the altercation and had to bend over to pick them up. "Sir, do not interfere with operations while…" He stopped in mid-sentence as he put his glasses back on and focused on the image in the screen before him. "Shit! Surface Defence, Surface Defence! We are under attack, eight targets, bearing two seven zero, one mile, closing at… sixty knots!"

A sudden roll of distant explosions rattled the bridge's windows. Even inside the bridge, the sound of the artillery was so loud it shook the deck. On the adjacent radar screen, eight tiny high velocity blips sprouted from the large blips and headed straight for them.

"Incoming portside!" the now-terrified sonar operator yelled.

The operator's warning was cut short as a glowing white ball with a trail like a meteorite flashed into view and entered the bridge's first story right below them. Triumph braced for the explosion but surprisingly there wasn't one. Instead the fireball went right through and flew out the backside of the conning tower. Another flew in on the starboard side, passing through the lower decks and emerging to port. A third flew right into the bow and emerged from the stern.

"No explosions!" observed Triumph with a grin. "Cannonballs! The fossils' guns just shoot cannonballs! They think they can hurt steel ships with cannonballs? What a joke!"

Everyone on the bridge had frozen in place, waiting for explosions and shaking that hadn't come. But suddenly an excited crewman at a screen yelled, "Fire in forward munitions bay!" Then a fourth ball flew right down the flight deck, hitting an F-35 on ta catapult, igniting its fuel in a mushrooming orange fireball. A second later its bomb load went off, shaking the entire ship and throwing flaming debris everywhere, destroying the bow catapult and blowing a big hole in the deck. Everyone on the bridge was bounced around, most falling to the deck. Triumph grabbed onto a column and managed to remain upright.

Alarms started whooping as crewmen jumped up and returned to their screens. Within seconds they started yelling out the status of their systems.

"Reactor room taking water port and starboard!"

"Catapults one and two out!"

"Fire spreading fast in forward munition bay!"

That last report set off alarms in Triumph's brain. Fire in the ammunition? He was surrounded by losers that had just fucked everything up, and he could smell a disaster coming. He always followed his instincts, and they now told him to get the hell away from these has-beens—quick! He moved as fast as he could through the nearest door, without even alerting his security detail, leaving them behind. He hustled down an outside stairway, past a growing fire on the flight deck, and over to the port side where lifeboats were being uncovered. Panting heavily, he wobbled up to the nearest lifeboat where several sailors were preparing the boat for launch.

"Sailor, get me into this boat and off this carrier. Now!" He yelled to the man in charge.

The young petty officer saluted and responded in a wavering voice. "Ah… yes sir, but… we 're just preparing boats,… we have no order to abandon ship, sir."

"Sailor, your commander-in-chief is giving you that order! Let's go! Can you drive this thing?"

"Yessir, yessir," he replied, nodding repeatedly, then turned to the other sailors." Crewmen to boat four!"

"Wait! Victor!" It was Bamming, trying to run down the stairs, losing his balance and bouncing off the railing. He managed to get to the end and slowly jog over to the boat, gasping for air, his ample belly shaking. Right behind him were several of the president's security guards.

"Let's get the hell out of this clusterfuck," he panted, trying to catch his breath. "It's a mess up there. No way those clowns are saving this ship."

"Yeah, I could smell the trouble brewing. Get in! Don't slow things down! We got to move!"

With a leg up from the sailors, Triumph and Bamming were helped into the lifeboat, followed by some of their guards and two crewmen. The boat was hoisted up, swung over the side, and lowered into the water. Just as they unhooked the lowering cables, a massive explosion above them shook the whole carrier. Triumph's lifeboat sped away as the ship lifted up in the center, then sagged back down into the water, its spine broken. Finally, it slowly rolled over and capsized as jet planes tumbled down the tilting deck. Dozens of sailors survived by going over the side or running up to the keel as the ship settled upside down.

"You really fucked up this time, Stan! Should've shot the Goddam whales. Next time I'm taking the pig's advice!"

The Battle of Whale Bay

SURPRISINGLY, RIDING INSIDE a giant whale had been quite comfortable. Wyckham and his gun crew had been able to settle down in the soft tissue area between cheek and gum, where it was reasonably dry and very soft, like a settee stuffed with jellyfish. And cool fresh air was coming in from the blowhole every three or four minutes. The creature was obviously moving at fantastic speed, its entire body pulsing in long powerful strokes. The whole mouth was in constant rolling motion, but no one was seasick, everyone aboard was an experienced sailor, some of the gun crew were even dozing. But apparently the whale was busy, because it was constantly clicking in communication with dolphins and the other whales.

About two hours in, the creature slowed its pace for a few minutes and started turning back and forth. Suddenly the creature's swimming motion picked up again and it started squealing. "Beat to quarters!" yelled Wyckham as he tapped the roof of the whale's mouth. "This is it. We're there. On the gun, lads." All six men leaped up and took their stations on various ropes, except for Crawford, who grabbed the lanyard and half-cocked the firelock. "Get ready for the mouth to open, could happen any moment now. Fire on my order, not before." The sailors all knew their work and didn't need that warning, but Wyckham wanted to settle them down with routine instructions—nothing to worry about, just another fight. But this was something different and they all knew it.

The whale opened its mouth to reveal a large bay surrounded by low hills, which outlined the enemy. Moored in the bay were over a dozen large ships, many with cannon protruding from metal boxes on their decks. Above, white trails from fireballs already shot from other whales spanned the bay, and the enemy ships were replying with rapid-fire rifles and small cannon. The scene was one of explosions, somersaulting debris, gunfire blasting from several ships, fountains of water exploding from the surface, and the trails of white-hot shot. Looming right in front of him was the mother ship, dwarfing all the others. The whale had brought him up right on target. "you may fire when ready, Mister Crawford."

Crawford was siting the gun, his right eye bulging out even more than usual, yelling to his crew. "Four fingers starboard!" Two men on each side yanked on a block and tackle, pulling the rear of the gun carriage sideways along the whale's tongue. "Back a finger!" Crawford shouted, the crew gave a small tug on different ropes, and he pulled back the hammer to full cock. He paused a moment, waited for a pause in the whale's motion, then yanked the lanyard. The gun fired with an ear-splitting report and a blinding flash, sending its Greek fireball flying towards the mother ship. The creature obligingly raised the rear of its tongue to absorb the big gun's recoil, then slid the gun back to its firing position. Crewmen jumped to reload as Wyckham watched through his telescope and saw their shot impact the huge vessel amid-ships.

White balls from other whales were also arcing through the air and striking the gigantic mother ship—the huge craft was hard to miss. While most just passed through it with no reaction, a small explosion erupted on the rear of the deck, followed immediately by a much larger one.

Wyckham lowered his glass and commented to Harrison, "She's hurt. Hit some ordnance, I'll warrant." Harrison nodded without com-ment. He was alertly searching through the telescope of his long-range rifle for targets.

Just as the gun crew completed reloading, a massive explosion shook the entire bay as something on the mother ship blew up. The center of the massive ship lifted up from the water, then settled back down onto the surface and began to capsize.

The size of the explosion astonished Wyckham. He'd been in bat-tles where ships blew up, but this was like Armageddon.

"Snapped her spine like a twig. Fire got to the powder stores, I'll warrant. Jesus, she carried enough explosives to level a city! Alright, let's see if we can find another target."

Wyckham tapped the big tooth to his left and the creature tra-versed to port. Immediately another large ship came into view, one of the amphibious assault ships Cochrane had told him about. They carried troops, landing boats, and the heavily armed flying ships which could hover in place. And sure enough, there was one of the damned flying things about two cables off, hanging in the air, facing Wyckham and his whale, clearly about to fire.

"For what we are about to receive, may we be truly thankful," said Wyckham grimly, making the stoic statement of Royal Navy officers when facing death. Fire started flickering from the front of the little craft, stitching a line across the water to slam into them. The big whale took at least four hits, one above its open mouth, its explosion blowing rammer Barrows and chunks of the whale's jaw into the water. The little flying ship dropped a few feet and prepared to open fire again.

But the Yankee Harrison hadn't been standing idle. Resting his long rifle on the cannon's barrel, he squeezed off a shot, and a little fireball streaked through the air. Damn if it didn't hit the hovering craft dead center! Immediately the little ship started spinning and fell the short distance to the surface, its twirling wings splashing in the water.

"That was one hell of a shot," commented Wyckham, his hands clasped behind his back like he was on *Righteous's* quarterdeck.

"Not too hard when you're firing a load that goes through anything," replied Harrison as he reloaded his rifle. "Just aimed for the middle, figured I'd hit something, either fuel or the propulsion system."

And Crawford wasn't done with this fight either. Gunner Crawford had been in many a brutal battle, and the loss of his rammer didn't distract him for one moment. Leaning again over the breech with one eye open, he muttered "Barrows, 'is one's fer ye," then spun away and pulled the reloaded gun's lanyard. The gun fired with another earsplitting blast and a big fireball flew across the water to bury itself in the hull of the assault ship. But before his crew could even start worming the barrel out, the whale started taking additional hits from unseen sources. A large caliber bullet clanged off the 32 pounder's barrel and imbedded itself in the creature's tongue. Blood started gushing from there and other holes in the creature's cheeks.

Time to retreat and fight another day. Wyckham tapped the whale's tongue and it responded by inhaling some air, closing its mouth and tilting down into a dive. Blood was pouring into its mouth, both from its throat and from its blowhole. It was sloshing around Wyckham's boots up to his ankles. After a few brisk strokes of its tail, the whale's motion slowed, and it seemed to lose strength. Then it stopped moving altogether.

Jesus, did this creature just expire? Were they stuck beneath the surface with no way to get out?

Hold on! Wyckham could hear the whale communicating in its clicking language. It wasn't done yet! Though how this wounded whale could get them out of this fiery hell eluded him. They were goners.

Then the whale's opened its mouth, but before water could enter it blew a mighty blast of air through its mouth, shooting everyone out into the bay, light from the surface just a few feet above. Wyckham was painfully bounced off one of the creature's big fangs but managed to keep his breath held as he tumbled out into blue water. Coming to rest, he started to swim for the surface but a strong current immediately grabbed him and rushed him backwards towards a dark shadow that was moving quickly up on him. Suddenly he was spinning again, buffeted right and left by rushing waters, then quickly coming to rest with something solid beneath him. It was soft tissue—another whale's mouth! Their whale had spit them out and another one had sucked them in! This creature gently exhaled though its teeth and all the water in its mouth was blown out, revealing his crew splayed about, with none other than Alistair Cochrane helping them up! Cochrane recognized Wyckham, his face registering astonishment as he raced over.

"Governor! You of all people. Welcome aboard HMS Wet Foot. Are you alright? What happened?"

Wyckham started to reply but the pain in his ribs on his made him gasp.

"You OK?" asked a concerned Cochrane.

"Christ, cracked a rib. Not the first time and probably not the last."

"So what just happened?" asked Cochrane. "I was about to take a shot at that assault ship when my whale clammed up, spun around, next thing I know she opens it and here you are."

"Our whale took some hits from a rapid-fire cannon on a flying craft, then Harrison here dropped the thing with a superb rifle shot, put a fireball right through the thing and she spun down like a dead duck. Before she died our whale started clicking away, apparently communicating with yours. With her dying breath she spit us out and yours sucked us in. She died valiantly. Saved everyone, except crewman Barrows, who was blown out into the bay."

"No sir, cap'm. Me leg be fooked but I be alive." There lay Barrows, apparently sucked into the whale as well, layed out on the whale's tongue, getting a bleeding leg tended to by one of Cochrane's crew. "Guess I'll be seein' the Slick surgeons when's I gets back. Mebbe they throws this leg away and sews on another one. Hope it be a nice one. I liked this leg."

"We'll make sure 'ey takes good care of ye," commented Crawford as he watched Barrows get a tourniquet tightened on his mangled leg. "I'll ask 'em t' sew on a horse's leg so ye kin run a gun out faster. An' while they be at it, mebbe they cuts off yer dingle and hooks on a horse cock so ye kin ram loads home wif it."

"Barrows, a simple man, didn't grasp the jibe. "Why would's I need a horse cock? Jest me leg got shot! Tell 'em not t' cut off me dingle!"

"Don't worry, Barrows," said Wyckham, patting the man on the back. "I'm sure your member functions admirably, no one's going to cut it off. Gunner Crawford was only jesting. Thank God you're here and whole."

Celebrations ended as the whale accelerated and made a sharp right turn, throwing everyone to the floor of the beast's mouth. Its whole body started bucking as it strained to increase speed. A strange whirring noise passed by to port, then an explosion rocked the whale as it sped away. Same strange weapon had just missed them.

"That was a torpedo," stated Cochrane. "A self-propelled explosive that can guide itself to target. But it seems our girl here evaded it by swimming at high speed right at it, passed it before it exploded. Same way our fighters—combat aircraft—evade flying missiles in the air. Someone explained to her how to deal with it. Quite amazing, actually. I suspect DiCarpaccio and his military advisors used the dolphin chain to relay military information to our whales during the trip out here. Our whale was clicking way to somebody… grab hold!"

Everyone grabbed for a handhold as the whale jerked. For the next few minutes she swam with everything she had, violently jinking and diving, obviously to avoid enemy fire. Finally, to everyone's relief, she settled down into the same long slow stroke that she'd used on the way out. Crawford immediately checked Barrows's tourniquet while Wyckham, Harrison, and Cochrane discussed the short, fierce battle.

"What did you two see of the fight?" asked Wyckham. "Did our shot on that assault ship stuck home? Were any of their other ships hit?"

"We surfaced and put our first shot into the carrier," started Cochrane. "She blew up just as we got the gun reloaded, so we fired at a missile frigate in front of the assault ship. Then our whale turned on her own and I saw a helicopter right in front of us, right before our whale closed its mouth and dove after you folks. In the distance I also saw that assault ship you shot at was smoking, can't say how serious the fire was. I didn't see much else, there was too much spray in the air from all the enemy's rounds splashing about."

"I didn't see any other ships get hit," added Harrison. "But the air above was certainly filled with smoke trails, lots of ordnance was going back and forth. I did see two more little flying craft firing away on our left. I guess we initially surprised them, but they sure became unsurprised very quickly. I fear we lost some crews."

"And some whales, too. Stalwart creatures, these whales." Wyckham pursed his lips thinking about the animal that had died saving him.

Cochrane nodded. "Yes, very stalwart creatures. Magnificent sailors."

"Yes, and have you noticed ours is chatting away?" Their whale had been clicking since exiting the bay. "Something's up. When we get back, we'll have the Fireflies report."

Once back in New Venice the Fireflies would translate information from all the whales, providing more details of the fight. He needed to know how hard they'd hurt this enemy. The three settled down for the long trip back. They did notice that their creature was swimming even faster than on the way out.

The Confederacy Strikes Back

I F YOUR SONAR man had installed NC-23-467," stated the admiral, "this fleet would still have its capital ship!"

Triumph was furious. A bunch of impotent old Brits and some goddam FISH had sunk Texas's only aircraft carrier! Not to mention the amphibious assault ship *Peleliu* as well, a ship that Texas had spent a fortune on recommissioning. Two missile frigates and a destroyer had been badly damaged as well. Fuck, some old jerk with a goddam musket had even shot down a helicopter!

The Confederate force had over 3200 dead and another 5100 wounded, mostly casualties from the carrier *H. W. Bush*. Fox news had been transmitting everything in real time, so everyone back on Earth knew of this catastrophic fiasco—with him in command! And here he was in a meeting aboard *Mobile Bay*, the remaining assault ship, watching all the Navy admirals sitting on their asses blaming each other. Enough of this shit! He stood up and banged his fist on the conference table.

"That's it, Goddammit! You're all a bunch of idiots! I'm taking over operations. Admiral Jackson? And your staff? You're all fired! Get out! Captains, you stay. You just got promoted."

Stunned silence swept the room. Admiral Jackson and several older officers with medals all over their uniforms got up and left, no emotions readable on their faces. The remaining officers likewise showed no joy at their immediate promotion. Triumph leaned on the table and addressed them.

"You all know me, I hate firing people, but they deserved it, they really screwed up. I'm sure you guys will do a terrific job. And here's what we're going to do. I promised to come here and get Schillings out of here, and that justifies a combined arms attack on their New Venice! We've got a modern task force, they got a bunch of antique popguns! We don't need the jets, we have all we need to obliterate this pack of old zombies."

Triumph stopped and his eyes lit up. Another great nickname! He turned to the cameras. "That's right! Zombies! This planet and all its trade are run by a pack of Brits over two hundred years old! It's time to clean house and free this world! And we're going to start with the chief zombie himself, this ancient Captain Wyckham, a little ship captain who thinks he's king of the world!"

He turned back to the room. "I want a full assault on this Venice of theirs. Get the submarine, the destroyers and helicopters out in front of the fleet. They're all trained to take out submarines, for Christ's sake, they can take out a few whales, right?" All the captains nodded affirmatively—now that they knew what to look for the whales would be no problem. "Then we'll soften up this fake city of theirs with artillery and rockets. First from the fleet's guns, then from the helicopters. Create enough chaos in the streets and this Wyckham will be out there organizing relief, then commandos brought in by submarine can take him out and this war is over!

"So that's it. You guys get together and figure out all the details, I'm sure you'll do a fantastic job. Head to New Venice, shell the place, land troops, take control, and bring me chief zombie Wyckham!" He turned back to the cameras. "And just the zombie's head would be fine."

The booming voice of the Dreash liaison came in through the window where the creature had been listening.

"We Dreash approve. Allow us to send in our Krag minions right after your first artillery attack. For those of you who do not know, Krag are crabmen, about four feet tall, with a long spearing claw and a short crushing one. They are very fast and hard for puny humans… ah, just habit, I meant to say puny British… to shoot with their single shot weapons. Use your undersea craft and your hovering ships to clear the waters around New Venice of whales. Then the Krag can swim up undetected to the city and be ready to swarm onto the main plaza as soon as the bombardment ends. Their attack will cause chaos among the tourists and hamper Wyckham's defense. His troops will still be engaged with the Krag while you make your main attack. Use your automatic weapons to slay everyone. Your men will suffer few casualties. We do not care about losses among our Krag."

A pleased Triumph responded, "An excellent idea, big guy! Thanks for your help! You guys been fighting the zombies for years, haven't you? Nice to have you on our team." He glanced around the room. "Hear that? He's willing to sacrifice his own beloved troops. Now that's loyalty."

The captain of the assault ship, Zachary Rogers, one of the old navy men still left in the Confederate navy, was shaking his head. "Mr. President, this attack would violate Naval guidelines on collateral damage, not to mention the Geneva Convention. Plus, sir, it's immoral. You want me to shoot up a city filled with American tourists? Probably some from our own states? Then send in a mercenary army of giant crabs? A bunch of vicious creatures not under our control? You've got to be shitting me."

Triumph was simmering. "New Venice is full of our enemies, Captain. Not just Wyckham's zombies, but secessionists from the Pacific and New England states, not real Americans. You think any decent person in Iowa is going to travel a thousand miles to a horribly liberal city, either New York or San Francisco, where the transporters are, just to come here? Hell no, those good people go to my luxury resorts for vacations. New Venice is filled with our enemies from the coasts! Well, maybe a few visitors from Austin, but to hell with those liberal jerks. We're at war, we've got enemies all around, we need to take it to them, we need to win! So you on board or what?"

Rogers did not respond.

"Alright, who's second in command on this tub?"

"Lieutenant Wilkes, sir," Rogers answered.

"Lieutenant Wilkes? Where are you, Lieutenant Wilkes? Ah, there he is. Lieutenant Wilkes, will you obey every order from your commander-in-chief?"

"Absolutely, sir," came from the young man with a strong Texas accent.

"Congratulations, you are now Captain of the *Mobile Bay*. Captain Rogers, you are under arrest for refusing to follow my orders. Security? Take Captain Rogers below and find him a cell. See if you can find an old one that smells bad."

Triumph turned back to the meeting. "Listen up, everyone. We're at war, and all you sailors have to follow the commander in chief—me.

This Rogers guy didn't do that. Now you guys meet without him and get the attack plan ready. We sail through the night and we attack at dawn—better light to see our targets. And makes for better video, too." He looked at the camera crew. "See, Fox News? I didn't forget you! Tomorrow, for the first time ever, we will bring Americans a live battle, with really great production values.

Now I know some people will be saying, 'Oh no, Triumph shouldn't have broadcast this, why reveal your plans to the enemy?' But I don't care about that. I'm going to give the bad guys a chance, let 'em know I'm coming, even though they don't deserve it. No one can ever say I'm not fair. Zombie Wyckham, we're coming! See you tomorrow morning."

Triumph turned back to his officers who nodded and mumbled, "Yes sir". The Emperor's security guard put cuffs on Rogers and walked him out. Triumph again addressed the cameras.

"Besides freeing President Schillings, we came here to negotiate a fair deal with Freeport on interplanetary commerce. Dozens of planets get to use their transporters to sell their goods to distant worlds, but not us. Totally unfair. And I have to ask you, have you ever seen any-thing uglier than these aliens this Wyckham has around him? People are saying they're rapists, they're murderers, they sell illegal drugs on dozens of planets. And these aliens get to keep Americans out of fan-tastic new markets? Not gonna happen, folks, not gonna happen. We came here to talk and get a better deal, and they attacked us without warning. But you don't mess with Texas, and we're going to show them the errors of their ways, believe me. However, since I'm a nice guy, I'm not going to simply destroy this New Venice with my artillery, since it is a beautiful place and I don't really want to hurt tourists, just the fos-sil Brits and their illegal aliens. So, I'm warning all you tourists in this Venice right now, you need to leave. And everybody back home, when we win this war tomorrow, watch how quickly we get the jobs in inter-planetary trade that these things on Freeport have rigged in their favor. I'm telling you that you're going to make so much money, you'll be sick and tired of money!" Triumph left and three dozen officers started reviewing their plan for a combined arms attack on New Venice.

Sitting off to one side, Bamming couldn't be happier. This attack on New Venice would kill and injure many residents of the liberal-globalist Pacific and New England states, making war in North America a sure thing. It would force people to choose sides, and everyone would be astonished at how many citizens of the two liberal nations would defect to the nationalist side. He had Confederate agents in New York and California that would come out against the coastal states' support of Freeport, working Triumph's slant that the new world was stealing interplanetary business from them. A few TV ads showing ugly aliens gloating over their gold was all it would take. He could just imagine the header; "Aliens being illegal? America First can take care of that!"

His America First party would rack up big gains on both coasts in the 2030 elections, possibly taking both liberal presidencies if he could come up with the right candidates. Time to survey Fox News again and pick out some stars with large followings. After the USA split up in 2020, the blue states had foolishly allowed alt-right radio to remain on their air, citing the first amendment, and now America First had plenty of followers in the two supposedly liberal bastions. Last time he looked there were a host of good-looking talk show fanatics who with a little direction could be elected president on the coasts. This would be too easy.

And now he had not only Earth as a stage, but the entire universe! With a little help, his populist message would resonate with every world in the cosmos. Their message would get spread to every planet. And he'd be running the whole thing.

This was real power.

The Big Weekend Blows Up

Though Emmie wobbled a bit as she exited the changing station, she was ready for another grand entrance. This time she was really going to show everyone, especially those goddam Fire-fucking-flies! Three times now she had found an interesting guy to dance with, only to have one of the holographic women walk up and steal the dude away! Each time, after knocking back another Sailor's Slam, she'd gone into the nearby changing station and ratcheted up the outrageousness factor on her body and clothes. Looking at herself in the full-length mirror outside the station, she now saw a cross between Wonder Woman, the Hulk, and a young Angelina Jolie. She was now over seven feet tall, with tanned skin, broad shoulders, taught biceps and thighs, pointed breasts the size of basketballs, a butt like steel, long legs, and a face with the sculpted lines of Phidias's Athena. She was wildly dressed in a slashed white t-shirt, a fringed brown leather vest, stiletto-heeled riding boots, and a long leather loincloth like Princess Leia's. Alien date-snakers, watch out! Emily the Conqueror was here!

Emmie made her way unsteadily back through the front door and managed to get to the gilded railing on the stairway and clamp on. Time for an organizational pause. Don't think about the heels, woman. Distract yourself. Check the place out again.

She raised her head to look at the scene below. It was like the annual Halloween Ball that the San Francisco Hookers Union threw every year, times ten. Over the past two hours the crowd had grown. Now she had to be looking at over ten thousand in the main hall alone. Not only had many of them changed their bodies several times over as well, the outfits they wore had gotten crazier as well. It was an extra-terrestrial costume ball, with vampires, cat women, lion guys, comic book heroes, movie stars, and sports stars, not to mention hundreds of actual aliens as well.

Every bar and the dance floors around them were packed. Emmie needed to find a spot quick—her experience with club hopping told her waiting lines would be forming soon. Time to rally! This special long night was in its eighth hour, another eight hours before the first of Freeport's dual suns arose. To Emmie the night was still young. Soon this place would really start cooking.

But the first obstacle was this grand staircase she had to get down, not an easy feat with six Sailor Slams on the night's tally. After taking a few deep breaths, she took a firm hold on the central railing and started down. The mental discipline she had learned in competitive fencing took over and she made an elegant though extremely slow and careful descent. Just like Venice's costume balls in the 15th century, every new arrival got scrutinized, and many in the hall were checking her out as she arrived, both humans and aliens. Tourists were leaning out of the luxury suites, yelling and applauding. The suite that was scoring attendees with number signs even gave her all tens! The noise attracted the notice of people at the nearby Slicks' bar, who turned to see what all the commotion was about. Her latest image was a hit, no doubt about it! Many eyes followed her across the floor as she headed further back to the Fireflies' bar. This was too cool! Emmie Bahtia, daughter of an Indian immigrant, was Belle of the Ball at the first Outer Space Halloween Gala!

As she walked by the staired pedestal around the mudmens' bar, she heard someone laughing and screaming, "Eee-ee-hah-hah-hah!"

Connie! Though the voice was shaky, Emmie could tell it was Connie. Emmie looked up and there she was, at least there was her head, the rest of her submerged in a mudman, definitely buzzed and having a good time. So, no sense in climbing up there, Connie was going to be busy for a while. Beside, Emmie's goal was the Fireflies' bar, the happening place in this club. Weaving slightly, she managed to forge ahead.

She finally made it to the Firefly's bar and started to saunter up its stairs but stumbled and almost fell. Damn heels. She recovered with a smile and made it right up to the bar as the crowd parted like the Red Sea, clapping and shouting approval. Vanoune emerged from the packed mass of people and aliens, laughing and applauding as well, and walked over.

"Look at you, girl! You're going home with me!"

"But oh my God, check you out!" Emmie replied. Vanoune, too, had changed her image again and was now even taller than Emmie, her biceps and thighs bristling with muscle, piercing yellow eyes, still wearing nothing but Mystique's blue mutant skin. "you are unbelievable!"

"Pretty hot, huh? The stations sure work well. C'mon over here, I'm hangin' with a cool group, all from Pullman." Pullman, named after the luxury railroad cars of the early twentieth century, was a start-up that looked like the hot company of 2028. Their expensive self-driving automobiles not only had the now common foldaway bed and work station, but also a gourmet kitchenette and a four-seat mini theater. The cabin was lushly appointed in top-quality woods and leather, and amazingly quiet, even on the nation's new 120 MPH self-driving lanes for self-driving vehicles. Coast to coast, Pullmans were the most popular poster in college dorms.

"Wow! Pullman? Lead on, Mystique! Be sure to point out the CEO!" They laughed and high-fived as they approached a group, males and female, who were standing at the other side of the bar. Emmie immediately noticed a stunning Samuel Adams, brown hair tied in a ponytail with a black ribbon, dressed in a brown frock coat, white lace cravat, tan breeches—and riding boots! She managed to squeeze through the throng and get to his side, making sure she didn't poke him with her protruding breasts, which were right at the shorter guy's eye level.

"Sam! My hero! A founder of our country and makes great beer too! I'm a big fan!" Emmie was a student of history and always thought Sam Adams was a true patriot, not to mention ruggedly handsome. "So nice you rose from the grave just to meet me!"

Sam gave her a big smile and nodded. "Yeah, I've always wanted to be him, and up here I could do it. He fought the Brits by lecturing in taverns. My kind of guy! But I'm Josh, nice to meet you," he said as he extended a hand, carefully avoiding her right breast. "So, who are you?"

"I'm really Emmie from San Francisco, but as far as who I'm supposed to be in this image, I'm not really sure. Just a holograph I've morphed into over the last couple hours," she replied as they shook hands. "Maybe Emm-an the Barbar-ian?"

He chuckled. "Well, you sure look like you could kick Arnold Swartznegger's ass, that's for sure."

He was into her! They chatted for a while, the usual small talk about jobs and politics. He had strong feelings about Triumph and the division of the US.

"We have a war coming, the biggest in history. I'm ready to fight for what's right. The whole world is at stake." He certainly sounded like a modern Sam Adams.

They danced a few songs, the wild energy of the dance floor affecting them as well, working up a serious sweat. Josh couldn't seem to take his eyes off her body. Alright! Finally this night was taking off!

Time for a break and a drink. They made their way back to the bar, and had no sooner ordered another drink when once again a Firefly strode over and went right up to Josh. Emmie was seething. *The date-nappers run like clockwork around here!* This one had the face of a Fifth Avenue model but was dressed in a ridiculous little school girl outfit, despite being over six feet tall. Shit, she'd scanned Josh's mind and found this image in it? Fantasies about teenage girls were a deal breaker for Emmie. Another familiar wave of disappointment washed over her, a meteoric crash from so high to so low.

"Josh! Great to see you! Remember me? Greta Taylor, we were in Mr. Stokes's sophomore math class together."

Fucking thief! Taken the image of some girl Josh had a crush on when he was fifteen. How do I compete against that? Emmie was about to tell both of them to fuck off and walk away, but Josh spoke up first.

"Yeah, Greta, sure. Listen, great job, you look terrific, and it would be fun to talk about old times, but Emmie here is a real human and we're going to enjoy this drink and then dance the night away."

The Firefly responded like a greeter at Wells Fargo. "I understand, have a wonderful time in New Venice, maybe next time," she stated with a corporate smile as she suddenly morphed into Kim Kardashian and walked up to the guy next to them.

She'd won! Josh took her hands and looked her in the eye.

"OK, so we both found something about me just now that's a little embarrassing. I guess my brain still stores dreams of Greta and that alien picked them up. But it's just a childish leftover." He put his arm around her. "Sure, you look wild too, but you're a real person, not just a lump of energy."

This guy was a dream date! Feeling relief and fueled by all the Sailor Slams, Emmie pulled him closer.

Just then there was a powerful explosion right above them. The roof suddenly disappeared, replaced by broken white plastic shingles and mangled metal supports. The blast had taken out the building's hologram projector and now the real roof was visible, all lightweight temporary construction, much like a Hollywood movie set. There was now a twenty-foot hole in it, and the metal framework that had been there was now falling into the hall. Screams filled the air and dust billowed up as the crashing debris hit the floor.

WTF?

The Battle of San Marco

IT ONLY TOOK two and a half hours for Wyckham and the four other surviving whales to return to New Venice. Wyckham's creature was clearly tired and under severe stress, its breathing labored and wheezing, and there was blood in its mouth from an unseen wound. It was performing heroically, like the Greek runner bringing the news of the Battle of Marathon to Athens. Hopefully this wonderful animal would not expire from his run like the Greek hero did. He would make sure that the best Slick surgeons were immediately summoned for all these whales as soon as they made New Venice.

The whale suddenly slowed to crawl. They were home. But the muffled sounds of explosions audible through the animal's thick hide told Wyckham not to expect a side party welcoming him home. He tapped the roof of the creature's mouth, it opened, and he got a view of the docks.

Clearly, New Venice was being attacked by the long-range artillery in Triumph's distant fleet. Dust was in the air and two more explosions rocked Piazza San Marco as Wyckham watched. One hit the Doge's palace, its holographic projector went down, and the palace's ornate facade disappeared, turning into a mangled mess of metal struts.

Scanning the docks, he saw *Trinidad* leaving under all plain sail, riding high in the water. Along the quays and in the piazza, hands were working furiously, moving guns, powder, and shot off the dock and across the piazza, helped by hundreds of the industrious ants. Wulfe's little scout ship was parked nearby in the piazza. Right in the thick of things was his old friend Captain Rawlins, shouting orders to both the humans and aliens preparing defenses and to Slick medics rushing about. Also present was the Lycan, Wulfe, wearing some sort of padded suit and holding onto another one. Surprisingly, he had two flintlock pistols strapped to his waist, weapons Wyckham had never seen the wolfman carry. DiCarpaccio was also here with his group of American generals. Looking about, Wyckham saw the head Firefly and Slick number 2256 waiting for him and beckoned them both over.

First, he needed the battle reports. "Firefly Tracy, I'd admire you communicate with all the whales that were with us, find out what they saw in our recent attack. But do not interfere with the medical efforts of Mister 2256 here." He turned to the Slick surgeon. "These whales were beyond courageous today. I know my creature here is wounded and I expect all returning whales will need immediate medical attention."

The Slick seemed to be ignoring Wyckham's instructions as he waved a buzzing device over the governor's chest.

"Fractured bone in chest," he stated as his translating device crackled to life. It then grabbed Wyckham's hand and pressed another device into his wrist which injected something into a vein. "Pain eliminator and bone mending solution. You may now continue fighting." He then surveyed the five whales in the lagoon and turned to the Firefly. "Will need help. Need octopi to assist with surgeries. Very competent with large marine mammals. Eight arms, extra fast." The Firefly nodded and looked to the shore, where several octopi immediately dropped into the lagoon and started swimming over.

The head Firefly also moved towards the dock where more whales had just arrived while Wyckham was speaking with the medic.

Wyckham then addressed Rawlins. "Seems I'm late to the party. How long has this been going on?"

"The shelling just started," replied Rawlins. "We knew it was coming. DiCarpaccio here and his generals told us that without their fast airships, the foe might use their artillery to soften up San Marco before landing troops. Dolphins strung out from here to the enemy let us know their fleet was heading this way two hours ago. Took us by surprise, they did, we thought they'd attack Port Wyckham. But right away we started preparing. First, marines and mudmen started moving tourists out of the main plaza into the underground ant nests. We're still doing that but there are hundreds more trapped in the rubble of destroyed buildings. At the same time, we unloaded sixty guns off the Trinidad and put them around the plaza, along with all her swivel guns for battery protection. You can't see most of them, they're hidden in the rubble of the loggias lining the square. And the ten guns here in the stone battery are fully manned. Should give them quite a surprise when what they thought were fake guns open up on them just as they disembark."

Right after meeting Triumph months ago, the planetary council had decided to replace New Venice's holographic saluting battery with ten real 32 pounders in an actual stone bastion, realizing that the Confederate President might just be crazy enough to somehow attack the city. The work had been done in secret by the planet's ants at night, who were not only tireless workers but superb stonemasons as well. Fireflies had provided a holographic fog every night to hide the efforts from any spies among the city's residents or visiting tourists.

"And Wulfe has an idea for another surprise," Rawlins continued. "Where's Captain Harrison? He's part of it."

The Yankee had just climbed up onto the quay, carrying his rifle. Wulfe walked over, grabbed him and started to haul him off. "I need you and that weapon of yours." He handed Harrison the strange suit he was carrying. "I will explain as we walk to my ship. Put this on while we walk."

Captain Harrison hefted the suit in his hand, looking completely bewildered, then nodded his head in acceptance. "Wulfe, you crazed canine, I have no doubt you can accomplish more miracles in that remarkable little ship of yours. Let's go." The two headed off towards Wulfe's ship, the big Lycan helping Harrison put on the suit while he explained his plan. Within a minute, the captured Dreash vehicle roared to life, four jets of flame coming from its underside in a thunderous roar, and took off straight up from the plaza.

Wyckham turned back to Rawlins. "What's our troop strength?"

"We have Trinidad's four Marine companies plus the three hundred fifty marines that were on duty in New Venice, total 825. We also have around four hundred sailors that were here on shore leave, though I'm not sure how many are sober enough to fight. But we emptied Trinidad's arms locker, so they're all fully equipped, including Greek fire for their small arms. We have most of our troops staged just outside the city, away from the shelling.

"On top of that, we have *Leviathan*, *Indomptable*, and *Righteous* hiding in coves along those thermal islands to the southwest, soon to be joined by the *Trinidad*, a total of 216 guns, all under Captain Badoin with his Firefly countess." Capitaine Jean Badoin was a French captain who had blundered onto Freeport 200 years ago and didn't leave, having fallen for one of the Fireflies in the image of a Burgundian countess with whom he was completely besotted.

Continuing, Rawlins described the strategy. "Earthly naval ships have devices that can locate and engage enemy ships at vast distances. However, DiCarpaccio and his military attaches have assured us that our wooden ships and clay guns would be invisible to their devices if we blend into those islands. The islands' constantly erupting geysers will confuse the foes' heat locators and the clouds of steam makes their thermal and visual devices useless. Additionally, he states that the islands' land mostly consists of iron ore, various clays and trees—the exact materials our ships are made of. To the foe's sensors our ships simply look like the land around them—they will be able to hide in the many coves and straights among the islands.

"Badoin's squadron is headed to an area about one and a half miles from the main channel used to approach New Venice. Should be the naval ambush of all time. However, DiCarpaccio informs us that he will probably only have time for one broadside due to the enemy fleets' speed, plus the continuing flash and sound of our guns would show our position."

So in total, about 1225 men on land and four ships on the water—a substantial force, fully equipped with small arms and heavy artillery. Wyckham nodded his approval. Rawlins knew his business and had reacted just as he would have. Wyckham wasn't sure about the outcome of the coming battle, but he was going to put up one helluva fight, that was for sure. While his foes had all sorts of powerful weapons, they didn't have Greek fire.

As if Triumph had read his thoughts, the shelling suddenly increased to a hellish crescendo, with explosions blanketing the entire plaza.

"Take cover and get ready, lads", Wyckham bellowed as loud as he could, waving his sword to everyone in the plaza. "The foe will attack any minute now! Let's send them all to Hell!"

Emmie had just stood there, watching the chunks of metal roofing fall on top of dozens of partygoers, too shocked to move. Just as suddenly as it had begun, the explosions ceased for a moment and wreckage stopped falling. The sounds of nearby explosions told Emmie that other buildings were being hit. She shook her head and slapped herself in the face. *Get moving, woman!* She didn't know what the hell was going on, but she had to get out of this place before the entire roof fell in. She saw Josh under the bar where he'd taken cover.

"Josh, let's go! We have to get outside!"

But the young man who had just talked about fighting a war wasn't going anywhere. He seemed shell shocked, holding both hands over his ears and yelling.

"Ahhhhg! No! Please make it stop! Please make it stop!"

She tried to grab an arm and haul him up, but he thrashed around wildly and after a few tries she gave up. So much for the fighter Sam Adams. Emmie looked up and saw Connie and Van getting up from under a table, looking around through the settling dust. Another shell hit the roof above the Slick's bar, its explosion sending more metal supports and roofing tiles crashing to the floor.

"Connie! Van! Over here! We gotta get out of here. NOW!"

Her two friends ran over, and the three athletes sprinted for the main entrance as fast as they could over a floor covered with wreckage. With additional explosions now dropping more debris to the floor, they had to periodically stop and take cover under tables. The three continued towards the exit whenever breaks in the shelling occurred.

With the building's holographic image generator apparently destroyed, the building had been transformed into its real physical self, mostly open space with only flooring and roof supports. Though the women had real shoes on and not the holographic stilettos they appeared to be wearing, it was hard to override what they saw and run. Not to mention the fact that their minds were also telling them that they all had absurdly heavy breasts bouncing around on their chests.

After ten minutes with several stops to avoid more shelling and falling roof tiles, they reached the foot of the main stairway, which was still clear. Ignoring more explosions behind them, they vaulted up the stairs three at a time and emerged into Piazza San Marco.

Gone was the San Marco that they had passed through just hours before. In the constant yellow flashes of exploding shells, the night was a panorama of flying wreckage, swirling dust, and mangled metal framework, all frozen in brief glimpses like a huge disco with giant strobe lights. While most of the buildings had also lost their image projectors to the bombardment and were now just twisted skeletons, others still appeared as 15th century buildings, adding a surreal touch to the deadly scene.

The toll on the tourists and aliens was considerable. Tourists from Earth were running every different direction, looking for cover in buildings only to have them disappear as another holographic projector was hit. Prostrate humans and aliens were strewn about the plaza, many screaming in pain, others not moving. Many of the red-coated soldiers that had provided security in the plaza were now casualties, screaming in pain, tending to their own wounds, or motionless. Dozens of Slick medics had responded, the extremely strong seven-foot beings carrying off the wounded, often two at a time, somehow anticipating the fall of each shell and jigging left and right to dodge the explosions.

Paralyzed with fear, Emmie had no idea where to go or what to do. *Shit, I'm in a goddam war zone!* Was anywhere safe?

But then her competitive energy took over. She would beat this threat! Then it hit her—the Slicks! Follow them, they're taking the wounded to a safe place!

Suddenly the bombardment ceased. For a few seconds all was quiet except the moaning of the wounded and the continued efforts of the Slicks. Just as Emmie was going to suggest they help evacuate the wounded, the air was filled with the sound of whistles, shrilling insistently—some kind of alarm?

It was more of the red-coated British soldiers. Files of them came running into the plaza, heading to the loggias lining San Marco, the docks, or joining the Slicks to aid the many wounded. Hundreds of grimy sailors like the ones that had brought her here were also running into the loggias surrounding the square, though most of the area was now just tangled piles of metal scaffolding.

"It's all over, I think," said Emmie. "Let's ask a soldier how we can help. C'mon, Connie, Van! We can't just stand here."

"Yeah, look," responded Van as she pointed across the plaza. "Over by the docks. They look like the commanding officers." A group of men with blue coats and pointed hats had appeared next to a little stone fort and appeared to be giving out orders. "Let's go ask what we can do to help."

A red-coated soldier noticed them and stood up from a body he'd been checking. "Wait, let's ask him what we should do."

"Officer, we'd like to help," stated Emmie. Can we help get the wounded out? Where should we take them?"

"Best clear the area, mum. Be a scrap comin' any time now, ain't no place fer a lady. Best follow the Slicks t' th' hospital, ye can be o' help there."

Emmie wanted to press him further about what the hell was going on, but Connie grabbed her arm to drag her off. "You heard him, Em! Let's get the fuck outta here!"

But it was too late. Just as Emmie started to leave, a huge wriggling orange mass erupted from the bay and swarmed over the docks. *Oh fuck, now what?* It was something out of a Steven King novel, an army of monsters, all clicking loudly, like a biblical swarm of giant locusts. Emmie squinted into the dark to try to figure out exactly what she was looking at.

As the swirling mob grew closer, she was able to make out individual creatures. It was a giant horde of crabs, big ones about four feet tall with mismatched claws, running sideways and spitting clicking noises from their mouths, attacking any beings they could get to. Paralyzed for a moment, Emmie watched them reach some scattered marines spread out near the docks who had been helping the wounded. Some were able to grab their muskets and fire at them, and a few of the crabs dropped, but the others attacked in overwhelming numbers. They used their long, barbed claws to hook marines and pull them close, then they crushed limbs and heads with their short thick ones. When all the marines had been killed, they went after tourists and the wounded, gripping heads and twisting them off like they were popping champagne corks. Within moments half the plaza was covered in gore. It was the most horrifying sight Emmie could have ever dreamed up. She had to swallow to keep from throwing up.

A crab looked up from the massacre, saw the three women, and alerted the others, clicking and bubbling. Several crabmen looked around, then took off right for her, waving and clacking their claws. Emmie turned to run but there were crabs behind her as well!

As soon as the shelling stopped, Wyckham climbed up on the roof of the stonework battery, quickly joined by Captain Rawlins and crews for the five great guns mounted there. Rawlins immediately started repeatedly blowing a brass whistle, which echoed through the city, to be met by blasts from many answering whistles. Hundreds of sailors appeared, running into the plaza and heading for the big guns placed in the skeletal ruins of the loggias, while marines ran to form lines along the waterfront.

The artillery barrage had been destructive but Wyckham wasn't that concerned. Most of his troops had been safely away from the plaza. He was more concerned about beating the Confederacy's heavily armed and technically advanced human soldiers that were sure to be coming next. He and Rawlins scanned the lagoon, looking for signs of an amphibious attack.

"DiCarpaccio's people say they'll come ashore in landing craft that fly across the water on a cushion of air," stated Rawlins. "Don't see any yet."

"Yes, strange that," answered Wyckham. "We should be seeing them by now. They should have gotten in closer before stopping the bombardment. I've heard Triumph commands this fleet himself, takes little advice from his officers. Mayhap his force doesn't run like a Swiss watch?"

They looked at each other and grinned. Both had been in battles commanded by aristocrats in the Royal Navy's officer core and both knew what terrible field commanders they could be. But maybe this

American aristocrat listened to his experienced officers? Probably not. Anyone told since childhood that they were better than others didn't listen to anyone.

But Wyckham was starting to feel uneasy. Had the foe landed further down the coast and was now approaching the city from the landward side? The back side of New Venice was undefended—all his guns were aimed into the lagoon. Anxiously he pulled out his telescope to scan the land horizon.

Suddenly an immense horde of Krag, the four-foot crabmen that fought for the Dreash, erupted out of the water right underneath Wyckham's battery, splashing and swarming up onto the quay. Christ, there were thousands of the vicious little bastards! And all of them were below the maximum depression of his guns, which had been placed to target ships in the lagoon. Not to mention the fact that his guns were loaded with six-inch balls of Greek fire for destroying ships instead of troops. If they shot these unstoppable fireballs from the battery down at the Krag, the rounds would just burrow into the ground instead of ricocheting all around the plaza like field artillery should. To fight a Krag attack, the guns needed plain old iron canister, tin cans loaded with thousands of iron musket balls that would skip all over the battlefield.

The Dreash had brought these beings to the planet centuries ago as servants, but they also used them when fighting the British. They were sprightly creatures, difficult to shoot, constant bobbing and jigging around. After Wyckham took the planet, he took pity on the starving creatures and used them for servants as well, though they were rather idiotic and hard to train for much of anything. He had no idea that the few Dreash on the planet had assembled this Krag army that was attacking them now. The bastard Dreash had fooled him again!

But almost every battle had a surprise—Wyckham just needed to react quickly to this one. "All gun crews, turn your guns around to target the main plaza, support the marines. First iron canister over the fireballs you've got loaded now, after that double canister. Quick now! Like rabbits!"

His gun crews started untying the great guns from the wall facing the water and moving them over to gunports facing inland to bear on the square behind them. Other hands shoved the big tin cans full of musket balls down the guns' muzzles and rammed them home. But it was taking minutes to bring the guns around, during which thousands of Krag ran past the elevated battery Wyckham was on and flooded into San Marco. Wyckham watched with dismay as the orange masses headed for the vulnerable marines, trying to form squares of leveled bayonets before they were overwhelmed.

However, there were still the fifty big guns around the square manned by sailors, and they were already loaded with canister in anticipation of an amphibious landing by Confederacy troops. They opened up in a steady rolling volley, blasting over a hundred thousand musket balls into the packed Krag, with devastating results. Any balls that were shot too low just bounced back up off the stone pavement into the running Krag. Parts of the brittle crabmen were flying everywhere, their claws, heads, and body parts spinning into the air, their white blood turning the air so milky it was difficult for Wyckham to observe the field.

But after two centuries, the crabmen and their Dreash masters were familiar with British artillery, and the fanatical Krag were clearly committed to this fight. Scores of them ran to the sides of the square, working their way through the twisted rubble of buildings destroyed by the Confederate bombardment, preparing to rush the flanks of the sailors' positions. Marine commanders, recognizing the threat, had their squares moving back towards the sailors' exposed flanks. But harassing Krag made it a slow retreat, attacking the square's vulnerable corners, knowing the artillery would not shoot into the packed marines.

A tough scrap and it's just beginning, thought Wyckham. "Pierce, I believe this fight will be decided on the far side of the plaza, it requires my presence. You stay and command the sailors in this battery. Keep an eye to the lagoon, I expect the foe will attempt a landing very soon."

Rawlins nodded his agreement. "Marines with me", Wyckham barked, and he set out at a run, accompanied by the battery's squad of marines.

Emmie's entire life flashed before her in less than a second. She was about to be buried in an orange mass of killer aliens. Should've listened to her mother and stayed home.

A ground-shaking explosion close behind Emmie almost knocked her over. It was immediately followed by dozens more from all around the square. Looking behind her, she saw sailors working big cannons that had been concealed around the piazza. Their fiery blasts tore into the packed mass of crabmen like tornados in a trailer park, shredding hundreds of crabmen into little bits of orange shells flying all over the place.

But a group of them near the three women and the marine had been spared, since the gunners wouldn't shoot cannister near the four humans, and now the vicious crabmen bolted towards them. Over the roar of the guns the helpful marine with them yelled, "Mum, ye best run t' the sailors o'er there, I'll try t'…"

But his advice was cut short as the first crabman caught up him, a large one with an aged bronze garland of seaweed around its head. It hooked the marine's arm with the barbs on its long claw and pulled it into his fat small claw. With one snap it severed his hand at the wrist, sending it and the sword it was holding flying to rest at Emmie's feet. Before the poor man could even scream, the brutal little crabman unhooked his long claw, cocked it back, and stabbed the marine right through his throat. Then, adding insult to injury, the evil crustacean clamped its short claw around the man's neck, gave it a quick twist, and severed the marine's head from his body. The poor man's blood spurted all over as his headless body collapsed in a heap.

Vicious little shit! Watching this considerate man die at her feet filled Emmie with righteous rage. All she had wanted was a fun weekend in this beautiful cool city but then this jerkoff, apparently the commander with his fucking green headband, leads an army of brutal monsters right into Venice and starts killing everybody?

The dead marine's sword was at her feet. As a fencer, she was familiar with historical swords, and this was a hanger, a short sword carried by infantry sergeants and good for hand-to-hand combat. It got its name because it was usually carried hanging from the waist. A short, light sword, much like the foils she had fenced with for years. Before she realized what she was doing, she bent down and picked it up. It felt good in her hands—reasonably light, well balanced, not tip heavy. She pinched her right thumb and forefinger snug up against the guard, wrapped her other three fingers around the leather-wound grip, flexed the tempered blade rigorously with her other hand to warm it up, and came *en guarde*—body sideways, knees bent, point up, blade in line with the forearm, left arm high and behind for balance.

The big crabman stopped, its eyes on their foot-long stalks checking her out, then held up its claws and started clacking them, the sound like a string of Fourth of July firecrackers going off. Several nearby crabs stopped fighting and gathered around—evidently this was a challenge and they were going to watch. And damned if the big alien in front of her didn't give her a knowing smirk! Emmie knew that look—a guy who thinks he's got an easy bout because he's up against a woman! Now Emmie was really mad. *Smirk at me, you little piece of shit?*

She started tapping her point on the ground, making an irritating invitation for the foe to attack. This was a move she often used in competition to provoke aggressive opponents to attack, and defense would beat offense when one knew an attack was coming. Seeing the apparent opening, the alien lunged at her, its long claw extended, trying to hook her just like it had done with the marine. Emmie sprung backward in a one-step retreat, just like she was taking a lesson, getting time and distance to go for a parry in *Quarte*. She missed as the crabman dropped its claw, avoided the parry, and thrust at her flank. But Emmie retreated another step, dropped her point in a contra-sixte parry, and closed the line, guiding the foe's claw past her. She held the parry for a moment, not pushing too hard on the crabman's claw so it didn't even realize it had been parried. She even arched her back a little, letting the creature's claw slide past underneath, then dropped her point and extended it back at the crabman's *Quince*.

Even though her opponent wasn't human, she could read the change in her foe's body language. The confidence of imminent hit changed to the realization that it was in trouble. Kicking off her back leg into a powerful lunge, her right arm locked straight out, Emmie's point struck her attacker square in the head, puncturing the thing's shell with a crack. Her point punched all the way through and blasted out the back of the thing's head. White blood ran down the fuller in her blade as the crab collapsed and slid off.

That woke up the watching crabs. Two of the little monsters extended their long claws and ran right at her. *Didn't enjoy the show? The ending upset you?* She moved to her right, putting the nearer one in front of the other so she could deal with them one at a time, following Napoleon's battle dictum. *Defeat your enemy in sequence.* The first foe with its long claw extended gave Emmie just what any fencer wanted, a motionless weapon just begging to get beat aside. She went to knock the tip of the claw aside, but the damn thing was so fast it got its claw past her defense before she could hit it. Though her sharp blade did whack into its arm, shattering it, which allowed her to extend her point in low *Quarte* and lunge. The crabman tried to parry, but its claw just flapped about on its broken arm as Emmie drove her point into its body. The Krag folded over and dropped to the ground, taking Emmie's sword with it. While she went to yank it free, the third crabman ran up and cocked its long claw to thrust right into Emmie's guts. *Oh, fuck!*

But the threat suddenly disappeared as a pointed axe head came swinging into view. It was Connie! She'd picked up a six-foot halberd from a dead marine and swung it in a wide arc. The heavy axe head hit the Krag just in time, sending it flying, its body almost broken in two.

"The cavalry's arrived!" yelled Connie as took a position on Emmie's left, extending the menacing point of her weapon at more approaching crabmen.

"Make room!" It was Van, pulling up to Emmie's left, *en guarde,* holding an officer's saber she'd found. From her *en guarde* stance, she lunged and made a backhand cut from *Quinte,* coming up to slice through the tubular neck of another crabman on the right, severing its head. "Me too for you two!"

The line of armed women gave the rushing crabmen pause. Each of the women had found a weapon that suited their fencing skills— Emmie had a light, fast defensive weapon like the foils she was used to, the muscular Connie had a long heavy weapon like her own epee, and Vanoune's was a sabre, the cutting weapon she competed with. The comfortable stance of the women, their prepared weapons, and the dead crabs at their feet convinced the attackers to spread out and encircle the three, jabbing and feinting, trying to push the women apart. Connie and Van slowly turned to face them, forming a triangle with the three women standing back to back. There they were—Marilyn Monroe, Jennifer Lawrence and Emman the Barbarian, dressed for a Halloween night on the town, ready for a desperate fight with dozens of deadly aliens.

Emmie started dancing on her toes, looking for an opening while watching for an attack. But it was almost impossible to move well with the large breasts her mind told her she had, bouncing up so high they hit her cheeks!

A crab across from her had been bobbing back and forth, but suddenly it lunged forward instead of dancing back. It feinted in *quarte*, immediately pulled its claw back to avoid Emmie's parry, planning a lunge in *sixte*.

But Emmie didn't go for his feint and had the crab wide open for a low lunge in *Septime*. Realizing the danger, the crabman leapt backwards but was still within fighting distance. Emmie went for a jump-lunge, but her mind told her she couldn't move quick enough—her boobs were holding her back! *Fuck! Just forget about the goddam boobs, they're not there!* Her fencing discipline took over and she pushed the perceived weight of her holographic chest from her mind. She made a lightning-fast jump lunge, hitting her opponent in the groin. Both of its right legs buckled, and it fell spasming to the ground.

"Ye ladies there! Ye women!" It was a sailor, standing about fifty yards away in the line of cannons. "Try t' work yer way o'er 'ere!" As he spoke, another sailor next to him fired a small cannon into the growing mass of Krag in front of them, carving a ten-foot hole in their ranks. Other sailors were firing their rifles, and a dozen or so marines jumped from the rubble lining the square, formed line with leveled bayonets and started advancing, slowly pushing the crabmen aside, occasionally shooting the ones that hesitated in front of their rifles. Sailors followed on their flanks, hacking away with naval cutlasses at the crabs between the women and the British line. The women started a fighting retreat, backing towards the British line, but the going was slow. And more crabs were rushing into the space between them and the Brits, an area where the cannons weren't shooting for fear of hitting the women.

Shit, how did I get into this clusterfuck?

◆ ◆ ◆

Wyckham and his marines were halfway across the plaza when the gun battery he'd just left finally got their guns around and opened up on the rear of the massed Krag. Over a hundred thousand balls of cannister swept the piazza clean like mops across the maindeck, bouncing across the stone plaza and shredding the soft-shelled crabmen. Along with the canister, each gun fired one six-inch fireball they'd been loaded with for shooting at the Confederate ships they'd been expecting. The big fireballs added an element of terror, roaring across the square to make a long cut through the packed Krag, instantly turning a dozen into ash and melting body parts of dozens more along the ball's passage.

"Yell, lads, yell!" the marine sergeant bellowed. "Let 'em know we're bringing 'em hell's fire!" The usually quiet marines bellowed threats as they bayonetted Krag from behind and fired their musket loads of Greek fire. With the sudden artillery and marine's musketry exploding from behind them, panic took hold of the dimwitted crustaceans, and hundreds started running away from the charging marines, only to run right into the sailors around the square firing canister from their great guns and swivel cannon. With no place to run, the guns mowed them down. The battle for the plaza took a pause.

However, Wyckham's gallant charge was too late for most of the marines that had been caught helping the wounded in the plaza. As he rushed towards the sailors' lines, he'd had to step around dozens of red-coated bodies. Wyckham stood on his toes to see if there were any marines still holding out in the piazza that they could rescue. At the far western side he saw a group of crabmen surrounding a few desperate defenders wielding blades. There were three of them, not wearing marine uniform coats nor sailor's striped shirts. Civilians? Well, whoever they were, they were still fighting and could use some help. Though their fighting stance and the pile of downed Krag in front of them showed they were swordsmen of the first order.

"Marines, this way!" He pointed towards the three battling civilians. "There's still fighting over there."

As they neared the three scrapping swordsmen, the crabs were concentrating on their three surrounded civilians, and Wyckham's marines were able to come up behind them unobserved and start hacking away. After bashing two unsuspecting Krag from behind, Wyckham yanked his Moroccan sword out of a third and looked up to see if the three civilians still stood. What did he see but three young women, clearly modern tourists dressed for the American Halloween holiday, fighting off a pack of Krag with cold steel! The big muscular one on the right was naked, covered in blue painted skin and clusters of warts, thrusting with a six-foot halberd like it was a big rapier. On the other side was a dark-skinned blond woman, wearing a filmy white dress fit for a ball, making precision cuts with a sabre. The center one in the Celtic warrior costume was bobbing on her toes, lunging with her point extended and recovering with the speed of a cat.

All three fought with the same athletic style of sword fighting that Wyckham had learned from bouting with Lieutenant Moore back when he was a midshipman. But where the hell did these women learn it? Rather than standing in place using hand speed and blade control to make attacks and parries, the three were dancing back and forth, knees deeply bent, ready to lunge or retreat, moving constantly like pugilists, darting in to strike whenever their feints created the opportunity. In particular he noticed the woman with a hanger as she lunged over ten feet to pick off a retreating Krag, punching a hole right in its head. How she could be so athletic astonished Wyckham, because she was doing all this despite an immense pair of breasts bouncing around on her chest! As she completed her powerful lunge and her front leg hit the ground, damned if the things didn't bounce up and hit her in the face! While he knew they weren't real but just a holograph, the fact that she could override the false message her brain was getting about a big weight on her chest and fight like hell was quite impressive.

By now the fight had backed up close to the sailors in the rubble of the loggia. Their carefully aimed swivel guns were able to hit the Krag from behind without hitting the three women, and several blasts cut rows through the foes around them. That was followed by a rush of screaming sailors waving cutlasses and pikes that slammed into the rear of the encircling Krag, resulting in the remaining ones rushing to flee the field. The foes in front of Wyckham's squad also realized their fight was lost, and they scampered away as well, leaving only three crabmen who were already engaged with the women.

The crab on the right went down as the tall blue woman advanced, slid her halberd along the crab's extended long claw, brushed it aside, then released and thrust so hard that it blasted a foot-wide hole through its body. She then flicked the corpse off her weapon like a farmer bailing hay and looked around for the next foe. At the same time, the woman on the left lunged and made a cut in *Quinte* that severed both of the stalks that the Krags' eyes were mounted on, its sudden blindness causing the bewildered creature to freeze in place for a moment, wondering why it could no longer see. The woman quickly stepped forward and nonchalantly swung her sabre through the creature's neck, sending its head spinning to the ground.

Before her two compatriots could help the woman in the center, she stretched out in a long lunge at her opponent, forcing it back a step. But rather than run off with the other Krag leaving the plaza, this fanatical little crustacean made a last-second inside parry with its short claw and launched itself back at the American tourist, leading with its long claw in a running *fleche'* attack. In a remarkable ballet-like move, the woman countered by standing straight up and dropping her point downward to close the line in *prime*. As the running crabman's claw passed by on her left, she bent over and slowly turned along with it, pushing her blade out to shove the claw's tip away. Now half bent over with her back to her opponent, she thrust her point under her own armpit and out behind her back, unable to see the crab but apparently knowing exactly where it was. Unable to stop, the flying crabman ran right onto her extended point, skewering itself in the chest and falling to the ground.

Wyckham raised his eyebrows and shook his head in appreciation of the woman's sword fighting skills. Where had she learned this incredible athletic way with a blade? And why? Wyckham didn't know much about modern Earth, but he knew that everyone carried pistols for self-protection. No one carried swords anymore nor even gave out presentation swords.

The fight was done in San Marco. The ground was pulsing from the hundreds of wounded Krag spasming around and a score of marines moaning in pain. By Wyckham's guess there were another 70-80 British dead lying across the plaza, along with a thousand or so Krag. And this had just been the enemy's first punch, a softening attack. Looking around, Wyckham searched for the foe's next move.

He didn't have long to wait. There was some sort of strange pounding noise in the air, and it was growing louder by the second. Looking westward towards the source of the sound, his worst fears were realized. It was an attack from those flying ships that could hover in the air and fire all sorts of advanced guns and explosives. As he watched, they fired a volley of rockets, making big whooshing sounds just like the Congreve rockets that Wyckham's squadron had fired at Baltimore's Fort McHenry so many years ago. They slammed into the sailors' lines around the edge of San Marco plaza, detonating in tremendous explosions. Massive 32 pounders were thrown into the air like toys, along with many somersaulting bodies.

An air attack had been the one thing Wyckham had no plan to deal with. How could an 1814 naval squadron deal with a 2028 air attack?

Dogfight Above Venice

"WE MUST LEAVE here quickly, an attack is coming soon," stated Wulfe through his translator as he helped get Harrison into the strange balloon suit. He then strapped him into the right-hand seat in the front of his small interstellar scout ship. "We have to get away from here and hide before the enemy attacks with his airships."

Harrison had ridden in this craft before, the only flying ship on Freeport allowed outside Port Wyckham, though he'd never had to don this ridiculous suit. The League of Worlds had banned flying ships from Freeport, along with most other advanced technology, believing that airships could be easily weaponized. But since this one was famous for winning the Battle of Hollow Mountain that established Freeport, this ship had been allowed to stay with its weapons removed as a tourist attraction.

Wulfe pulled a lever and the little space ship blasted vertically into the air, flaming and roaring, pushing Harrison down into his seat. Wulfe twisted another knob and the ship accelerated horizontally, heading for a group of islands Harrison could see about twenty miles to the south.

"So here's my plan, old friend," said Wulfe as he kept his eyes on the horizon with his translator at full volume. "We know that they lost the ability to launch their high-speed air craft thanks to Wyckham and his whales taking out the mother ship. But they still can use their low speed hovercraft, which they can launch off any ship. These things will be arriving over New Venice as soon as the artillery stops. While these little craft are heavily armed, they are not very fast, certainly not compared to the "Flying Pup' here," he said, using the name Wulfe had given his little ship. He'd even painted a winged canine on the fuselage. "We can outrun them and their weapons."

"I understand, we can run away. But exactly what capacity for offense do we have against a squadron of these well-armed hovercraft?" asked Harrison. "I'm flattered you think I can shoot them down with my rifle here, but I just can't. I have to be stationary and so does the enemy for me to hit anything. In the coming fight I expect everyone will be flying around like diving falcons."

"Actually they won't and neither will we," responded the big Lycan. "DiCarpaccio's generals told us that they have to hover or at least slow down to fire their weapons, and that's when we strike. My ship is faster than theirs. We scream on up right next to them, come to a stop a few yards away, you put a fireball into them, then off we go. Hit and run, shoot and scoot, what an outnumbered force always does against a superior enemy."

Was Wulfe looney? Harrison knew how miraculously fast this ship could accelerate and stop. He'd be crushed like an olive in a press, certainly unable to shoot accurately.

"Have you gone daft? We'll be tossed around like dice in a cup. You won't be able to fly this ship and I won't be able to shoot a thing."

"Now you know what this suit is for. It's a gravity suit, inflates to cushion the body from violent maneuvers. Hold still while I plug you in." Wulfe leaned over and inserted some thick hoses dangling from Harrison's suit into holes on the control board. Then he pressed some knobs, and with a hissing sound Harrison's suit inflated until it hugged every part of his body. Harrison moved his arms around to make sure the suit did not affect his movement as Wulfe inflated his suit.

Their ship arrived at the islands and Wulfe brought it down between some trees, landing while they waited for the foe to appear. "Now we wait," proclaimed the big canine, and damned if he didn't close his eyes and take a snooze! *This here wolf's gonna sleep right through the fight!* thought Harrison. But within a few minutes, the wolfman's nose started twitching and he awoke with a start.

"They're coming. I can smell them. Earthmen really stink, I think it's their diet. You loaded? I'll rush up behind the squadron and pop open the porthole in front of you. Put a round into some vital part, then reload quick. If we get threatened, I'll zoom off a hundred miles before they can get a shot off, then come back in from another side."

Well, this was going to be one helluva crazy fight. Harrison had no idea if Wulf's plan of attack would work, but he did know that this craft could travel at blinding speed. Wulfe had told him once that it could travel at over three thousand knots! Shaking his head at what he was about to get into, Harrison leveled his rifle in front of him, checked the firelock, and settled down in his seat, his body sideways in shooting position.

He didn't have long to wait. Over the low hum of their own idling vessel he heard it—the same rhythmic pounding he'd heard just hours ago. "Hear that? That's them a'right." Wulfe had his eyes on a screen, which Harrison knew showed a moving illustration of all nearby ships in the air or on the water. It showed eleven little dots moving east towards the outline of New Venice's shoreline. Wulfe yanked a lever and the scout ship took off like a cannonball. Harrison was pressed into his seat, but his inflated suit kept him in control of his limbs. Within a few seconds Harrison guessed they were up to over 500 knots. The speed was simply astounding.

"I'm staying low over this string of islands, avoiding their sensors, they missed us as they flew by, now I'm going to pop up behind them. Get ready," the wolfman declared and zoomed his ship straight up, turned to starboard, brought his craft level and headed for the group of enemy hovercraft. Harrison could see the ones in the lead were already attacking San Marco, shooting some kind of rockets into the edges of the square. Wulfe headed their little ship right into the rear of the nearest hovercraft at ferocious speed. Just as Harrison felt they were about to crash into a stationary enemy ship, Wulfe slammed the vessel to a stop a mere twenty feet behind it. The force of the rapid deceleration shoved the Yankee forward into the straps holding him in his seat, but his inflated suit spread the force across his body and he was ready to shoot. The porthole in front of Harrison popped open. "Shoot! Now!" the Lycan yelled.

Harrison needed no urging. Before Wulfe had even finished his words, Harrison squeezed the trigger and sent a fireball burning right through the target filling the sky in front of him. He must have hit its commander or its rudder controls, because the craft slowly nosed over and headed towards the sea, flames licking its sides as it went down. Immediately Harrison began reloading his rifle, ramming down a paper wrapped cartridge of the planet's black ooze propellant and the two powders that made Greek fire. He flipped the frizzen up and tapped a few grains of gunpowder into the pan just as Wulfe moved their vessel up behind a second enemy. One pull of the trigger, a little lower than his previous shot, and something in the enemy hovercraft immediately exploded. The craft went tumbling downwards, its thin spinning wings broken and flapping about like a wounded pheasant. *Ah. Low and center for their fuel storage. That's where to hit them.*

But now they had earned the attention of a nearby pair of hovercraft which turned to point their weapons at them. "Neighborhood just got unfriendly. Time to get the hell out of here," stated Wulfe, and the craft accelerated straight up with astonishing force, thrusting Harrison back into his seat. His lips were pushed halfway down his throat and his cheeks were pushed back, flapping over his wisdom teeth, but the inflated suit managed to keep everything else in place as Wulfe put the ship through violent rolls and turns to dodge enemy fire. Looking back over his shoulder, the slow flying enemy hovercraft looked stationary, but they had fired four rockets which were now chasing them. Wulfe accelerated the little ship even further to fantastic speed, leaving the rockets and even the planet behind. The next thing he knew they were in the darkness of outer space! Harrison had heard what space looked like, but this was his first trip above Freeport's atmosphere. As a lifelong explorer he had taken in many breathtaking views, but the sight of the vastness of outer space almost took his breath away. The sky was dark but for the twinkling stars all around them and Freeport's three moons. It gave Harrison a sudden feeling of inner peace, despite having just burned men to death moments ago. Below him, Freeport was a gigantic blue and green sphere curving beneath him, with vast stretches of white clouds swirling in its atmosphere. Harrison wondered if Earth looked like this from above. He suspected it did, with lots of oceans and forestland just like Freeport. It was the most peaceful of scenes. A heartwarming pause right in the middle of a vicious fight.

"Well, that worked out well," Wulfe declared. "Those slugs of theirs can barely move. Can't do shite compared to the "Pup" here.

He looked over at Harrison. "Back we go. You loaded?" For the first time ever, Harrison had forgotten about reloading in the midst of a fight. "Ah, a moment if you would," replied a flustered Harrison as he quickly rammed a load down his rifle's muzzle and primed the forelock. When he nodded that he was ready, Wulfe nosed the "Pup" straight down and accelerated to blinding speed in a heartbeat. Within seconds they'd flown back through the planet's atmosphere and into the midst of the enemy squadron, fat cows awaiting slaughter, and slammed to a stop right in the middle.

"This time we really hit them," Wulfe declared. Harrison's portal popped open again, he fired to starboard and the hovercraft there immediately started spinning like a leaf in a whirlpool. Meanwhile, Wulfe had pulled out one of his pistols, cocked it, and fired at an airship right in front of him, the little pistol's fireball blowing the craft to pieces just like Harrison's rifle had. Then he dropped it, pulled out his second pistol, and fired through a porthole that had opened portside. Harrison watched as the terrified pilot, staring at the snarling wolfman, quickly disappeared in a burst of flame as the hovercraft fell away, billowing smoke and spinning down to the surface.

"Well that was fun," bluntly stated the Lycan. "But in case you've forgotten again, we have to go reload now." Wulfe yanked a lever and the ship flew off again, climbing vertically back into space for another moment of serene beauty, getting ready for another moment of bloody slaughter. But after they'd reloaded their weapons and started back down again, they saw that the fight was over. Terrified by the repeated sudden death from above, the six remaining aircraft were flying off in different directions, bobbing and turning, frantically trying to avoid Wulfe's little tiger of a ship. None had continued on towards New Venice—they were all heading back to the safety of their fleet.

Wulfe slowed the ship a bit and leveled off. "They're done. So long, assholes. Shouldn't have fucked with the 'Pup'. He looked over at Harrison. "Now back to San Marco. Whatever is going on back there, I'm sure someone can use our assistance."

They both knew that the whole enemy fleet must be about to attack New Venice. "I 'spect that to be an understatement," replied the Yank.

◆ ◆ ◆

Triumph slammed his fist down on the gilded formal French table he'd had installed in the conference rooms of all his ships. "You had a dozen Apache helicopters with Hellfire missiles and Gatling guns, and they couldn't take on two British zombies with antique flintlock pistols?" Though the table bounced up from the force of Triumph's blow, mostly the officers around the table stayed quiet. They all knew that a comment during one of the Emperor's tirades could cost them their jobs or worse.

But one foolishly spoke up. "Actually, it was an alien and an American, and they had quite a rifle, too," replied Gonzalez, the veteran Marine air wing commander. "And that ship of theirs…"

Triumph's fuming response overwhelmed the soft-spoken general. "Oh, they had a rifle! A fucking zombie and an alien defeat an entire Apache squadron because they had a rifle?" He stood up fuming and started pulling his hair. "What's your name, general?"

"Gonzalez, sir," he replied, knowing what was coming.

"Gonzalez! Well, no wonder! General Gonzalez, you're fired. Who here is number two in the air wing?"

A colonel about forty years old uncomfortably raised a finger. "Taylor, sir."

"Taylor! Much better. Officer Taylor, you now command the air wing. Your first order is to assign Bad Hombre Gonzalez here to janitorial duties." Two of Triumph's burly security detail moved over and escorted General Gonzalez from the room. Triumph gazed slowly around at the assembled officers.

"Gentlemen, we are going to attack this little town with everything we got—now! So we couldn't soften them up with our helicopters—so what? We've got an entire fleet here full of big cannons, rockets, missiles, cruise missiles for Christ's sake, and a million machine guns! And all they have is single shot antiques? We can't lose! There's no reason we can't conquer this little loser of a town! For starters, we're going to level this New Venice with a huge, terrific artillery bombardment, not another lightweight shelling. Then our troops can walk right in. To Hell with all the west coast tourists that may be there! No more Mister nice guy!"

The Dreash leader, whose name translated to Pig Prime, was outside on the deck monitoring the planning session. He spoke up in perfect English.

"My race will join this attack. While your forces execute the frontal attack, dozens of Dreash will swim around to the far side of New Venice, down the Rio di Noale and into the Grand Canal, then rise from the waters and attack the enemy's rear. They will be unable to move their cumbersome artillery in time to face us. We will devour all in our way and meet you in San Marco."

"Now that's a great idea, big guy!" Triumph said and turned to his officers. "How come nobody here's come up with something like that? You need to be more like these guys!"

Several officers gave the big Dreash uncomfortable looks as the creature started drooling at the thought of eating so many souls. Though Triumph didn't seem to have any problems with the big monster's proposal.

"Anyone have any objections to the plan?"

Unsurprisingly, no one in the meeting spoke up. And then came the carrot. Triumph turned to the ubiquitous TV cameras.

"And for all my hard-working soldiers and sailors in the fleet watching me on your ships' monitors, here's another reason you want to win today. Victor Triumph today declares that we will fight this fight just like they did centuries ago in the real Venice. Back then, if a town refused a terrific surrender deal like we've offered them, soldiers of the attacking force were allowed to loot the place for three days. That's right! Every one of you who fights in the coming battle can take whatever he finds! Over three days! And I hear the place is loaded with gold! Now, keep away from government buildings, my personal security force will be securing them. But the rest of the city is yours—you earned it! Grab any girl that suits your fancy and head for the nearest bar or hotel—it's all free to you guys! And you gals too—you can grab any guy you like! When this city falls, it's yours! I give it to you! Now go get your orders, good luck, and God bless you all."

During all this the Fox News cameras focused on a middle-aged blond woman, Triumph's official translator, who addressed the cameras and explained what her boss had actually just said. They missed the raised eyebrows and nervous shuffling among the officers in the room, especially the older ones. But as none were interested in a janitorial career, there were no objections. And they also missed the almost uncontrolled glee on Sam Bamming's face.

Wyckham stood erect, watching rockets slam into the sailors' batteries. British naval officers did not drop down like ducks in the middle of a fight—it was important for his sailors to see him right in the thick of it. But standing there wasn't going to win this fight. He needed a miracle.

Obujimi appeared from nowhere and handed him his telescope for a close-up look at his opponents. Snapping it open and putting it to his right eye, he made out about a dozen of the flying craft like the one Harrison had downed in the earlier fight, about a mile off. But a different kind of airship, quick as a lightning bolt, had flown up from an offshore island and taken position behind the enemy squadron. Adjusting his telescope, he recognized the little craft—Wulfe's space ship! Before he could even exclaim out loud, the enemy craft in front of it burst into flame and spiraled downwards. Captain Harrison had taken his rifle with him and Wulfe had maneuvered close enough to make it deadly! None of the other ships reacted, apparently unaware of what had happened behind them, and within a few moments Harrison fired again, and another ship exploded. This time the other ships noticed and began maneuvering to bring their weapons to bear on Wulfe's ship. But with the mighty roar of flames coming out its stern, the old Dreash scout ship headed straight up at incredible speed, creating reports in the air so loud that the ground shook, then flew out of sight before any of the enemy even craft got off a shot.

The enemy craft broke formation, ships turning every which way, looking for Wulfe, apparently unable to locate him with their electric sensors because he was probably halfway to Earth by now. But a few moments later, two more booms in the air announced his return as he moved deftly to the opposite side of the squadron, flying right up behind three of them and stopping like it had hit something. This time there were three quick shots, two of them from what had to be Wulfe's pistols, and three more craft fell to the sea while Wulfe's vessel again sped upwards and disappeared into the heavens, chased by four of the hovercrafts' rockets. Then, choosing discretion over valor, the remaining ships bolted for home like panicked horses, and the scrap was over. For now. But Wyckham knew the fight for San Marco was far from over.

Wyckham saw Firefly Brashton suddenly reappear in front of him as she was wont to do in a crisis. He approached her with a request.

"Firefly Brashton, well met. Might I ask you to do a little of your electrical magic and raise a mast here flying 'CAPTAINS REPAIR ON BOARD?' I need to see everyone right here, right now." Though this message was generally used at sea, all Wyckham's officers and civil officials would understand its meaning.

The Firefly conjured up a holographic mast with signal flags, and within twenty minutes all of Wyckham's commanders were there at the quayside. The leader of the ants, Worker Queen, was present, along with Bubbler, the chief mudman, Slick number 2256, the head Firefly, and representatives of the sightless Gorillas, the stickmen, the big octopi, and all the other alien groups who had prospered on Freeport. Wulfe landed his ship in the plaza, finding a spot with minimal rubble, and he too joined the meeting along with Captain Harrison. Also present were Captains Rawlins, Hamilton, Randolph, Badoin, and Marine Captain Kenworthy, along with Prime Minister Cochran and President DiCarpaccio with some of his uniformed military advisors. A crowd of resident aliens and American tourists was also gathering about them, the only functioning authority they saw, trying to find out what was going on.

"Alright, we all know what comes next. They'll make an amphibious landing with lots of artillery support from their fleet. Thanks to Wulfe and Captain Harrison, I don't believe we will see any more of their hovering gunships. Now let's get ready, I expect matters to heat up very soon. I will command from this battery. Captain Rawlins, you have the sailors and the guns along the square. Captain Kenworthy, keep your marines just outside the plaza until the artillery stops, then get into the square right quick. Move up in skirmishing order, DiCarpaccio here informs us that the foe will be spraying bullets all over the place from their fast firing rifles. Wulfe and Captain Harrison, get aloft and see what you can do, try to take out any boats landing troops but don't get shot down, DiCarpccio tells me that even their boats carry guided rockets. Don't worry about their big ships, Captain Badoin and the fleet have that responsibility." He paused for a moment and scanned the faces of all his subordinates he'd lived with for over 200 years. Then he addressed the noncombatants.

"To our residents and visitors I see about me, good luck surviving the artillery bombardment. I wish I could recommend a safe place to ride it out, but there is nothing of substance in this entire city except this small stone redoubt here, and it can only hold so many. At least get out of the plaza. Though I expect the enemy will bombard the entire area, I'm afraid no place is safe".

Queen's Favourite, the head ant, was twirling his antennae, always an indicator of an ant with something to say. "Use ant tunnels. Big ant city under plaza."

Thousands of the big ants lived in warrens under Port Wyckham and around Venice. The industrious creatures apparently had dug similar systems under San Marco!

"Most welcome news, that. You have enough room for everyone? We have over a thousand sailors and marines, not to mention several thousand tourists."

"Yes," replied Queen's Favorite. His species was not known for loquacity, preferring work to talk. "Entrances being cleared now." Wyckham looked around the square and sure enough, there were several groups of ants throwing mangled building framework around to reveal cave-like entrances to the underground network.

"Cracking good work, Mr. Favorite, absolutely cracking! Alright, everyone, follow Mister Favorite here and get below ground. Quick, like rabbits now!"

"We'll go round up tourists." Wyckham looked for the source of that suggestion. Damn if it wasn't the warrior woman, standing with her friends, all three of them still carrying their weapons, splattered with white crab blood. "There's a bunch back around Brashton's club, all in shock, I'm not sure they'll follow directions from ants." She turned to her two companions. "You guys down with this?"

Her friends nodded assent and slapped hands the way tourists often did, then headed off towards Brashton's. Wyckham admiringly watched them leave. *Strong women, those.*

What Fate New Venice?

EMMIE, CONNIE AND Van ran all the way back to Brashton's Club with several ants for guiding the civilians below. The club was as they had left it, a tangled steel framework with roof supports and tiles scattered about. While many club goers had wandered off into the surrounding forests, hundreds were still there, many of them wounded. Tall Slick medics were carrying the seriously hurt off to their hospital, while others administered to the lightly wounded. Other tourists, mostly friends of the suffering individuals, were assisting, slathering Slick anti-blister agent on those with burns and cycling tourniquets on wounded limbs.

Emmie climbed up on a real stone fountain and called out to everyone as loud as she could. "Fellow Americans and other tourists—listen up! I'm Emmie, just another tourist. I just came from Governor Wyckham and he says we're about to be attacked by a fleet from the Confederacy. He says we must take shelter underground—now! Everybody follow these ants, they'll lead you into tunnels they've dug under the town. And those who can, help the wounded up and get them to safety as well! Hurry!"

The alien medics immediately picked up the wounded they were working on and started along the line of ants leading to a burrow entrance just a few yards off. But some of the tourists moved slowly, those wounded or still dazed by the recent shelling. Emmie and her friends did their best to get them moving.

"Come on people, you got to go! Now!" Emmie shouted. "This plaza is about to get leveled by artillery! You've got to get underground right away! Follow the ants! Follow the ants! Go, go, go!" Her entreaties got a few more moving but not with the haste Emmie thought necessary.

The problem was solved when the first explosions rocked San Marco plaza. Compared to the earlier barrage, this one was even heavier. Tourists leapt to their feet and started running towards the ants, for the most part helping the wounded along as well. Emmie helped a few get up who were then immediately grabbed by ants or Slicks and carried off. The shelling paused momentarily, and she took a last look around the plaza before she followed them underground. As the smoke started dissipating, she made out some shapes lying on the ground across the plaza. Should she run over and check them out? She had to, couldn't live with herself if she didn't.

"You guys go now, I'll be back in a sec," yelled Emmie to Connie who were both helping some elderly tourists. "I'm gonna check out the square one last time." She started off and got about halfway when the barrage resumed, even heavier than before. She couldn't continue, the entire area she was heading into became blanketed with explosions. Going further would just be a dangerous waste of time anyway, nothing could have survived in the area she was looking at. Turning back to get to safety, another line of explosions walked across the burrow entrance, ripping up the plaza and sending paving stones flying. Now there was no way could she make it back, and the ants' tunnel entrance was buried anyway. She looked around for a refuge and the only one she saw was the stone artillery bastion she'd left only minutes ago. Off she went, running like hell to the only safe place she could see in this hellish rain of destruction.

Emmie had seen plenty of war movies and knew that the safest way to cross the plaza was to run from one shell hole to the next. While she'd never been in the army, she'd seen enough war movies to know to stay low in an artillery barrage and the safest places were the holes just made by exploding shells. Waiting in the first crater during a particularly heavy series of explosions, she was almost overwhelmed by the train-like roar that the descending shells made. *Forget it, Emmie! Get ready to move!* When it momentarily stopped, she dashed to the next crater to wait for another momentary break before climbing out and dashing to the next shell hole.

Despite some close calls and the flying debris, she managed to get to the bastion with just a few scratches. The one-story structure was big, about a hundred feet per side, with five cannons on the roof and five more poking out of portholes below. In addition, there were several small swiveling cannons mounted on the roof. Not seeing any door, she flew up a wooden ladder on the land side and onto the little fort's roof. And there, with his telescope out calmly scanning the lagoon like a spectator at an America's Cup event, was Rodney Wyckham, along with a black man in fancy Georgian-era clothing.

Just as she arrived, a nearby explosion blew a spray of little stones across the roof, knocking off Wyckham's bicorn hat. He turned around to pick it up and started when he noticed Emmie.

"The young warrior herself! Well, mum, I know you're handy with a blade, but unless you're handy with a 32 pounder as well, I suggest you go back across the piazza to an ant tunnel entrance and get underground. This is no place…" He stopped his warning and flinched as rubble from a nearby explosion sprayed the roof.

"Yeah, that ship has sailed," replied Emmie as more explosions blanketed the plaza.

It took a moment for Wyckham to understand the metaphor. Was this woman a sailor? *Ah, she means it's too late.*

Suddenly the thunderous din of detonating artillery stopped. But there it was immediately replaced by the buzzing of rapid-fire rifles. Bullets danced across the stone face of the redoubt, sending stone chips flying. Wyckham stepped over to the top of the interior stairway and yelled down to his men sheltering below.

"Gun crews up! All hands man your guns—the foe has arrived. And Gunner Crawford, get this woman below." Men in striped shirts started running up to the big cannons on the roof, pulling stoppers from their muzzles and running the guns out between the roof's crenellations.

Emmie looked over the ramparts into the lagoon. Flying across the water were several large hovercraft, boats that American marines used to land troops. Machine guns mounted on their sides were firing away, their tracers flashing across the plaza. An older sailor ran up onto the roof and grabbed Emmie. "Me pardons, mum, best to get below. Quick now, gots t' work me gun."

Emmie couldn't argue with that. As the last man climbed the stairway, Emmie ran down into the fort. Surprisingly, the stone walls were really thick, like thirty feet thick. This place just might stand up to modern weapons. She moved back behind the big cannons, trying to keep out of the way of the scurrying gun crews.

"Ahoy le pont!" It was the lookout in the crosstrees of *Leviathan*, the French 80-gun ship-of-the-line that had also entered the portal in the English Channel 200 years ago along with Wyckham's British squadron and been transported to this planet. The ship was anchored in the middle of some small islands where it hoped it would be invisible to the enemy's electrical vision and sensing devices. Her lookout aloft could see the vast lagoon through a space between some trees. *"L'enemi! L'enemi!"*

French Capitaine Jean Badoin snapped open his brass telescope and scanned the lagoon. Over a dozen grey shapes had emerged over the horizon, firing huge guns as they rapidly advanced, moving east towards New Venice. "Merde, but zey are fast!" Badoin exclaimed in his heavily accented English to his British First Lieutenant, Carlton Moore. "Signal zee othaires, 'Enemy to stairboard'."

Without waiting for the order, a French midshipman ran signaling flags up the mainmast as Lieutenant Moore bellowed out, "Leviathan will clear for action!" Bosuns pipes whistled, French and alien sailors in their striped shirts ran to run out the great guns, and within minutes the ship was ready to fight. Behind them, *Indomptable*, *Righteous*, and *Trinidad* were preparing as well, their gunports banging open as they too cleared for action. Signal flags flew up their mainmasts showing they were ready for battle.

The experienced French captain quickly ran his eyes over the spider's web of ropes running from *Leviathan* to trees on the small rocky islands around the ship. It was a network of springs—cables used to move an anchored ship around so its guns would bear on a foe. "Forward capstan 'aul ayway, stern capstan pay off! He watched for a moment, then yelled, "Stop!'" He walked over to another cable running sideways off the stern. "Pool zees one een twenty metres!"

Badoin and Moore watched the enemy ships move closer. "Must be making 25 knots," Moore commented. "No way we hit can ships moving that fast."

"Yas, but DiCarpaccio say zey must stop to lower boats for zee aytack on zee citay. We can onlee hope zey stop zoon where we can heet zem."

As if on cue the the enemy ships came to a stop. A strange-looking large boat burst from the bow of the largest one, roaring across the waves, spraying huge plumes of water behind it.

"Zere! Zee gran sheepe in zee centaire has zee landing boats!" yelled Badoin. "Fire on zat sheepe!"

Leviathan's veteran gunners aimed their pieces and guns started firing off, reaching a crescendo as the last dozen crashed out at once. The big French ship mounted 32 carronades per side, big 65 pounders made by the ants out of the planet's amazingly strong clay. They used Freeport's highly combustible black ooze for gunpowder and bundles of grapeshot, egg-size Greek fireballs, which could penetrate steel even from miles away. While bundles of grapeshot generally sprayed all over the place and weren't accurate over a hundred meters, these clay guns were rifled and kept the spread of the small balls much tighter. White flaming streaks crossed the lagoon slamming into the CSA *Mobile Bay*, setting off secondary explosions that rocked the ship. Within moments the amphibious assault ship was in flames from bow to stern. A further thunder of artillery erupted around Leviathan as Badoin's three other ships opened up on the rest of the enemy fleet.

"Bon shooteeng, citizens! Now 'aul zee sheepe back behind zee eyeland! Queek! Queek!"

Prersident DiCarpaccio had warned Badoin to only fire off only one broadside, then get back behind the tree-covered islands. As with Wyckham's previous attack on the fleet, once the element of surprise was lost, the Confederate fleet would open up with their advanced weaponry and destroy any of Badoin's squadron they could target. "Shoot and scoot", DiCarpaccio's advisors called the strategy.

But three of the fast landing craft had made it out the *Mobile Bay's* open bow before the ship has been rendered inoperable. Badoin and Moore grimaced as they watched these three landing craft, blasting out a torrent of seawater behind them, sped off towards New Venice, filled with hundreds of troops carrying God-knows-what deadly weapons.

Badoin muttered solemnly, "*Bon* luck to Capitaine Wyckham. 'Eee faces ay deeficult fight."

<hr>

"Sorry ye gots mixed up 'n all 'iss, mum," said the old sailor who seemed to be in charge on the lower floor of the little fort. "But Peter Crawford'll keep ye safe. Jes' stay back o'er there inna corner, don't want t' git run o'er by a jumpin' gun".

Emmie stepped back just as the five big cannons in the room fired with a resounding crash and recoiled back, one of them running right over the spot where Emmie had just been standing a moment ago. *Shit, he wasn't kidding.* Sailors quickly serviced the cannons, swabbing them out with wet mops, ramming paper-wrapped bundles down the muzzles, and grabbing ropes to haul the guns back up to the gun ports. Crawford was standing next to her, not saying much. It seemed the sailors all knew their business.

Emmie was puzzled. "No cannonballs? What's in those paper bundles you're loading?" she had to ask.

"Special dirts f'um this world, makes Greek fire whens 'ey touches, mum," he replied, switching his attention to peer out a small window. "No hits, lads. One more load o'roundshot fire, then grape fireballs." Guns started firing as they reloaded with no reaction from Crawford. Suddenly the men on the roof started cheering. Crawford stepped back from his view out the window, upset for some reason.

"Lucky shot t'was all," Crawford said to his crews. Noticing Emmie standing there looking puzzled, he stepped further back and motioned for Emmie to come take a look. "Lads on th' roof got one. Come see."

Emmie moved up to get a view at the lagoon. About a mile off, dominating the scene, was a burning ship, one of those big marine hovercraft that she'd once seen practicing off Pendleton Marine Base in California. One of the guns on the roof had apparently hit the ship with Greek fire, and it was completely consumed with fire, bobbing like a dead fish. Two other landing ships were flying at high speed towards the docks, turning back and forth to evade the flying fireballs, giant rooster tails coming out of their sterns. Flashing orange lights sparkled from machine guns mounted on their sides. Bullets smacked into the wall across from Emmie's window, spraying stone chips around the redoubt. Emmie instinctively reacted, her fencing training taking over as she ducked below the windowsill for a moment, then stood up unscathed.

Peering back out at the quay, she was disappointed to see the two big troop carriers had stopped at the dock, mostly hidden below the stone quay. Though she couldn't see what they were doing, the two ships were doubtlessly unloading troops in this spot protected from the Brits' artillery. It seemed Crawford realized that as he spat out a quick order.

"The foes be 'ere, lads. Add a load o' canister, run out, 'old fire til I sez so."

The gunners around Emmie grabbed tin cans the size of half-gallon juice containers and rammed them down their guns' muzzles. From the way they rattled, Emmie guessed they were filled with small bullets. Loaded with both the Greekfireballs and the added tin cans, the guns were run out to stick their menacing muzzles through the square gun ports. Gun captains squinted down the barrels and waited for targets to appear above the docks.

They didn't have long to wait. Yelling "Ee-hah!" in southern accents, dozens of uniformed soldiers burst onto the plaza along the quay and started running for the little fort, firing M-16's with grenade launchers like the one in the movie "Scarface". Before they got the range, two of Crawford's big cannons fired. Most of the attackers were swept away— they just disappeared, apparently shredded by all the stuff Crawford's gunners had stuffed down their barrels. But from the roof above came frantic yells and the sound of hand-to hand fighting.

"Swivels! Look west!" It was Wyckham's voice from above her on the roof. Emmie looked out an empty rear gunport and saw a submarine moving back out into the lagoon. It had landed attackers on the west side of the little fort who had emerged unnoticed while the British had been focused on the foes in front of them. On the roof the little swivel cannons barked but sounds of struggle above indicated that the enemy had gotten some men onto the roof. Looking up the stairs, Emmie could see men in close quarter fighting, American soldiers firing M-16's and British sailors shooting flintlock pistols.

A hissing grenade bounced down the stairs and landed at Emmie's feet. While Crawford and his gunners just stared at it uncomprehendingly, Emmie had seen enough war movies to know what to do. With a fencer's hand speed, she grabbed the thing and flipped it out a nearby gunport where it exploded harmlessly.

Now an M-16 muzzle appeared at the top of the stairway, followed by a helmeted head peering down into the room. But before the man could fire, the point of a cutlass burst from his neck as he was stabbed from behind. His head slumped down and his M-16 clattered down the stairway.

The competitive fighter in her took over. She'd shot M-16's at Las Vegas gun ranges (everybody who went to Vegas did it, it was really cool) and knew that an automatic rifle could help the Brits in this desperate fight. She grabbed it, made sure its safety was off, switched it to full auto, and went up the stairs to peek out over the roof.

Bodies were strewn across the roof, both American and British, some moaning with bloody wounds. About thirty feet in front of her, several soldiers in helmets and flak jackets were hunkered down behind two of the large cannons, holding up their M-16's and firing blindly across the roof. At the other end, the remaining Brits crouched down behind other cannons, occasionally firing their flintlock pistols but clearly overwhelmed by the Americans' firepower.

The Confederate soldiers had their backs to her; none of them knew she was there. *Do this quick, don't give 'em time to react.* Emmie put the rifle to her shoulder, took aim at the soldier nearest her and gave a quick squeeze on the trigger. *Three shots at a time, just like they told you in Vegas, don't want the rifle bouncing around.* The soldier dropped like a bag of laundry and Emmie squeezed off three more at the next one. With all the firing on the roof, no one noticed her, and she just kept walking her bursts down the line of soldiers crouched behind the cannons. When she went for her fourth, only one shot was left but luckily it hit her target. Fortunately, the gun's previous owner had taped a second magazine to the one she'd just emptied, and Emmie just popped the magazine out, flipped it over, racked the slide and resumed firing.

As the last Confederate in the line slumped to the ground, one she hadn't seen rose up from behind a cannon and ran towards the British end of the roof, spraying bullets from his rifle. Off to his side, none other than Governor Wyckham himself stood up, fired a beautiful old pistol at the man, but missed as the man ducked. Emmie stood up as the soldier swung his M-16 around at Wyckham, but before he could fire Emmie fired a long burst into him, blowing him right off the roof. The scene suddenly went eerily quiet. Emmie and the Governor just stood there for a moment, staring at each other.

Before either could get a word out, a soldier emerged from somewhere behind Emmie and tackled her, knocking the M-16 from her grip. They both fell to the ground as the Confederate cocked his arm to stab Emmie with a huge knife. Her fencing reflexes took over. She grabbed his wrist, straightened her left arm to keep it at bay, at the same time drew the hanger from her warrior's sash and pulled it across her waist, keeping it low and out of her opponent's vision. Once Emmie had it free, she dropped her hand low, raised the point and made a quick thrust under the guy's chin. The sharp point went up through his head, jarring Emmie's hand when it struck the underside of his skull. The Confederate went limp and fell off Emmie, his gushing blood spurting all over her. Slowly she sat up, pretty shook. *Jesus, did I just do all that?* She'd just killed or wounded several human beings, not just some big crabs. *Snap out of it, for shit's sake! They were the assholes that started this shit.* Finally standing up, she looked around the rooftop and out over the plaza. While there was still some shooting over on the far side of San Marco, it seemed this fight was over. And in front of her was Wyckham, calmly standing there like nothing had happened.

"The warrior princess saves the day," he commented dryly. "Quite remarkable—I had no idea anyone in the cosmos was proficient with both a 19th century sword and a 21st century raped-fire rifle, much less a woman. My gratitude for your skill with both."

Emmie usual riposte to chauvinist comments like this was, "Virgins never appreciate women," but this wasn't an argument in a bar. *Take it easy, Ems, take it easy. He's 200-some years old and wasn't on Earth during the women's movement.*

"Sorry to astonish you. Lucky for you a woman was around to save your ass, huh?"

"And while wearing quite a… ah… cumbersome costume? Frankly, I am quite amazed that you could even walk bearing those… appendages, much less dance around with that hanger and make such lightning-like lunges. Is this how women dress for battle on Earth these days?"

His comment cooled Emmie's resentment at Wyckham's sexist comments. She almost laughed out loud, realizing she was standing on a field of death covered in blood but looking like a porn star. "Yeah, seems every hologram generator in this city got blown up except the one projecting my boobs. Hopefully I can find an intact changing station and get rid of these things."

Boobs? Well that was an interesting word. Wyckham had thought that after centuries of living among sailors he would be familiar with every word on the subject, but this one was new to him. Why were they given that name on Earth? Maybe because they flopped about without purpose? Or because they always gave one a blank stare? He didn't know why, but for some reason the appellation seemed appropriate.

The Lady Brashton Firefly suddenly appeared. Probably she'd been present all along, hiding in case any Dreash had been present during the battle. Accompanying her for some reason was Piglet, the juvenile Dreash that Jamison had brought back and been given that name. It now had a translator installed on its head.

"Governor, we have an emergency," she blurted out. "The little Dreash here says that a group of Dreash is swimming towards the Grand Canal from the north to attack the plaza from the rear."

"She right she right!" the little pig yelled through his translator. "Old mommy coming, wants to kill me and new mommy! Don't let her get me!" The juvenile monster cried, covering his ears in a vain attempt to remove his mother from his thoughts.

The news hit Wyckham like a roundshot. He had no doubt that what the little beast had just said was absolutely true. It was well known that everything one member of the Dreash knew was communicated to other members if close enough, and this little fellow knew whatever his mother was thinking. And with all Wyckham's defenses facing west towards the open docks, he had no idea what he could do before the Dreash arrived. His mind raced to think up a viable counterattack but came up empty. Christ!

But the Firefly had been searching as well and blurted out a plan.

"Mademoiselle Emmie! Your device! We must contact Wulfe!" She pointed to Emmie's waist at the small communicating device that all tourists used. "Please enter following message!" Fireflies were pure energy and could not do anything physical, so she had to have Emmie manipulate the device.

"Address message to 'Wulfe'." He will pick it up on his scout ship's communicator. State 'Dreash force in Grand Canal or Rio d' Noale, approaching San Marco'."

Wyckham was puzzled. What could Wulfe or Harrison do in that little scout ship against a landing force? As Emmie entered the message, the Firedly image of Lady Brashton answered his unspoken question.

"I saw Wulfe loading his scout ship with mortar bombs from *Vesuvius* yesterday.

Of course! Captain Randolph of *Vesuvius*, a bomb ketch mounting two thirteen-inch mortars, packed his shells with the planet's powerful black ooze explosive. When Wulfe dropped them onto Dreash forces in in Port Wyckham back in '15, their huge explosions won the fight. With these mortar rounds Wulfe could certainly wipe out a Dreash attack. Wyckham just hoped he wouldn't blow up the whole city.

◆ ◆ ◆

The airspace beneath them was clear. Wulfe and Jamison were in the little scout ship, cruising slowly back and forth several miles above the planet, scanning the skies around New Venice. What they saw conformed what the little screen on the space ship's control panel indicated—there were no enemy flying craft within twenty miles of New Venice.

Earlier, when they saw troop ships heading towards San Marco, Jamison had wanted to fly down and attack them, but Wulfe had persuaded him that they needed to stay where they were. "Those fast landing craft will be hard for us to hit even if we slow way down, but then their rapid fire weapons could take us out if pretty easy. Plus the bastards on the command ships are watching us on their own screens, the minute we leave high cap their hovercraft will swarm over San Marco. Have faith in our Captain Wyckham, he doesn't need us to win this scrap. His opponent is no field commander, just another one of those psychotic politicians that thinks he knows everything but doesn't have a clue about commanding a fight."

It now looked as if Wulfe had made the right call. Jamison could see that the bright flashes of artillery fire and exploding shells in San Marco had stopped and the enemy ships were retreating. It looked like the Brits had won the fight. Suddenly an alarm bell started ringing and a message appeared on another screen in characters that Jamison recognized as the Lycan tongue.

Wulfe immediately started pushing buttons, shutting off the alarm and putting the ship into a steep dive. "Dreash are in the canals. Get aft and prepare to drop mortar shells. Cut fuses for a thousand feet. We'll drop them from five hundred, want them to blow up underwater."

Jamison undid his restraining belts and stepped to the rear door behind Wulfe, his sea legs keeping him upright in the hurtling spaceship, to a rack of thirteen-inch shells by the closed door, their fuses dangling. Jamison pulled out his hunting knife and cut the waterproof fuses at the spots marked 1000, then switched on a heating coil mounted on the wall that quickly glowed red-hot. He also pulled back the hammer on his rifle leaning against the wall to half-cock. The rear door opened as Wulfe leveled the ship out over the New Venice lagoon and rocketed north over the city.

◆ ◆ ◆

Mawg pulled ahead of the school of other Dreash swimming underwater towards the Grand Canal's northern entrance. She wanted to be the first out so she could find and devour her son, the little bastard that had run away and joined the enemy, just because she had given him a little discipline. The Dreash were a tribe and any disloyalty was punished severely. She would take her time dismembering and eating her ungrateful offspring, inflicting as much pain as possible.

With a final kick of her massive webbed feet, she launched out of the water onto a walkway and started running towards San Marco. It would be much faster than swimming and she didn't want the others to get to San Marco eat her son first.

The roiling waters three cables north of the island were a dead give-away. Wulfe yelled over his shoulder to Jamison.

"Enemy in sight. You ready? Start rolling them off when I count three."

Jamison grabbed the glowing coil off the wall with his right hand and the first release lever on the rack with his left. "Ready."

Wulfe now clearly saw the giant shapes of Dreash in the water ahead. He slowed his ship and dropped to 500 feet. "One, two, three."

Jamison lit the first fuse and yanked the lever. The first bomb rolled out the door as Jamison lit the second. Within a few seconds, he'd rolled six of the big iron balls out the side door. Wulfe called to him to halt and sped the ship away before the entire area turned to Armageddon.

Tremendous explosions shook San Marco, even though they were coming from at least a mile away. Wyckham counted six as they went off just a few seconds apart in evenly spaced intervals. Wyckham knew what they were—mortar shells packed with the planet's high explosive, dropped by Wulfe from his little ship. Quite impressive. Maybe the tourists' little communicators weren't so bad to have around after all. Looked like this fight was finally won.

But the little Dreash was even more agitated. "Mommy coming! Mommy coming! She want to eat me! Save me!"

Wyckham didn't think anything could've survived those explosions. But this little Dreash would know exactly how his mother was doing, and he seemed to think she was alive and close. Wyckham nervously pulled out one of his Nocke pistols and cocked it. Its load of Greek fire would burn a six-inch hole right through these huge demons, but when running they were hard to hit—with their muscular legs they were quick and evasive. Hitting a running one with a pistol required a superb shot.

Sure enough, around the northern corner of San Marco came the mother Dreash, snarling as it stopped for a moment. Her son started yelling, "Save me! Save me!" and jumped behind Wyckham. Catching sight of her son, the huge creature roared and took off in a blindingly fast run right at them, crossing the entire plaza in a couple of seconds. Wyckham sighted his pistol and pulled the trigger but knew he didn't have a shot—as it ran the beast was bobbing and weaving like a fish evading a shark. It dodged the shot, then bent down and reached out a massive arm to grab them. *Christ, I'm about to be eaten. I couldn't have gone in a real naval fight?* But Wyckham didn't move. Captains in the Royal Navy stood in the face of death rather than running like a barnyard chicken.

Suddenly the beast's head blew apart and flew forward, looking like a wine barrel dropped by a dockyard crane. As the immense body fell to the ground and skidded to a stop in front of him, Wyckham saw the source of his salvation behind it—Wulfe's ship, hovering in the air, with Jamison's smoking rifle still sticking out a front porthole. He could see Wulfe and Jamison up front talking, but with the roaring of the ship's engine Wyckham couldn't hear their comments.

◆ ◆ ◆

"Nice shot,' said Wulfe, nodding in admiration.

"Right where the filthy devil deserved it," observed Jamison as he pulled his rifle in. "Right up its arse." The fireball had indeed entered its buttocks and burned all the way through its body to burst from its forehead.

◆ ◆ ◆

The little Dreash was spinning around, its webbed hands in the air, happily singing, "Old mommy in pain, old mommy in pain… Oh! Now she bye-bye, she go bye-bye…"

Emmie's communicator made a chiming sound. She looked down and read aloud, "From Wulfe. 'Caught foes in the water. Shock waves took them all. Rio d' Noale clogged with corpses. Fresh pork for your sailors tonight'."

Emmie laughed, thinking Wulfe was jesting. But Wyckham knew that Wulfe was not joking. Dreash meat was actually quite tasty, and for sure the pickets in the area would already be harvesting it for dinner. He shook his head at the thought. *The royal Navy did not eat its foes, for God's sake!* But a victory was a victory, and he reveled in both the enemy's destruction and the salvation of the planet. While there were still foes to be dealt with in the plaza, with their relief force destroyed, they were beaten and they knew it. All thanks to the young Dreash.

Wyckham bent down to the still-dancing alien. "Well done, my little man. You warned us in the nick of time. I'm sure that new mommy here will give you a nice fresh rat treat for this. Isn't that right, new mommy?" The Firefly smiled and nodded.

"Of course." Immediately a rat popped up from some debris and ran right up to the Dreash, which immediately scooped it up and threw it into its mouth. The sight of a being submitting to suicide shocked Wyckham. *Jesus, but the Fireflies are getting powerful.*

Wyckham stood back up and looked about the square to assess the battle. The enemy's artillery had stopped when they landed their troops and had not resumed. On the west side of the square, British artillery was still banging away at Confederate soldiers who were hunkered down among the collapsed building framework.

"Mister Crawford, my compliments, and can you get the guns here aimed at the backs of those foes in the plaza? Maybe a look down the cave-like maws of our thirty-two pounders will persuade them to surrender?"

He turned to ask Obujimi for his speaking trumpet, but there he was already, offering the brass instrument to the governor. Wyckham put it to his mouth and called out into the plaza.

"Lads! Belay firing! Our fight is won. To all our gallant foes, your cause is lost. Stand up without weapons and your hands in the air and surrender. You will be treated fairly as prisoners of war. You have one minute, then the guns in this battery will fire upon you."

San Marco went silent as the British guns ceased firing. The only sound was the creaking of naval carriages as the redoubt's sailors pushed their big guns around to bear on the square. The ominous groaning sounds of the wooden trucks convinced the Confederates to start standing up and surrendering, their hands in the air as instructed. Red coated marines ran into the piazza and began taking their weapons. Wyckham was finally able to turn back to his rescuer.

"Well, you certainly did save my arse, and with a remarkable display of swordplay, shooting, and courage, I must say. Not to mention that handy little device you carry. Allow me to formally introduce myself," said Wyckham as he made a leg. "Governor Rodney Wyckham. As pressing events have been successfully concluded, it is extremely nice to meet you."

Emmie smiled back and extended a hand for a shake. "Emmie Bahtia. American, from San Francisco."

The Firefly walked up close to Emmie and spoke softly in her ear. "May I be of some assistance?" Immediately Emmie's image changed and there she was again, a five-nine San Franciscan woman in the jeans and t-shirt she had put on for her vacation. "Your clothes now appear fresh, but please be aware that the clothing you are wearing is badly ripped and soiled from your recent activities. You probably want to go change into different clothes".

Wyckham seemed to approve the image change. "Well, that's better." And then he took her proffered hand and put it to his lips! "At your service. I must now attend to the needs of the city's residents and visitors—medical care, food and shelter. But a dinner after a victory is Royal Navy tradition, and I will be dining tonight with those who fought so gallantly today. You are certainly among that party. Might you join us at eight this evening? The dinner will hopefully be aboard the *Trinidad,* which should be back here at the docks by then. Are you alright until then?"

Emmie finally relaxed and realized she was exhausted. "Ah, yeah, sure, I'm down with that. Right now, I need to go find my friends, see how they're doing, make sure they're OK, but shit yeah, I'll be there."

"Ah, yes, the other two women also so handy with their blades. Of course, they are invited tonight as well."

"OK! I'll let 'em know!" replied a more excited Emmie. They were heroes going to a victory dinner! How cool was that! She headed off to where she had left Van and Connie, the thrill of victory and recognition helping her cope as she walked through the American bodies. *To Hell with them. They attacked a fucking Halloween party.*

Wyckham watched her leave. *Fascinating woman, that one.*

◆ ◆ ◆

Aboard the CSA destroyer *Spruance,* a celebratory dinner was not on the evening's schedule. *Crappy little ship probably couldn't even cook one anyway,* thought Triumph. The *Mobile Bay* had been sunk and now he was stuck aboard this scow, sitting at a small conference room table, listening to the ridiculous excuses his officers were making about why they had lost another battle with this joke of an enemy.

"… And our sensors were unable to target the enemy ships, hidden among these islands made of the same wood and ceramic material that the ships had. After losing *Mobile Bay* and taking hits on three other ships, we had to cease the bombardment and retreat over the horizon, out of the enemy's visual range."

Triumph was simmering as he sat there listening to Admiral Taylor, the newly promoted air wing commander. *Fucking idiots all around me! How can I make the cosmos great with all these losers?* He fought to keep his anger in check.

"So, Admiral, you're telling me that with all our high-tech targeting equipment you couldn't find a bunch of wooden ships in plain sight? How come THEY could hit YOU without having any of this shit?"

Wilkes shifted uncomfortably in his chair. "Well, while our lookouts could see the enemy, there is no longer any way for our naval artillery to be manually aimed. Visual engagement is accomplished with satellites, something we don't have here. The enemy is used to firing by visual identification, and clearly, after fighting this way for over 200 years, they're pretty good at it."

That was the final straw for Triumph. At home he'd be better at self-control, since his daughter was always at his side to keep him from lashing out, but she didn't come on this trip, citing a lack of good nannies.

"We lost what, our one remaining assault ship, three destroyers and almost a thousand men, and all you can do is make ridiculous excuses! Get the fuck out of here—you're all fired! This meeting's over!"

Bamming came over and sat down next to his emperor as the last of the naval officers left the room.

"Take it easy, Vic, this thing's not over. Take out their leader, this puffed-up Wyckham, and the planet's yours."

"So just how do we do that? You got any ideas?" Triumph's depression evaporated at the suggestion of a solution by Bamming, his long-time confidant, the only one who had assured him of victory in 2016 when everyone else said he should drop out. Bamming had also saved him in 2019 when videos from 2011 had surfaced showing him in the check room of the White House Correspondents Dinner urinating on the previous president's overcoat. Bamming's label of "Fake DNA Evidence" had worked and even flipped some independents.

"First, go on Fox and tell everyone back home about the battle we just won. We lost a dozen or so, enemy dead in the thousands, advanced Confederate weaponry and our brave American patriots won the day, your condolences to the families, thoughts and prayers, yaddah yaddah yaddah.

"But the night's big statement is that you are unilaterally calling a ceasefire and offer peace talks. The battle was so one-sided, it was such a slaughter, it really upset you, you wanted to avoid further bloodshed, so you stopped the fighting. You only want two things—you want the opportunity to trade with other planets using Freeport's portals, just like all the other planets, and you demand we get Shillings back. Now, they are not going to give us a fair deal and probably still can't even find our Christian friend, much less persuade him to return to us. But with negotiations proceeding it will be easy for you to get the Brits worked up, they focus on your messaging and don't watch the back door in the real world. We just slip in our submarine with the Seals aboard and grab Wyckham on his way to one of the scheduled peace talks. Then we'll see how tough all these creatures on this planet are without their leader. Bunch of immigrant animals from shithouse planets can't possibly fight against us like the old Brit has. Say what you want about the old man, he's been fighting battles for 200 years and he knows what he's doing.

But the rest of this planet's population doesn't know anything about human beings or how to fight them. After Wyckham's out of the picture, we make a show of force, maybe win a skirmish, they'll make a deal."

Triumph nodded his head in agreement. It would work. Thank God for Bamming, the man's a real saint, and loyal. Aside from that little squabble years ago when he'd had to fire Bamming to appease the Secretary of State, (had to be done), and Bamming got pissed and said some bad things. But when the Confederacy got started and Bamming rejoined him, he'd been invaluable.

Now he just had to prepare a statement for the Fox news cameras declaring the day's fight as a victory. Shouldn't be hard since he'd kept the reporters aboard ship away from the fighting, they'd go with whatever he told them. Bamming had again proved his genius.

"Stan… you… mutha… FUCKA!" Triump yelled as he shoved Bamming like a football player after a touchdown. "Brilliant idea! Brilliant! I'll beat them to the facts and get the lead on this story. Easy. These ancient idiots won't know what hit them. Get Fox News in right here now. I'm know what I'm going to say."

He was right about that, thought Bamming. The man was the master of impromptu facts. "Go get 'em, Emp!" Bamming said as he whipped out his phone. Moments later the quiet conference room exploded in activity as if some omniscient being had pushed a button. First, several navy officers arrived, posing like combat commanders though they were really clerks grabbed from the nearby accounting offices, and lined up behind a seated Triumph. Then a four-man TV crew arrived and set up, ready to broadcast in less than a minute; they'd done this before. Everyone turned to the monitor on the wall which was showing a broadcast from earth, the afternoon Fox News show. The TV screen changed to show Triumph and the accounting clerks.

"Sorry I have to break away, Rush," said the glamorous raven-haired woman on the TV, "but we have to end this interview. Fox News has an exclusive interplanetary message coming in right now from Confederate President Victor Triumph, who is currently on the planet Freeport. Mr. President, good morning. How have things been going up there?"

Triumph was sitting behind the conference table holding a stack of blank papers he'd just picked up off the nearby copy machine, with the solemn officers behind him, everyone looking like they'd just been involved in a very important meeting. "Good morning, Kimberly. On this day I have a major announcement to the world. Americans have just won their first victory in outer space. Only a few hours ago, Confederate forces engaged the aliens who were illegally restricting trade. With our amazing advanced weaponry and the incredible bravery of our warriors, we were able to defeat the ancient zombie colonists and their rapist, murdering, drug-dealing alien allies. My cabinet members will have a news conference in a few hours to give you all the details. But I can tell you that I, Victor Triumph, intervened with our generals and stopped the battle early. I was on the battlefield, directing the fight, and it got to the point where I just couldn't let the slaughter continue. It just wasn't a fair fight, the way we were killing them, and I only fight fair. So I ran in front of our troops, right in the middle of the battle, risking my neck to save our enemies, and commanded our troops to cease fire. I want to give these zombie Brits and their illegal aliens another chance to make a deal and end this war. So now Victor Triumph calls out to the Brits and aliens up here to start peace talks. We only want to trade with other worlds using the space portals, just like they do. Hell, you've given more rights to aliens than us humans! Recently, you even let our enemies here on Earth use it, but not us. This is a disgrace. The Confederate States of America is not being treated fairly.

"Also, I demand that you release President Shillings to us immediately. You say you can't find him, he's gone into hiding—you really expect anyone to believe that?" He slammed the deck for emphasis and raised his voice. "There are only two puny cities on this planet, you have to know where he's at, get him and let him go home to his family and his own country! Period!

He quickly settled down. "So, Captain Wyckham, or governor, or whatever you call yourself, contact us here on the *Spruance*. We'll meet with you anywhere, anytime. Do not make me resume this fight. If you do, make no mistake about what will happen. You will lose this fight, there will be regime change on Freeport, and the cosmos will get a government here that is competent and loyal."

Triumph made a slight nod to the cameraman and the broadcast ended. The navy officers went back to pore over their accounting spreadsheets and Bamming went into discussions with the TV crew.

The Confederate leader sat back, knowing he'd just grabbed the lead in this struggle. Maybe it was time to find a good painter who could portray the victory he'd just made up? He could just visualize it—a panoramic fresco with Victor Triumph in the middle of the battle in San Marco plaza, a smoking M-16 in his hands, one foot on a prostrate Rodney Wyckham, dead aliens everywhere. Something to post in the White House when he conquered the other Americas and returned to Washington. He would have to find a true modern master to do it, a new Norman Rockwell. It had to be really terrific. Probably cost a fortune, but he could have the Victor Triumph Foundation pay for it. Much better than throwing his own money to some loser artist like some idiotic do-gooder billionaires did.

Bamming came over, looking at his phone.

"Snap poll shows your anger over Schillings disappearance went over real big, even with Dems. Keep working that issue."

"Yeah, I got worked up there, didn't I?" He lowered his voice and moved closer to Bamming. "No chance they'll find him, is there? Super hooker has him in a safe place?"

"No fuckin' way," Bamming responded. "She knows every corner in this city and has the big pigs screening her whereabouts off from those Goddam Fireflies. They'll never find him. We get to discover him when we need a push."

The two men slapped each other's backs. Bamming went off to talk to the latest round of fleet captains, while Triumph settled in to watch the discussions about him on Fox.

Sherlock Bahtia and the Case
of the Missing President

VICTORY DINNERS HAD been common in the 19th century Royal Navy, and the tradition had continued here on an even grander scale. Present at this one were all his officers, civil administrators, alien leaders, and the three brave young women. Also present was the American president DiCarpaccio, his military advisors, and, last but not least, British Prime minister Alistair Cochrane. Altogether there were nearly forty attendees packed around a large banquet table that had been set up in *Trinidad's* spacious great cabin.

The last of many courses had been served, the copious toasting was over, and the cigars had gone out. British seamen in white jackets and black breeches (Obujimi had tried using ants but they looked ridiculous in service uniforms) whisked away the last remains of dinner as Wyckham prepared to begin the discussion on the battle and its aftermath (discussing issues was considered impolite during dinner).

The butcher's bill had not been that bad, with only 56 marines and 23 sailors dead, but many were men who had been with Wyckham right from the beginning of this wild adventure, all men whom Wyckham knew well. In addition, 52 civilians (both human and alien) had lost their lives. The wounded tally was in the hundreds, but Slick medical care would make all of them whole again, thanks to mechanical body parts or alien replacement organs. New Venice had been rapidly cleaned up, which wasn't hard, since only the framework for holographic images had been there in the first place. And the Fireflies had quickly gotten the hologram projectors functioning so that the city looked completely back in order.

The enemy had not fared so well. Cannister rounds had killed or wounded over 250 enemy soldiers in the plaza, with another 400 or so prisoners. On top of that, Badoin's ships had achieved remarkable success. With one volley of Greek fire they had sunk four Confederate ships, including the big assault ship *Mobile Bay*, probably causing over two thousand enemy casualties, if DiCarpaccio's staff was to be believed. Proposing a toast to himself earlier, Badoin had bragged about it.

"Everyone say to me, 'Shoot ball, *non* grape,' but I know, zee sea eagle knows, zat ay seengle ball of fire grape weel burn through decks and seenk any sheep. Eenstead of onlee two 'ondread roundshot, my carronades shoot thousands of grape, and we ween zee day!"

The biggest surprise after the fight had been the immediate surge in tourism. Not only had few American tourists canceled their trips, but in a show of solidarity to Freeport, thousands more humans who had heard about Triumph's attack were signing up to visit. Many were even ex-military wanting to join the fight. Triumph's electronic messages may have excited his followers, but they had certainly stirred up his enemies as well.

"Now, gentlem… ahhh, ladies and gentlemen." Wyckham nodded to the three women, "Time to discuss our next move. What will this fellow Triumph do next? With his military forces decimated and humans flocking to Freeport in rejection of his twats, what options… yes, Madam Emily?"

Emmie had interrupted him and whispered in his ear, trying not to burst out laughing. "Ah, I am informed the correct word is 'tweets', Wyckham corrected himself as the three American women snorted in an attempt not to laugh. "Whatever you call them, it seems to me that he has no choice now but to give up and return to Earth. I'm actually surprised he has not done so already. Your thoughts?"

While he had expected DiCarpaccio to be the first to speak, the somewhat inebriated Emmie Bahtia spoke out. "Don't count this guy out. He may be a real jerkoff," she stated nonchalantly as she pumped her fist up and down in a recognizable motion, "but he has able to outmaneuver his enemies again and again."

Emmie's hand sign for masturbation caused Wyckham and other humans to shift uneasily in their seats, but some of the aliens were curious.

"I am puzzled," inquired the Firefly. "Clearly you use this gesture as a negative. Why is that? The giver of spermatozoa receives physical pleasure and others can collect and benefit from such marvelous life energy."

Wyckham, now visibly uncomfortable, interrupted the Firefly before matters got out of hand. "A topic for another time, what?" He turned to Emmie. "Madam Bahtia, please tell us all you know about this man, possibly with no more portrayals of self-satisfaction?"

The intoxicated Emmie couldn't understand what he was upset about but continued. "Triumph is a master at shaping public opinion. You may think Earth has turned against him, since you're seeing such a jump in people coming to Freeport, but I've checked Facebook and Twitter, and millions of people in the American south, midwest, and even around the whole world have been fired up by Triumph's media blitz. On TV and social media, he's pushing angry messages about unfair trading and illegal aliens, and he's getting lots of traction over the alleged kidnapping of President Shillings. And by the way, he's telling all Earth that he won the recent battles here. As a result, not only are thousands of individuals signing up with the Confederacy's armed forces, but the nations of Russia, Prussia, the Philippines, and several countries in Africa, all the ones with brutal despotic rulers, are pledging their armed forces to join the war. Lemme tell you, the last thing you want is these armies arriving on Freeport. Many of their soldiers think God wants them to shoot every alien they can find."

Wyckham addressed DiCarpaccio. "He's assembling more forces to replace his losses here? Have your military men seen evidence of this as well? Any estimate of the numbers and capabilities?"

A clearly embarrassed DiCarpaccio struggled to answer as he quickly scanned the faces of his advisors. None spoke up. "Ah… well, we've picked up some unverified background chatter about Turkish and Russian fleets exiting the Black Sea, but we don't know where they're heading. Understand that Russian hackers took out our surveillance satellites several years ago, and many have not yet been replaced."

Wyckham was puzzled, his mind a bit puzzled from drink as well. "Your scouts need saddle lights? Hell, I just give my scouts good mounts and they always can find the enemy, no matter how dark."

Cochrane shook his head and spoke up. "I suggest you hire this woman here to find out more about the enemy's forces, she seems able to monitor communications from all manner of sources."

He stood up to ask the basic question for the current circumstances. "But let's assume she's correct and Triumph is being reinforced and resupplied thanks to all these people responding to his erroneous claims. How do we respond?"

The Firefly Lady Brashton answered. "We must find and dismantle this new portal that brought this enemy fleet to us before more of their forces use it. Clearly the Dreash are involved. I will employ all the animal resources on this world, especially the whales and dolphins, to help us locate the enemy's fleet and their portal. We will start at the bay where the Confederate fleet first arrived. We must assume that the portal controls will be well hidden and protected. Once found I will bring you a tactical assessment for its destruction."

"Thank you, Firefly Brashton," said Wyckham. "Let's hope you can keep the foe's reinforcements from coming to Freeport." He turned to rest of the room. "For our part, we will continue to fight the New Confederate forces over every step. Other than that, I don't know what else we can promise."

"You need to hit back on social media" It was the American Emmie Bahtia again. "So far Jerkoff's false claims have gotten resonance since there's no one disputing them. We need to counter every text and tweet. First, I'll post videos of the recent battles showing what really happened. I'm sure I can find videos the tourists made. My friends and I will Google our brains out, and we'll also start canvassing people in San Marco's restaurants and clubs as soon as they're back open.

"Also, we've got to diffuse the 'Kidnapped Shillings' issue. More than Triumph's battle claims, which even his followers mistrust, the statements about Freeport abducting the president of the Midwest are gaining traction. We need to find Shillings as soon as possible and return him to Earth."

"I have no idea what 'posting videos' encompasses exactly," stated Wyckham to the entire party, "and 'Googling' sounds dangerous. But I feel quite confident relegating these tasks to this capable American woman and her friends." Turning to Emmie, he continued, "And if I might, I would ask you to help us find Shillings. You can pose as a tourist and go to the shadier areas of Venice where few will speak to our marines. Go to the smaller canals where the brothels are, work the longshoremen's bars and restaurants, keep your eyes wide for any information concerning this president. Last we saw of him, he'd gone ass-over-tit for Tracy Brashton and went off with her. Our marines have searched for him everywhere in New Venice but couldn't find him nor Lady Brashton. Every time they found one of her secret brothels it was deserted, despite signs of recent occupation. Obviously, they have lookouts and devices that warn them if we get near. We need someone who can blend into every neighborhood. You can, posing as a wandering tourist.

"We will pay for your efforts. I assume payment in gold would be acceptable? Where's Thomas? I'll have him draw up a contract for your fee."

Wickham turned and almost bumped into Obujimi, already at his side with a blank parchment in one hand and an inked quill in the other.

"Would a daily rate of one pound of 24 carat gold per day be acceptable?" the imposing African asked.

Emmie's heart was thumping so hard she hadn't even heard the offer. All her life she'd been a big Sherlock Holmes fan. She'd read all Sir Alfred Conan Doyle's books and seen both the old and new movies about the world's foremost consulting detective. And now she'd get to work on a mystery in one of history's most mysterious cities!

Wyckham interpreted her momentary delay in responding as a lack of interest. "Alright, how about two pounds per day?"

That got her attention. *Two pounds of almost pure gold per day? Shit, wasn't gold at two thousand an ounce? And I get to play Sherlock Holmes?* "Damn right that would be acceptable!" She turned to Connie and Van.

"Baker street irregulars! The game is afoot!"

* * *

Three days later found Emmie in the Cannaregio district along the Rio de la Muneghete. It was not one of Venice's nicer canals. The buildings had few windows to light up the foggy night and the area even smelled worse than the rest of the city, which in Venice was really saying something—did they really have to replicate medieval Venice's odor when they built this place? And even the canal's name sounded nasty—Google wouldn't translate it.

Emmie had already been in several of the canal's taverns and none had any human tourists, just aliens. And not the smiling corporate types that served tourists in San Marco, but an array of scaly, slimy creatures fresh out of the new "Doom 12". When New Venice opened, all the criminal elements across the bay in Port Wyckham, mostly those involved in smuggling and all its related nefarious activities, had moved into this remote district of the new city, where it was easier to hide from competitors' muscle, upset customers and Obujimi's agents.

However, they didn't scare Emmie. After the battle in San Marco, Emmie Bahtia felt ready for anything. The hanger at her side, the weapon she'd shown herself that she could handle, gave her the confidence to deal with anything in this bizarre city. While all weapons were banned from New Venice, the city council not only gave her special permission to carry the small sword she'd just used so heroically in the recent battle, but they even had the city armory sharpen it. With its rigid screening at its portal, Freeport had been remarkably successful in keeping weapons off the planet, so Emmie was better armed than everyone on the entire world other than the military. Fingering the leather grip, it was with a sense of confident caution that Emmie descended from the *fondamente*, down a short stairway and into a basement establishment, passing under a wooden sign proclaiming "il Contrabandieri"—the Smuggler's Den.

Yesterday, Emmie and her two friends had uncovered much useful material. The three of them had returned to the quickly repaired Lady Brashton's dance club, packed with new tourists that had arrived in a show of support for Freeport, and in just an hour spent mingling at the bars, they'd found several American tourists who had videos of the San Marco battle and were happy to share them with the three fellow Americans. One of them even had a video interview of a captured Confederate marine.

"Yeah, we just got our asses kicked pretty damn good," the wavy-haired twenty-something Texan said. "I gotta say those old English guys n' their outta-space buddies could fight, that's fer sure. But Triumph said he was right 'n the thick of it? Buncha hot air. Big gasbag never left his fancy-ass ship's cabin."

Emmie and her friends had sent about a dozen videos to CNN, CBS, NBC, ABC, and even Fox News, though they didn't expect that station to air it. But within minutes of posting, the video of the Confederate marine had gone viral.

As for President Shillings, the three had split up and started looking for clues in the many taverns, but nothing had turned up yet. It was now late evening of a long Freeport night, and Emmie was mentally and physically drained. The adrenaline from the battle had gotten her through the past two days, but now it was gone. This day had been a long one, talking to dozens of chatty bartenders and random aliens, but she hadn't even turned up a rumor concerning Shillings's whereabouts.

She got to the bottom of the steps but stopped. Maybe it was time to just bag it and get back to her apartment for a good night's sleep? Try again another day? But then she thought of Sherlock Holmes. He often went sleepless for days, investigating every lead, until he solved the case. She just took a deep breath, slapped her cheeks to wake up, and took the last steps down to the cellar's door.

The tired fencer entered a stone room lined with alcoves and the typical vaulted ceiling common in medieval construction. The main room was not only dark but smoky from pipes and small cigars. What the hell it was that they were smoking, Emmie had no idea, but it sure did stink. Every alcove had aliens that eyed her suspiciously, clearly not interested in talking to any strangers. And for Emmie, most had at least one deal breaker for engaging in conversation, such as facial tentacles or foot-long drool. A lot them weren't wearing translators, either, so she couldn't talk with them anyway. But she had to try.

"Hey there handsome, buy you a drink?" she asked the first one as she headed down the bar.

The troll-like creature staring at Emmie with his one bulging eye hawked up a green ball of phlegm the size of a grapefruit and spat it at her feet.

"OK, I'll take that as a 'no'. Thanks so much for that lovely response, made my day." She approached a booth in an alcove. "How about you guys? How we doin' tonight? You come here often?"

The two aliens she was addressing, one a snowman-like thing made of featureless stone balls, the other a giant made of buzzing bees in a human-shaped swarm, stopped their conversation to stare for a second at the annoying tourist. The stone guy swiveled his round head around, looking at her from dark holes that made up its soulless eyes, while the thousands of bees making up the second alien stopped their buzzing and turned to look at her. The entire tavern was then rocked by a blast of a million bees farting. The two turned away and resumed their animated discussion. *Strike two. But one hell of an impressive rejection.*

Well, there was always the bartender, in this case one of the blind gorillas who used their empty eye sockets as sound amplifiers. And he was even wearing a translator. Emmie leaned on the bar and ordered a Sailor's Slam, now her favorite drink. There was a green lizard-woman at the end of the bar (Emmie knew it was a female from her eight-breast décolletage), shouting in a strange hissing language at the bartender.

"What's her problem?" Emmie asked the gorilla as placed the bright blue concoction in front of her. "You run a clean place, no bugs for her to eat?"

Noticing the pile of Wycks, Freeport's printed currency, that Emmie had placed on the bar, the big furry alien gave her a ragged smile and responded through his translator. The device had seen better days and sounded scratchy, but Emmie was able to understand the ape's English. "She courtesan, comes here a lot, works in brothel across the rio. Wants drink but no money."

Emmie nodded, downed her drink, left a few Wycks and headed for the door, the lizard woman still yelling. This place was just too scary, and no one would talk to her anyway. Maybe to smugglers, but not to her. It was time to call it a day.

As she reached the door, she heard the green reptile right in the middle of haranguing the bartender hiss the word "Shillingsss". Without pausing, Emmie turned right around and returned to the bar, cozying up alongside the fuming lizard.

"Get her whatever she wants," Emmie told the barkeep as she put the pile of Wycks back on the bar. "And tell her my name is Emmie from Earth and I think she is so awesome."

With his long arms, it only took a few seconds for the simian to whip up a complex red concoction requiring several liquids and powders, topped off with a live beetle skewered on a little plastic sword. Fuck, it looked like it had enough alcohol and drugs in it to kill one of the local Triceratops. The lizard woman took the tall glass in her claws, held it up in front of her, then out snapped her tongue and the beetle was gone. The drink was gone a moment later and she pushed the glass back to the barman, in her slurred language clearly asking for another. She didn't even acknowledge Emmie's presence.

"Sure, make another," said Emmie to the big ape, while smiling at the lizard woman who had no idea what she was saying. "Just make it virgin, you know what I mean? No alcohol or drugs or anything that might affect her ability to talk, you got that? Don't think she'll notice, do you? And hand it to me," she said while she kept up the smiling and nodding.

She had a lead! Emmie had plenty of experience with drunks and junkies on the streets of San Francisco and was going to work this one for info.

She took delivery of the second drink, smiling at the slumping lizard, and spoke to the bartender. "So, tell her I'm interested in getting brothel work, I want to hear about her clients." She gave the lizard her warmest smile.

The gorilla translated Emmie's message into her hissing language and the lizard perked up, babbling and showing Emmie a haughty smile, then arching her back in a glamourous pose that didn't really work for a shitfaced lizard. The bartender's translator sputtered to life again.

"She laughs at you, says you would not be successful. Who would pay to mount a female with only two breasts, she say? You will never be like her, Vanessa, Queen of Lizards. She makes more than any courtesan in Venice. Says your race especially goes wild for her."

"You're Vanessa? The famous Vanessa? Tell her I had no idea. Isn't she President Shillings's favorite?"

The gorilla translated. Vanessa got off her barstool and stood up like she was modeling a beautiful outfit instead of a ragged shift with most of her eight breasts hanging out, nodding knowingly at the American. She took the drink from Emmie's outstretched hand and swirled along the bar as she rambled on in a "faux salon" voice.

"She say yes, she Shillings's favorite. Many women try to win him from her but he always return because she so beautiful, such great dancer, wears most beautiful dresses, blah blah, more nonsense..."

Emmie's long shot question had struck gold! She'd found Shillings!

"Could you take me to work? I would like to... ah... learn how to be a courtesan. I'd especially like to talk with President Shillings to learn what such an important man likes from a whore. Shit, no, courtesan—from a courtesan."

Vanessa shook her head slightly as she responded to the gorilla's translation. "She say no, she no longer welcome there, they falsely accuse her of skimming life units, she get angry, breaks things, mean Madam throw her out."

Shit! So close! "The great Vanessa, thrown out? Outrageous! I'll go set that woman straight! I'm friends with Governor Wyckham, I gotta lotta juice around here! Just give me her name and address."

But the drinking and dancing around had taken its toll on Vanessa. She muttered a few words, collapsed back onto her stool, put her head on the bar and passed out.

Shit! What were those last words? Did she get it out? She turned inquiringly to the bartender.

"She say brothel underneath wine shop at end of *fondamente*. Madam is human Tracy Brashton—the Baroness."

The woman who went off with Shillings the day he arrived! Obujimi had been looking for her for months, without success. Originally courted by Rodney Wyckham, she had instead married a baron in 1812, a young girl excited by money, status, and the intrigues of the salon. She had come to Freeport in 1815 but stayed behind when her husband left, hoping to snare Wyckham, the Governor of an entire planet, rather than stay with a mere baron, and a baron with no future after Wyckham defeated his efforts to colonize Freeport. Quickly rejected, she had opened up a brothel for both humans and aliens, which soon developed into a cosmos-wide chain of such establishments, harvesting the life units in sperm cells and selling them to almost every planet. But while on the day Shillings arrived she had taken the injured president to the Slick medical facility, it was a group of humans that had picked him up when he was discharged, and she seemed innocent in his disappearance. In the course of Wyckham's seven-month search for Shillings, no evidence against Lady Brashton had turned up. With her far-reaching business, she had forged relationships with powerful local factions on both Freeport and other planets and no one had even come forward to reveal her whereabouts, much less accuse her of anything.

But now a location had come up! The intergalactic brothel titan had the missing president hidden in one of her establishments. And did she know the humans who had taken Schillings from the hospital? Was she working with them? From what she'd heard about Baroness Brashton, she'd work with anyone who could increase her power and fame.

Emmie dashed up the stairs and started running down the walkway along the canal. The cool air was welcome after the smoky atmosphere in the Smuggler's Den, and it brought Emmie back to her senses enough that she stopped running. *Shit—slow down, girl!* She didn't want to draw any attention. Brothels had to have lookouts that would shut the place down if anything looked funny. And a human tourist, here in the shitty side of town, running like hell towards a brothel, with a sword at her waist? That would certainly be cause for concern if you were harboring a kidnapped diplomat.

What would Holmes do in this situation? The answer hit Emmie immediately. He'd put on some brilliant disguise whenever he had to slip into a lion's den. And what was sitting on the *fondamente* right in front of her but a personal holographic image projector—a changing station! She went inside, touched the screen to activate it, and entered "At the Oscars" in the search box. She emerged a minute later fully made up, bejeweled, and clad in a sleek red evening gown. The silk roses that angled across the dress from shoulder to ankle did an excellent job of concealing her sword.

Another five minutes of walking brought her to a little plaza at the end of the canal and its *fondamente* sidewalk, with no sight of anything that looked like the entrance to a brothel. What the hell was she looking for anyway? A building with a red candle? She'd just have to hang around here for a while, try to figure out which ancient building in the piazza was one of Lady Brashton's establishments. Emmie pretended to be a wandering tourist checking out the view of the rio, then slowly turned to study a small bridge that spanned the canal. *Wow, no railings on the bridge. Guess this planet doesn't have lawyers.*

Across the tiny plaza was the wine shop, doing brisk business with both humans and aliens. Ahah! Three British sailors were milling about, making boisterous comments. Now did these humans come all the way out here just to buy a few bottles of wine? Sherlock Emmie turned away to study the canal again but kept her ears open. When the Brits' chatter suddenly fell off, Emmie knew they were walking away and turned to watch them, just in time to see them approach the warehouse next door. The big double-doored cartage gate had a small personnel door cut into one side. One sailor stepped up to the little door, grabbed the brass doorknocker and gave it a long, complicated knock. Emmie counted—one, eight, one, four. *1814!* The year Wyckham came to this planet! A little viewing slot popped open, someone or something inside checked out the two sailors, the small personnel door opened, and the two humans went inside.

Emmie waited a few minutes and then approached the door. She paused for a moment—time to get in character. She reviewed her quickly devised lines, decided she was ready, and grabbed the door knocker. Repeating the 1-8-1-4 knock brought a pair of bloodshot eyes with diamond-shaped pupils to the little viewing window. The guard must have liked what it saw, since the door opened before Emmie could blurt out her just-concocted introduction.

But relief turned to revulsion as the door guard was revealed to be one of the snakeman, his head as big as a human's, flicking out his nasty forked tongue to give Emmie a sniff. She had read about the alien snakemen on Freeport's website, but this was the first one Emmie had seen. They were essentially giant snakes that slithered about upright, though they did have two tiny arms. They fancied themselves corsairs and wore pirate vests that looked ridiculous on their serpentine bodies. While they were allowed use the planet's transporters for trade, they weren't liked or trusted by other alien races, suspected of both weapons smuggling and conspiring with the Dreash. They were the only race that did not hold any positions in Freeport's diverse government. Clearly Obujim's agents did not know about this place.

The snakeman slithered up into Emmie's face and gave her a once-over. His eyes widened like he'd just won the powerball. His translator hissed suggestively. "What do you wishhhh?"

She forced herself to smile at this slimy POS. "Well hello there, big fella! Ah'm Bridgette, ah'm from Texas, and ah am ready, willing, and able to take over this place! Ever since ah heard about Lady Braston's, ah been dreaming about working here! Ah will bring in the best clients and ya'll's business will double! Ah was the hottest gal in the whole Dallas-Fort Worth metro and I'll be the hottest gal on this 'ere en-tire planet!"

The bouncer's eyes narrowed at her response and his tail started to coil up on the floor. "You heard about thisss place? Nobody just hears about thisss place." The frightening serpent moved his face up to hers. "You must tell me how you just heard about usss?"

"This friend of mine, Abigail? Well she found a video on her husband's phone? It showed him, right here, in one of your rooms, gettin' it on with a eight-breasted lizard? Now understandably she was pissed, put it on Facebook, got a dee-vorce with a tee-riffic settlement, jury said they'd never seen the video but y'all know they had. Ah sawed the video, he'd videoed th' outside, too, it showed me how to git here. An' here ah am! Yee-hah!" Emmie finished with a poke to the reptile's body. Yuch! Its skin was greasy as a grimy frying pan.

Before the big reptile could stop her, she walked inside and descended a stone stairway down to a small entrance hall that was filled with Persian rugs, gaudy Louis 14th furniture, heads of unrecognizable animals on the walls, and large jungle plants in the corners. Some of which were even moving! *Jesus!* Keeping a wide distance from the plants, she came to the entrance of a ballroom, filled with light, strange music and the background hum of a dozen alien tongues. The doorman, now more relaxed, motioned her ahead.

"And it's even more bee-yootiful than ah ever thought possible! Ah am done with all them new hotels in Houston and they-ah borin' billionaires, who cares 'bout they-ah stupid 'awl fields? Ah wonna have some worldy 'speriences, diff'rent cliants, exsatin' cliants, an' lord ah 'spect y'all got 'em here!" she stated as a creature that appeared to be a branch with giant seed pods passed her on its way out the door. Ignoring the hesitant snakeman, Emmie reached the next room's entrance, entered what appeared to be the main salon and looked around.

Sulieman the Magnificent's harem meets Star Wars. A menagerie of courtesans was lounging about, clad in all sorts of suggestive outfits designed for humans that looked absurd on aliens. She tried to keep babbling without any visible reaction to the alien sex workers, but it was hard. Not only were their gross faces right out of a low-budget horror film, but the various appendages these creatures were seductively waving around—in front of her were nothing but tentacles, claws, fins, suction cups,—were certainly not designed for anything amorous. *Em! Get back in character!* "An' land sakes alive, look'it all the… ah… stunnin' gals ah'm gonna be competin' with? Is that OK to call 'em gals? None o' that silly PC stuff here, raht?"

The snakemen just smiled at her with a "I'll have some fun with this one" look. Emmie had to prompt him. "Ya'll gonna show me aroun'? Maybe see the rooms, meet some clients?"

"Yes, of course, mademoiselle", it hissed with barely disguised malevolence. "Let me show you around Lady Brashton'sss, the most famous house in the cosmosss."

He led her through the main salon and down a hallway, nodding at another snakeman posted at the hallway entrance. The first door was open and the two entered a spacious suite. One side had a cheery fire crackling in a freestanding Swedish fireplace, the opposite wall had a miniature waterfall falling into a meandering stream lined with bonsai trees. "This suite isss for humans, our best customersss." He touched a dial on the wall and the room instantly transformed into a nighttime desert scene, with friendly prairie dogs running around and a sky filled with stars that rivaled San Francisco's planetarium. Emmie saw the opening she'd been looking for.

"Humans? Ya'll got impawtant men clients? Now ah mean real men, men from Earth? Ah don' think ah could… ahh… properly entertain clients what look lahk monsters? How's would ah know wheah theyah thingies are? An' ah'm int'rested in impawtant men, men what's good to know? You got any congressmen, senatahs,… maybe even a president?"

The snakemenman's smile disappeared and it edged closer to Emmie, getting in her face again. "Now why would you asssk such a question, mademoiselle? Sex workers care only about the size of clients' pursesss. But maybe you're not a sex worker? Maybe you are lying to me? Maybe you are one of Obujimi's agentsss? Or an employee of an American information company?"

Oh shit. Emmie was tired and had just made a real dumb mistake. *What had she been thinking, asking a security guard about presidents? This snakeman wasn't just some bouncer.*

The snakeman's tail coiled up underneath him as he opened his jaws and prepared to spring. *Emmie, you are truly and completely fucked.*

Just then the door across from them opened and who walks out but Lady Brashton herself. Emmie recognized the face from all the TV commercials that Lady Brashton's Club ran on west coast TV, in which she posed in outrageous outfits promoting her New Venice nightclub. Here she was, dressed in modern business attire but carrying something unusual—a bejeweled riding crop with nasty-looking barbs down its sides.

And right there through the open-door Emmie saw the man she'd been looking for—Mark Shillings himself! He was seated on a couch with what looked like the San Diego Zoo all around him. Most puzzling was the array of buzzing devices right next to his bed, with hoses running all over the place. Was it medical equipment? Shillings certainly didn't look sick. As a matter of fact, while Emmie was not an expert on the subject, he appeared to be having an orgasm right now! Probably thanks to the ministrations of a big pink squid on his lap, all made up with lipstick and finger-long fake eyelashes on its huge eyes, its tentacles whirling all over Shillings's body.

Lady Brashton gave Emmie an angry look and slammed the door behind her. "Who the fuck is this?"

"She said she wantsss work, but now I think she already has a job," the serpentine bouncer answered. "Like working for an information company from earth? Are you wearing a recording device, lying human?"

The big snakemen moved right into Emmie and pinned her against the wall, its long tongue flicking out, looking for the scent of anything that could record images or sounds. Just as Emmie thought she'd passed inspection, the snakemen's body bumped into her sword and the scabbard peaked out from her holographic dress.

Only assassins or Obujimi's agents carried swords in New Venice, and both were hostile to Lady Brashton's business interests. "She's armed!" the baroness yelled. "Kill her!"

The reptile drew its head back, coiled its body, and lunged at Emmie, nasty three-inch fangs bared in its wide-open mouth. Emmie spun right and the snakemen missed, its head disappearing into the holographic wall. It only took a split second for it to pull back for another strike, but that was all the time Emmie needed to reach across her body, pull the hanger from its scabbard and continue upward into a hard-backhand cut, slashing across the beast's exposed neck. The blow severed the snakemen's spinal cord and it plopped down at her feet, a puzzled look on its face. *Jesus, they sure did sharpen this blade!*

Lady Brashton was already gone, halfway to the salon, her exit covered by the second snakemen who was slithering quickly down the hallway toward Emmie. It cocked its head to strike at Emmie, but she beat him to the punch with an extension in high *Quinte* pushed out by a full lunge, getting her point right into the creature's open maw. Emmie just held her lunge as the committed serpent sprung at her, only to impale its head onto her extended blade.

Commotion behind her alerted her to another threat. A quick glance over her shoulder revealed three more snakemen rushing towards her from the other end of the hallway. *Time to get the fuck outta Dodge!* Emmie yanked her blade out of the second snakemen's head and took off for the front door. Amazingly, the first snakeman, though paralyzed from the neck down, tried to bite her as she passed, flapping its jaws like those toy wind-up dentures. Without losing a stride, Emmie planted her left foot on the floor, kicked hard with the right, and booted the offending head down the hall, with its body flapping around behind it. Adding a little incremental punishment, she made sure to stomp her right heel right between its eyes as she passed by.

She flew through the salon without a glance. Fortunately, none of the aliens lounging in the salon seemed concerned by someone running by all covered in blood, (probably not an uncommon event in this establishment), and without further delay Emmie was able to make it up the stairs and out to the *fondamente.* Where she didn't stop running until she got to the safety of San Marco plaza.

The Artful Dealer—Rodney Wyckham

ND ALL THESE spacemen at the table, some of them were like, drooling, I swear to God one even farted so loud it shook the furniture. Reminded me of the circus in Madison Square Garden when I was a kid back in New York City." Triumph waved his hand and shook his head. "Of course I don't go there anymore, the city's a horde of liberal snowflakes. But back to these aliens at the meeting, their females were even begging to hook up with me—like I'd be interested? I've seen better looking females on 'The Walking Dead'." That got a laugh out of the television crew. Triumph let the laughter die down and resumed.

"But I had an outstanding meeting. I made it clear that if the Zombies don't return President Shillings to his wife and family, they will face fire and fury such as the world, and I mean any world, has ever seen. I also gave them a list of my demands for interplanetary trade and technology transfers to earth, they've got a rigged system up here, it's unfair, they trade with the American coastal states but cut out the working families in the heartlands, the ones that are making America grand again. The fossil Brits and their illegally acting aliens say they are going to consider our offers and get back to us tomorrow. It's a good deal, it's a fair deal, let's hope they're smart enough to take it."

Fortunately for Wyckham, he had agreed not to wear his sword at his meeting, or he would have thrust it through Triumph's gut right now. Wyckham had not wanted to appear with the American leader, but DiCarpaccio had persuaded him to do it, saying that he needed to "push his brand." Wyckham wasn't sure what that meant, but he had accepted the Pacific president's advice, and here he was, getting insulted and humiliated in front of millions on Earth.

But then this Narcissus, convinced that his plotting had won the day, gave Wyckham the opening to use his own mass communication service against the pompous *poseur*.

"Governor Wyckham, anything you'd like to say to Earth? You use my own TV coverage. Unlike you and your aliens, I fight fair and give my opponents the opportunity to explain their beliefs, no matter how flawed. Here, step up to the mike."

At first Wyckham froze. How did one address millions of people?

Triumph jumped at the opportunity to demean Wyckham further.

"You okay, old man? You paralyzed? Too old to walk when you're stressed?" He looked at the transmitting crew and smiled knowingly, then back at Wyckham. "OK, I'll help help you, guide you through this." Triumph extended his hand. "Just take my deal. Shake on it and this war is over.

The additional slurs woke Wyckham up from his momentary reverie and he stepped up to the sound-recorder on its stand. Avoiding the American's hand like it was poxed, he faced the picture devices.

"Thank you, I actually do have a reply." Wyckham started pulling off his right glove at his small finger. Wykham's hands were heavily calloused from 200 years climbing ships' rigging and hauling ropes, and he'd always worn white calfskin gloves at formal events after his snobbish, arrogant father once referred to him as "Our family's common laborer".

He continued pulling the glove off as he started speaking.

"President Triumph here has made up lies, falsely slandering me, my government and the residents of Freeport." Off came the glove's fourth finger. "Here on Freeport, and on Earth when I left it, immoral and boorish behavior is simply not tolerated among decent people." He grabbed the middle finger. "So I demand satisfaction". With a sudden final tug, Wyckham whipped the white glove off the remaining fingers and right across Triumph's cheek. The American was momentarily astonished, then responded by throwing a punch at Wyckham's face. Wyckham effortlessly caught the blow in his left hand like he was catching a child's ball, the seasoned captain's hands capable of holding onto wet ropes in a full gale and his joints strengthened in several surgeries by the technically advanced Slicks.

"And the choice of weapons is yours," Wyckham continued softly, slowly pushing Triumph's hand down.

"That's it!" yelled Triumph. "Take him!" Triumph's uniformed military guards reacted immediately. A big one got a headlock on Wyckham and pulled him away. He was quickly joined by a dozen other guards, several more pushing the resisting governor while others pulled pistols and crouched in a protective line. But then five of the big mudmen rolled to a stop in front of them, bringing the abduction to a sudden halt.

"Would any of you gentlemen care for a bath?" It was Obujimi, appearing from nowhere, standing there in a white suit and ruffled cravat, with his hands clasped in front of him like a butler. "I can offer you a trip inside a ball of mud to our famous lagoon, which is a delightful mix of festering food scraps, transmittable diseases and fecal matter. If you do not fancy such a toilet, I suggest you remove your hands from Governor Wyckham—immediately."

One look at the mudmen and the guards released their captive, holding their hands in the air as they backed away. They had all seen the videos of mudmen absorbing Triumph's security guard and spitting them into the lagoon during the San Marco riot months ago.

Wyckham spoke as if nothing had happened. "May I present my second, Thomas Obujimi? You may arrange details with him, but I insist on dawn tomorrow." With that, Wyckham shot his cuffs and headed to the palace, with Obujimi at his side, his hand on his sword and walking backwards so he could keep an eye on the President's guards.

Immediately upon entering the office, Obujimi went to the sideboard and poured Wyckham a whiskey. Just as he finished, British Prime Minister Cochrane entered, shaking his head, clearly bewildered, and asked Obujimi "Sir, if you would, a stiff one for me as well? Trying to abduct a leader at a negotiation! That man can drive anyone to drink."

"Driven to drink? I suspect you docked at that port a while ago," observed a smiling Wyckham. "You know, your ancestor Thomas refused to suffer fools as well. Probably before he was in britches."

Still too shocked to comment, Cochrane downed his drink in one gulp and held his glass out for a refill.

Within a few minutes, all of Wyckham's governing council had arrived, along with DiCarpaccio, his advisors, the planet's alien leaders, and the three young American women. Most of them also made for the sideboard, feeling a sudden need for strong drink as well. Finally, everyone was seated and Wyckham spoke.

"So first of all, I have one question for those of you from Earth who are familiar with my antagonist. Just answer one question—has he ever been in a duel or personally fought in a war?"

"No, he hasn't," answered DiCarpaccio. "We no longer fight duels on Earth, and Victor Triumph avoided martial service with a spurious claim of bad feet."

"Spurious? How could you doubt the veracity of your fellow American president?" jibed Cochrane. "His poor feet are all chewed up from putting them in his mouth his entire life."

"Well I don't care what weapons he chooses," remarked Wyckham. "I looked him straight in the eye and I saw no steel in his spine. I doubt he'll show up tomorrow. If he does, I'll just take a few practice shots with whatever he hands me and I'll be ready, though I expect that will scare him away. After 200 years of fighting the Dreash, I'm reasonably handy with anything that shoots."

"I agree that he probably won't show," stated DiCarpaccio. "He certainly didn't say so, and like all bullies he avoids fair fights. But you can bet he'll be fighting you viciously in the media. That's his preferred weapon and he's quite good at it. And each outrageous post he makes brings more recruits and military assets coming through their transporter to join their fleet.

"Though I think you just scored a few points out there. Made him look weak, and that's something that hurts his image of 'Victorious Victor'—he constantly talks about his 'wins'. But he'll surely bring up Shillings again and again. Polls show that the issue of the missing Midwest President still works for him. You need to find Shillings and get him back to earth."

"Yes, I know. We almost had the randy old boy just yesterday", commented Wyckham with a shake of his head. "Our new agent, Mademoiselle Bahtia here," he made a short bow to Emmie, "actually found him in a Cannaregio brothel, apparently having one hell of a time. The place was full of snakemen and run by the international madam herself, the dream woman of my youth, Baroness Brashton. But Emmie here was discovered and had to flee for her life. When she reached San Marco and told us her story, we assembled a marine company and got back there within minutes, but we were still too late. By the time we got there it was an empty warehouse, covered in dust and cobwebs. Looked like it hadn't been used in years, but of course it had all been holo-graphs, they could have left and changed its appearance in a single minute. So, our search must start again from the beginning. However, with our American sleuth here back on the case, I have confidence she will once again find our man."

"Well, until then we will be forced to fight him in social media," said DiCarpaccio, "where he'll be a tough opponent. I suggest Ms. Bahtia's friends continue to find and post true eyewitness accounts of the recent fight while she continues the search for Mr. Shillings. With her proven undercover abilities, she can blend into the tourist population and find our man."

Emmie nodded acceptance. "Sure! Love it!"

"And I will accompany her for communication and her own protection," stated the head firefly in her usual form of a young Lady Brashton. "While I would remain unseen for the most part, should the courageous young American get in a dangerous situation, I can immediately appear in whatever form that might settle things."

Wow! I'm going to be accompanied by an alien leader with almost magical powers! Emmie's concerns for her own security dropped to zero. This alien could do just about anything.

"Awesome!" I'm honored to have such a wonderful… ah… female being to watch over me."

"We should be assured of the success of your mission with such a capable guardian," commented Cochrane, "but meanwhile we must consider our military options should the Confederacy resume hostilities. Above all, we must begin the effort to find their transporter and take it out. If Triumph gets enough reinforcements he will certainly renege on any agreement and attack."

"Sounds like a job for our native leader Prince Dreashpalone here, whose name translates to 'Dreash killer'," Wyckham said as he turned to the tattooed bronze native. "Might I impose upon you to organize a search with your well-mounted tribesmen? I suggest you start with a thorough investigation of the shoreline around their bay."

The loincloth-clad native nodded acceptance. "Without delay, o' conquerer of the Dreash." Dreashpalone's tribe loved Wyckham like a god ever since the British had taken over the planet from the hated Dreash, which freed his people to return to their ancestral homes along the coasts. "I leave now to start the search." He stood up and ran out, making a chirping sound to call his mount, one of the Triceratops that his people had domesticated.

"I will send some of my race with him," added the Firefly. "They will communicate with the local flora and fauna which must surely be aware of this transporter's location."

"I'll go with him as well," said Jamison. "I spent a week exploring that area, there are some caves there that would be ideal for sheltering a transporter. Saw some signs of Dreash there, too." Jamison was an experienced explorer, perfect for the task.

"Capital idea, no better man for the job," stated Wyckham. "But for God's sake take a horse from the stable." Wyckham had appropriated cavalry mounts from the British force that had invaded Freeport two centuries ago and had bred some magnificent riding stock. "Just not right for a council member to go riding off on a big ugly Dinosaurus."

"Well, as you know I've never put much truck in looking British proper," commented the American frontiersman as he left the hall. "And those big bird-lizards make much better time through the forest country where we're going. They don't have to go around anything. And I've trained one, 'Tootsie', she'll be mighty handy in a scrap. So thank you, but I'll take my own mount." He left with Dreashpalone and the firefly, leaving Wyckham and Obujimi with slight frowns on their faces.

The council then settled down to the details of assembling a stand-by mobile force for an attack on the transporter once it was located. It would consist of two hundred sailors, a hundred marines and thirty guns, again using whales to carry the force into battle. An hour later the meeting was adjourned and everyone headed out for their assigned tasks. DiCarpaccio walked up to Wyckham with a final suggestion.

"If he does show up for the duel, it would be best if you just wounded him. Killing him would make him a martyr, galvanize his supporters, and both you and I would have even more shit to deal with."

DiCarpaccio walked off as Cochrane came to Wyckham's side.

"Don't listen to him. American naivete'. You get the chance, you put one in his head".

Back on the Case

EMMIE LEFT THE Doge's palace with her Firefly escort and emerged into the bright light of Freeport's two suns. The always-crowded San Marco plaza was filled not only with tourists but also with four snaking lines of men and women leading to makeshift tables manned by red-coated British marines.

"So what's going on there?" Emmie asked herself aloud.

The holographic Lady Brashton seemed to concentrate for a moment, then answered, "Those are volunteers from the American coasts, signing up to fight for Freeport. I have monitored their memories, they are mostly military veterans. I expect they will be every effective fighters, despite the unfamiliar weapons they must learn to use."

Jesus, this alien made of pure energy had just read minds from fifty feet away. She must have read all the embarrassing memories of Emmie's own past as well. Even that time back in college when she took a shit in that asshole's bed after he'd posted she was a bad lay? *Shit!*

"Any idea where to start?" asked Emmie, trying not to think of other instances from her wild past that were now in the head of a mind-reading alien wired up to millions of others.

A commotion to her right got her attention. The leader of the planet's ants, Worker Queen, had also left the meeting and been met by an agitated group of her own kind, their antennae whirling in excitement. The queen noticed Emmie and the Firefly and quickly rambled over, her six legs churning like a military robot.

"Diggers working on ant city below ground," she said through her translator. "Find large spaces under Arsenale filled with humans. Maybe Shillings there. You investigate now." That done, she immediately took off at a brisk pace towards the southeast of the city. Ants believed in activity more than discourse.

The Arsenale had been the shipyard where medieval Venice had built its fleet of war galleys, and it had been faithfully reconstructed here. Dry dock pits were dug out to build ships which could be flooded to release the completed galleys. If no ships were under construction, wooden covers were placed over the pits. If someone wanted a large hidden space to do something illegal in New Venice, the Arsenale would be perfect.

In a remarkable instance of dialog for an ant, the queen continued explaining as they rapidly crossed the square. "Diggers were enlarging ant quarters, come upon big rooms. Many human males connected to machines run by snakemen".

Connected to machines? Just like Shillings was at the brothel! "Did they see your digger ants?" asked Emmie. If they did, the facility would be quickly abandoned just like the one in Cannaregio was.

The queen waved her antennae and her ants responded the same way. "Workers say no. They observe through small hole, did not enter facility."

"Then let's beat feet over there and take a look," responded Emmie. "If Shillings is there, we try to sneak him out. No waiting for marines, I'm sure they have sentries posted that would see them coming. We need to sneak in there, get him out, then call in the troops."

With the Arsenale not yet in view, the digger ants led them into a warehouse and down a stairway to the entrance of a freshly dug tunnel. Surprisingly, the tips of the digger ants' antennae lit up like LED's and they were able to continue through the winding tunnel at the same brisk pace. After about a hundred yards, the leading ants stopped to communicate with their queen.

She turned to Emmie and reported. "Diggers say view hole around bend. Follow quietly. We look."

They all headed slowly around the bend, with Emmie struggling to move as quietly as the ants who unerringly avoided placing their spindly legs on any loose rocks. After a few seconds they came to the end of the tunnel where light came through a small hole about two inches wide. The queen motioned for Emmie and the Firefly to take a look.

Putting an eye to the hole revealed what looked like a vast hospital ward. But it wasn't. Though beds were lined up into the distance and alien attendants were administering to human patients, the first giveaway was the fact that all the patients were male. The second was the presence of patrolling snakemen, clearly there to keep order. And the "nurses" weren't wearing uniforms: the ridiculous outfits they were wearing, clearly attempts to mimic Earthly lingerie, didn't have enough material to qualify as clothing. Emmie shook her head, unable to believe what she was actually looking at. Female lizards, wolf women, squid-headed humanoids, all dressed in Frederick's of Hollywood, climbing all over dozens of men on their beds—San Diego Zoo meets lap dancing bar.

But there was one thing happening that didn't happen in a men's club or anywhere on Earth. Besides IV feeders hung next to the beds, each "patient" had clear plastic tubing running from under the covers to a clear plastic bag at the side of the bed. It looked like an IV feeder, but Emmie knew what it was, and it wasn't giving the men anything, it was taking something away. Yuck! The room reminded Emmie of her summer with the Girl Scouts working on a dairy farm outside Stockton. Except this facility was milking humans.

News reports back on Earth had covered the fact that most alien races could harvest "life force" from eating living beings. Millennia ago, planets attacked each other to devour the inhabitants, just to get these units of living energy. After countless races had been wiped out from this practice, a League of Worlds was formed to stop this and bring a halt to the endless wars. The only holdouts had been the ferocious Dreash, who continued to conquer other planets and consume their residents. After Wyckham arrived and took control of the Dreash home planet, the last practitioners of this interplanetary cannibalism fled into the planet's vast interior and the universe had been at peace ever since, though at times a fragile one. But the League hadn't banned the collection of sperm cells, which had the same unit of life that grown beings had and didn't fight back.

With the arrival of Wyckham and willing humans, sperm harvesting had reached industrial levels. As a reward for assisting the British in taking the planet, the Fireflies had been allowed to set up "taverns" which collected spermatozoa from eager British sailors. With over 30 million sperm cells in a typical human discharge, the Fireflies were easily able to gather more life units than from devouring entire planets' populations.

While what she was seeing was certainly distasteful, it was certainly better than devouring living beings, so if it worked to keep the peace in the universe Emmie had no problem with it. But many of the men seemed comatose, even as they were still filling the plastic bags hanging next to their beds. What she was looking at wasn't a brief romp between sexual partners, but sperm collecting on a giant scale. The lingerie-clad nurses were constantly removing little filled bags and taking them to some kind of electronic scanner in the center of the ward. Emmie watched as a walking octopus in a neon orange bikini placed a bag on the device, which then flashed through some numbers until settling on 32,581,007. A humanoid woman with the ears and facial features of a rabbit and wearing a fishnet body stocking placed her bag on it next and it flashed 37,077,151.

"Beat you again, Inky," the rabbit squawked through her translator, surprisingly in English. "Can't say I blame these human males for not getting aroused by a smelly fish. Maybe you need to go jump in the ocean for a quick bath, 'Stinky Inky'?"

"You just jealous, Jessica," the squid responded. "I get forty million from American president every time, I most valuable courtesan here Baroness tells me."

Shillings was here!

Suddenly Inky's head shot forward from a blow, quickly followed by Jessica's.

"Oh really?" It was Lady Brashton, brandishing her riding crop, who had emerged from behind a bed curtain and clouted both the aliens with it. "If you two want to keep working here, you can stop your prattle and get back to work. Especially you, madam Inky. Shillings is calling for you. Move!"

The big squid moved down the aisle, spiraling its legs along the floor, leaving drops of blood from open cuts left by the barbs on Lady Brashton's riding crop.

"And you had best get the forty you just bragged about," Lady Brashton called after her, slapping the riding crop on her thigh. "And make it quick, we're moving him soon. You have twenty minutes. Drain him." With that she moved down the ward and turned a corner, out of sight.

Emmie and the Firefly continued watching as the squid moved five beds down the aisle to pull aside a bed curtain and disappear behind it.

"There you are, my many-armed beauty," they heard coming from behind the curtain. It was Shillings voice! Emmie had heard him speak many times in that same monotone voice in his constant harangues against abortion. "Where have you been? Yes, climb right up here! Yee-hah!" For once he sounded a little excited. Two snakemen quickly took up positions in front of the bed.

Emmie motioned the Firefly to leave, and they both silently went back around the bend to the waiting ants where it was safe to talk.

"So Shillings is here," declared Emmie. "Now what do we do?"

The ant queen was twirling her antennae, communicating with her fellow ants. "My ants brave, say they will enter Arsenale main entrance, fight their way here. But they digger ants, not soldiers, too many snakemen, if they try they just die. I send for soldier ants and human marines."

"No, that won't work. Super Bitch said they're moving him soon, and for sure she has other exits to this secret complex she's constructed. As soon as she hears a commotion, she'll escape with Shillings."

"I believe the American here is correct," commented the Firefly. "Lady Brashton has proven elusive. I suggest we watch to see when she leaves, I will take her form, find the exit up to the Arsenale's tourist area and take Shillings there where you can meet us. I will have to accept a snakeman escort to make matters believable. I will try to accept only two. Be prepared to overpower them."

"You think you can get away with impersonating her?" inquired Emmie. "Gotta think those snakemen know her pretty well."

"Snakemen are not the most brilliant of species. Besides, I have impersonated her for years and have frequently fooled her fellow humans." With that, there was a flash of light about her and she re-emerged as a perfect clone of the older Tracy Brashton, even wearing the same red business suit and white shirt that the real Lady Brashton had just been seen wearing.

"Don't forget the riding crop," noted Emmie. "You won't fool anyone if you're not as nasty as that fucking bitch."

"It is here," answered the Firefly, pulling back her jacket to reveal the barbed instrument protruding from an inside pocket. "Right where she usually carries it."

"OK, so you can fool them but how do you plan get in there? We make the hole bigger, they're gonna hear it."

"That will not be difficult", and with another flash of light she was gone. Emmie stood there puzzled.

"I am here," the Firefly's voice came to her, but where the hell was she? "Down here, the cockroach."

Sure enough, there was a cockroach at Emmie's feet. "I will enter through the view hole," said the cockroach, "and change into Lady Brashton where no one can see. I suggest you now head above into the public area of the Arsenale."

Worker Queen nodded acceptance. "We go to public area of Arsenale, spread out, find you wherever you emerge." The ant queen and her minions scurried back down the tunnel, heading above to cross the canal and enter the Arsenale.

"I'll catch up with you, just wanna watch for a bit and make sure this con works out," said Emmie as she followed the cockroach down the tunnel and watched her climb up and get through the hole. It scurried behind a screen, only to emerge a moment later as Baroness Brashton in the red business suit. She quickly moved down the aisle to Shillings's bed, ranting away in the Baroness's loud, abrasive voice.

"Everybody, listen up! Drop your cocks and grab your socks, we're outta here! Shillings has to go, now! Get him unplugged!"

She pulled aside the bed curtain and there was the squid woman riding Shillings like a scene from a psychedelic horror movie. The big cephalopod stopped humping the convulsing American president and complained. "He wants more of me. Can't take him now."

The Firefly Baroness wound up her right arm and cuffed the lizard with a vicious backhand. Her brain receiving a message of pain from the Firefly, the alien screeched and her head snapped sideways in reaction.

"Get off him and get him ready to walk, you slimy slut! Now!"

A snakemen with a flintlock pistol in his red pirate sash walked up, repeatedly yelling "Security escort to bed 25." He made the bow that the Baroness always insisted on, then spoke.

"I will get a security detail here in a moment, madam. Why the sudden rush?"

"Fangs!" The Firefly addressed the snakeman by his name, probably a fact she'd just discovered with a quick sweep of his mind. "We've been found out! Goddam ants found our tunnel in the Naval Museum, and now that fuckhead Wyckham's got a squad of his marines heading through it right now! So we're going up and leaving through the Arsenale. No security detail, it would attract too much attention, the place is filled with tourists. Just you and your lieutenant."

"As you wish, madam." The snakemen yanked the squid woman off Shillings, revealing the old human with his member still erect, ready to party on, though a little groggy from the nearly empty whiskey bottle on his end table. The snakeman lieutenant arrived with a Slick medic to unhook Shillings from a variety of medical devices, a male squid orderly got Shillings dressed, and the four of them headed across the room and ascended a crude stone stairway. Emmie dashed back down the tunnel, her sword banging around on her hip, up into the sunlight and all the way to the Arsenale entrance. She dodged tourists as she raced through the main gate with its two brick towers and the big winged lion above it.

Immediately she sighted several of the ants, spread out about the complex, keeping an eye out for Shillings and his escort. She nodded to them and they dipped their antennae back in acknowledgment. Emmie continued down a line of ships under construction in dry pits along the quay while the ants pretended to be construction workers, poking around in corners with piles of masts and other construction materials.

When she reached the fourth ship in the line, she heard some shuffling noises from the bottom of its pit. Emmie walked a complete circuit around the dry dock, noticing some loose rubble being scattered over the ground from beneath the galley's hull. Was there a tunnel right under the ship as a hidden entrance? A tunnel there could allow workers at Lady Brashton's sperm farm to come and go right through the holographic warship.

Sure enough, the big head of an alien snakemen now popped out of the main hatch, gave a quick look around, then disappeared back into the hull. A moment later up came, Shillings, two snakemen and the Firefly Lady Brashton.

"Where we going?" asked Shillings. "Why did you take me away from Tiffany? She was really hot. Almost as hot as Vanessa, my cute little lizard tart. I really miss her. Can you take me to Vanessa?"

"What a coincidence," said the Firefly. "We're going to see Vanessa right now. It will just be a short walk."

"Oh boy, Vanessa!" responded Shillings with enthusiasm. "I've so missed that ravishing little reptilian. She was really class."

Emmie joined a crowd of tourists fifty feet behind them and followed them towards the Arsenale entrance, trying to blend in as she walked around the docked ships and displays. If they could just make it to San Marco plaza, they could turn Shillings over to the marines on duty.

"There they are!" *Shit!* Emmie knew who was shouting even before she turned around. It was the real Lady Brashton, running as fast as she could in her red high-heeled boots, emerging from the same ship, yelling to the dozen or so snakemen with her. "Don't let them leave the Arsenale!"

The Firefly turned to the two snakes with her, feigning shock and anger. "It's a trick by the Firefly scum! I'm the real Baroness, you know that! Stop them!"

The snake lieutenant, quite confused, just stood there. Not so for Captain Fangs, or whatever his rank was, who hissed in derision and went for his flintlock pistol.

Emmie drew her sword and her training took over. She came *En Garde,* made a graceful *ballestra* to close distance, and lunged in *quarte.* While the snakeman was still cocking the hammer back on the big horse pistol, an open target if ever there was one, her point went through the snakeman's back and out his chest. Arterial blood spurted as she withdrew her blade, and the thrashing reptile tried to spring away but fell into an outdoor café, crashing into a large group from Nebraska celebrating grandma's birthday. Everyone at the table stood up in shock as the beast's wild death spiral sprayed blood all over their cake as well as grannie.

The group of horrified tourists headed for the exits, yelling up a storm, and within a few seconds a general panic was underway. Tourists and aliens jumped from their seats in the nearby cafes, running every which way. Emmie was looking around for the next threat but had trouble seeing through the terrified crowd.

Ants! She saw several of them, running up and jumping onto the group of snakes around Lady Brashton. Though outnumbered, the ants fought ferociously, piling on the big reptiles and trying to rip them apart. But Lady Brashton, steadfastly focused on preventing Shillings's escape, broke free of the fighting and headed after him.

As concentrated on Shillings as she was, the Baroness almost missed seeing Emmie. But suddenly her eyes opened wide in recognition and she jolted to a stop. "You! Wyckham's agent in the Rio Muneghete house!" The infuriated madam turned towards Emmie as she reached into her jacket. "I'll do for you right now, you little cunt!"

Emmie didn't know what the madam was reaching for, but she wasn't going to just sit there to find out. Emmie ran at her in a *fleche'* attack but pulled up *en guarde* when she came within distance. And just in time, because the furious Baroness had pulled out a modern automatic pistol, racked the slide, and leveled it at Emmie.

But Emmie was ready. She made a lunge and a beat on the pistol in *quarte*, whacking it with her *forte*, the thick lower part of her blade, and sending it flying. With her blade still in *quarte*, her point was upright and pointing right at Lady Brashton's throat. Emmie snapped her right arm into a full extension and placed her point right under the oncoming Madam's chin.

To Lady Brashton's credit, she managed to pull up before she ran completely onto Emmie's sword, only getting a half inch of Emmie's point thrust up into her mouth. She tried to back off, but Emmie grabbed her jacket lapels and held on, keeping her point on the madam's throat, and Lady Brashton's reward for all her thrashing around was just a larger wound.

"So, I'm a little cunt?" asked the fencer with an angry sneer. Pent-up anger at this horrible woman welled up inside Emmie. "Well, how about a little prick from this little cunt?" And with that she pushed her point up into the roof of Tracy Brashton's mouth.

"That's just a taste! You move again, your tongue's a pincushion. Freeze!" Lady Brashton immediately froze in compliance "Now, I want you to tell your snakes to back off, let us out of the Arsenale, the ants too. Tell them to stay here."

Emmie pulled her point from the madam's mouth so she could issue the commands. "Everyone, back off... glug!" was all she could manage as blood dripped down her throat, making her gag and cough. All attempt at communication ended as she pinched the wound around the blade in an attempt to staunch the bleeding.

"You snakes got that? She says leave us alone and stay here," Emmie yelled out. She turned to Lady Brashton. "Isn't that right? You can just nod your head."

The baroness nodded frantically, anything to prevent Emmie's sword from going any deeper. Emmie headed towards the Arsenale gate, walking backwards, with one hand gripping Lady Brashton's lapels and the other holding her sword tight to the British woman's throat. More ants arrived and fanned out around the three women, protecting them as they all backed out the gate and headed for the palace.

Wyckham's First Date

WELL, IF IT ISN'T Lot's wife herself!" said Wyckham as he looked up from his desk to see Baroness Tracy Brashton entering his office, escorted by Emmie along with the Lady Brashton Firefly, Shillings, and a group of ants. "Taken from your house in Sodom, were you, you poor thing? Maybe about to be turned into a pillar of salt?" He got up and walked over to where she stood. "Well, don't worry, I can't turn you into a pillar of salt. Though I certainly would if I could." But Wyckham's light tone changed as he moved closer and got into the captured spy's face.

"You are what the Americans call a real POS. A piece of shite," he stated as his anger surged like a sizzling grenadoe about to explode. "First you plot with the Dreash for decades—yes, we knew it was you—in all sorts of crazy plots to take over this world. And then you contact this lunatic Triumph and his crowd and persuade him to invade the most peaceful and prosperous world in the history of the universe? Why? So you could parade me through Port Wyckham like a conquered barbarian and then torture me to death? All because I rejected you since you grew up into a vicious, power-mad manipulator?"

While Wyckham was fuming, Slick medic 2256, had pulled one of his miraculous devices from his belt and sealed up the hole inside Lady Brashton's mouth so she could speak.

"You insignificant country squire!" she erupted, blood droplets spraying from her mouth as she screamed at Wyckham. "You chase me for years, then when I finally accept your courtship, relinquishing my Baronetcy for you, you snub me in favor of some lowlife alien who takes my image? Just what greater insult can there be to my family, one of Britain's oldest and most respected? What noble woman wouldn't seek justice? You little popinjay, you think…"

"Mister 2256," Wyckham interrupted. "The poor woman is clearly exacerbating her wound with this tirade. Might I recommend one of your injectable sedatives? She clearly needs rest and relaxation."

The Slick medic touched the ranting ex-baroness with another small device and she immediately fell asleep on her feet, the medic catching her as she fell.

"Thank you, sir. Once again, your admirable medicinal skills help the suffering. Not to mention the suffering of everyone here in her presence. If you would be so kind as to take her to your San Marco medical facility? One of your secure rooms for lunatics? Hopefully she will regain her wits under your expert care. Corporal, would you be so kind as fetch a litter and escort our medic and his patient to their facility? Make sure you take several of the duty sentries with you, an attempt at her rescue might be made by any one of her factions. After she gets settled, maintain guards on her room, if you would."

"Sah!" The marine corporal stamped his musket on the floor and went off to get a litter. Within minutes the prostate Lady Brashton was on her way across town. Wyckham turned to Emmie and the kidnapping party.

"So, allow me to make a wild guess. Our esteemed Madam Bahtia has saved the day again? I imagine that wound in the traitor's mouth is a result of your blade?"

All eyes in the ornate Doge's office turned to Emmie as she stumbled over a response. "Well… uh, yeah, she was going for a pistol, what the fuh…, ah the heck was I supposed to do? Just my fencing reflexes I guess, I did it without thinking. Only a flesh wound, she'll be OK, right?"

"Ah, even concern for a fallen foe," replied Wykham. "Another admirable quality surfaces in the young woman. Do all American women have the morality of Queen Elizabeth and the martial skills of Athena?"

Emmie didn't know what to say. Receiving compliments from a 200-year-old world leader who'd seen everything in the universe wasn't a usual event in her life. "Ah, shit, just doin' the right thing," was all she could manage.

"Well, we are indebted. But now we must get President Shillings back to his own country."

Wyckham was interrupted by the arrival of DiCarpaccio and his aides, who always seemed to know about important political developments as soon as they happened on Freeport, thanks to their little communicators. Right behind them were many of Freeport's leaders, including Captain Jamison, Bubbler the mudman, Captain Rawlins and counselor Obujimi, all of whom had seemingly already heard of Schillings's return.

"Way to go," the American president said. "I heard you'd found the Midwest's missing president, and here he is. We've contacted the Confederates and they are ready to send a small party to pick him up. They can arrive by helicopter in a few minutes, but they ask for assurances that your tiny but quite effective air force will stand down. I've told them to land on the middle San Marco dock."

"You can assure them that our air battalion is not currently airborne, since the pilot of our sole flying machine is right here," replied Wyckham, nodding to Wulfe who had just wandered into the office.

"Well, well, so they are afraid of me," commented Wulfe dryly. "Guess they're not as stupid as I thought."

Jamison walked over to Wyckham, turned his back to the assembly, and whispered in his ear, "And we should not be stupid, either. I'm sure Mister Triumph's word is above question, but just in case, me and my boys 'r gonna take up sniping positions around the docks, all loaded up with fireballs. That ship fires one shot, we'll drop her."

Wyckham nodded approval as the American privateer left the room. The Firefly Tracy then walked up and spoke into Wyckham's ear.

"I have received communication from the dolphins. Whales intercepted an undersea craft about two miles away headed towards San Marco. The ship shot motorized bombs at them which they easily avoided. They then chewed up the rotating propulsion device on its stern, so it now sits immobile. They hear troops inside. Do you have any instructions? The whales can destroy it and eat everyone aboard if you wish."

"No, for God sakes! Once again, we do not... eat... our... foes! Tell the whales to leave them alone, let their own ships rescue them."

Wyckham turned his attention back to the issue at hand. Shillings was minutes away from rejoining his fellow Americans, ending the reason for their invasion and hopefully resulting in the Confederate forces returning to Earth. But a problem emerged from an unexpected quarter.

"Where's Vanessa? You said you were taking me to Vanessa?" It was Shillings. "What's going on here? I wasn't born yesterday, you know. I think you're lying to me. I don't think you're taking me to Vanessa at all!"

Christ, just when everything looked resolved, Shillings threatens to cock everything up. Wyckham had to get this settled right quick. "President, you've been through quite a lot. Your fellow Americans are coming for you, I suggest you return to your friends and family on Earth."

"Listen here, young man, I'll go back when I damn well please. I don't know what kind of world you're running here, but in my country, people travel when they wish and not when some dictator tells them they have to!"

Wyckham had been briefed on Shillings and it was well known that he worshipped his wife. Wyckham would try that tack.

"Sir, I understand that your wife back on Earth has been sending out electrical messages, begging for your return. You want to put an end to her stress and return, right?"

"Yes, she's a good Christian but she's no lizard and no Vanessa. Where's Vanessa? I want my Vanessa!"

Wyckham shook his head in disgust. This supposedly devoutly religious man was governed by his genitals. How could Americans elect such hypocrites as their leaders? Thank God he'd been able to keep such unmanageable democracy off of this planet. But what the hell was he going to do now?

"And just who is this Vanessa?" He asked the group around him. "One of Lady Brashton's courtesans? Now we have to find her as well?"

Emmie responded. "She's a lizard that used to work in the brothel on Rio Muneghete, I talked to her there in a nearby bar. Said she was Shillings's favorite. When we found him at the Arsenale brothel, I… uh… told him we would take him to Vanessa."

The now familiar beating of an American hovercraft let everyone know that the Confederates were arriving. *Shite! No time to find this Vanessa creature.*

"Well, President Schillings, your fellow Americans are arriving," said a resigned Wyckham. "Shall we meet them on the docks? Ahh… maybe they brought Vanessa with them?" A bit of a lie but he had to move things along.

Schillings's viz brightened at the mention of Vanessa and everyone headed out to the docks. As they walked out the palace door, Wyckham leaned over and spoke to Bubbler. "Get a few of your mates and stay close. Never know what this wanker Triumph and his guards might try to pull off."

"Aye, a smart move that. Don' trust this bunch far iz I kin spit, an' I spits fair far," the muddy mass answered in its cockney English.

They arrived at the docks just in time to see one of the flying hovercraft settle down onto San Marco in a thunderous pounding and a storm of dust. Immediately Triumph's ubiquitous electronic communications crew emerged and began setting up their transmitting devices. After just a few moments, the electronics people nodded to the ship and Triumph appeared, talking to the recording crew as he walked towards Wyckham and his group.

"Once again, I managed to make a deal that settles everything and gets Americans a fair shake. With the threat of our forces hanging over them, we've forced these British and their illegal alien friends to release President Schillings from his captivity here. God knows what sort of torture and depravations they put this wonderful Christian through, but now he can return to a God-fearing America and his wife and family. Next, we'll be negotiating trade arrangements, and I can assure you they will give us a fair deal, or they will regret it."

Good Lord, does this man's mouth ever stop? Wyckham was going to warn Triumph that Schillings was refusing to leave New Venice, but to hell with that. He'd let Triumph get embarrassed in front of the watching millions back on Earth. "Welcome, Mr. President. President Schillings is right here."

Before Triumph could address Wyckham, Bamming whispered something in his ear which caused Triumph to grimace and turn angry. Wyckham suspected he'd just been told that whatever mission their undersea ship was on would not be completed. But Triumph quickly shook it off as if nothing had happened and addressed Wyckham as he walked over to Schillings. "Whaddya think of my personal helicopter here? Never seen anything like that, huh?"

"Oh, it's amazing. Congratulations, you must be so proud," responded a droll Wyckham. "All we have in Port Wyckham are a few dozen interplanetary spaceships that fly at the speed of light." But Triumph wasn't listening as he reached Shillings, gave him one of his famously impressive handshakes, put his arm over the Midwesterner's shoulder and faced the cameras.

"Mark, you must be so happy to be free again and returning to America. Tell everyone right now, on live TV, all the horrors these nasty Brits and their viscous monster friends put you through during your captivity."

But Schillings acted like he hadn't heard a word, not even looking at Triumph as he scanned the newly arrived group of Americans.

"Where's Vanessa? Did you bring Vanessa?"

Triumph's mouth dropped open, but nothing came out. Finally, he managed, "Vanessa? Who's Vanessa?"

"You didn't bring Vanessa? Then what are you doing here?"

Triumph turned to the recording crew and tried to smile but his face showed tension. "We're here to take you back home, Mark. You're now freed from the illegal aliens. Isn't that great?"

Shillings turned angrily to Triumph. "Listen, Vic. I'm not going anywhere. Vanessa is here, I like it here. When Vanessa's not around she sends her friends, and they're all wonderful. Hell, they got a frog woman, got a tongue a mile long. Suck the chrome off a bumper hitch! You know, my wife is great, but I never realized what I was missing until I came here." He looked directly into the recording device. "Betty, you were a great mother for our kids, but you were terrible in bed. Christ, sometimes I thought I was fucking a nun! But up here, all the women really know what they're doing. I'll send you some videos, maybe you can learn a few things. And don't send me any of your nonsense about God's disapproval. Jesus never said it was wrong to get laid."

A frustrated Triumph stepped in front of Schillings and addressed the recording crew.

"Don't worry folks, he's been through a lot, we'll get him home and once he sees his dear wife and family he'll be good as new." He looked at his guards, waved them over, and mumbled into the ear of one of them, apparently their commander. Immediately two of them grabbed Schillings's arms and started pulling him towards their flying ship, despite his loud objections. "Goddamit, Triumph, tell your goons to release me! I am not going back! Let me go!"

A man was being abducted right in front of Wyckham. He was not going to let that happen on his planet. "Mister Triumph, you must let him go," Wyckham called out. "We protect personal freedom on this planet. No one on Freeport may be seized and forced to go anywhere against their wishes. I insist—release him immediately."

Ignoring Wyckhjam, Triumph kept walking towards his hover-craft as he nodded a signal to his guards. They immediately pulled out pistols and formed a moving screen, escorting the kidnappers as they walked away with Schillings. Wyckham heard Triumph speaking under his breath, "Yeah, well let's see you stop me, old man."

Hummmph! "Mister Bubbler, please detain Mister Triumph and any of his guards that resist, if you would." Bubbler replied with an abrupt guttural sound, undoubtedly some affirmative word in his own farty language, and rolled right at Triumph along with several other mudmen. The American guards started firing with their pistols, which had no effect at all on the mudmen, and except for the two holding Schillings were quickly rolled over and absorbed by the surprisingly fast mud creatures. Bubbler picked up Triumph himself and started towards the bay with the orange-haired head of the Confederate leader sticking out. Triumph yelled and cursed as he was spun around until the third roll, when his head got bashed on the pavement.

Uh! That must have hurt.

At the point of losing consciousness Triumph managed to get out a shout.

"Oh-fuck! OK! I release Schillings! Lemme out of this shitball!"

Wyckham nodded to Bubbler and Triumph was expelled from the mudman's body with a crude sound and a rush of foul-smelling gas. He got up groggily but shook himself awake and headed right at Wyckham, but thought better of it when the two marines at Wyckham's side leveled their bayonets right at his chest. Wyckham didn't flinch an iota, remaining motionless with his hands clasped behind his back in the classic captain's pose.

With Triumph momentarily at a loss for words, a rare event, Wyckham couldn't help but add to the blusterer's discomfit.

"You poor man." He gave Triumph an up and down glance. "I'm afraid that very expensive raiment of yours needs immediate replacement. Good God, man, you look like a stable hand, and with an odor to match! You don't want your all followers on these message devices seeing you like this. Go back to your ship and get some fresh clothes—maybe one of those cowboy suits you favor?"

Triumph looked down at himself and indeed his suit was in dismal shape. Mudmen picked up all sorts of filth rolling around all day, and Triumph's suit bore all sorts of rotting food, bird droppings, horse 'apples', and even a couple of decomposing rodents picked up from the streets of New Venice. And worst of all, the sulfurous odor of decomposing street refuse was all over Triumph's clothes, the smell easily detectable even from Wyckham's distance.

"Whew! And your odor trumps all," added Wyckham. "You will excuse me if I move upwind?" Wyckham pulled out his lace handkerchief and coughed violently into it, then waved it in the air to dispel the noxious vapors. "Good Lord!"

The sight of his carefully groomed appearance gone to hell put Triumph at a loss for words. "You little, ancient,… unfair! You're not treating me fairly! You're a dead man! Dead! I accept your duel! Weapons will be AR-15's, my choice since you challenged me, and I'm going blast you into hamburger! Then… then I'll cook you up into a Big Mac and feed you to those big shitballs of yours! You fucking…, you…"

Wyckham was done with the man and interrupted his tirade. "Yes, yes, I understand, you've been treated unfairly by mean old me, just because you invaded a peaceful world, killed hundreds of residents, how dare I get upset?" *Christ, the cheek of the man!* "Good day to you sir, I will see you here in the plaza at dawn. But I suggest you get that turd out of your hair before tomorrow, wouldn't want that seen by all your followers at such an important event."

A sausage of fecal matter, probably excrement from one of Freeport's raptors, was indeed resting on Trimph's bright orange hair, picked up from the mudman's insides. Triumph, known for his extreme concern over his appearance, immediately started grabbing at his hair. Finding the offending shite, he gave it a forceful yank, throwing it to the ground. Unfortunately, the turd was apparently quite sticky and pulled off the toupee that the man was wearing as well. A bald Triumph just stood there, staring at his wig on the ground, his head covered in unflattering liver spots, the image being sent to millions of viewers back on Earth.

Wyckham couldn't resist a parting shot. "A lovely pate you've got there, Mister President! Lots of delightful liver spots. Impersonating a leopard today? You look quite ferocious, I must say. I'm very frightened. See you at dawn. Don't avoid it again like you did last time, you despicable coward." With that, Wyckham turned away and headed back to the palace, his party following him, as Triumph started fuming again.

"Wasted Away Wyckham!" Triumph turned to the recording crew. Yes, that's him. Everybody! His new name! Wasted Away Wobbling Wyckham! I've just given him a great new name! I really got him there!"

Wyckham just shook his head as he entered the palace for an hour-long meeting with Freeport's leaders to make plans for the morrow's duel, including troop deployment in case of treachery. After a few minutes of arranging duties, the governance council departed to follow the orders, leaving just Emmie and Wyckham's valet Obujimi.

"Some dinner, Governor?" The valet asked. "Let me see what the kitchen can come up with and I'll prepare the table."

"No," replied Wyckham. "No, I want you to go work with Jamison tonight on preparing the plaza for whatever the yellow-haired magician might come up with. Your obsession with my safety should be a part of all planning. I'll find something to eat." Nodding understanding, the African left, leaving just Emmie there with Freeport's governor.

"And Madam Bahtia, thank you for all you've done, feel free to go out with your friends tonight in New Venice and have an enjoyable evening, you've certainly earned it. I hear this town is a wonderful town for celebration."

Emmie suddenly felt the man's loneliness at this moment, which had to be a frightening one, the night before a duel. He hears it's a wonderful town? This guy, this hero, had never explored the amazing city he'd created? No way Emmie was going to leave this hero all alone on what might be the last night of his life.

"Forget it, Governor Wyckham, you're going out with us tonight, not staying alone in this big empty palace waiting for a duel at dawn." She stood up and grabbed Wyckham's hand. "C'mon, we're buying you dinner at the Café Florian. Then we're going dancing at Brashton's. You know you gotta rename that place? We can think up a new name over dinner."

Wyckham faced up to the fact he'd been avoiding for the past two days—he was entranced by this woman. She was a vision from a future time with all its knowledge, twice able to find Schillings after he had failed, could shoot a deadly rapid-fire rifle and handled a blade like a fencing master. And cared deeply about doing right. Not to mention she certainly wasn't hard on the eyes. Wyckham wanted nothing more than to spend an evening chatting with this remarkable young woman.

"Done on both counts. I accept your invitation to this 'date'. Isn't that what you call it? Though shouldn't I have been the one to propose the outing? And as for the club we'll name it 'Emmie's'. He stood up and motioned Emmie towards the door. "And no more 'Governor Wyckham', for God's sake. Call me Rod."

Life Stories and Pasta Florian

Tᴴᴇʏ ᴄʀᴏssᴇᴅ ᴛʜᴇ plaza and entered the Café Florian. When Emmie had asked Consuela and Vanoune to join them for dinner, they'd refused, making lewd comments about not wanting to interfere with Emmie's attempt to hook up, and her friends went off to Brashton's to meet up later. Recognizing the governor in his formal Navy uniform, the fishman Maître D' took them to a special outside table near the musicians, his nose arrogantly in the air despite the fact that he smelled like an old bait bucket as his kind did when on land. Octupi musicians were playing a brisk waltz on several instruments, continuing a century's-old competition between the Café Florian, the Ristoranti Quadri and Caffe Lavena, the two other cafes across the plaza that had live music as well.

Emmie recognized the song being played and started singing along. "When the moon hits your eye, like a big pizza pie, that's *amore*", she crooned, like the ubiquitous grandpa at an Italian wedding. "Dean Martin—1953," she informed Wyckham. "See the kind of thing you missed out on over the last two centuries?"

"I must admit it sounds like Mozart compared to the racket most alien musicians play in the portside taverns," Wyckham complained. "The worst are the mudmen. They always seem to start up just as your dinner arrives, and once they start caterwauling in that farty language of theirs, one's appetite immediately flees in abject terror."

Emmie chuckled and pretended to be absorbed in the menu, which she didn't need to do since she knew it from her earlier visit with Van and Connie. It wasn't hard to remember since along with a few sandwiches there was only one entrée, Pasta Florian, the café's famous soup with shrimp, mussels and pasta.

But keeping her eyes on the menu helped hide the childish thrill she was feeling about the man before her. Here she was in 2028, sitting next to the ruler of an entire planet who dressed in an 1805 naval uniform, listening to him describe in proper Georgian English an alien language that sounded like farts. A man who looked around 30 but was actually over 200, had defeated monstrous aliens that threatened Earth, founded a planet that was a haven for the oppressed, fought off Triumph's Confederacy, and was about to fight a duel tomorrow! And they were on a date! It was hard to get her head around all this.

She noticed the date on the menu's cover. "Wow, it says '1720' here on the cover. This restaurant is that old? For us San Franciscans, that is just so fly. We don't have any buildings that old in California."

"Interesting. For an Englishman, a restaurant only three hundred years old is the new place on the block. When I was here in 1805—in the original Venice—the Florian was just a hundred years old, the newest place in Venice and talk of the town."

A waiter, one of the blind Gorillas in a white tuxedo, took their orders and soon returned with two bowls of the Pasta Florian brimming with pasta and shellfish, along with fresh crusty Italian bread and olive oil. Surprisingly hungry, Wyckham tucked into his feed with relish, the flavors reminding him of the first time he'd eaten here back in the 19th century.

"Cracking good food, cracking," he commented as he ladled the hearty broth into his mouth. "Tastes just like it did when I was here 200 years ago. Actually, 223 years ago, to be exact."

Despite the man's reminiscences of 1805 Venice, Emmie still had trouble believing Wyckham was over two hundred years old. He looked thirty something, and without the weathered face from a life at sea he would have looked even younger. But there was something in his eyes and speech that spoke of vast experience, understanding and self confidence that young men usually lacked.

"But tell me of your life," Wyckham asked just before Emmie asked about his. "I've been away from Earth for several lifetimes now. You must tell me about life for a young woman growing up in twenty-first century America. I can only imagine how different it must have been compared to Georgian times."

"Shit, where do I start," Emmie pondered aloud. Before she could answer, Wyckham asked a question.

"Well, let's start with that. How did it come about that 21st century women use words like 'shit' that only streetwalkers would use when I grew up?"

That sort of startled Emmie. "Actually, that's a question I've never thought about." She had to think for a second.

Wyckham filled in the silence. "Didn't your mother teach you not to say such words?"

"Yeah, sure, but at the same time my mom was saying 'shit' and 'fuck' and all the other swear words whenever she got pissed off in traffic—that would be when she was taking us somewhere in her car… automobile… uh, a coach with an engine, no horses."

"Yes, women drive vehicles on Earth now. I must say I have a hard time imaging that. There certainly were no coachwomen when I grew up. Managing a team of horses at high speed was something that everyone, including women, thought was just too difficult for a woman to manage. Yet now you women drive these 'cars' that I understand are heavier and faster than any horse-drawn coach. Jesus, I understand that they routinely race along over a mile per minute! I don't believe I could safely do that, yet apparently women back on Earth do it with ease."

Emmie nodded and tried to put herself in Wyckham's shoes, a man raised in the 1700's, with the views on the frailty of women that were common at the time. Usually she gave a sharp rebuke and the contents of her glass to any guy making such comments, but she would cut Wyckham a break.

"Cars, our coaches, are actually pretty easy to drive, what with power steering—uh, that would something in the car that helps you steer it. You really should come to Earth and go for a drive!" Without realizing it she'd made an advance. The Hell with it, she'd keep going! "Really, don't you want to visit your old world? I could show you around, there's so much that would amaze you. We'd have a great time!"

Surprisingly, Wyckham shook his head and pursed his lips, not too interested in the idea.

"No, I don't think so. My presence on Earth would create an uproar. All the factions intent on invading Freeport to milk its resources would just love to get me out of the way. There would be thousands of people stirring up hatred for Rodney Wyckham on your 'social media'—what is it, that 'Headbook' or whatever it is—all those Americans that are adherents to Triumph's message of unfair treatment by Freeport would put a price on my head. Hell, they all walk around armed with those rapid-fire pistols, they'd all be competing to put the first bullet in me! You would not want to be anywhere near Rodney Wyckham, 'King of the Evil Illegal Aliens'."

"C'mon," said Emmie, "we're not that bad. Aren't you curious about all the technological advances we've made back home? There are self-driving cars that can take you anywhere, robots that harvest our crops, fantastic screen entertainment, electronic books available on every subject. I know you'd enjoy it, you'd be amazed."

"Yes, yes, I understand that Earth has made remarkable advances since I left. But understand that for two centuries I've been up here with aliens from a thousand different planets, each with technology well ahead of Earth's. If you want to see technology on display, check out the docks in Port Wyckham.

"Plus, frankly, I'm not too impressed with technology. It certainly hasn't seemed to make Earth such a great place. Between your deadly wars and your climate change, it seems technology has made Earth a far deadlier place than backward Freeport. Actually, I've done my best to keep advanced technology off this planet. Our wind-driven ships and single shot muskets have worked for us just fine. We have a peaceful world; our only violence comes from occasional invasions by Earth—Triumph's attack is the third. Thousands of immigrants have come here over the years, just to get away from the wars and environmental prob-lems caused by their own technology. And without your Democracy in control, I can make sure everybody here gets along, despite the fact that Freeport's population is far more diverse than Earth's. Christ, Earth still fights wars over religion or skin color? Up here half our population isn't even humanoid. We have stick people, figures that are swarms of bees, fish people, stone people, but nobody attacks their neighbors because they look different. They come here fleeing all that nonsense."

Emmie couldn't help but think about the millions of people on Earth whose lives had been destroyed by technology. The automation taking jobs, the rising oceans swallowing their homes, the pollution making them sick, the advanced weapons taking their very lives—the problems caused by the advances in technology had steadily grown, es-pecially over the last decade. And the advances in mass communication had been misused to elect a true despot as US President, breaking up her country and causing world chaos.

This date was getting too serious. Time to change the subject.

"Well, I can't argue it hasn't caused problems. You're not alone in questioning technology's contribution to society. But enough of that difficult question—tell me about the past." Emmie the history buff wanted to hear more of life 200 years ago. "When you visited Venice in the early 19ᵗʰ century, what was it like? Was it still the party city with Carnivale and all the masked balls?"

"It certainly was. Though Venice had declined by the nineteenth century, it had become a popular place to visit. Every young rake and eligible dam just had to spend some time here on their Grand Tour, and the city became the center for traveling young aristocrats. While there were no establishments like the dance clubs here now, there was a spring schedule of parties that anyone seeking social advancement in Europe just had to attend.

"It became quite a randy place, probably even more so than during the Renaissance, when Casanova and all the carousing attracted the attention of the Inquisition. The goings-on I witnessed..." Wyckham shook his head in near disbelief, "let's just say they're not for discussion with a lady."

Now Emmie's historical curiosity was aroused. "Shit, you can't do that, you gotta tell me some stories, don't be a cock-block... uhhh...". Emmie stopped before she uttered a 21ˢᵗ century term that would not be proper for a lady to utter around a Georgian-era man.

Wyckham looked at her with a smirk, shook his head and said, "Alright, so be it. I must accept that morals have changed here in the 21ˢᵗ century and women are free to be as crude as men. I will describe some of the incidents I witnessed in Venice in '05. But first, what were you about to call me? A cock on the block? You must clarify the accusation, or I may have to assume the worst and challenge you to a duel, right after Triumph."

Emmie smiled back and explained, "The term I was about to use is 'cock-blocker'. It's refers to a person who does something to ruin an enjoyable moment."

Wyckham's smirk gradually widened into a smile. "So, I'm a cock-blocker. Please refrain from telling anyone else here in New Venice, a cockblocker is not what New Venice wants as its leader, I can assure you." He snorted derisively but it turned into a chuckle. "Cock-blocker. Governor Wyckham the cock-blocker."

Sitting there in an 18th century café, watching a world leader dressed in an impeccable 19th century naval uniform and hearing him call himself a 21st century "cock-blocker", everything a pinnacle of incongruity, it all suddenly hit Emmie as just too funny and she burst out laughing. Wyckham as well couldn't control himself and laughed out loud as well. Pretty soon tears were coming from both their eyes.

"A cock-blocker!" Wyckham managed to get out. "That a woman would use such a term!"

"You… are!" responded Emmie, gasping for breath. "Tell me some juicy stories of 19th century Venice or you're"—her laughter made it hard to talk—a… goddamned… cock-blocker!"

A large group of nearby diners, an outing of Baptists from Alabama, stopped eating and began muttering under their breath. "Disgusting up here. We should have stayed home." Emmie decided it was time to leave.

"I think we better get out of here and hit the club where I can call you a cock-blocker and not get any shit." She stood up, threw some money on the table before Wyckham could object, and grabbed his hand. "Let's go dancing, cock-blocker!"

Much to the relief of the Baptists, they left and headed across San Marco towards Brashton's. The square had been miraculously cleaned up and all the buildings restored, which actually wasn't that hard since the debris from the battle was all lightweight framework and the buildings were only electrical images anyway. Tourists filled the square as usual, the outpouring of visitors after the attack reassuring to Wyckham. The fact that thousands of Americans had come to New Venice right after the recent battle, despite the possibility of open warfare, placing their bodies on the line to support Freeport and reject Triumph, showed that many people on Earth still had morals as well as some spine. As he walked across the square in his naval uniform, many tourists called his name with congratulatory exclamations like "You showed that asshole!" and "Go, Gov, Go!" After politely declining their requests to record his image on their communication devices, he and the young American entered Brashton's dance club.

Despite it being a Monday night, the place was packed. Fiddling quickly with her communication device, Emmie was able to locate her friends at the Firefly bar and they joined up. Van and Connie had drunk their dinner and the ribbing started immediately.

"Hell, I thought the governor of this planet would date some classy bitch, and here he is with some ugly alien! Where's she from, the dooky planet?" asked Connie.

"Nah, she's from Earth. East Shitkicker, Kentucky, right honey?" asked Vanoune. "Moved to Dallas to work for your idol Triumph?"

"Yeah, aren't you Triumph's latest fixer?" added Van. "Triumph needed a woman to pay off his latest groping victims, and you had no problem taking that job, right girl?"

"Excuse my friends, Rod,' said Emmie with a grin. "They get stupid real quick when they've been drinking. I know the solution. We need to catch up! Barkeep, four Sailor Slams!"

The Firefly bartender that looked like the offspring of Chris Evans and Selena Gomez smiled seductively at Wyckham. "In a flash, and free for the Governor and his party." Her arms started flying about in a blur, faster than the eye could follow. Within a few seconds the drinks appeared in her hands and she slapped them down on the bar. The fact that the drinks were only holograms and the Firefly would send the appropriate messages of inebriation to their minds didn't seem important.

"That was fast! We could use her in San Francisco," stated an impressed Connie. "Wouldn't be so hard to get a drink at Brixton's on a Saturday night."

"A toast," proposed Vanoune, and the four of them hoisted their drinks in the air. "To Triumph's last day on Earth. Or I guess I should say on any planet?"

Wyckham lowered his glass slightly. "Can't drink to that. The man is certainly a boor, but my days of killing someone for that flaw are long gone. Instead might I propose, 'May I survive, and my foe get a bit wounded'?"

The women all laughed, and Emmie yelled, "Very painfully wounded!" Glasses clinked and the four knocked back the blue colored concoctions. After a few coughs and headshakes, the conversation continued on the topic of tomorrow's duel as the bartender readied four more Sailor Slams.

"Now Rod," inquired Connie, "Or is Emmie here the only one who can call you that? You don't seem stressed about your duel tomorrow, even though I guess you've never shot an assault rifle before."

"Actually, that is not correct. After the battle here, I did some target shooting with one. As commander, mademoiselle, I was obligated to fully examine my foe's weapons, and I took some shots with a captured rifle. Also, understand that most young members of the aristocracy in Britain were pretty good shots to start with. We all assumed we would be in duels occasionally, must be able to defend yourself from the inevitable social offense and all that. And shooting is all the same no matter what weapon you're firing—take a breath, exhale slightly, lower the sight onto the target, squeeze the trigger.

"Another reason I am not concerned about the outcome of this duel is that I smell coward's fear. Triumph reeks of it. All of us in the 1800's had lots of experience with cowardly rulers. Most of the kings of England and France were completely ass-over-tit lunatics—they broke their own laws whenever they felt like it, murdered and imprisoned thousands, and most damaging, they constantly warred with their neighbors. But they all stayed behind their palace walls during these conflicts as they sent thousands to die. Like them, our friend Triumph doesn't seem to lead from the front as he orders his troops into danger. I understand he never served in the military?"

"No surprise there," stated Emmie. "He didn't. He was called up to fight but had some doctor say he couldn't fight because of some bullshit disease."

"ED!" proclaimed Vanoune. "His dick didn't work!" The women laughed together, clinked glasses and emptied them again as Wyckham sipped at his.

"So! Despite your supposedly 'classless' democracy," continued Wickham, "the powerful get special treatment just like the royal classes did back in England. Well, let's see if this man Triumph stands for a duel. I doubt he will. I'll suspect that *Righteous's* crew are currently placing bets on whether he soils himself on the field tomorrow."

The three women cracked up. "Wouldn't that be the best!" yelled Emmie. "Right in front of the Fox News cameras!" But Connie, further into her cups, decided there were more important things to talk about.

"Enough about the duel. Let's talk about something even more important. Van and I are Emmie's chaperones, and we need to make sure you're acceptable date material for her. Isn't that right, Van?"

"Goddam right!" agreed Vanoune. "The first thing I need to rule out—have you ever sent any woman a dick pic?"

Connie and Van laughed and high-fived each other as Emmie rolled her eyes. Wyckham was puzzled.

"A Dick pic? A portrait of a Richard? One of the British kings from the House of York? No, I haven't. But why in the galaxy would anyone do that? I know that modern Americans love the British royals, but you even gift paintings of the royal Richards during courtship? Absurd. Well I hope that at least you do not revere Richard the second, a murderous lunatic by any measure."

With that explanation, Connie and Van almost fell on the floor from laughing so hard. Finally, Connie regained enough composure for further inquiry. "OK, so never mind about that. You need to tell us about the stories we've read about concerning your involvement in Firefly orgies during your first year here. How do you plead, guilty or not guilty?"

Wyckham's eyes went high as he pursed his lips. "I must confess my guilt, Magistrate Consuela, and throw myself upon the mercy of the court. Understand that on the two instances that I succumbed to the entreaties of Eros, I had just fought two desperate battles only to be slighted by aristocratic arses that had either played no part in the fighting or were bitter losers. I felt they needed a good shock to their supposedly higher morals. And 'twere a long time ago, I was a typical sailor, a bit randy."

Connie laughed again but demanded more. "Is it true that at one affair where women were flying back and forth between your officers, landing impaled in their laps? This court must have the facts! Every salacious detail!"

Emmie had had enough. "Fuck them, Rod, you don't need to answer their shit. We're outta here—let's dance!"

She grabbed Wickham's hand and led him onto the elevated dance floor surrounding the bar. Fittingly, the Firefly DJ, a Jaylo clone, was playing classic rock, the Beatles' "Back in the USSR." Emmie knew that Wyckham didn't have a clue about dancing to such music and would need some help.

"Now there's no rules about dancing to our music. Just move to the beat, however you feel it." She started bobbing her head and stepping back and forth just to give him the idea.

"Well one certainly can't avoid the beat in this music, can one?" replied Wyckham as he started stepping bck and forth in time to the music. "It very much reminds me of the music in African tribal celebrations. I attended one in Mauritania in '01 after my squadron put an end to the local Arab slavers. The local tribes were quite grateful and threw us a week-long celebration."

"Yes, modern American music traces its origin to the enslaved Africans of the 19th century. Most of our best music is by African-Americans."

Wyckham looked about him, surveying the gyrating mass of bodies that surrounded him. "Yes, it definitely reminds me of that African celebration. The dancing is very similar." He started to move with more energy, bobbing his head, mimicking the actions of those about him.

"Now you're getting' it! Lookit those moves!"

Wyckham raised his hands and started clapping along with the music. "Look at me! I'm a savage! Next I'll be cooking up Anglican missionaries for dinner!"

Jesus! Emmie grimaced at his metaphor. Luckily the music was too loud for a nearby black couple to hear his comments.

"Uh, Rod, these days we don't refer to Africans as savages. We'll talk about that later. But boogey on!"

They danced the next two songs, returned to the bar for another Slam with Connie and Vanoune, then all four danced together for several more songs. After an hour at the club, Wyckham decided it was time to end the night and get some rest for the morrow.

"Whew! Very invigorating! I must say your music releases the inner muse. But I must call it a night. Might I walk you to your room or do you wish to stay here longer with your friends?"

Emmie didn't want the evening to end so abruptly. "I'd love it if you walked me home." With all the alcohol she'd consumed, how the night should end wasn't quite clear to her, but a romantic night time stroll along the canals of Venice with this dashing Governor certainly couldn't be passed up.

"Let's go. See you guys later." She wrapped both arms around his arm and hugged him close as her two friends hooted their approval.

"Woo-hoo!" yelled Connie. "Have a nice night, girl!"

"Yeah!" added Van. "Don't forget to post the video before you go to sleep!"

Emmie ignored her friends' catcalls and headed out the club's main entrance. Vanoune and Consuela turned back to the bar, their glasses desperately needing refills.

"Where's Selena?" Connie banged her glass on the bar and looked around. "Need a drink here!"

But not only was there no sign of the Selena Gomez bartender, but in the entire Firefly bar there wasn't a single one of the shape-shifting aliens in sight. Not only were all the bartenders gone, but the dance floor no longer had any of the ravishing holographic Fireflies trying to pick up male humans.

"Shit! Just like home! You can't get a fucking drink when you need one!

◆ ◆ ◆

Emmie and the governor emerged into the cool night, Emmie leaning on Wyckham for support and warmth. Four of Freeport's nine moons were out, their different colors giving the scene a holiday air.

"The moons are beautiful tonight. Which ones are these?" she asked.

Wyckham pointed to each one as he named them. "The red one there we named Ares, the Greek name for the god of war, after Earth's nearby red planet Mars. The bluish one is Pacifica, the tiny little one there is Bonaparte," (Emmie laughed at the denigration of the diminutive French emperor), "and the gray one covered in craters is George, named after our king, whose face suffers from boils."

With that last vivid description, Emmie decided the moons weren't so romantic after all. Before she could stop herself, she asked about the thing that had been bugging her ever since she'd met Wyckham.

"But tell me more of your life up here over the past two hundred years. Did you ever marry? Or just lots of mistresses?"

"*Hummph.* No. After my brief, ahh, as you would say, "physical" involvement with the Lady Brashton Firefly, my social life here pretty much ended. It was impossible to develop real feelings for Fireflies, just balls of energy taking false images, and unlike many of the hands who married aliens I found no alien race that interested me amorously. And the only interesting female human who came here until now was the real Lady Brashton, and she had turned from a delightful young woman into quite the shrew."

Until now? In his relaxed state had he let something slip out? But she had to ask about the fact she'd just heard. "You haven't had sex for over two hundred years?" she blurted out before she realized that such a question was way too much for a first date.

"Well, there was that octopus woman fifty years ago. By God, her hands were everywhere!"

Emmie elbowed Wykham in the ribs. "Yeah, bullshit. No way you'd fuck a fish. The smell alone would have been too much for an aristocrat like you."

Wyckham persisted. "She reminded me of my life at sea!"

"Sure!" responded Emmie. You must'a just loved it, in the sack with her, watchin' her slimy head flap around like a sack of laundry."

Wyckham laughed. "Caught lying again. You modern women are just too smart." He then squeezed her arm with his free hand. "I must say that you are very different and more... ah... stimulating to be around than the women of Georgian England."

Emmie felt her pulse ratcheting up at the sign of interest. The entrance to her Airbnb loomed in front of them. Should she ask him up? She really shouldn't; he needed to be well rested for his life-or-death event tomorrow.

"This is it, right here, "she said as they walked up to the iron stud-ded wooden door. "I'd invite you in, but I expect you want to call it a night with what you face at dawn tomorrow."

Wyckham took her hands and stared deeply into her eyes, search-ing for what he wanted to stay. But that look was all Emmie needed.

"You know what, fuck that! It's still early. Come on in."

She produced an ancient-looking skeleton key, unlocked the big door, and led Wyckham right to her bedroom. She closed the door be-hind them, turned to Wyckham and immediately put her arms around him. He wrapped his arms around her, and gave her a long, soft kiss. Her pulse racing higher, she finally broke off the kiss and sat down on the four-poster bed, unbuttoning her shirt.

Wyckham looked astonished for a moment, then took off his jacket and started unbuttoning his breeches.

"Frankly, I am at a loss for words right now. But I do find you an absolutely absorbing woman." Her shirt off, Emmie stood up and dropped her skirt to the floor, stepped out and approached Wyckham for another embrace. That brought a look of incredulity to Wyckham's faced as he stared at the underwear Emmie was wearing.

"What's that, a slingshot? Can't be knickers, way too small for that function. Modern women keep a weapon handy in case of an aggres-sive male in their bed?"

Emmie chuckled, gave Wyckham a quick hug, then sat back down on the bed to continue disrobing. "Yeah, it's a slingshot. But you don't have to worry about it, I like you." With that she whipped the gar-ment off, drew back on it like a slingshot, and shot it into a corner. Wyckham shook his head with a tender smile and removed his own undergarments.

"You are physically delightful," he stated as he saw Emmie's athletic body. "I just hope I can perform my duties as a man. It's been decades since I have conjoined with a woman." Now, naked as well, he approa-ched Emmie on the bed.

His well-toned body looked just fine to Emmie. "I doubt you'll have any problems," Emmie said as she reached for him. His growing manhood certainly seemed ready for sex.

But she stopped as it started growing even faster, ridiculously so! It was as long as her forearm and still it kept growing, right towards her head! She tried to jerk her head back to get out of its way, but it smacked her in the forehead! She leaped off the other side of the bed, but it kept expanding towards her. Shit, it was now the size of one of the bedposts!

And then it went wild. As Wyckham too watched in bewilderment, the end of his now gigantic member started pulsing like a jackhammer, vibrating back and forth in a blur almost too fast to see! Fucking thing was going to pound Emmie into mush! It would kill her! The whole evening was a huge betrayal—the man she had been obsessed with was really some kind of alien!

Emmie's fear quickly turned to anger. *Sonovabitch got me all excited and he turns out to be some kind of date rapist, and not even human!* Well, goddam it, he'd picked the wrong mark on this night!

Emmie had left her sword in its scabbard hanging from the near bedpost. She grabbed it with both hands, yanked the blade out of its scabbard and came *en'guarde* with her point up, at the same time throwing the heavy scabbard at Wyckham's face with her unarmed hand.

It hit him square in his right cheek, but he didn't even notice. Instead he was looking around, back and forth, yelling and cursing as if there was someone else there.

"Damn you! Who's here? You cannot do this! Turn this thing off and show yourselves! Now! Or you'll lose every business you have on Freeport, I swear it!"

But Emmie hadn't heard a word of it. She was in pure competition mode, focused completely on getting a hit. She lunged with point straight out and hit right on her target—the monstrous phallus's peehole! Her point went straight in, driven two feet deep as Emmie finished the lunge with a push off her muscular back leg. Surprisingly, she felt no resistance—apparently the alien's flesh was very soft.

But this alien that looked like Wyckham didn't act as if anything had happened! It just kept yelling into the room. "Stop this disgusting ruse and show yourselves, damn you!"

Suddenly the thing's huge member disappeared. With the pounding threat no longer in her face, Emmie leapt for the door, keeping her point extended as she ran by Wyckham. In a snap she grabbed her robe and was out the door, heading down the street, running like hell and calling for help.

Just after Emmie exited the room, women magically popped into view, Fireflies that had been magically hiding. The room was full of them, the hall was full of them, even the bathroom had three of the energy-based aliens in it. All were in the form of human females, all dressed in the provocative outfits they'd been wearing at Brashton's club just minutes before. The Lady Brashton Firefly stood at the head of the group.

"You!" shouted Wyckham. "Why am I not surprised? What were you hiding as, a bug?"

"Actually no, just a floor molding over the real one," replied the guilty alien.

"And look at all of you!" continued an enraged Wyckham. "What were you doing, selling tickets to witness my bedroom activities? Like I was the main show at the Lyceum? And you gave my sex the image of a pile driver at the London docks? Some things are just not done, for God's sake! What were you thinking?"

"The mating of Freeport's leader is something that hasn't happened for over two of your centuries. We all wanted to assist you on this special occasion, so we made your genitalia appear large and active, attributes which we believe females of your species find desirable. And, of course, there was always the possibility that you would leave some of your production about for us to harvest." She moved closer to Wyckham, trying to explain things.

"Two hundred years ago, you donated some of your seed to our race. They were remarkable examples of human life energy from which our race benefitted greatly. They were used to obtain additional abilities that we used to help you defeat the Dreash. Each one of us here wanted to be the member of our species that absorbed the unique and revered Wyckham spermatozoa."

Wyckham didn't think he could get any angrier, but he did. He clenched his teeth and clapped his hands to his head as if he was afraid his brains might explode.

"Christ all-fucking-mighty! This was about my seed? Has your species no sense of decorum? You've lived on this planet under proper Georgian laws and moral principles for centuries—did you learn nothing of what human standards of decency are?"

"We are all so sorry. We thought it would be something you'd want, since we made your genitals appear this large on a previous occasion and you seemed to appreciate it."

She was referring to a dinner party in '15 that included some French officers he'd just defeated in battle, at which Wyckham decided to shock the French after they'd accused him of all sorts of unscrupulous actions during the fighting. After they' invaded him for Christ's sake! So he'd had sex with her image right in front of everyone and even had the Firefly give his member a gigantic image for all to see. While Wyckham usually smiled at the memory, he was far too infuriated to smile at anything right now.

"That was two centuries ago! I'm an older man now and don't pull such shenanigans! You must apologize to Emmie here, she is quite shocked and frightened as would anyone be who's visiting our planet for the first time."

He started explaining everything as he turned to Emmie. "Madam, I am so angry about what..." He only stopped when he realized she was gone.

Biggest Greatest Most Tremendous Duel Ever

EVEN THE TWIN SUNS of Freeport seemed interested in the day's event. The two came up over the horizon almost simultaneously, first the smaller Apollo spreading bright white sunlight racing over the assembled thousands in Piazza San Marco, followed immediately by the larger yellow Helios, giving the plaza a warmer glow. The Fox News crews were waving light meters in the air and adjusting their cameras just in time to catch Triumph, in his usual starched cowboy shirt and stiff jeans, and his second, Sherman Bamming, slovenly as usual, as they emerged from a large helicopter along with their security detail at the main San Marco Vaporetto stop. Triumph immediately walked up and faced the TV cameras.

"This is a great day in history, the day that will go down as the day that Victor Triumph conquered another world in one-on-one combat, ending its unfair trade practices and its illegal alien activities. The days of this planet keeping us from interstellar markets are over!" He waved to a few cheering human tourists and turned to look for Wyckham. "How about we get this thing over with right now!"

He looked around the plaza for Wyckham but didn't see him. "Well folks, I guess the coward didn't show!" he proclaimed, turning back towards the cameras.

"Wrong again, Mister Rodriguez," yelled out Wyckham, using Triumph's real name. He was seated at a table with a white linen tablecloth in front of the Doge's Palace, with Obujimi serving him breakfast on finely decorated china. "Not showing up for duels is your specialty, not mine. If you can recall, you missed one two days ago, another of the inconvenient facts you seem to forget. Now I'd offer you a spot of tea, but you may not be able to keep it in once your ample stomach gets a hole in it."

Triumph's ebullient mood quickly dissipated upon hearing his actual Hispanic name and seeing Wyckham relaxed at breakfast. "You piece of shit. Just get your ancient ass out of that chair and we'll see whose stomach gets a hole," he called across the plaza. With that he spun and walked back to ha group of Americans, including Bamming holding two AR-15 assault rifles.

Wyckham didn't react. A hovering Obujimi asked, "One more scone while it's still warm? Scones should never be eaten cold."

Wyckham stood up. "This won't take long. I'll be back before it cools." Obujimi immediately began preparing Wyckham's coat for the duel, folding the lapels over to cover the bright target of Wyckham's white shirt. That completed, Wyckham began to stroll over towards Triumph, but was interrupted by a shout from the gathered crowd.

"Rod! Be careful!" It was Emmie, standing next to the Lady Brashton Firefly. Surprised, Wyckham walked up to her.

"Dearest Miss Emmie. Please let me explain the reprehensible goings-on of last night. I assure you I had nothing to do with the crude and fabricated display of my... ah..."

"Yeah, fuck, don't worry about last night, the Firefly here explained everything. Now it all seems pretty funny! So just go out and save the world from this man. Hell, you can save the whole universe from this schmuck! But be careful!"

"Have no fear. This man is nothing. I doubt he'll stand."

"But he's tricky! He sure fooled a lot of smart people on Earth! He's probably got some shit planned!"

"Of course I expect some sort of treachery. Whatever foul play he intends, my staff and I are prepared to sniff it out. Rest assured I will return momentarily."

As he started to turn away, Emmie grabbed his arm, pulled him close, wrapped her arms around him and gave him a long kiss. The crowd erupted wildly—huzzahs from Wyckham's sailors and aliens cheering in all sorts of chirps, clicks, buzzes, animalistic roars, including the usual crude noises from the mudmen.

Wyckham was joined by his second, Captain Jamison, and his medic, Slick number 2256. Triumph and his second, Bamming, met them in the middle of the plaza, where a Firefly in the form of George

Washington was waiting as the duel's director. Triumph had accepted this alien in the form of America's first president as umpire, even though he considered all aliens objectionable. The live appearance of America's founding father in his duel would probably break all records for a single-show TV ratings, something Triumph just couldn't pass up. *Probably more views than even the Super Bowl!*

Bamming approached Jamison and held up the two rifles for his inspection. "Standard AR-15's, all checked out," he said. "Pick whichever you like."

But instead of examining the weapons, Jamison simply picked up the nearer one and passed it to the Slick, who pulled a little electrical device from his accessory belt and began waving it over the weapon. Almost immediately the device emitted a high-pitched alarm. The Slick pushed some buttons on his device and the alarm abruptly stopped.

"Personalized trigger lock. Weapon would only fire in opponent's hand. Will work now," said the Slick through his translating device as he handed the AR-15 back to Wyckham.

Triumph immediately denied any wrongdoing. "You really expect people to believe that?" He turned to the cameras. "This alien friend of his makes some beeping noises and says the weapon was tampered with? Witch hunt! We did not tamper with these rifles! No collusion!"

Wyckham rolled his eyes but said nothing about the expected ruse. "May I test the weapon to make sure it has no more interesting modifications?" Wyckham asked. Without waiting for an answer, he turned around and scanned the sky. One of the Tarren, the dimwitted raptors that kept trying to eat the plaza's holographic Pigeons along with occasional tourist's scalps, was passing about 300 feet overhead. Suddenly it went into a steep dive, heading straight down towards the plaza, targeting God knows what. Wyckham put the rifle to his shoulder, followed the bird down and squeezed off three quick shots. Three puffs of feathers popped off the bird, confirming that all three of Wyckham's shots had scored hits. The third shot tore the Tarren in half and the remains fell to the ground right in front of Triumph. "One less of those unpleasant avians," Wyckham commented dryly as he lowered the weapon.

Triumph for once was speechless, clearly impressed with Wyckham's marksmanship. And clearly frightened as well. The old foreigner had successfully brought down a bird in a high velocity dive! To fill in the noticeable silence, Wyckham commented, "I must say your weapons are quite impressive. I practiced with one that we picked up from the battle here two days ago. Only it took a few shots to get used to. Accurate, light kick, light trigger, what?"

As usual, Triumph lost control when confronted with a setback. He turned back to the cameras and yelled, "He's treating me very unfairly! He was supposed to be unfamiliar with AR-15's, that's why I picked it! People told me he brought in California snipers, gave him expert instruction on the AR-15! If I'd known he was going to act this way I would have chosen a different weapon! This is a disgrace!"

Wyckham leaned over to speak in Triumph's ear. "Let's just shut up and get matters underway. You keep complaining instead of fighting, you'll look like a coward in front of your electrical audience. Don't want them to question your well-known courage, do you? Must keep up the image of strength, mustn't we?"

Bamming now leaned into Triumph's ear. "Don't do it, Vic, don't do it. Too risky. Get out of this deal," he said, loud enough for Wyckham to hear. "We can walk everything back later."

Wyckham was keeping Bamming's hands in view, especially the right one. It was nonchalantly stuck in his jacket pocket with the thumb hanging over its edge, just how an assassin would place his hand before pulling a pistol. Seconds were armed in case of foul play, and with Bamming being right-handed, most likely he had a pistol in that pocket. Maybe his words about quitting the fight, strangely said loud enough for Wyckham to hear, were a distraction to get Wyckham to focus on Triumph's response? Sure enough, Bamming's thumb suddenly disappeared, his hand dipping deeply into the jacket pocket. Wyckham was about to lunge and smack Bamming's chin with the AR-15, but he was beaten to the punch by Jamison. Standing behind Bamming, his second thrust a big flintlock pistol right between Bamming's legs, jamming it up his derriere. Bamming's eyes went wide and his right hand froze.

"Yes, you better stop," said Jamison, his mouth in Bamming's ear. "Smart move. 'Cause that bullet absorbing shirt you're wearing's not gonna help you down there. I've got a big load of Greek fire in this horse pistol and it'll roast yer nuts and blow them out your ears. Now pull your hands out to your sides, slowly, and keep them there, I'm gonna be right here by your side 'til all this gets settled. But feel free to go right on advising your man here. I'm just dying to see you get out of this."

Bamming had lost his tongue and said nothing. "Opponents take your positions," bellowed the Firefly Washington. Wyckham turned his back to Triumph and pointed his gun's muzzle straight up, taking the proper position to begin pacing off the ten steps before turning and firing. Triumph just stood there, unsure of his next action. Over his shoulder Wyckham made a final suggestion to his opponent.

"Time to turn your back and take in this stunning view. Appreciate it. Your last view of anything."

An increasingly alarmed Triumph slowly turned, scanning the crowd as he brought his own weapon up. All the aliens were shouting things that Triumph didn't understand but were clearly predicting his immediate demise. *Aw, fuck, I'm gonna die! Shot down by some ancient foreigner? In front of a crowd of loser aliens cheering for my death?*

"Gentlemen, your last chance to avoid bloodshed," Washington continued. "Is there no chance to come to some sort of agreement?"

Relieved, Triumph opened his mouth but Wyckham immediately squelched his hope for a deal. "I insist we go through with this. This man has never made an honest deal in his life, an arrangement acceptable to me is impossible since I cannot trust anything that comes out of his mouth. Besides that, I believe eliminating the man will end a threat to the entire universe."

Over a spluttering Triumph, George Washington loudly began counting out the steps. "One." But Triumph was frozen in fear and just stood there. The crowd started yelling in all their respective languages, clearly booing the hesitant Triumph. Finally he took the first step. Washington continued. "Two! Wyckham began to whistle the British national anthem. The watching British sailors began singing along. "Rule, Britannia, Britannia rule the waves…" The entire crowed joined in, every alien in the cosmos familiar with the British national anthem—"Britons never will be slaves…" To Triumph, who didn't like music to start with, there was some incomprehensible power in his enemy's victory song. It blasted him like collapsing poll numbers. It was his funeral dirge. "Three!"

That was it for the American. The call of "three" jogged his memories of the Wharton track team, and he did what he used to do back then when he heard "three". He took off as fast as he could. While there were still seven more steps for George Washington to count off, Triumph was gone, headed for the open door of his helicopter.

Wyckham had was still stepping off the count, his back turned, unaware that Triumph had run. The count reached nine and Wyckham tensed, prepared to spin, aim, and fire. "Ten!" Wyckham whirled around and lowered his weapon to put the sight on Triumph. But he wasn't there! However, fleeing in a duel was punishable by the oponent's second, and Jamison now pulled his pistol from Bamming's derriere and took aim at the fleeing American. But Bamming, now relieved of his concern about the pistol shoved up his buttocks, elbowed Jamison in the face and gave him a shove. The pistol fired off, but the flaming ball went high over the crowd.

Wyckham, however, had no one interfering with his aim. And there in front of him was the fleshy Triumph, jiggling along on his tiptoes, going nowhere fast. Wyckhm had plenty of time before the large man got to the safety of his airship. Dropping his muzzle further, he put the sight over Triumph's ample right buttock, enough to give the man a flesh wound to remember this day for the rest of his life. For one who constantly bragged about his courage and strength, it would be a life-long embarrassment. He placed the sight on target and went to squeeze the trigger.

But he couldn't do it. A duel was an affair of honor; no one shot an opponent in the back. It just wasn't done. Besides that, duels were fought for satisfaction, and watching Triumph run in front of millions watching back on Earth gave Wyckham all the satisfaction anyone could ask for. Triumph's career was over, and he would have to go through every day owing his life to an enemy's act of decency that he certainly wouldn't have granted. Maybe he'd learn something about decency from the occasion.

He lowered the weapon and clicked on the safety. Triumph was lurching along as fast as he could, finally making it through the booing crowd to dive headlong into his parked helicopter. It was over.

Almost immediately, Wyckham was knocked down. It was a charging Emmie, hugging him tightly even as they hit the ground.

"Way to go high! That asshole owes you for life!

Wyckham wanted to respond, but the wind was knocked out of him as an additional pile-up of aliens and British sailors landed on top of him. Just as he started to worry about his survival, the pressure went away, and he was hoisted up onto the shoulders of several large gorillas and even some of the stoic Slicks, who were certainly not prone to emotional celebration. Followed by dozens more in the crowd, a parade began around the square, the festive mood enhanced by British sailors passing out tall glasses of ale they'd grabbed from the nearby cafes. Along with the cacophonous cheers of the various alien species, there was loud cheering and celebratory dancing as well by hundreds of the Human tourists.

Finally, after much complaining and some stern orders to his sailors, Wyckham was eased down to the ground where he was given another ferocious bearhug from the athletic Emmie.

Looking about for any security issues, Wyckham saw none. Mudmen had kept the crowd away from Triumph's party, who were now boarding their flying ship and leaving. Mostly, the crowd was just celebrating, delighted that their beloved governor had survived and that Triumph and his crowd had been humiliated. Aliens and Humans were now dancing with each other, celebrating in their different ways. He even saw Dreashpalone and some of his Garoshen, Freeport's natives, running around and slapping hands, their traditional gesture of celebration, with both humans and aliens.

"Oh my God," yelled Emmie. "Look at them! Your natives know how to high five!"

Wyckham didn't know about high fives but he did know the existential invasion of Freeport was over. He doubted any of Triumph's officers would continue the fight after having their leader's cowardice shown to everyone back on Earth. He gave Emmie a return hug as he stood there, finally able to relax for the first time in days. Only one alien seemed unhappy, a lizard woman standing alone, desperately searching the crowd for someone or something.

"Look!" yelled Emmie. "That's Vanessa, Shilling's beloved hooker! Gotta get the young lovers back together!"

Emmie broke away and ran to the confused alien, grabbing a scaly hand and pulling her across the plaza, yelling to Schillings who was standing back behind Wyckham. "President Schillings! Look who's here!"

Schillings turned, saw his true love, and started running towards her, surprisingly quickly for a man his age. Vanessa broke into a smile, something frightening to see on a giant lizard's face, and began running to meet him as well. Emmie almost expected them to go into slow motion like young lovers in a movie. Finally, Vanessa ran into Schilling's arms and began smothering him with kisses, her forked serpent's tongue even exploring a nostril. That was more than Wyckham and Emmie could bear watching further, and they turned to each other.

"So I'm forgiven?" he asked her. "The Fireflies told you that they were wholly responsible for that shocking manipulation of my… ahh… image in your room last night? Please understand that I was as surprised as you."

"Yeah, they explained everything," Emmie replied. "They're embarrassed at what they did—that surprised me, I didn't think Fireflies ever felt embarrassed. But looking back on it now, it was really funny." Emmie's eyes glanced sideways. "Think you could persuade them to do it again so I could make a video? Be really bitchin' on my Instagram page. It'll get more hits than any sex video in history! Everybody will have to check it out!"

Good Lord! While the duel hadn't perturbed him, Wyckham was now stunned. Just seconds ago, when Wyckham had turned to look into Emmie's eyes, seeing Emmie's forgiveness and Triumph defeated, he'd felt an overwhelming need be in a relationship with this remarkable young woman. It had swept through his mind without any conscious thought on his part, almost magically. But this made it clear that there were insurmountable differences between him and a woman from 2028. The young woman had just showed that she had complete-ly different customs, so different as to be abominable. He could never be a part of her life. Show pictures of himself naked with a monstrous phallus to billions of people? Not for him.

Wyckham, shocked, couldn't formulate a response, and for a couple of seconds they just looked at each other. Then Emmie broke into laughter.

"Got you with that one!" she cried out. But then she read the shock on Wyckham's face and felt guilty.

"Aww, maybe I shouldn't have? Not funny? Hey, I'm sorry. Sometimes I'm a bit much." She put his arm through his and turned him towards the Canale l'Bacaroli and her apartment. "But you'll get used to it." She called over her shoulder to Obujimi. "Sir Thomas?" she asked, using the name *Righteous's* crew had given him for his refined manners and formal speech. "Could we put the planet in your very capable hands for a few hours? Your captain needs a few hours away from all this shit."

Obujimi smiled broadly and nodded. "I could not agree more. My Captain, forget your duties for as long as you wish. Whenever you re-surface you will find all Freeport's shit in hand."

Back at the Krag

A WEEK LATER, WYCKHAM was across the bay in Port Wyckham at his table in the Ruptured Krag, the tavern popular with arriving intergalactic traders looking for business opportunities. With the threat of invasion gone, the place was busy, crowded with aliens from both the nearby galaxies and some very distant ones as well. One of the human-size spiders from the Arachnid Galaxy was trying to trade spider silk for living beings to feed its rapacious population.

"Industrial silk!" it called out, waving a roll of fabric in the air. "Stronger than any metal and soft as a larva's butt! Big orders, small orders—let's talk! You know your planet has trouble makers—get rid of them in exchange for something useful!

A group of ants were at a nearby table, staring at the spider making his irritating sales pitch. Ants and spiders did not get along. Spiders had been one of the first civilizations to develop space travel, and over millennia had raided the ant planet, Industria, abducting their tender young. The practice had ended decades ago with a truce arranged by the League of Worlds, which both ants and spiders had joined when the intergalactic threat of the Dreash took precedence over all other squabbles. But centuries of warfare had left deeply imbedded hatred between the two races.

One ant had heard enough. A large female stood upright and threw her dinner, a melon-size ball of hard crystalized sugar, right at the spider, hitting the big insect right in the middle of his clustered eyeballs. The big spider gave out a high-pitched shriek, dropped his roll of silk and began rubbing his eyes with several of its legs. The offending ant got up from its table, scrambled over, picked up the ball of sugar and popped it into its mouth. "Sorry, dropped my dinner."

Wyckham smirked and returned his attention to the daily shipping notices, pretending he hadn't seen anything. The big arachnids were constantly trying to barter their silk for living beings, though despite the usefulness of their silk, most species would not do business with them. Wyckham wished he could ban their commerce, but the trading occurred off planet and he couldn't do anything about discussing business on Freeport, where free speech was protected.

He looked up as someone approached his table. It was Dreashpalone, leader of the planet's native population, clad in fringed skins like an American frontiersman. He bowed and made a leg like a page in Lords. "Good news, governor. May I sit?"

Wyckham put his paperwork down and leaned back in his chair. "Most certainly, my good man. Always well met."

The rugged yet refined native sat down and formally addressed Wyckham in perfect English. "I am happy to report that the transporter used to bring the recent invasion to Freeport has been destroyed. We located it thanks to the head Firefly's efforts in intelligence gathering. By communicating with animals in the area around Whale Bay, she was eventually led to some bats that told her of a new cave about two miles inland. My people scouted it out and saw several Dreash going in and out. We waited for a moment when they were all inside, then rolled one of *Vesuvius*'s mortar rounds into the entrance. It brought down the entire mountain on them. None escaped."

"Well done, Prince. Do you know if the deceased included the Dreash leader, Brak?"

"No, we do not. The cave is now inaccessible forever."

Hummph. The leader of the Dreash could still be afoot and capable of more mischief, including the construction of another transporter. After some more small talk, Dreashpalone left and Wyckham returned to his shipping notices.

A rousing commotion brought his attention back up to scan the tavern. Entering to a hero's welcome was the head Firefly, in her usual image of Tracy Brashton, making her first visit to Freeport since the end of the recent hostilities. Wyckham settled back in his chair, twiddling his pen, a large feather from a Tarren, watching as every alien in the tavern vied for her attention. Over the past few years, even before the recent war, he'd noticed the increasing species-wide admiration of the Fireflies. Certainly they had helped repuse the invasion from Earth, but one discovery from the recent events could explain their growing popularity, and today he meant to confirm his suspicions.

Wyckham stood and made a leg. "Lady Brashton, your servant. A moment of your time? Please have a seat."

"Of course," the alien replied with a suggestive smile as she took a seat. "I always enjoy catching up with my old friend and lover."

Wyckham ignored that comment. The days of giving this being his seed were over. "First of all, I must thank you for your recent efforts on behalf of Freeport. In the fight against Triumph your supply of intelligence was crucial. But this fight also exposed a disturbing industry here on Freeport, the large-scale harvesting of human seed, run by your human counterpart, Baroness Brashton. Knowing your race's large demand for this product, I must ask you if you are involved in this sordid business. Did you do business with her or help her establish and operate the business?"

"Yes, we are involved," she replied, her smile still in place. "Baroness Brashton was hurting our tavern business with her competing taverns—her use of actual Human females had appeal we could not match. So we proposed a joint business in seed collection using gleaners from all planets. We Fireflies worked with every planet in the League, sending eager workers here to New Venice to accommodate the desires of all, aliens and humans alike, while Baroness Brashton operated the facilities. Please understand we did not know of her working with the Dreash and the Americans to invade this planet. The Baroness, with assistance from the Dreash, was very competent at hiding this from us.

"But our business with her turned out to be very successful. Shipments of living energy units to our galaxy increased tenfold. The increased supply of life energy was extremely useful to my race, you must have noticed our increased abilities in intelligence gathering during this recent conflict. And other planetary systems received energy units from the tavern business as well, production is shared with all League members. Since we understood that most humans found the business distasteful, we kept the business hidden so as not to affect tourism in New Venice. We saw no laws of yours prohibiting it, and since we have openly conducted the trade in our Port Wyckham taverns for centuries, we did not think you would object."

Wyckham had expected this but still became enraged at hearing it confirmed.

"Behind my back you set up sperm factories across my city? You get humans so obsessed with sex that they abandon their normal lives, their families unaware of where they are or what's happening to them, living only to have constant orgasms so your race can milk them? Like cows on a farm? Is there no depth of depravity you will not descend to? Good Lord! Some things are just not done, for God's sake!"

"I'm sorry you find this industry offensive," the Firefly replied, the cordial smile still gracing her face. "Realize that we force no one to do anything they object to, contributors are free to leave our stations at any time. You repeatedly state that Freeport guarantees personal freedom, yet you object to them choosing the life of physical pleasure we offer them? When most Human males, even you, constantly leave this valuable seed on their bedsheets only to dry out and die? When we can use it to expand our abilities in all sorts of positive endeavors, especially fighting the Dreash?"

Still smiling, she stood up to leave. "We wish to continue our military and intelligence cooperation with Freeport. If you pass a law banning this commerce, we will obey it and close our facilities." With that final comment she left.

Hummmph! Fat chance that Freeport would pass such a law. While there was no public voting for anything on Freeport, Wyckham knew that the planet's population, especially his own sailors, would riot if they felt there were to be any restrictions on the Fireflies' taverns. They loved the saloons where Fireflies in seductive holographic images plied customers with free food and drink just to have sex with them. Her commitment to abide by any future law on the subject would never be tested.

Not to mention the fact that the he didn't want to damage relations with the Fireflies. She was correct in bringing up the importance of the intelligence they supplied on every other planet, even those in distant systems. Without them on his side, he would never have won the conflicts with the Dreash, French, British and now the Americans. And he never would have even known about the problems on Earth, which had resulted in the construction of new Venice and the immigration of much-needed Humans.

His mood ruined for the day, Wyckham looked around for a Firefly to order some strong drink, but his sulk dissipated immediately as Emmie Bahtia enter the room! A few days after the duel she had boarded *Indomptable* for its afternoon departure to San Francisco, saying she had to return to Earth "to get her shit together," whatever that meant, and would return within a week. Here she was back in just three days! Should he be heartened that she had returned early?

He stood up and made a leg, only to be crashed into once again by the energetic Emmie giving him a hug. At least this time he managed to keep his footing.

"I'm back!" she declared. "To my captain and his planet! Now my planet!"

An interesting statement that Wyckham would have to ask about in a moment. But good manners were in order first.

"So glad to see you," he stated. "A welcome-back glass? I was just about to order one myself."

Emmie released him but held his hand as she sat down next to him. "You betcha," she answered, her eyes not leaving his.

A Firefly in the image of a buxom blonde woman whom Wyckham did not recognize appeared at their table. "What can I get for you lovebirds?

Wyckham was a little embarrassed by this Firefly's recognition of his relationship with the earth woman. Did everyone on Freeport know? But he made no comment. "The Armagnac brandy for me. For you as well, Emily?"

Emmie finally took her eyes off Wyckham to order a drink but was immediately overwhelmed with mirth when she looked at the waitress.

"Squally! O my God, you look perfect!" She put her hand in the air and the Firefly slapped it with her own in the "high five" celebration so popular on Earth.

"You know this woman?' Wyckham had to ask.

"Sure! Squally Gales, the porn actress that had an affair with Triumph and got paid off for keepin' quiet." She turned to the Firefly. "Hysterical! And I bet you're gettin' get lots of attention in this image, huh?"

"Yes, it's true, I am very popular like this with Earth males. My seed shipments to my home world have been excellent."

Wyckham was unfamiliar with Emmie's description of the Firefly. A 'pourin' actress? What type of theater was that? Some kind of ritual bathing where actresses pour liquids? And this was so sexually stimulating to Earthmen that Triumph had taken one of the pouring actresses as a mistress, even though he had to pay her to stay mum? Wyckham's desire to visit Earth, already at low ebb, declined even further.

Emmie's celebration of the Firefly's image over, she ordered a Sailor's Slam and turned he attention back to Wyckham, their hands clasped together on the tabletop. "So, tell me how much you missed me," she demanded.

"Well, I did. And so did my planet. I have an offer of employment for you."

"Really? I'm all ears."

"This planet needs you. Just moments ago, I confirmed that the fireflies, my allies for centuries, have been involved with Baroness Brashton in a massive sperm harvesting business right here on Freeport, and I didn't know a thing about it. It's clear that I need another source for domestic information. While Obujimi is an effective Minister of Civilian Affairs, he is only one man and cannot stay on top of all the intrigues that are cooking both in Port Wyckham and New Venice.

"Now while you were gone, I obtained a copy of the book, 'The Collected Sherlock Holmes,' a book about this fellow you try to emulate. Freeport needs a person like him, an investigating detective. In the few days you were on this planet, you found this Shillings fellow that we'd all spent months searching for. Twice! Would you be interested in accepting the position of Chief Detective for the entire planet? Not only have you proven your abilities in this area, I expect you can bring some 2028 methods to crime fighting, especially in the use of electrical information… as you call it, 'social media'. Compensation would include…"

"Would I be interested? Shit yeah I'd be interested! I just finished saying goodbye to my friends and family to move up here where there are no jobs for programmers? Hell, I was planning on looking for a waitress job, and instead I get to be the Sherlock Holmes for a whole planet? Done deal!"

Wyckham smiled and gave her hands an extra squeeze.

"You didn't let me finish. Compensation would include a wing of the palace with offices and living quarters. With, of course…"

"Lemme guess, "laughed Emmie. "with a secret passage to your bedroom?"

Wyckham was overjoyed. "Well, the old palace does have many concealed stairways, so, sadly, I may be unable to find a suite for you that does not have one. Shall we leave this den of ill repute and head across the bay to my palace? My cutter awaits." And with that he stood, extending his arm which Emmie took. She momentarily considered a dig about his "cutter", but wisely realized this was not the time. They headed out the door, passing under the tavern's 200-year-old wooden sign depicting a crabman getting bayonetted in the groin by a red-coated marine. Following them as they left was a cacophonous approval from the barful of the usual astonishing alien creatures.

About the Author

Vince Scully is a retired class clown, fencer, engineer, drag racer, furniture designer, and sales rep who lives in Long Beach, California, with his wonderful wife and two dogs. With his two children out of the nest, he spends his time writing, staying in shape, and tinkering with his treasured cars, a '32 Ford and a '31 Lincoln. He often pretends to be Dodger announcer Vin Scully in order to get better reservations at restaurants. His friends describe him as indescribable. This is his third novel.